P9-DGN-075

BETWEEN THE NOTES

Between the Notes

BY SHARON HUSS ROAT

HARPER TEEN
An Imprint of HarperCollinsPublishers

HarperTeen is an imprint of HarperCollins Publishers.

www.epicreads.com

Library of Congress Control Number: 2015933430
ISBN 978-0-06-229172-1

Typography by Kate J. Engbring
15 16 17 18 19 CG/RRDH 10 9 8 7 6 5 4 3 2 1
❖
First Edition

TO RICH, SEBASTIAN, AND ANNA

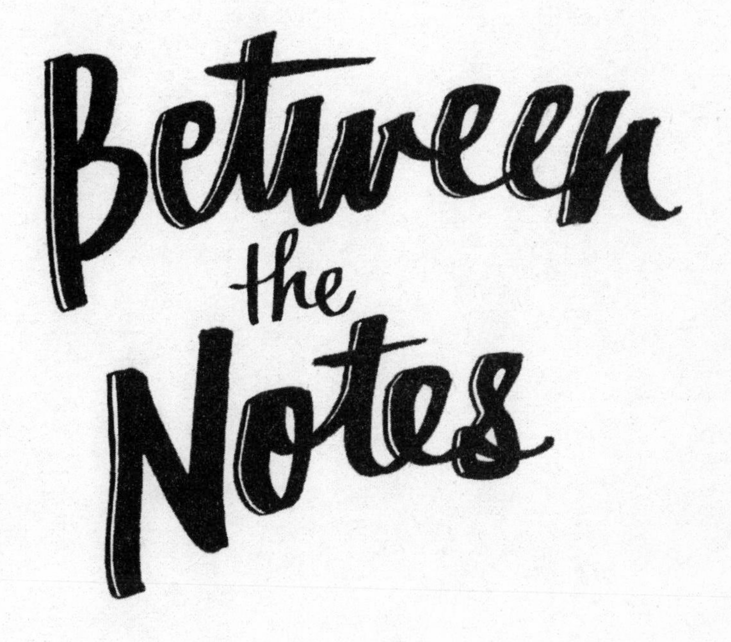
Between
the
Notes

ONE

I came home from school on a Thursday in early September to find my parents sitting on the couch in the front room, waiting for me. I knew immediately something wasn't right. We never sat on that couch. We never even walked into that room, with its white carpet and antique furniture. And what was Dad doing home from work, anyway?

My mother was wringing her hands, literally, like she was squeezing water out of her fingers, too preoccupied to ask me to take my shoes off in the foyer.

"What's wrong? Where's Brady?" I naturally put the two together before I realized it couldn't be him. They would not be sitting here so calmly if something had happened to my brother. There'd be a note on the kitchen counter, a frantic phone message from the hospital.

"He's at school. He's fine. Kaya's fine," said Mom. "Everything's fine."

Dad squeezed my mother's hand. "Have a seat, sweetie.

There's something your mother and I need to talk to you about."

Clearly, everything was not fine.

I dropped my book bag on the carpet with a thud that mimicked the feeling in my stomach, and lowered myself into one of my mother's favorite wingback chairs.

"What did I do?"

Mom laughed, about an octave higher than usual. "*Nothing!* Nothing."

Then Dad cleared his throat, and they broke the news like it was a hot potato, tossing it back and forth so neither of them actually had to complete an entire, terrible sentence.

"You know, my business . . ."

"Daddy's business . . ."

"It hasn't been good."

"This economy . . ."

"The whole printing industry, really . . . It's been . . . a difficult few years," said Dad, nodding and then shaking his head.

"And with Brady's therapy bills . . ." said Mom.

My spine went stiff. My parents never blamed anything on Brady's disability. It was an unspoken rule.

"We got behind on some payments," Dad was saying.

"And the bank . . ."

"The bank . . ."

They paused, neither one of them wanting to catch the next potato.

"What?" I whispered. "The bank what?"

Then Mom started to cry and Dad looked like the potato had slammed into his stomach. "The bank is foreclosing on our house," he said. "We have to move."

I suddenly felt small amid the lush upholstery, like the chair might swallow me whole.

"Huh?"

"We've lost the house," Dad said quietly. "We're moving."

I couldn't seem to process what he was saying, though it seemed plain enough. "This is *our* house," I said. They couldn't take *our* house. We couldn't move. Not away from my best friend, Reesa, who lived next door; and my lilac-colored room with its four-poster bed; and the window seat with its extra-fluffy pillows; and my closet where I could see everything; and . . . and my piano room, and . . .

"We can't move," I said.

They shook their heads. They said, "We're sorry," and "We hate this, too," and "There's nothing we can do," and "It's the only way . . . ," and "We're sorry. We're so, so sorry."

I threw a dozen what-if scenarios at them: "What if Mom gets a job?" "What if I get a job?" "What if we just stop buying stuff we don't really need?" "Get rid of my phone?" "Sell the silver?"

"Your mother *is* getting a job," Dad said. We wouldn't be buying anything but necessities, the silver had already been sold, and yes, they'd be canceling my cell phone service. Even with all that, we still couldn't afford the mortgage. In fact, we'd barely be making ends meet in the way-less-expensive apartment we'd be renting.

"What about Nana?" My grandma Emerson lived about two hours away in a farmhouse. She had chickens and made soap from the herbs in her garden. Lavender rosemary. Lemon basil. She always smelled like a cup of lemon zinger tea. "Can't she loan us money?"

Dad dropped his chin to his chest.

"Ivy," said Mom, "she lives off Social Security and the little bit she makes selling her soap at craft fairs. She can't help us."

"Aunt Betty? Uncle Dean?"

My parents shook their heads. "They have their own problems, their own bills, their own kids to send to college," Dad said.

The air went out of my lungs; my bones seemed to go out of my limbs. I couldn't even lift an arm to wipe my tears.

"I know this is hard, but it's necessary." She paused. "Please don't cry. The twins will be home soon. We don't want to upset Brady."

I took a shuddery breath, but the tears were refusing to stop. Mom looked nervously out the front window.

"The bus is coming," she said. "Here." She offered me a wad of Kleenex.

I nodded, took the tissues from her hand, and sniffled my way to the stairs. We didn't cry in front of Brady. We didn't raise our voices or have freak-outs of any kind if we could help it.

My little brother had a seizure disorder when he was a baby. His brain had been wracked by spasms for months, and while they had finally stopped, he now struggled to walk and talk and understand the world around him. If you got angry or emotional in front of him, he thought you were upset with him or, as the doctors said, he "internalized." Then it took hours to pry his hands away from his ears and calm him down.

I went upstairs to the music room and closed the door. It had taken a special crane to get the baby grand up here through French doors that opened onto the balcony. I sat at the piano bench and played a tumble of scales and chords until my hands turned to heavy bags of sand and I dragged them over the keys. The resulting noise was satisfying. It sounded exactly how I felt.

Out the window, I saw Brady and Kaya walking up our long driveway. They were six years old and I was sixteen. I remembered when my parents brought them home from the hospital. Brady was perfect then. The seizures didn't start until six months later. We were so worried Kaya would get them, too, but she never did.

She held his backpack for him. It always took a while for them to make their way to the porch, because Brady stopped every few steps to pick up a pebble or stray bit of asphalt and throw it into the grass. We had the cleanest driveway on the planet.

When they neared the house, Mom and Dad walked out to greet them with hugs and pasted-on smiles. I wasn't ready to pretend everything was okay, not even for Brady.

I just continued to play my piano.

When I saw where we were moving a week later, my throat closed up and I could barely breathe. Mom made it all sound like a fabulous adventure, like camping in a deluxe cabin.

"It's really very nice," she said. "Three bedrooms, two baths, walk-in closets. Even wifi."

"Golly, Mom. Do you think we'll have running water? And heat?" Sarcasm was one of the few ways I could say what I truly felt in front of Brady, as long as I paired it with a smile.

"Of course, sweetheart." Mom smiled sarcastically right back. "Refrigeration, too. And bunk beds!"

"Brady get bunk bed!" he exclaimed with a sweet smile.

It was amazing how easily six-year-olds could be won over by the promise of narrow sleeping surfaces stacked on top of each other. Mom and Dad were just relieved he wasn't traumatized by the whole thing, and made no attempt to redirect him to a new topic or coach him to speak in complete sentences like they usually did.

I ruffled his soft, blond hair, the hair I wished I could trade for my mop of brown, frizz-prone curls. "Bunk beds are cool." We'd been talking up the benefits of the bottom bunk in particular, so he wouldn't want the top. It was too dangerous for him.

He hugged my leg. "Ivy bunk bed!"

I kissed his head and quickly turned back to the dishes I was wrapping in newspaper. My bags and boxes were packed with what little I was allowed to take to our new home. Essentials and favorites only, Dad had said. The rest would go into storage or be sold, because the new place was "more economical." I was pretty sure that was code for "crappy little apartment," but I wouldn't know for sure until Dad got home and took us to check out the place.

The phone rang and I heard Mom answer in the next room, a den with a circular fireplace we always sat around on New Year's Eve to roast marshmallows.

"Oh, hi, Reesa. . . . Yes, she's here. Why don't you come over? Ivy's just—"

I lunged for the kitchen phone. "Mom! I've got it. You can hang up."

I waited for the click. "Hey. I'm here."

"I kind of noticed that when you screamed in my ear. You want me to come over?"

"No!" I closed my eyes and took a calming breath. "No, I'm . . . Mom has us all doing chores. She's, um . . . she's giving a bunch of old dishes away. For a charity thing."

I wasn't quite ready to tell her that *we* were the charity thing. I kept thinking if I didn't tell anyone, it wouldn't happen.

"Then you totally need me. I know how to pack china so it won't break," said Reesa. "Remember my job at the antiques store?"

"You worked there for one day. They made you dust."

Reesa laughed. "Okay, fine. But I did learn how to wrap flatware before I quit."

"That's okay," I said. "I'm almost done, and we have to go out when my dad gets home, anyway."

I managed to rush her off the phone before she could ask where we were going. When I hung up, Mom joined me across the table. She slid a dish onto newspaper and folded four corners to its center. "You haven't told her?"

I shook my head. "Not yet."

She wrapped another plate, and another, alternately stacking hers with mine. When I placed the last plate on the pile, she rested her hands on top and sighed. "We're moving this weekend, sweetie. You should tell your friends."

"I will. I'm just waiting . . ." I didn't know what I was waiting for. That sweepstakes guy to show up with a gigantic check for a million dollars and a bouquet of roses, maybe? "I want to see it first. That's all."

As if on cue, Dad walked into the kitchen and laid his briefcase heavily on the counter. He didn't say a word. He didn't have to. His look of nervous resignation was enough to announce it was time to go see our new place, ready or not.

We loaded into the Mercedes SUV, which now sported a handmade FOR SALE sign in the rear window. Mom chattered on about how nice the new apartment was. Her voice sounded thinner than normal, like she couldn't get enough air. "It's smaller, of course. But plenty of room for the five of us. Three bedrooms . . ."

She kept saying "three bedrooms" like it was a huge deal. I should've known the sleeping accommodations were the least of my troubles. It was like worrying that your tray table is too small on an airplane that's about to crash.

I hid my face behind the FOR SALE sign, picking at the tape that held it in place, while Brady and Kaya bounced in their booster seats. My father steered the car down our long, curving driveway. The wrought-iron gate swung open as we approached, triggered by a motion sensor that was perfectly timed to release us without a moment's delay. My parents hadn't installed the gate or the fence around our property to keep people out, but rather to keep Brady in. He had a tendency to wander. Still, it kept visitors from stopping by unannounced, so none of my friends had discovered we were moving yet. I was hoping to keep it that way.

My nail polish, a glossy fuchsia, had started to chip. I scraped one thumbnail against the other as we passed Reesa's house. Their gate was sculpted of copper with an ornate letter M for Morgan in the middle. It was flashy and curvy and shiny like she was. But more important, it was right next door. The distance between her kitchen door and ours was precisely seventy-seven steps—or fifty-three cartwheels. Though we hadn't traveled via cartwheel in a few years, we had sworn to always live next to each other, even when we went off to college. Even when we got married. "Our kids will be best friends," we always said.

I lifted my head like a prairie dog. "Maybe the people who buy our place will rent it back to us."

Daddy darted a warning glance at me in the rearview mirror. Brady and Kaya didn't know the house was going to be sold. "Nobody's buying our place," he said.

My parents wanted to spare the twins the full details of our situation, so they wouldn't be overly traumatized. (Was there such a thing as moderate trauma?) We were telling them this was a temporary move while work was being done on the house.

A big fat lie, I'd said.

A little white lie, Mom insisted.

"Oh, yeah." I winked at Kaya, who squinted back. She was totally onto them, but also very well trained in the ways of the let's-not-upset-Brady bunch.

I twisted around to watch the rolling hills of Westside Falls disappear behind me as we headed toward the city of Belleview, then slouched back down in my seat. Maybe the new place wouldn't be so bad, after all. Small, but cozy. Like Brady's bunk bed. Maybe it would be located on one of those cute streets in the city where the houses were like Manhattan brownstones, and I'd be close enough to walk to my favorite shops.

We hadn't been driving long, maybe six or seven minutes, when my father turned left at an intersection we usually went straight through. I sat up taller, the fine hairs on my arms standing at attention as we passed some industrial buildings and warehouses, an abandoned gas station, and a vacant parking lot with weeds sprouting through crumbled asphalt. "Wait, we're not . . . where is this place, exactly?"

"It's in district." There was definitely something weird about my mother's voice. "You won't have to change schools or anything."

I froze, swallowing hard. "But it's . . . it's not . . ." Another warning glance from my father confirmed what my arm hairs had been trying to tell me.

We were moving to Lakeside.

Like Westside Falls, Lakeside was a suburb of Belleview. But that's where the similarities ended. Lakeside was a bad neighborhood that had been added to our otherwise posh school district a few years ago when they redrew the boundaries. There wasn't even a lake there, only a reservoir where they'd flooded a valley years ago to provide water to the nearby city of Belleview. I'd never actually been to Lakeside myself—we never drove this way when we went downtown to shop or go to restaurants—but I'd heard plenty. Somebody's cousin's best friend's mom got carjacked when she took a wrong turn and asked for directions. And everyone said if you wanted to buy drugs, all you had to do was look for a corner where a pair of high-top sneakers were dangling from the phone wires above.

The worst part was how all the Lakeside kids who attended Vanderbilt High rode a single bus to school, and everyone joked that it came from the state penitentiary, which was on the other side of the reservoir.

No way was I riding that state pen bus to school.

We slowed down as an exceptionally ugly apartment building loomed ahead, its sign promising GARDEN TERRACE ESTATES though there was neither a garden nor a terrace in sight. It did have balconies, though, which were strewn with deck chairs, grills, and . . . was that a giant, inflatable snowman drooping over the railing? I closed my eyes and didn't open them until the car bumped to a stop and Daddy said, "Here we are."

The twins scrambled out, squealing. I opened my left eye, and it immediately started twitching . . . as if trying to protect me from what it was about to see. I pressed my palm to the lid to make it stop and squinted through the other eye. Mom pulled my car door open and held her hand out to me. I finally lifted my arm and slipped my fingers into hers.

I was relieved, at first, that what stood in front of me didn't have balconies full of deflated Christmas decorations. It wasn't an apartment building at all, but a tall, skinny, brown house on its own little plot of land. It looked like a row home that had lost its neighbors and might teeter over sideways in a stiff wind.

"I thought you said we were moving into an apartment." I stayed close to the car, figuring they'd made some kind of mistake.

"We are." My father pulled some keys from his pocket and strode up the steps to the front porch. "Top two floors are ours, plus the attic. The owner lives downstairs."

He jiggled a key in the lock and held the door open as the twins scampered inside. Brady almost tumbled over backward craning his neck to view the steep flight of stairs in front of him before turning around to scoot up on his bottom. I wanted to turn around, too. And *run*. My feet shuffled backward until I was leaning against the car, staring at the exterior of our new home. The vinyl siding was the standard Crayola shade of brown (no chestnut or copper or raw umber for us). The fake shutters were painted a slightly lighter brown, like a chocolate mousse, and the front steps were the color of mud. The lawn was more weeds than grass, but at least it was green. Ish.

I walked toward the porch steps but couldn't bring myself to go any farther. It was my mother's face that stopped me. For the thinnest whisper of a moment, her brave smile had slipped, and I caught her reaction. The same panic and dread that clenched my stomach were reflected back to me in her eyes.

She was as scared as I was.

"Coming in?" Mom held the screen door open, her everything-will-be-just-fine mask back in place.

"Sure," I said. "In a sec."

I waited for her to disappear inside before attempting my escape but only made it as far as the edge of our yard, all of ten paces away. I stood there, looking around. The neighborhood didn't appear to be laid out in any sort of grid. Houses were scattered at random angles, as if they'd sauntered up the hill, spied an empty lot, and plopped down. A gravel road meandered between them. Our house was the only one taller than two stories, dwarfing the squat little houses and cabins around it. Bungalows? I wasn't sure what to call them.

Some kids on bicycles came tearing around the corner, skidding on the gravel road. They headed for the playground across from our house, bumping over the grass and dirt and hopping off their bikes to make a pass across the monkey bars. They noticed me standing there, and one of the little girls stared for a minute, then said something I couldn't hear to the others and they all leaped back on their bikes and rode away.

I vaguely registered the creak of door hinges behind me and expected to hear my parents calling me inside. But they didn't. Nobody was there when I turned. I looked toward the neighboring house, a small brick ranch surrounded by a tall hedge. Nobody there, either, but I noticed for the first time an older-model Jeep parked out front. It was bright red and immaculately clean, the only vehicle I'd seen so far that wasn't covered in a film of dust from the gravel road.

I was staring at the Jeep, thinking it didn't belong here any more than I did, when its engine revved. Jumping back, I fell against the rear bumper of our car. The Jeep lurched forward and rumbled my way. I regained my balance and stood there like I'd never seen an automobile before as it covered the short distance between us and rolled to a stop in front of me.

A tattooed arm, lean but muscled, stuck out the window. It

looked familiar, and when I lifted my gaze to the driver's face, I knew where I'd seen it before. Or, rather, where I'd *ignored it before.*

The tattoo—an intricate pattern of chains and gears—belonged to none other than Lennie Lazarski, a senior at Vanderbilt High School and its most notorious druggie.

His black hair, always tied in a short ponytail at school, hung wet and loose around his face like he'd just showered. He drummed his fingers on the outside of the Jeep's door, flexing his tattoo as he looked me up and down. Then the corner of his lips curled into a lopsided grin.

"Ivy. Emerson." He punctuated my name like that, slowly, in two parts.

I didn't think it necessary to acknowledge that I was, indeed, Ivy Emerson. Or that I knew who he was. Not that I could've spoken if I'd wanted to. My mouth was suddenly very dry, and my throat . . . my throat was doing its squeezed-tight thing. I stared at him, blinking. Hoping he'd disappear.

Lazarski's eyes darted from me to our car to the brown house and back to me. He let out a single, raspy snort of laughter, then gunned the Jeep's engine again and drove off, stirring up a cloud of dust that billowed at my feet.

TWO

"Thou hast thine period?" Reesa said in a British accent. She was trying to guess the source of my agony as we sat in her bedroom after school on Friday.

Moan.

"Thy mother hath readeth thine diary?"

Reesa had been talking like this since we started studying Chaucer in AP English the week before. I shook my head, moaned some more. I didn't keep a diary, exactly. It was more of a journal, where I scribbled bits of poetry and song lyrics and occasional rants I couldn't rant about in front of Brady.

"They didn't have the dress thine wantedeth in a size zero?"

Already I felt the wedge, a little sliver of a thing at first, start to wiggle its way between us. In Reesa's world, the one I'd lived in until last week's big foreclosure reveal, the worst imaginable causes for distress were things like cramps. And a dearth of cute dresses.

"Not even close," I said.

She plopped down next to me. "I giveth up."

I took a deep breath. "You need to swear you won't tell anyone or laugh or stop being my friend. And you need to promise you will lie, if necessary, to protect me."

"Oh, my God, yes, yes, yes," she said. "Tell me. What is going on?"

I lifted a stuffed koala bear from her bed and pressed it to my face, peering over its fluffy head to gauge her reaction as I spoke the horrible words. "We're moving. To Lakeside."

Her eyes got big. "Uhhh . . . what?"

"We're moving."

"Yeah, I got that part, which is just . . . wrong. But I could swear you said you're moving to Lakeside. And that's insane."

"We're moving into an apartment over there. In a house. It's behind a long-term storage place off Jackson Boulevard, you know?"

Reesa did not know. Her blank stare got blanker.

"There's a Save-a-Buck store at the corner. Or Save-a-Cent. Whatever it's called. It's . . . it's over there." I waved feebly in the general direction of my new neighborhood.

"B-but, why?" She could not have looked more shocked and disgusted if I'd announced I was pursuing a career as a pole dancer.

"My parents are totally broke. The bank is foreclosing on our house. We're . . ." I lowered my voice. "We're *poor*."

"That's not possible. How is that possible?"

I tried to explain what my parents had told me, how my father had put our house up as collateral on a business loan right before the economy tanked. It hadn't seemed like much of a risk at the time because sales had tripled the year before. Then everything bottomed out, and Brady started having all kinds of therapy. My mom had to stop working to take care of Brady, and they couldn't keep up.

"It came down to paying our mortgage or paying for Brady's therapy," I said. "And they couldn't exactly stop teaching him how to talk and stuff."

Reesa squeezed her cheeks between her hands, nodding. She knew. Outside our immediate family, she was one of the few people who knew the challenges Brady faced, how hard everything was for him. She watched him take his first steps, applauding along with the rest of us. She helped me teach him how to clap. He still claps whenever he sees her.

"Couldn't they, like, declare bankruptcy or something? That's what my uncle did and he didn't have to give up his house or his boat or anything," said Reesa.

"I don't think it's an option." Or, at least, not one my father was willing to consider. I had overheard my parents arguing about it months ago, one of many signs of our impending doom that I'd ignored. When I walked in and asked what was wrong, they said everything was fine. *Nothing for you to worry about, sweetie.*

Maybe they'd thought they could fix it, that something would come up. But it hadn't. They'd put off the inevitable as long as they could. "Dad said we just have to live within our means. Make it work."

"Like *Project Runway*."

"I wish." I flopped back on the bed. "Try 'Project Poverty.'"

Reesa crinkled her nose as if she'd just taken a whiff of the girls' locker room at school. I had thought it would make me feel better to tell Reesa, to hear her say everything would be all right, that it wasn't so bad, that nobody would even notice or care. But she didn't say any of those things.

She said, "That sucketh."

I hadn't even described the house yet—its overwhelming brown-ness, my closet-sized bedroom. "It's not that bad," I lied, suddenly afraid of scaring her off entirely. "Kind of cozy, actually."

Reesa pouted. "I'll never see you. You'll be too busy smoking pot. And getting tattoos."

I rolled my eyes. "No, I won't." I had already decided not to mention Lennie Lazarski. Even a friend as loyal as Reesa might run screaming if I mentioned that he lived next door.

"Move over." She put her head next to mine on the pillow and we both stared at the ceiling. There were still a few of the glow-in-the-dark stars we'd stuck up there in the shape of constellations when we were twelve. "I can't believe you're leaving me."

"I'll see you at school every day, and I'll get Mom to drive me over here on weekends, and you can . . ." I almost suggested she visit me, but I didn't want to trigger that smelly-locker-room sneer again.

"I'll call you," she said. "All the time."

I pulled my phone out, dialed her number, and showed her the NO SERVICE message that popped up on the screen. "I'm officially a total loser. Just, please . . . don't tell anyone. Okay?"

"Someone might notice if you never answer your phone again."

"I'll make up some excuse. Nobody has to know I moved. *Nobody.*"

Reesa nodded, knowing exactly who I was talking about: Willow Goodwin and Wynn Davies, a.k.a. Wicked and Witch. We ate lunch with them every day, went shopping together, attended the same parties. They were among our closest friends.

And we couldn't stand them half the time.

Willow's mother was "old money" and her dad worked as an attorney, not that he had to work at all. *The only reason my dad works is so he doesn't have to hang out with my mom all day,* Willow told us. She insisted that she hated her mother, but she didn't mind the perks that came with being Frances Goodwin's daughter, like getting the role of Clara in *The Nutcracker* after her mother donated a million dollars to the Belleview Ballet.

Wynn was spoiled, too, but more so by the absence of her parents. They took their role as socialites seriously, and that meant Wynn was practically raised by a revolving door of nannies du jour. Her parents bought her whatever she wanted to keep her happy.

The two of them sat at the tippy top of the social ladder of Vanderbilt High School and made it their business to know *everything* about *everybody.*

"They'll find out," said Reesa. "They always do."

My throat tightened. I knew girls fed gossip to Willow and Wynn, simply to avoid being targeted themselves—a preemptive strike of sorts.

"Can't your parents borrow money from someone?" Reesa reached for the Tiffany-blue, polka-dotted piggy bank on her nightstand, as if its contents would make a difference.

I shook my head.

"My parents are packing up the last of our stuff right now, so we can move this weekend," I said. The bank wasn't officially foreclosing on the house for another month, but it would take a few weeks to sell all the furniture we weren't taking with us.

"This weekend?" Reesa sucked in a sharp breath. "As in tomorrow?"

I closed my eyes. "Yeah."

"This is bad."

Duh.

"But it's not, like, permanent, is it?" Reesa was going through the same five stages of Oh-Shit-This-Can't-Be-Happening that I had: denial, denial, denial, denial, and denial.

I could only shrug. My father had assured me the apartment

was a temporary fix. We'd find a regular house in Westside Falls once the debts were paid and some of our savings replenished. But he wouldn't say if "temporary" meant a few weeks or a few months. I didn't want to consider that it might be even longer.

THREE

Saturday morning I rode shotgun in the truck Daddy rented to haul our stuff. Mom was planning to follow in the car with the twins and Brady's little fish tank once she packed up the food from our fridge. I hadn't showered. My hair was knotted into the same messy bun I'd slept in, and my sweatshirt had toothpaste down the front. Not that it mattered. Nobody important would see me today.

"The red couch from the den will go in the living room," said Dad, seemingly oblivious to my unenthusiasm. "Your mother's little writing desk will fit in your room. That small dresser of Kaya's will be yours, too. . . ."

I zoned out on his detailed inventory of what we'd brought from our old house. My piano hadn't made the cut, of course. None of my bedroom furniture had, either. All of it was too big to fit in the tiny attic room that would be mine.

". . . and Carla asked one of the neighbor boys to put together a moving crew to help us unload, so it shouldn't take long."

"Who?" I said, panic rising in my throat.

"Carla Rodriguez. Our landlady. She's very nice. Your mother's already spoken to her about watching Brady and Kaya from time to time. I think you'll like her. She's—"

"No, what neighbor boy?"

"Hmm?" He bent over the steering wheel to see out my side-view mirror. "I think I just cut that guy off. Sorry!" He waggled his hand toward my window. "Give him a wave, so he doesn't think we're jerks."

I leaned out the window and offered what I hoped was a we're-not-jerks sort of wave. In the side mirror, I saw an arm shoot out of the passenger side, wave, then give me the finger.

"I'm pretty sure he still thinks we're jerks," I mumbled. I rolled up my window and ducked down in my seat.

The car continued to follow us into our new neighborhood, stopping in front of the Lazarskis' house as we pulled in front of ours.

"Uh, Dad? I think the guy we cut off is part of our moving crew . . . or he wants to kill us," I said. I slid down in my seat even more.

"Oh, great. I can apologize in person." Dad jumped out and strode over to their car. The whole embarrassing scene was visible in the driver's side-view mirror.

"Sorry 'bout that, boys," Dad said, sounding like one of those annoyingly reasonable and cheerful fathers on a 1960s sitcom. "It's harder to drive that thing than I thought." He gestured toward the truck and I ducked down farther—I was practically on the floor at this point—so they wouldn't spot me.

There was some muttering among them that I couldn't make out, and the squeak of a screen door. Someone shouted, "Lazo, my man!" A voice that I presumed was Lazo's said, "Gentlemen." And the decidedly-not-gentlemen laughed.

More muttering. Then Dad was back, opening the door to the truck. "Are you coming? Do you want to meet the boys?"

"No." I shook my head. "No way."

"Ivy, please."

I shook my head again and Daddy sighed, closed the truck door, and walked up to the front porch. I heard a woman's voice, and the door to the house closed.

Then laughing. Hooting. "'Sorry, boys,'" someone mimicked my dad's deep voice. More laughing. Then, "Shut it, dickwad," "I need a smoke," and "Are we gettin' paid to carry that asshole's furniture, or what?"

I pulled the hood of my sweatshirt up and pressed it to my ears. When Daddy came back to the truck, I would tell him to make them go away. I'd rather carry every single box up three flights of stairs myself than let any one of them step foot in our apartment.

Suddenly, the passenger door I was leaning against was yanked open, and I nearly rolled out backward.

"Shit, Emerson." Lennie Lazarski caught my shoulders from behind and shoved me back in. "What the fuck are you doing?"

A kid with a scar under his lip stood behind him laughing.

"Nice language," I said, scrambling onto the seat.

"Yeah, nice language, Leonard," said Scar Face. "Is that any way to talk to such a fine piece of Westside ass?"

Lazarski smirked. "She's not a Westsider anymore, is she?"

I wanted to shout that I was not a Lakesider and never would be, but I was *here*. In a moving truck. Waiting for my belongings to be unloaded. It was kind of hard to claim that I wasn't one of them. I reached for the door handle instead and slammed the door closed, punching the manual lock down with my fist.

"Go away," I said through the glass.

Lazarski crossed his arms over his chest and tilted his head back so he could look down his nose at me. "You gonna carry this stuff inside all by yourself?"

I took a deep, shuddery breath and cranked the window down a couple of inches, to make sure he could hear me. "Yes, we are. Your services are no longer required, so you and your friends can go home."

A slow smile spread across his lips. He uncrossed his arms and did a deep, exaggerated bow, swishing his hand in the air like he was bowing to the Queen of England. "As you wish, Your Royal Highness."

Sauntering away, he threw an arm over Scar Face's shoulder and called out to the guys, "Hear that, gentlemen? Our services are no longer required."

They all started talking over one another. "Great." "I got out of bed for this shit?" "What'd you say to her?" "This is bullshit, man." "Dude, I'm hungry." "Yeah. Let's eat." "Vinny's?" "Yeah, Vinny's."

I lay on the truck seat with my arms wrapped around my head until I finally heard four car doors slam shut and the sound of tires spinning out on gravel.

A few minutes later, the front door to our house swung open. I lifted my head to see Daddy step onto the porch, followed by a slender, dark-haired woman. Carla, I presumed. They looked toward the puff of gravel dust the car had left in its wake.

"Where'd everybody go?" said Dad.

Carla took a few steps toward Lazarski's house. "Leonard?"

I scrambled to the driver's-side door and pushed it open, jumping down to the road. Lazarski was nowhere to be seen.

Dad turned a befuddled face toward me. "What happened?"

"Nothing, they . . ." I lifted my chin, refusing to cry. "We don't need any help. We can do it ourselves."

I walked shakily to the back of the truck and pulled the lever to open the cargo doors. A box of pillows tipped over and spilled its contents onto the road. A single bark of laughter came from Lazarski's backyard. My sincere hope that he'd left with his friends was dashed. Slowly, I bent to collect the pillows and put them back in the box. I would *not* cry in front of that jerk-off. I would *not*.

Dad joined me at the truck. "Ivy," he said gently, "are—"

"Let's just get this done, Dad. Okay?"

He nodded, and we quietly started carrying things upstairs.

By the time Mom and the twins arrived, we had already made twenty trips each. As soon as I dropped a box in whichever room Mom had marked it for with her blue Sharpie, I turned around and went down for another. Carla helped us wedge the couch up the stairs and kept an eye on Brady while we hauled everything else up. We took a break a few hours later, ate sandwiches standing around the tiny counter of our new kitchen, then went back to hauling boxes.

I overheard Mom hissing at Dad when she didn't think I was listening, "We should've hired someone ourselves. Or asked some of the guys from the shop."

Dad gave her a funny look. He obviously didn't want his employees to see our new neighborhood any more than I wanted my friends to. "Too late now," he said, heaving another box from the truck. "Won't take much longer."

Six hours later, it was done.

Brady was happily introducing his fish to their new room. The tank was so close to his bed, they were practically sleeping with him. He was thrilled.

I made a final climb to my attic room, lay down on the bare mattress of my single bed, and stared at the boxes filled with the remains of my life. I didn't even have the energy to search for my earbuds and plug them into my not-a-phone-anymore to listen to music. As I closed my eyes, the noise of the neighborhood drifted in—car doors and dogs barking and the pounding bass of a passing car stereo. I took pride in being able to find music in nearly every sound. The rustle of leaves, a squeaky swing swaying in the breeze, the slamming of lockers . . . laughter, footsteps, sighs, even sneezes. Finding my own voice was sometimes hard, but I could always hear the music around me.

But here, in Lakeside, I wasn't sure I'd ever hear it again.

FOUR

Someone had slipped off my shoes and unpacked a blanket to cover me. I'd slept in my clothes on that bare mattress straight through to Sunday morning and didn't wake until the sun hit my little dormer window at just the right angle to shine in my face.

I went down to use the bathroom, which was next to my parents' room on the third floor, and down again to find my family unpacking the kitchen. Mom fussed over me. Made me eat an egg. Brady wanted me to see his bunk bed. My legs ached. But I followed him up, huddled with him on the bottom bunk for a while.

I really needed to brush my teeth and shower, but the thought of climbing stairs again to get my stuff made me want to cry. The apartment was so vertical, I wondered if we wouldn't have more space if we laid the building on its side. Carla lived on the lower level, which had a kitchen addition out the back that made it a bit more spacious than the upper floors. A narrow stairway led from the front door to the second floor, which contained our living room and kitchen, and there was a little landing out the back with another set of stairs to the backyard.

Mom was not amused when I referred to the staircases as "two means of escape."

Next to the twins' bedroom was a little hallway where more stairs led up to my room, a.k.a. the attic, the fourth floor, the tippy top. Somehow, when I'd imagined living in a penthouse someday, this wasn't exactly what I'd had in mind. There wasn't even a proper door, just a rainbow-striped curtain I could pull across the opening at the top of the stairs.

The "walk-in closet" my mother had promised consisted of a bar mounted between the sloping walls of my attic room. It was more of a dive-in closet, since the single bed occupied the entire width of the room and I had to leap over it to get to my clothes. The tiny desk and dresser sat on either side of a dormer window that looked out the back.

The view out my window wasn't as bad as I'd expected. No snarling dogs pulling against chains. No yards littered with broken-down cars. There were some lawn ornaments you might not find in Westside Falls—like the small flock of plastic pink flamingoes a few houses down. But the yards were neat and tidy for the most part. People were out on their stoops or hanging their laundry or fixing their cars, talking or laughing or arguing.

Nobody I knew ever hung laundry outside or fixed their own cars.

On the road behind ours, sitting next to someone's trash, I

spied the answer to at least one of my problems: a bicycle with a FOR SALE sign taped to its spokes. My parents had sold mine in a last-ditch online auction frenzy, thinking I wouldn't care since I hardly ever rode it. But now that I faced total humiliation on the state penitentiary bus, I cared.

Our new neighborhood might have been light-years away from my old life, but it was only 3.5 miles to Vanderbilt High. So I pulled the last of my dwindling cash from my purse and walked over there.

"How much for the bike?" I asked the elderly man who answered the door.

He limped outside, leaning heavily on a cane, to size me up. I wished I'd thought to put on scruffier clothes. "Fifty," he said.

"For that old thing?" The bike was rusty. I didn't even know if the tires could hold air. "How about twenty?"

The man gasped and held a hand to his chest. "You insult me," he said. "That's a classic Schwinn. Vintage. People pay a lot of money for bikes like that."

I nodded slowly. "Well, thanks, anyway." I smiled and headed back toward the road. I had fifty dollars, but that was *all* I had. Considering the man had sat the bike so close to his trash, I had a feeling he'd take my twenty bucks. Nobody else had come up to make an offer in the hour I'd watched out my window. And from what I could tell, every other kid around here already had a mode of transportation.

The man cleared his throat a few times as I walked away.

"Now, wait up. Just a minute. I didn't say I wasn't willing to negotiate. You can have it for twenty-five."

I stopped and turned around. "If you throw in a tire pump, you have a deal."

He paused, then shuffled over to a little shed and dug around in it until he found a tire pump. I took it, gave the man his twenty-five dollars, and wheeled the bike away. It squeaked and rattled, but it rolled.

I searched for a place to hide it. The playground across from our house was surrounded by woods. I found a path that cut through the trees and tucked the bike behind a snarl of vines a few feet off the trail. Secrecy was my new best friend, apparently. It was a matter of survival, I told myself. My parents would never let me ride that thing to school. They'd have plenty of good reasons: too dark, too bumpy, no headlights, no helmet. And there were stretches where the road to school had no shoulder.

But the bus? So much scarier. I might survive the bus trip itself without being physically harmed (I heard an armed police officer rode along), but I'd be seen. And everyone would know. And that would be worse. Westsiders and Lakesiders did not mix at our school. We sat on separate sides of the cafeteria and in different sections of the bleachers at football games. It was bad enough Lennie and his friends knew I lived here, but I could be fairly certain they wouldn't be chatting with any of my friends about it. Stepping off the state pen bus in front of the building, though? I might as well announce it at a school-wide assembly.

Satisfied that the bike was sufficiently concealed, I turned for home—or, rather, that brown thing we were living in. I spotted Lennie walking from his backyard toward a pickup truck that was idling along the gravel road in front of our houses, so I lingered in the shadows of the tree line. He handed something through the driver's window, and the guy took a few bills from his wallet and flipped them into Lennie's hand. They chatted, laughed. I couldn't hear what they were saying, but had a pretty good idea what they were doing.

And it happened three more times that day. I saw out of our window a vehicle arriving, Lennie going out, an exchange, and the car driving off. Each transaction took less than five minutes.

"Shouldn't someone report that?" I asked when the fourth one had come and gone.

"What?" Dad continued ripping tape off empty boxes and flattening them under his foot in the backyard.

I told him what I saw.

"Don't jump to conclusions. You have no idea what's going on there."

Oh, I had ideas, all right. I just couldn't believe the guy was so bold about it.

By the afternoon, we were settled in. When your living space is roughly the size of a shoe box, it doesn't take a whole lot of time to unpack. Clothes were jammed onto that bar across my room and shoved under the bed in plastic bins. Still, I'd left at least half my wardrobe behind. "The half you've worn once and never looked at again," my mother pointed out. I could've added, *Because Willow or Wynn said it made me look fat, or wasn't the right color, or was frumpy or bunchy, or OMG their cleaning lady had the exact same blouse!* Mom was taking it all to a consignment shop, where other unsuspecting girls could relive my fashion faux pas at half the price.

The bunk beds and a marathon game of hide-and-seek had kept the twins entertained for most of the weekend. Kaya didn't even mind that Brady crawled under the exact same box whenever it was his turn to hide. She still searched and searched, calling out his name before finding him. I took them to the playground and helped him up the ladder and down the slide about eight hundred times, and he squealed with delight every single time. The monotony of it would drive most people crazy, but Brady's smile was probably the only thing keeping me from crying. So we kept on sliding.

Then came bedtime and we tried to go through our usual routine, but Kaya started noticing which of her toys were missing, like the sock monkey she hadn't played with for three years. Suddenly, it was her all-time favorite. Brady fixated on his train puzzle, one stupid train puzzle that hadn't made the cut when Mom packed their favorite things.

Kaya's shoulders quivered as she tried not to cry, but eventually, the tears came. She just couldn't hold it in anymore. I knew how she felt. Brady started rocking back and forth on the floor saying "train puzzle train puzzle" over and over again. I found a different puzzle, with dump trucks on it, but he merely clapped his hands to his ears and squeezed his eyes shut tight.

Dad appeared in the doorway to the twins' bedroom and pressed his forearms against its frame, as if he was holding the walls from crashing in on us. We all stared up at him. The crying and rocking stopped.

"Kids?" His tone was grave. "This isn't going to be easy, adjusting to our new home. It's a lot smaller. Everything we had before won't fit here. Okay? But we all need to try our best, and make do with what we have."

Kaya started whimpering again and Dad held up his hand like a stop sign, as if that would work. But, oddly, it did. She pressed her lips hard together and held her breath.

"We will make one more trip to the house. You may each pick one item to bring back. Just one. Then that's it. Got it?" His eyes locked on mine first, then Kaya's, then Brady's. We each nodded in turn.

"Get in the car," he said.

"Like this?" I gestured to the pajamas we were all wearing.

"Yep. Let's go."

Mom let out a huge sigh, and the air went back into the room. We all tumbled down the stairs and into the car. Nobody said anything the whole way there. Brady even stopped his puzzle chant. When we pulled up the driveway, our house looked so dark and empty, so lonely. So enormous.

I went to my room first, scanning the remains for that single left-behind item that would make my life in Lakeside bearable. The one thing I wanted wasn't in my room, though. It had a room of its own.

My mother had purchased my piano before I was born. It was one of the reasons they'd bought this house. She'd seen this room and known immediately it would make the perfect piano room. I started playing when I was three, but ever since the talent show debacle in fifth grade, my performances were reserved for the twins only.

Mom came up behind me then and laid her fingers next to mine on the keys. "We'll get you a keyboard for the apartment," she said. "I promise. Everything will work itself out. You'll see."

I nodded and closed the lid. We both knew it wouldn't be the same. Leaving my piano behind was like chopping off an arm. No . . . more like wearing a blindfold. Music helped me see things. Whenever I was confused or upset or frustrated, I went to the piano like it was my own private shrink. Reesa called it "Dr. Steinway."

"You're selling it," I said. It wasn't a question.

Mom nodded and stroked her hand along the curved body of the piano. "Not right away, though. The realtor for the bank said she'd find out if the people who buy the house want it."

"That's nice." I don't know why I said that, because it wasn't nice at all. But it gave me a little glimmer of hope. Maybe the house wouldn't sell. Maybe we'd get to come back and my piano would be here waiting for me.

Maybe I was still in denial.

"We have to do this for Brady," she said quietly. "We need the money. If he doesn't get the therapy now . . ."

"I know, Mom." I strode to my room before she could remind me how much the sacrifices we made now would mean for Brady's future. Even with twenty hours a week of therapy—speech and physical and occupational—his life would be a constant struggle. Without it, he didn't have a chance. Didn't I want the best for him? I would say, "Of course I do." Because I did. I only wished it didn't mean the worst for the rest of us.

I went to my wall of shelves to search for that special something to take with me and ran my fingers across the spines of my favorite books. I wanted them all, not just one. So I had decided to leave the lot of them behind. Good-bye, *Will Grayson*. Farewell, *Jane Eyre*. See ya, *Stargirl*.

I looked around. Resting on the top shelf was the ukulele my aunt Betty had given me. I hadn't played it much. It was too quiet. It could never make the entire room vibrate like the Steinway could. I reached for it and blew the dust off its frets, strummed a badly out-of-tune chord. Maybe I'd give the uke another chance. Maybe it was just the right instrument for our tiny apartment and the smallness of my voice when my throat felt tight. I tucked it under my arm and went down to the car. Dad smiled but said nothing.

Kaya got her sock monkey. After tearing through the entire house in his Superman pajamas, Brady had decided he didn't want his train puzzle after all. He chose a small, fuzzy accent pillow from the couch in the TV room. Dad raised an eyebrow, but he certainly wasn't about to argue. We'd made our choices, and that was that. Mom hadn't picked anything, though, so Dad disappeared into their room and came out with one of her slinky evening dresses.

"I don't think that'll fit you," she joked, but wrapped her arms around his neck. "Shouldn't you pick something more practical?"

He gave my mother a long kiss, long enough to make Kaya hide her eyes. "Just because we can't afford a beautiful house doesn't mean you can't have any beautiful things," he said. "It doesn't mean we'll never have an occasion to celebrate again."

Mom looked up at the house, swept her hand from one end to the other as if brushing it away. "We never needed all this," she said. "I don't know why we bought it in the first place."

The mother I knew, the one who took such pride in our home and fussed over every tiny detail of its décor—the fringe on every pillow, the angle of every chair, the potting of every plant—seemed to disappear before my eyes.

I knew our furniture would be disappearing soon, too. At least we wouldn't be there when it was carted off by the auction house. Mom said they'd get better prices than she could, but I had a feeling she just didn't want to witness our life being sold to the highest bidder, piece by piece.

Back at the apartment, my father tucked the twins into their bunk beds and read to them. Their room was directly below mine, and I could hear their soft voices filtering up the attic stairs. When Dad snapped the book shut and kissed their cheeks, I heard that, too. He flipped off the light. Click.

"Ivy sing," said Brady.

"Yeah," said Kaya. "We didn't get our song."

I'd been singing to them at bedtime since they were babies, when they'd finally put on enough weight to come home from the hospital. At our old house, the piano room was in between their two bedrooms. I would sit there and play and sing until they drifted off to sleep. It was our thing. I didn't perform anywhere else, or for anybody else. *Ever.* Not since my spectacular display of stage fright during the district-wide talent show when I was eleven. I had frozen onstage like some shocked victim of Medusa. After that, the mere thought of performing made my throat close up, like someone was strangling me.

But it was different at home—at our old home. I could play and sing there, safe behind walls of stone and layers of insulation and acres of yard and trees and space. Not these paper-thin walls.

Dad took a few steps up and poked his head in the opening to my room. I pretended to be sleeping. It was a decision my body made before my mind could convince it otherwise. I loved singing to the twins, and I hated to disappoint them. But I felt so exposed here. It was a warm night and the windows were open. People might hear me. People like . . .

"You awake?" Dad whispered.

I didn't answer. Because I'm a coward. And a liar, apparently.

Dad went back down and told the twins I had fallen asleep, that he would sing to them instead. Kaya said, “Blackbird,” and Dad obliged with his soft, breathy version of the Beatles song.

When he finished, I heard the rustling below as he tucked and kissed and closed the door. Then, through the thin walls, a tiny, off-key voice:

“La-la-la-la-la.” Brady was trying to sing his own la-la lullaby. That’s what we called the bedtime songs I made up for him that used only the sound “la” so that he could easily sing along.

He sang his la-las over and over again, eventually lulling himself to sleep.

FIVE

There was a split second when I first woke up the next morning that I didn't feel like I was going to vomit. But then I remembered where I was, and what I faced. I hadn't heard from Reesa all weekend. No calls, and no email since we hadn't had a chance to set it up yet. No cell phone meant no texts, either. Reesa and I always used to text each other in the morning—what we were wearing, how horribly our hair was behaving. Reesa saw things in her breakfast cereal and would send me pictures: DO THESE CORNFLAKES LOOK LIKE STONEHENGE OR IS IT JUST ME?

But she'd been silent, and it felt like I'd moved to another planet.

The morning was a jumble as my family got in each other's way dodging and reaching for cereal, milk, toothbrushes, shoes, coats, backpacks. I had calculated that our new home was about the same total square footage as my parents' bedroom, bathroom, and closet in our old house. We now lived in about one-tenth the space we had before. The strangeness of it confused Brady.

It must've reminded him of a vacation house we once rented in Sea Isle—which had an outside shower but only one bathroom inside—because he kept asking, "Which way the beach?"

"Which way *to* the beach," I said, tying his shoes.

My parents hadn't corrected his speech in days—which was bad because of the way he locked onto things. It was hard for him to unlearn something once he'd gotten it wrong.

"Which way to the beach?" He smiled, proud of his good sentence.

"No beach here, buddy. But I'll take you to the playground after school. Okay?"

He gave me one of his signature kisses—a press of wet lips to my cheek, followed by a smacking sound. He hadn't quite coordinated the two yet. I kissed him back, extra hard.

My plan was to slip out by six twenty, retrieve the bicycle, and get to school before the buses. I figured Mom and Dad would be too distracted to realize I was leaving a half hour early. But I hadn't counted on Kaya watching my every move.

"Where are you going?" She stood blocking the top of the stairs that led down to the front door, arms crossed and hip jutting out.

"School," I said.

"It only takes three minutes to get to the bus stop. I timed it." She tapped her pink glitter watch.

"I like to be early. Just in case." I avoided her lie-detector gaze.

"Since when?"

"What?" This conversation was wasting precious time. I pulled my backpack onto my shoulders.

"Since when do you like to be early?"

I sighed heavily. "Since none of your business. Can I get through here, please?"

She stepped aside and waited until I reached the bottom step to cup her hands and call down to me, "Have a nice ride!"

"How did . . ." I spun around but snapped my mouth shut. Maybe she was referring to the bus ride, not bicycle. I was being paranoid. "Thanks," I managed. "You too. Let the bus driver know if anybody messes with you or Brady, okay?"

She nodded and disappeared into the living room, and I flew out the door like a claustrophobe escaping an elevator. It was much darker at six thirty than I'd expected. I stumbled around the woods searching for the Schwinn, which I'd hidden so well, nobody would ever find it. *Including me.* Using my not-a-phone-anymore as a flashlight, I swept its beam across the trees until I spotted my trusty getaway vehicle. The handlebars were cold against my bare hands. I flung a leg over the seat and steadied myself, then kicked off and pedaled across the playground toward the road.

The bike groaned beneath my weight, rattling over the gravel. My legs seemed to be groaning, too, after all the stair climbing I'd done over the weekend. But I picked up speed once I hit the paved road, the wind whipping my hair into my eyes. I hadn't thought to tie it back. At the first stop sign, I yanked my hood up and cinched it tight around my face, tucking every last stray brown curl inside.

God, I hoped nobody saw me.

The transportation office at school had given Mom a map of our new bus routes, which I'd used to figure out the most direct route by bicycle. It seemed easy enough, only one right turn and one left . . . but it all looked so different on the ground in the dim light of dawn than it had on the map. Every car that passed sent a shiver through me. Nobody knew I was out here. Someone could knock me off the road or kidnap me, take me to a soundproof cell in their basement and imprison me there. I'd never see my family again.

Maybe I was exaggerating the dangers of bicycling through Lakeside. Or maybe I should've just sucked it up and taken the bus.

I pedaled faster, swerving to miss potholes I swear were big enough to swallow small children.

My thighs were burning as I made my final turn and saw Vanderbilt High looming ahead, the lights of the parking lot casting an eerie glow through the morning mist. No buses in sight, though. Still, I didn't want to ride up to the front of the school on this thing, so I headed to the loading dock out back by the faculty parking lot. There was a hedge along the side that looked like the perfect hiding spot. I swerved toward it, bumping onto the grass and squealing to a stop. The gap between the hedge and the wall was only about ten inches wide, but if I turned the handlebar sideways a bit, the bike slipped right in. I shoved it far enough back that nobody could see it, then scanned the parking lot to make sure I wasn't being watched.

A sleek black sedan pulled in, so I crouched low and waited, wondering which of our teachers drove such a nice car. But it wasn't a teacher who stepped out, at least not one I'd ever seen before. It was a guy. Tall-ish, blond-ish, cute-ish. If he was a new student, Willow would probably be dating him by lunch. He pulled a messenger bag from the trunk and threw it over his shoulder, then walked in my direction. I ducked farther behind the wall. Why was he parking there? Maybe nobody had told him this lot was for teachers and staff only. Or was he worried his fancy car would get scratched in the student lot? I heard his footsteps approaching and, realizing I was about to be discovered squatting behind shrubbery, leaped to my feet as he rounded the corner. He jumped sideways, his startled eyes flashing to mine.

"Sorry," I squeaked. My face felt so hot, I was afraid there might be steam rising from it. "I . . . uh . . . was just . . . um."

He took in the scene of me and my bicycle hiding in the bushes, and one of his eyebrows shot up.

I went catatonic. He was standing so close and he had beautiful, pale-blue eyes. They rested on mine for a second, then drifted up to my hair, which was crammed into my hoodie.

"Oh, God." I fumbled with the drawstrings under my chin and shoved the hood back. My hair sprang out like a can of rubber snakes. I tried to flatten it down.

He took a step back and looked at his feet, like maybe he was trying to give me a moment to collect myself. But I was pretty much uncollectible at this point, so I just stood there staring at him, all sweaty and panting like a dog.

When he looked up, he tipped his chin toward the bicycle crammed into the hedges behind me. "You, uh . . . do this every day?" A sweep of sandy-blond hair fell across his eyes, and he pushed it back.

My face went redder than it already was. I didn't need a mirror. I could feel it. "I, no . . . I just . . . my bike . . ."

He teetered back on his heels a bit, hands shoved in his back pockets.

"This is the first time," I said, finally managing to form a complete sentence.

"Oh. Cool." He looked anxiously toward the front of the school. Probably eager to get away from the crazy girl in the bushes. "Well, I better go."

I nodded. "Right. Okay."

But he didn't go right away. He hesitated, like he was going to say something more, then just smiled. "Bye, then."

"Bye."

As he walked away, I felt a trickle of sweat drip down the small of my back. He must have thought I was a complete idiot. At least he was new and didn't know anybody he could blab to about my unfortunate appearance and bizarre behavior.

I knelt beside the hedge to deal with my perspiration situation, unzipping my sweatshirt to let the cool air dry my damp skin. I found a tissue in my backpack and dabbed it across my face. When I pulled it away, I saw a brown smudge. With legs.

I whimpered, shoving the dead-bug tissue into my pocket and hoisting my backpack to my shoulder. School buses were arriving. I moseyed out of my hiding place like it was perfectly normal to enter the campus through a hedge, and merged onto the sidewalk.

I was almost home free, zombie-shuffling toward the building like everyone else, when someone fell into step directly behind me. I scooted to the side to let the kid pass. But whoever it was stepped sideways right along with me. Assuming it was Reesa goofing with me, I stopped abruptly.

And then Lennie Lazarski sidled up beside me and murmured in my ear. "Hi, neighbor."

I stopped, sucked in my breath, inhaling the dead-giveaway, burnt-leaf scent of a pot smoker.

"You really should wear a helmet, you know."

"I have no idea what you're talking about," I said, picking up my pace.

He laughed. "Okay. But I still saw you."

I stopped and glared at him. "Saw me what?"

"Hiding your bicycle."

"I wasn't hiding it. I, uh . . . don't have a lock, so I parked it back there so nobody would—"

"Steal it? You think someone's going to steal that thing?" He barked out that annoying laugh of his, a single, loud "Ha!" Everyone walking within a five-mile radius turned and gawked.

My face burned for the second time that day, and it was barely seven o'clock. "It happens to be a classic Schwinn. People pay a lot of money for vintage bicycles like that, you know."

He chuckled. "Looks more like something you found, oh, I don't know . . . lying in the trash by the side of the road?"

"It wasn't in the trash, it was . . ." I snapped my mouth shut. "Why am I even talking to you?"

"Just being neighborly?"

I ran up the stairs, hoping to distance myself from him before we reached the entrance. But he took the steps two at a time and lunged to open one of the double glass doors for me.

"Thank you," I muttered.

"You're very welcome." There were two sets of doors, and he leaped ahead of me to get the second one as well. I told myself he'd go away then. He'd go his way and I'd go mine, and . . .

"So, how's life in Turd Tower so far?"

"In WHAT?" I immediately regretted the volume of my reply as another dozen people registered me talking to Lazarski. I imagined tiny little cameras snap, snap, snapping away, like paparazzi. "What are you talking about?" I asked, trying to speak without moving my lips.

"Your house," he said. "Don't tell me you haven't noticed it kinda looks like a giant turd. A very tall one."

My mouth dropped open, but I was too stunned to cough up a

clever retort. He was absolutely right. My new brown-on-brown-on-brown home looked like shit. And I was living in it.

Having it rubbed in my face by Lennie Lazarski was more than I could bear. My eyes started to burn with hot tears. I spun around to escape him and marched down the hall toward my locker.

Where Willow and Wynn were waiting for me.

SIX

"I-vy!" Willow waved to make sure I'd seen her, in case I missed her shouting my name with her megaphone voice. Wynn greeted me with a more delicate wiggle of her fingers, lashes fluttering. I knew better than to be fooled by their sweetness.

"Hey." I continued walking, hoping they'd go back to their usual favorite pastime of admiring themselves. But the clomp of their heels followed in my wake. When I reached my locker, they pulled up on either side of me, like tennis players preparing to volley.

"New boyfriend?" Willow nodded toward the entrance.

"Huh?" My eyelid twitched.

"We saw you talking to Loser Lazarski," said Wynn.

I pressed the knuckles of my right hand to my twitching eye. "He's not . . . I wasn't talking to him. He opened the door for me and I said thank you. It's called being polite. You should try it sometime."

"To him?" Willow gave a fake shudder. "No thanks."

Wynn reached over and plucked something out of my hair. A leaf. "Nice. Were you rolling around in the grass with him or something?"

I grabbed the leaf from her hand and let it fall in crumbled bits to the floor. "No! I barely spoke to him."

"We're kidding," Willow said in a monotone. "God, lighten up."

I wasn't sure that was possible, what with the quicksand of my life swallowing me whole.

"Where were you this weekend?" Willow twisted a stray hair around the dancer bun she always wore. "You didn't return our texts."

Wynn made puppy-dog eyes. "Are you mad at us or something?"

"No, I . . . uh . . . lost my phone."

"That sucks," said Willow. "When are you getting a new one?"

I shrugged. "I'm thinking maybe I don't really need a phone—"

"Right." She laughed, then realized I might actually be serious. "Tell me you're kidding."

For a few seconds, an alternate conversation went through my head in which I confessed the truth of my situation, that my family was broke and living in Lakeside, next door to a drug dealer. But the look of disgust on Willow's face at the mention of no cell phone was so horrible, I just wanted to make it go away. I broke into a smile. "Of course, I'm kidding. My dad's ordering a new one through his work. It might take a few days."

Willow sighed. "Don't joke like that."

Wynn yanked me into a hug, then quickly pulled away. "Ew. You're all sweaty."

"I, uh . . . had to run for the bus."

They glanced sideways at each other. Willow put her fingertips on my sleeve. "Text us as soon as you get your phone, 'kay?"

"Sure."

Wynn air-kissed my cheeks, both sides as she had been doing ever since her family went to Europe last summer. Then they were gone.

An irrational sense of relief flooded over me, like I'd successfully tiptoed through a minefield. My hand smoothed nervously over my unruly curls, which seemed to have picked up even more altitude than usual. I quickly opened my locker, got the books I needed for first period, and hurried to the bathroom. Windswept was not exactly a good look for me. Wetting my hands, I combed through my hair, then dried my damp arms with a paper towel.

My exterior appeared almost the same as usual, but it didn't feel that way on the inside. In homeroom, I stood for the pledge and pretended to listen to announcements, certain everyone was staring at me. Was it on my face in some way?

I caught up with Reesa on the way to first-period AP English. "Do I look different to you?"

"What do you mean?" She dabbed some gloss on her lips.

"I don't know." I dropped to a whisper. "Poor?"

Her gaze swept from my head to my toes and back up again. "Nope. Same as always, you skinny bitch."

I smiled. "Thanks, Rees." Reesa was always complaining about her curves, and I was always complaining about my lack thereof. The only thing I had that wasn't straight was my hair, and Reesa was the opposite.

We walked into AP English and took our seats as the bell rang. Mr. Eli wrote *The Canterbury Tales* on the board and underlined it three times. There were a few sputters of nervous laughter. Our assignment had been to memorize the opening part of the prelude, as it was originally written in Middle English, and recite it in front of the entire class.

I sat as still as possible and kept my eyes on the floor. Mr. Eli strolled the aisles between our desks until everyone was settled and quiet. "Now, don't strain yourselves volunteering all at once," he said.

The door opened and I said a silent thanks for the disruption, then looked up. It was the guy from the hedge this morning. He had this adorable way of tipping his chin down and looking out the top of his eyes, through his hair. He was doing it to Mr. Eli right now.

"Can I help you?" Our teacher took a step toward him.

Sitting next to me, Reesa sucked a breath through her teeth. "Be stillith myith heart."

The boy handed Mr. Eli a paper. "I'm new," he said. "Is this AP English?"

Mr. Eli nodded. "Yes, uh . . ." He looked at the paper. "James Wickerton?"

James nodded. Mr. Eli said, "Welcome, James." Then he turned to the class and said, "This is James. Find him a seat."

There was an empty desk on the other side of Reesa's. She nearly dislocated her shoulder trying to alert James to its availability. He smiled at her and started walking toward the desk, his eyes sweeping the room. I dropped my forehead to my hand and looked down at my notebook in a classic don't-call-on-me-I-have-a-terrible-headache stance.

Mr. Eli picked up where he'd left off. "*The Canterbury Tales.* The first eighteen lines. Who's ready? Who hath learned thy Middle English?"

I peeked out over my hand to observe that I was not alone in dreading this assignment. While my stage fright only reached paralytic proportions when I was standing on an actual stage or otherwise attempting to sing for an audience, I still got very nervous for anything remotely performance related. In classes, going to the board definitely made my palms sweat. I was usually fine answering questions, as long as I could remain seated safely at my desk. It was best if I didn't have to sit there anticipating my turn and getting worked up over it. But that didn't mean I wanted to go first, either.

Mr. Eli lifted a book from his desk and walked over to James. He flipped to the correct page and laid it down. "We've been studying *The Canterbury Tales,*" he said in a low voice. "I won't make you memorize since you're just starting with us, but maybe you'd like to start us off today by reading from the book?"

James's face went slightly green. "Uh . . ." He licked his lips and squirmed under Mr. Eli's gaze. I knew that squirm, that heart-racing discomfort.

"I'll go." I jumped to my feet, knocking the desk with my hip so it scraped loudly across the floor. Everyone who had been watching James turned to gape at me.

"Miss Emerson?" Mr. Eli looked at me with surprise. Reesa looked at me with surprise. The part of me that hadn't gone totally insane looked at me with surprise. "Thank you for volunteering," said Mr. Eli.

I swallowed and began before my brain could fully process what I'd done, what I was about to do.

"'Whan that Aprill with his shoures soote, the droghte of March hath perced to the roote . . .'" My voice quavered, but the strange words spilled out in the proper order. I had put the poem to music in my head, a trick I always used to memorize things. Separating it now from that melody was like reading backward, but it kept my mind off the fact that everyone was watching me. Closing my eyes helped, too.

When I finished, there was a polite smattering of applause and I took my seat. Or rather, I fell into my seat as my knees gave out. Reesa was still staring at me like an alien had possessed my body. "What was that about?" she whispered.

I shrugged as Mr. Eli called on her next. She hopped up and launched into the poem. I let my eyes flutter over to where James sat. He was staring back at me, a curious eyebrow raised. I looked back at the front of the classroom and didn't budge for the rest of the class.

"Glad that's over," Reesa said after the bell rang. She linked her arm with mine and looked back over her shoulder as we left class. I followed her line of sight and saw James standing in front of Mr. Eli's desk, teetering back on his heels, now with his thumbs hooked through his front belt loops instead of shoved into his back pockets. "He's hot," she said.

"Who?" I said.

"Sir James. Me thinketh he's divine."

My throat felt dry. "You think?"

"Oh, yeah," she said. "Tall, dreamy. And quiet. You know what they say about the quiet ones."

"Um, they don't talk a lot?"

"Actually, I have no idea what they say about the quiet ones. But it must be good." She laughed at herself. "They have a secret. They're hiding something, like—"

"Bodies? The quiet ones are serial killers?"

Reesa put a hand on her hip. "Don't talk about my future boyfriend like that. I was referring to a secret passion. Quiet on the outside, crazy and sexy on the inside. Something like that." She gave a meaningful wink. "I'll let you know when I find out."

She sauntered off with an exaggerated sway of her hips, putting her dibs on James Wickerton. I didn't like it. The guy surely thought I was an idiot, and I'd rather my best friend didn't date someone who thought I was an idiot. But, to be honest, what really bothered me was that she hadn't even mentioned his eyes. How could she not have noticed how they were icy blue and warm at the same time?

Because he hadn't looked at her.

SEVEN

I didn't see James for the rest of the day. But Lennie was suddenly everywhere. Grinning, leering, sneering, materializing out of nowhere—like my own personal Cheshire cat. Sometimes he was surrounded by his friends, the moving boys from Saturday morning. But fortunately, Lennie was the only one who seemed to remember me.

Reesa noticed one of his more blatant stares when we passed him in the hall on the way to chemistry. "Who's that?"

"Nobody," I said too quickly.

She turned to get a better look. "What's his name, Lizinsky? Lewinski? Isn't he, like, a drug lord or something?"

"No idea. Can I borrow your psych notes? I kind of zoned out during that ethics lecture."

"Sure." She dug a notebook out of her bag as we were walking. "But why is that guy . . ."

"Can we not talk about him, please? He stared at me. End of story." I walked ahead of her without taking the notebook.

She hurried to catch me. "What's wrong with you?"

"Seriously?" I wanted to bang my head repeatedly against the lockers.

She rolled her eyes and handed me the notebook. "Don't be so sensitive."

"Easy for you to say. You weren't the one ripped from your home and thrown to the wolves. You act like nothing's changed, like I'm just . . . I don't know, having a bad hair day or something."

She glanced up at my hair. "Well, you kind of are. And you *told* me to act like nothing had changed. Remember?"

"I told you not to *tell* anyone. There's a difference."

Reesa took a deep breath and exhaled it loudly. "Obviously, whatever I say is going to be the wrong thing, so I'm just going to shut up." Now she was the one walking away from me.

"You didn't even call me," I mumbled to her back.

She spun around. "You don't have a phone!"

"Shh! Do you have to announce it to everyone?"

Reesa closed her eyes and spoke low. "You're in a mood. I get that, and I get why. But you need to stop acting like a crazy person. Okay? We're going to be late."

I followed her down the stairs to our last class and tried my best to act like a noncrazy person, fully engaged in the wonders of science. But my mind kept straying to my next challenge: retrieving my bicycle from the hedges at the end of the day without attracting further attention.

And when the final bell rang fifty minutes later, I dodged my way to an upstairs bathroom to avoid my friends, who might notice if I didn't head out to catch a bus or a ride home. I waited for a turn at the mirror. Reesa wasn't kidding about bad hair day. I scrounged through my backpack for something to tie it back, but all I could find was one of those big black-and-silver metal binder clips. I grabbed a fistful of hair and clipped it back. It looked . . . well, pretty stupid. But it would keep my hair out of my face on the ride home. My standards were clearly falling already.

The hallway had grown quiet. Aside from a few kids sitting around some lockers at the far stairs, the coast was clear. I started walking toward them, but Mr. Cook, the assistant principal, appeared at the end of the hall and started interrogating them. I dived for the nearest door and ducked inside.

Mr. Cook was notorious for giving detention, and that was the last thing I needed. The room I'd entered was pitch-dark. I stood, not moving, just listening for footsteps and trying not to breathe too loud. Behind me, in whatever this room was, something was dripping. It started to freak me out, so I swept my hand along the wall until I found a switch. A long fluorescent light flickered on, illuminating a storage room with floor-to-ceiling shelves stacked with cardboard boxes and big multipacks of toilet paper. The drip was coming from a utility sink in the corner.

Beyond the supply shelves was a long, narrow hallway. It was too dark to see exactly where that led, but I noticed another small room off to the side. It was a tiny little sitting room, a break room for the janitor, maybe? It had a table and lamp, which I switched on, and an orange faux-leather chair like the ones in the library (only this one had a tear in it that was patched with duct tape). The wall was lined with shelves that were empty except for a few boxes of paper clips. The discovery gave me a little tingle, like I'd stumbled upon the secret tunnels of Vanderbilt High.

I closed the door and sat in the chair, which was surprisingly comfortable. The cement walls blocked out every sound from the outside world. It was the perfect place to hide after school. All I'd need was a few good books to pass the time. I pulled out the beaten-up copy of *The Great Gatsby* I had in my backpack from a summer reading project and set it on the shelf—a little start to my secret reading room. I switched off the lamp and closed the door as I left.

It had been ten minutes, and the hallway was eerily quiet and empty now. My pink Chucks squeaked along the waxed linoleum. When I reached the double doors, I hesitated. Someone was in the stairway. I peered through the little window and saw the one person I least wanted to see: *Lennie*. He was talking to some guy wearing a black slouch hat.

"It's top quality," Lennie said, handing him a small paper bag.

Slouch Hat looked into the bag, then rolled it up and shoved it in his front pocket. "How much?"

"Twenty."

The kid took a bill from his wallet and handed it over. "I'll call you if I need more. I know some guys who might want to check out your stuff, too."

"You know where to find me," said Lennie.

Oh, my God. I ducked down so they wouldn't see me through the window. Had I just witnessed what I thought I'd witnessed? *Unbelievable.*

The door pushed against me and I jumped back. "Ahhh!"

"Emerson," said Lennie. "Can I help you?"

I stepped away. "No."

He came through the door, letting it swing shut behind him. "Were you spying on me?"

"Of course not." I glanced behind me, now wishing Mr. Cook would appear. "I was just leaving."

I attempted to walk past him to the door, but he sidestepped into my path, glaring down at me. "What are you doing here?"

I remembered what someone once told me about vicious dogs. They could smell your fear. I straightened my shoulders and lifted my chin. "I might ask you the same thing!"

He nodded. "You might. And I *might* have a very good answer."

"Such as?"

"Such as I help out in the au-to-mo-tive shop after school." He articulated the word like he was trying to sound aristocratic. "Fully approved and sanctioned by the administrative powers that be. And you?"

"None of your business," I said, desperately wishing I'd had a better comeback, something that seemed to escape me whenever I was in Lennie's presence.

"Better be on your way, then." He glanced up at the big, round clock that hung over the doorway. "Mr. Cook is due to pass through here on his daily rounds in approximately two minutes."

My eyes widened. He had it all timed perfectly.

"Unless you want a ride," he added, grinning.

"No, uh . . . I don't think so." I brushed past him to get to the door. As I started to pull it open, he slid his heavy boot in the way. I stared down at it, fingers squeezing the door handle so tight my knuckles went white.

"It's just a ride," he said in a low voice. "I wasn't asking you out or anything."

I swiveled my head to look up at his face, which was now inches from mine. "That's not what I thought. I would never think that."

The grin that had been taunting me through most of our conversation fell from his face. He pulled his foot out of the way. "Of course you wouldn't."

My heart was now thumping visibly through my shirt, I was sure of it. I yanked the door open and nearly flew down the stairwell. I was almost to the bottom when I heard the door above swing open again.

Lennie called out, "Love what you've done with your hair, by the way!"

I put a hand to my head, felt the giant binder clip, and groaned inwardly as I pushed through the doors to the downstairs hallway.

EIGHT

I pedaled home. Fast. My legs screamed. All I kept thinking was that I had to beat Lennie home. I didn't want him there waiting to taunt me again. I'd also nearly forgotten about the twins' bus, and the disaster it would be if I didn't arrive in time to greet them. Mom was usually there, but she had an interview today for a job at a newspaper. I bumped onto our gravel road just as the bus squeaked to a stop and deposited Kaya and Brady at my wheel, along with a handful of other kids from the neighborhood. A few gave Brady funny looks, but Kaya funny-looked them right back and they ran off. Kaya was Brady's fiercest defender, and most of the time he didn't even know it was happening. He automatically assumed everyone was nice, like he was.

"Hey." I panted. "How was school?"

"Fantabulous," said Kaya. She nudged Brady's arm.

"Fan-tah-lah-bus," he tried. Kaya attempted to teach him a new word on the bus every day. She was responsible for additions to his vocabulary including "chili cheese dog," "holy bagumba," and "butt head," among others.

"Fan-tah-*byu*-lus," she tried again.

Brady didn't respond. He was staring at his feet, then looking toward our house in the distance, and back down to his feet. His little mouth fell open as he squatted down, patting the stones with both hands.

"Oh, no," said Kaya. "The rocks. He wants to clean up the rocks. Like at home. The driveway. Remember?"

He picked one up. Just one bit of gravel from an entire road made of gravel, and threw it toward the grass. It didn't quite make it, so he went to where it had fallen and tried to figure out which one it was. He finally picked up a stone and threw it again, then squatted down for another.

"Brady," I said, "the rocks *belong* here. In the road. It's not like home." That was the understatement of the year. Our driveway at home was beautifully paved with an ornate brick border. Here it was just gravel that crunched when you drove on it.

"Come on." Kaya gently took his hand. "Let's go."

He let her lead him to the side so they could walk along the edge of the grass. I followed, pushing the bike. Kaya glanced at it but said nothing, clearly too nervous about the precarious situation with Brady and the gravel. You never knew what might set him off.

When we got to the house, I quickly wheeled the Schwinn around back and tucked it under the stairs. Brady and Kaya were standing out front. I watched from the side of the house. Sometimes it was best to just let him process things. He was staring intently at that gravel road, no doubt trying to figure out what he was going to do about it. The poor kid had spent all of last year clearing our driveway of every stray bit of stone, like it was the most important job in the world. *His* job. It was a huge source of pride for him, and now it was gone.

God, I hated this place.

As the three of us stood there, Lennie's Jeep rumbled to a stop in front of his house. He climbed out and started walking toward his front door, glancing from Brady to the road. He took a step toward the twins, and I was about to run out to protect them if he got any closer, but he didn't.

"Whatcha doin'?" he called out.

Kaya kept looking out at the road and said, "My brother is trying to figure out what to do about all those rocks."

"Ah," said Lennie, nodding. "They get everywhere, don't they?" Then he reached down, picked up a piece of gravel from his front yard, and threw it into the road.

Brady swiveled his head to look at Lennie, who bent down to pick up two more pieces. He tossed them one at a time, underhand so they arched up high before dropping with a satisfying clatter.

Brady watched each rock as it soared into the street. A big smile came across his face. He studied the grass around his feet, squatted, and selected one of several bits of gravel. He stood and threw it with all his might. It landed about three feet away.

Lennie laughed. He threw another rock, then Brady threw one. Then Kaya joined in, and they all took turns. The threat of a major Brady meltdown had been avoided. I kept watching from the side of the house, not sure what to do.

Lennie looked up and saw me, then let the rock he was holding drop to the ground. He turned to Brady. "Gotta go, dude. Keep up the good work."

Brady smiled at him, and waved—a perfectly normal exchange, which was *not* normal for my brother. It usually took him weeks of behavior therapy to master an interaction like that.

I waited for Lennie to go into his house, then hurried to collect the twins and take them inside. Brady was loath to leave his work unfinished, but I assured him he could continue later. There had to be at least a year's worth of gravel in our little yard to clean up.

"How was school?" Mom asked an hour later. She kicked off her shoes and opened the refrigerator.

"Fine."

"The bus?"

"Fantabulous," I said. "How did your interview go?"

"Also fantabulous," she said, not even realizing it was Brady's word of the day. "I got the job."

"That's great! Doing what?"

"Copyediting. Writing obituaries, the police report, stuff like that. It's just two afternoons a week for now. I'll need you home to get the twins off the bus those days. Okay?"

"Yeah." I heard the distinctive rumble of Lennie's Jeep and watched out the front window as he drove off. My chest unclenched the slightest bit, knowing he was gone. "You probably won't have to go very far to get stuff for your police report."

Mom raised an eyebrow. "Why's that?"

"Am I the only one who's noticed that our neighbor is a drug dealer?"

"Mr. Lazarski?" Mom chuckled. "He's sixty-five years old and disabled. I hardly think he's dealing drugs. He can barely feed himself, apparently. Carla told us a car fell on him, if you can believe it. He used to be a mechanic."

I peered out the kitchen window toward their little house. There was one broken-down car parked in the grass along the far side, and one of those prefab sheds shaped like a miniature barn. I'd seen Lennie coming and going from it, but nobody else had stepped out of the house.

"I wasn't talking about Mr. Lazarski, Mom. I was talking about his son."

Mom pulled a box of pasta from the cabinet. "Trust me. We checked everyone out thoroughly before moving here. It's not a bad neighborhood, sweetie. No arrests, no incidents at all in the past year."

"That just means they haven't been caught yet," I mumbled.

Mom gave me The Look, as Kaya came bouncing down from the bunk bed room and described the gravel incident in painstaking detail. In her version of events, Lennie hadn't absently thrown a few rocks into the road. He had practically swooped in wearing a superhero cape to save the day.

Mom turned to me and said, "See? He's not so bad."

"He knows how to throw rocks," I said. "Doesn't exactly make him a model citizen."

"I'm sure he's a perfectly nice boy." She disappeared upstairs to check on Brady.

I took the phone to my room and dialed Reesa's number.

She answered on the first ring. "You got a phone?"

"Landline," I said flatly. "Same number as before. Didn't you recognize it?" We must've dialed each other's home phone numbers a million times when we were kids, before we got our own.

"Oh, yeah." She recited the numbers, superfast. "Sorry about not calling. I didn't think they'd let you have the same number over there."

I know she didn't mean it as an insult, but it felt that way. "What, like there's a special number for poor people?"

"No, I . . . never mind. That was stupid."

An awkward silence fell between us. This phone call was not taking my mind off my situation as I'd hoped. "So, what are you doing now?"

"Deciding what color to paint my nails."

"Choices?"

"Sassy Librarian's new colors are out. I couldn't decide so I got them all."

We had discovered this teen boutique and bookstore in Belleview last summer that made its own nail polish, with literary-inspired names. There was "Shatter Me Silver" and "Lovely, Dark, and Deep Purple," and "Every Day Red." We loved them more for the names and the fun of figuring out which book they referred to. And if you bought the polish *and* the book, you got a 20 percent discount.

"How many?" I asked.

"Six," she said. "And books, too. Mom said we'd call it a back-to-school present."

I started calculating in my head what six polishes and matching books would cost, but stopped myself before I reached an exact figure. One polish was out of my budget now. "That's great," I said weakly.

"Wait till you hear the names."

I sighed. "I should probably do homework."

"Oh, okay. Fine." She sighed. "I'll show them to you this weekend. We're still going to Little Invisibles concert, aren't we?"

"Oh, crap," I said. "I can't."

"Ivyyy," she whined. "You told me we'd go next time they played at the King."

"That was before I became a person with an allowance of zero," I said.

"It's only twenty dollars!"

"It might as well be a hundred," I mumbled.

She paused. "I guess New York's out, too?"

I'd forgotten all about the trip we'd been planning—to take the train into the city to shop, maybe see a show. Even if I didn't actually buy anything and we stood in the discount ticket line at Times Square and walked everywhere instead of taking a cab, it would still be a four-hundred-dollar day. "I don't think so, Rees."

"I'll loan you the money. You can pay me back when things clear up."

"Things aren't just going to clear up, Rees. And I'm not going to be your charity case," I said. "I'll get a job or something."

"A job?" She was wrinkling her nose, I could just tell. "Then you won't have time to do anything. You'll always be working."

"Yeah, well . . ."

"I have two words for you," she said. "Rich. Boyfriend."

I sighed. "Because destitution is so attractive. I'm sure they'll be lining up outside my crappy apartment."

There was a rustle and clunk on the other end, like Reesa had dropped the phone. "Hold on," she said, then I was on speaker. She always put me on speaker when she was painting her nails. "Maybe James has a friend."

"Uh, James . . . who?"

"My future boyfriend. James Westerton. Wickering. Whatever his name is. The new guy who sat next to me in English. He of the golden, wavy hair."

I wanted to tell her his last name was Wickerton, not Westerton or Wickering, and his hair, while definitely worthy of running one's fingers through, was not his finest feature. But I was too busy feeling slightly nauseated at the thought of James and Reesa becoming an item. I didn't begrudge her a hottie boyfriend, but the guy had seen me with bugs smashed to my face. The last thing I needed was to hang out with him and Reesa all the time.

"Wonder what kind of car he drives," she mused.

I should've said something then, that I'd seen him in the parking lot. That he drove a nice car, a black one. Mercedes, or maybe a BMW. But I kept it a secret. Maybe because secrets were all I had left. Or maybe it was inertia . . . an object in motion stays in motion? Once you start keeping secrets, it's kind of hard to stop.

NINE

Tuesday. Lakeside, day four. I contemplated carving hash marks on the wall of my room, but didn't want to make the place feel any more like a prison sentence than it already did. I left the apartment five minutes earlier so James wouldn't see me bug-faced and shrub-hiding again, so Lennie wouldn't walk in with me, so the Witches wouldn't pounce. So, so, so many reasons. My hair was tied back. No looking like a possessed sea anemone today.

I went into our backyard to get my bike but stopped short when I saw a white plastic bag in the basket. If my parents had noticed the bike, they hadn't said anything. Maybe they assumed it was Carla's. But somebody had found it.

I poked at the roundish shape, then lifted it far enough to see the blue-and-green Ike's Bikes logo. My dad had taken us to get our custom bicycles there. It was a nice shop. Expensive. I reached in and pulled out a bicycle helmet. Had my parents . . . ? No. They definitely would've said something.

A light went on over at Lazarski's house. I saw a shadow pass in front of the window. Then a light in another room. My eyes went back to the helmet in my hands. I started to get that nervous feeling like when you think someone's following you on a dark street.

You should really wear a helmet, you know, Lennie had said.

I dropped it into the basket as if it was scalding hot. Why would he buy me this? What did he want from me? I couldn't wear it. Absolutely not.

But the cars did whiz by really fast.

I picked the helmet up again and turned it over in my hands. It was gorgeous, and that is not a word that usually appears in the same sentence as "bike helmet." The surface was smooth and cream colored, with pale gray-and-white flowers screen-printed on the side.

I hated that he'd paid for this . . . *if* he'd paid for this. I'd be indebted to him. Maybe I could wear the helmet until I had a chance to buy one of my own. Then I'd give it back to him. I wouldn't owe him a thing. I flipped the helmet onto my head and snapped the buckle under my chin.

It fit perfectly.

When I got to my locker, relatively nonsweaty in the fresh shirt I had packed, Reesa was waiting. She waved a sheet of paper in my face. "This is the answer to your problem. Right here."

"Which problem?" I said, pushing it aside to get to my locker. "I have several, you know."

"Your cash flow problem."

I took the flyer. The country club her parents belonged to was looking for someone to play piano and sing in their hoity-toity bar and restaurant, and to perform "light background music" at dinners and receptions. I pushed the sheet back into Reesa's hands. "I don't think so."

"What? It pays fifty dollars an hour. Plus tips."

"A, everyone we know goes to that country club; and B, I can't sing." I turned back to my locker.

"Yeah, and Adele totally sucks, too." Reesa was the one person, outside my family, who had ever heard me sing. And only because she was sneaky and had a key to our house.

"I can sing at home. That's it." And I couldn't even manage to do that anymore.

Reesa slapped the flyer on top of the books I had pulled from my locker. "Come on. People will start noticing if you never have spending money. And this isn't like a *job* job. You could totally do this."

A graceful arm swept over her shoulder and snatched the flyer. "Do what?"

I tried to grab it back, but Willow held it out of my reach as she read. "You sing?"

"No," I said, but Reesa drowned me out with a loud, "Yes! She sings."

Willow looked at us like we were crazy, which we probably were. "Like, in the shower?"

"Yeah. Something like that." I grabbed the flyer and shoved it into my backpack while giving Reesa a don't-say-another-word-under-penalty-of-death stare.

"God, Ivy. It's been six years," Reesa muttered. "Get over it."

Air hissed out between my teeth. She might as well have stuck a knife in my chest. I knew how ridiculous it must seem that I hadn't gotten over my stage fright from that stupid talent show yet. It should've been ancient history by now, but the further away I got from that day, the darker and more frightening its shadow became.

"Thanks." I stared daggers at Reesa. "Thanks a lot."

Willow tilted her head to the side and tapped her dangly earring. "Wait," she said. "Are you talking about . . . Oh, my God. I forgot all about that!"

I groaned.

"What was that song you were supposed to sing? Something about summer from the perspective of a butterfly?" She giggled and nudged me like I was in on the joke, not the butt of it.

"Summerfly," I mumbled.

"Awww." She pushed out her bottom lip, then her face brightened. "I won that talent show, remember? I danced Clara's solo from *The Nutcracker*."

"Yes." I gave a weak smile. "I remember." She hadn't actually witnessed my humiliation, thankfully. She'd been off somewhere "getting into character" or stretching her foot behind her head.

"Didn't some kid have to drag you off the stage because you froze up?"

I nodded, though "drag" was a bit of an exaggeration. There was a boy who gently took my arm and led me off. At least, that's what my mother told me. All I noticed were the bright lights and the front few rows of faces staring at me.

Willow pulled me into an awkward hug, my books pressed between us. Then someone down the hall behind me caught her attention. "Ooh, gotta go." She waved and sashayed off.

"Well, that was fun," I said.

Reesa grimaced. "I'm sorry."

I shrugged.

"I'm really, really sorry. You know I just want the rest of the world to hear your amazing voice. And for you to have spending money so we can have fun." She pressed her palms together, fingertips to her lips as if in prayer. "Forgive me? Please?"

I rolled my eyes. "You're forgiven. Just promise you won't throw me under the Willow bus again, okay?"

"I promise," she said.

We started down the hall, walking shoulder to shoulder and swerving to miss people without breaking contact. It was something we'd started in middle school as our own secret good-luck charm. If we made it to class without separating, we'd get whatever we were wishing for that day. As we approached the stairway, Willow twirled away from her locker and pushed straight between us with a laugh. We stopped and glared at her back.

"I hate her," Reesa growled. "Remind me why we're friends with her?"

"Must've done something awful in a past life."

"We're such losers," said Reesa. "It's sad, really."

"Really sad."

"Lame."

"Pathetic."

We went on like that all the way down the hall, belittling ourselves, turning it all into a joke. But as I sat down in homeroom, I wondered why we let her rule over us the way we did. It was just as much our fault as hers, I suppose. We were all complicit in the state of inertia that governed our friendship. It was just easier to keep going along the way it was than to change direction.

When we got to AP English, James Wickerton had not yet arrived and Reesa took the opportunity to scoot her desk closer to his. She did it casually, like she was just trying to get her things situated and comfy.

"Seriously?" I shook my head.

"What?" She smoothed all her hair to one side of her neck and adjusted the collar of her blouse so it displayed her décolletage.

I slouched a few inches lower in my chair and let my hair fall around my face like blinders. Reesa was an accomplished flirt, but I didn't like to watch. It made me feel like a third wheel.

The room got a little quieter when James walked in. Reesa waggled her fingers at him, and his face brightened with recognition as he walked toward the desk she'd saved for him.

"Good morning, James," she practically sang.

"Hey." He gave a quick smile and sat down.

"I'm Reesa."

James nodded, his eyes darting from her to me.

"Oh, and this is Ivy." Reesa leaned back so there was a clear line of sight between him and me.

"Yes," he said, "We've . . ."

"Nice to meet you," I said quickly, before he could reveal that we'd already met. He frowned, confused, but I ignored him and opened my notebook, paging through it like I was in search of some very important notes. I could still see them out the corner of my eye, though.

Reesa leaned over to rest her hand on James's arm. "If you need, like, help finding a classroom or the library or something, don't hesitate," she said. "You can ask me anything."

"Oh, uh. Thanks," he said.

We suffered through the remaining recitations of *The Canterbury Tales,* the words sounding like mush by the time we were done. Mr. Eli made one more attempt to get James to recite, but he politely declined.

And when class was over, I darted. I didn't want James to mention the bike, the bushes, or the bugs in front of Reesa. She wouldn't understand why I was keeping secrets from her. I didn't understand it myself, except it was all so embarrassing.

As soon as I reached my locker, I realized I'd forgotten my hoodie. I quickly swapped my English book for chemistry and hurried back, hoping Mr. Eli hadn't left for his free period yet.

I was relieved to find the door ajar. But someone was in there with him, so I hesitated before waltzing in.

". . . smale foweles maken melodye, that slepen al the nyght with open ye . . ."

It was a deep, rich voice that managed to put feeling into the words that had lost all meaning coming out of the rest of our mouths. I listened as if transported to fourteenth-century England, where my now-favorite poet was whispering the melodious verses into my ear.

". . . The hooly blisful martir for to seke, that hem hath holpen whan that they were seeke."

When the poem ended, a shiver shot down my spine, jarring me back to the present. I peeked through the narrow slit but could see only Mr. Eli, tilting back in his desk chair.

"Excellent," he said, looking more than a little astonished. "I wonder why you didn't want to do it for the class."

James?

"I don't know. Nervous, I guess. I'm not very good at public speaking."

"Our Shakespeare section should help with that. We'll be reading from various plays," said Mr. Eli. "If you want full credit, I'll expect you to participate."

"Yes, sir."

The warning bell for second period rang and I didn't want to be late. But I didn't want James to think I was stalking him, either. My hand was poised over the door handle when he pulled it inward. He caught me in an awkward, about-to-steal-a-cookie pose.

"Oh, hi," I squeaked, sounding like a helium addict. I withdrew my fingers from the handle and we did a little you-first, no-you-first dance in the doorway.

He laughed and stepped aside. "After you."

"I, uh, forgot my jacket." I pointed to where it was draped over the back of my chair.

He took three long strides back to my desk and snatched it up, and then held it out by the shoulders to help me put it on.

Mr. Eli cleared his throat. "Don't you have somewhere to be? I know I do."

The bell rang for second period. "Can I get a pass?" I asked Mr. Eli.

He nodded and I went to his desk. When I looked back at the door, James was gone. Mr. Eli scribbled out a pass for me and I hurried off. The hall was empty, except for a lone figure approaching the far end, messenger bag slung over his shoulder and a huge book under the other arm. I watched as he opened a door near the stairs and slipped inside.

Though chemistry was in the opposite direction, I followed

the path James had taken to see which class he was in. But when I arrived at the door I was certain he'd entered, it wasn't a class-room. It was the same unmarked door that led to my secret room. I put my hand on the knob and turned.

It was locked.

TEN

When I returned to the supply room at the end of the day to wait out the after-school rush, the door was unlocked. It hadn't occurred to me to lock it before, but James had done it, so I pressed the button to make sure nobody walked in on me. Then I quickly found my way to the secret room and switched on the lamp.

Everything was just as I'd left it, but my tattered copy of *The Great Gatsby* was no longer the only item on the shelf. It was now dwarfed by a three-inch-thick hardbound book. I pulled it down to read the cover: *The Complete Works of William Shakespeare.*

Not my first choice of reading material. But James was proving to be not-your-average cute boy. I sat and thumbed through the book. Almost every page had something highlighted, with notes scribbled in the margin. Words defined, explanations of what was really going on. I flipped to the front cover to see if James had signed his named, but found only the initials J.A.R.

I closed it tenderly and returned it to the shelf, gathering my stuff to go. But something called me back. I don't know if it was the secret feeling of the room or my new life of secrets, but I wanted to know more about the owner of that book. I took out a pencil and scrawled a note under the initials.

And what do you read for fun?

I smiled as I closed the book again and left. I avoided the stairwell where I'd seen Lennie yesterday, got my bike, and pedaled home as close to happy as I'd been all week.

Mom was sitting on the living room floor with papers spread out around her and all over the coffee table. She looked up as if she hadn't been expecting me and quickly scooped everything into a pile.

"What's all that?" I asked.

"Nothing." She shoved it all into one of those brown accordion folders. "Just paperwork."

"Bills?"

She smiled. "Nothing for you to worry about."

My stomach twisted. That was what she'd been saying for months. I knew better than to believe her now.

"Mom—"

"How was your day?" she asked brightly.

I told her what *she* wanted to hear. "It was great, Mom. Really great."

She sighed as if the weight of the world had lifted. "I'm so glad to hear that. Things have a way of working out, don't they?"

She disappeared into her bedroom with the papers, and I wondered what bad news they might contain. We'd already lost our house and most of our possessions. How much worse could it get?

The next morning I gazed longingly at some of my cute skirts and dresses and boots but again chose a more cycling-friendly outfit instead: a pair of skinny jeans, my Converse sneaks, a vintage T-shirt, and hoodie. My new uniform.

Mom and Dad were already in the kitchen when I went down, arguing in hushed tones. I stopped and stood on the middle stair.

"Please tell me we didn't lose everything for . . . for nothing," said Mom.

"If we get the university contract, we'll be fine," said Dad.

"And if we don't?"

"Something will turn up."

My mother was making coffee, noisily slamming the pot into place. "You've been saying that for weeks, Mark. And look what turned up."

The step I was standing on suddenly creaked, and their conversation came to a halt. When I arrived in the kitchen, it was all sunshine and roses again.

"Hey, princess." Dad smiled in his usual way, but I could see the sadness in it now. I wondered how long he'd been hiding it.

"Hey, Daddy," I said, snarfing down the jelly toast Mom offered. "Gotta go!" I left before the twins were up. Another sign my parents were distracted by their financial woes? They hadn't even noticed how obscenely early I was leaving for school.

It was my third day on the Schwinn, and everything was going okay until one mile into my ride, a car zoomed past so close I swore it brushed my arm. Someone thrust a hand out the window and gestured at me with an angry fist. *Jerks.* Like it would kill them to share the road with my elbow, which was the only part of me that might have crossed the white line. I gripped the handlebars tighter and veered to the side, leaving plenty of room between me and the car lane. But the loose, gravelly surface of the shoulder sent my wheels skittering and sliding. I swerved back onto the smooth road to get control of the bike.

Another car came up behind me, and I slowed to let it pass. Black BMW. What were the chances James took this road to school? Small, I told myself. Minuscule. He had to live in Westside Falls. Still, watching it go up the hill in front of me was enough to take my eyes off the road long enough that I didn't notice the rainwater drainage grate coming up in front of me. And when I did, it was too late.

My front tire dropped through the metal slats to a jarring halt, slamming me into the handlebars. I toppled forward and landed smack on the top of my head in a grassy ditch, then flipped onto my backpack like a turtle.

I lay there for a minute, the wind knocked out of me. My ears were ringing, and then rumbling.

No, that was a car.

I scrambled to right myself and discovered one of my shoes was missing.

"Looking for this?" Lennie sauntered up with my pink Converse dangling from his fingertips.

I nodded, and he tossed it to me. My fingers fumbled the laces as I tried to tie them. I was shaken up but uninjured—as far as I could tell—if you didn't count my pride. I stood and brushed myself off.

Lennie lifted my bike from the ditch. "Chain's off," he said, pointing to how it dangled loosely. Before I could think what to do about that, he had the whole thing flipped upside down, balanced on its seat and handles. I watched numbly as he returned the chain to its gears and slowly rotated the pedal until it was running on track.

"Should be okay now." He set the bike upright and rolled it over to me. "Are you?"

I nodded again and walked toward him, took the handlebars in my shaky fingers.

He didn't let go. "Could you say something so I know you're not brain damaged?"

"Something," I murmured.

Lennie pulled a cell phone out of his pocket. I was officially the only person in our entire school without my own functioning cell phone. He swiped his finger across the screen.

"Want me to call someone?"

I shook my head. "No, that's okay."

He studied me for a minute, his eyes slowly scanning my body from top to bottom, then settling on my face. He gestured back toward his Jeep. "Sure you don't want that ride? I could throw your bike in the back."

I shook my head again. "No, I'm fine."

"Of course." He snorted and backed away. "Wouldn't want anyone to see you with me, huh?"

It was true, I couldn't deny it. I stood there and watched him walk back to his Jeep. Before he got in, he turned back to me.

"Good thing you were wearing a helmet." He knocked on his head, then got in and peeled away, leaving me in the dust for a second time that week.

I arrived at school without further incident, hid my bike, and checked myself. No scratches, no blood. The bruises would show up later, no doubt. I'd given myself a complete pat down in search of rips or holes, and found none. Unfortunately, I wasn't contortionist enough to see my own rear end, so I didn't realize it was one gigantic grass stain.

Willow kindly alerted me to the situation at a decibel level roughly equivalent to the blast of a foghorn when I walked past her in the hall. "I-vy! What the hell is all over your ass?"

I instinctively went into defensive mode and leaned my back

against the wall. Wynn scurried over to spin me around. "Oh, my God!"

"What?" I said, twisting myself backward to see what everyone was looking at. For one terrifying moment I worried that I'd landed in dog shit. "What is it?"

Molly Palmer stopped to observe the commotion. Molly had been one of "us" until she and Willow had a huge falling-out freshman year. I secretly envied Molly for standing up to Willow. It had cost her nearly all her friends, but she didn't seem to care. She walked over now, looked at my butt, and shook her head. "It's just a grass stain," she said. "Haven't you nitwits ever seen a grass stain before?"

"Who asked you?" said Willow.

Molly snorted. "Like I need your permission to speak?" She pulled a sweater out of her backpack and handed it to me. "You can borrow this, if you want. To cover up."

"Thanks," I said, clutching it to my stomach.

Willow snatched it out of my hands and threw it at Molly. "She doesn't want your ugly sweater."

Molly shrugged and pushed the sweater back into her backpack. She glanced over at me before she walked away. "Don't be such a sheep," she said.

I watched her disappear into the crowd that continued to stare. *At me.* Reesa came pushing her way through. "Nothing to see here! Move along. Move along." She took one look at me and went into crisis mode.

"What happened?" she said.

My eyes started to water. It was too much to explain. "I fell."

Willow and Wynn were suddenly all "Poor Ivy, are you okay?" Neither one of them objected when Reesa handed me a sweater from her locker. "Here," she said. "Tie this around your waist."

I hoped she could read the gratitude in my eyes, because I was finding it difficult to speak. She helped me position the sweater to conceal the damage.

"Can't you call your mom and ask her to bring you something?" said Wynn.

I gave her a withering look. Her own mother was never home to bring a change of clothes. But she had the nanny. "I'm just going to use the bathroom," I said.

Reesa followed, as I knew she would. As soon as we were alone, she whispered, "What really happened?"

"I fell off my bike." I didn't mention that Lennie had helped pick me up.

"What bike?"

"The one I've been riding to school."

Her eyes widened. "I thought your mom was driving you."

I shook my head. "We only have one car now." And the complication of getting both of my parents to their jobs was difficult enough without adding me into the equation. Even if I had my license—I was still on the six-month learner's permit I got when I turned sixteen—we didn't have a second car I could drive, anyway.

Reesa's eyes went all "poor you" and she touched her fingers to my arm. "As soon as I get my license, I'll pick you up, okay? It's only three more months."

That was a lifetime. But I gave a quick nod and busied myself, pretending to fix my hair. Reesa fiddled with the sweater around my waist, trying to tuck in the sleeves, then giving up when she couldn't make it look like something it wasn't.

"You know, I read somewhere that downsizing is trending."

"What does that even mean?"

"I don't know. The headline was 'Hashtag Downsizing' or something. It was about people going off the grid, making do with less, shopping at thrift stores, using lemon juice instead of deodorant."

I crinkled my nose. "People do that?"

"I totally read that somewhere," she said. "Citrus has natural deodorizing properties. It's all very Bohemian."

My brain was starting to hurt. Considering how our own high school treated kids from Lakeside—even putting them on their own separate bus—I'd have to say being poor would never be trendy.

But I was too weary to attempt to set Reesa straight on that particular point. "Let's just go."

"I'll walk you to homeroom." She leaned her shoulder to mine as soon as we were out of the bathroom, but separated suddenly and squeezed my arm. "Oh, God. There he is. Should I talk to him? I should. I should talk to him."

"Who?" I swiveled my sore neck in time to see James striding toward us. His head was down, though. I did a quick spin-and-drop maneuver, crouching to tie my shoe. Then I dug through my backpack until he passed.

"Shit, shit, shit." Reesa stamped her foot on the last shit. "He didn't even look at me."

I stood and returned her "oh, well" shrug, hoping it hid the relief I was feeling. Maybe she'd lose interest in him.

"He drives a black BMW, you know," she said. "A really nice one. I saw him pull into the back parking lot. But I couldn't find any listings for a James Wickerton."

"Listings?"

"Google, Facebook, Twitter. It's like he doesn't exist. There's only one explanation I can think of."

"He's not into social networking?"

"He's a vampire," she said, breaking into a playful smile. "But still, probably loaded. Vampires always have money. Centuries of saving, stealing from their victims. It's all very lucrative."

"You should definitely stay away from him." I tried to make it sound like I was joking, but Reesa didn't take it that way.

"Why?"

I pretended to flip casually through my notebook in search of something. "He doesn't seem like your type."

Her bottom lip jutted out. "You don't like him?"

"No, it's just . . . I don't think he's right for you is all."

She gave me a long look, then patted my shoulder. "You

must've bumped your head in that fall. Because if tall, dreamy, and rich isn't right for me, then I don't know what is."

When I entered our first-period AP English class, Reesa was twirling her hair at James. "We go into the city a lot. You should come with us sometime."

"I'm not much of a city boy, actually."

"Not even to visit?" she said, looking slightly aghast.

He laughed. "Not if I can help it."

"Then what do you do for fun?"

He glanced over to me as I sat down. "I read a lot."

Reesa frowned. She loved to read, too, but I don't think that was exactly what she had in mind with James. What she wanted, I realized, was to ditch me and go to New York with someone who could afford it. So much for "hashtag downsizing."

Mr. Eli called us all to attention and launched into a soliloquy on Shakespeare that drew James's full and rapt attention, and put Reesa into a coma. About halfway through the class, she escaped with the bathroom pass and gave me an unobstructed view of James. I slid my eyes his way and found him looking at me, too.

He smiled a quick smile.

I quick-smiled back.

Mr. Eli gave the class an assignment to do at our desks. "Take five minutes," he said, "and write whatever comes to mind when you think of Shakespeare's plays. The characters, the language, the plots . . . What are your impressions? If you completed the eighth grade, you've already studied at least one of his plays. What are your perceptions of his work? How does Shakespeare make you feel?"

Kids started calling things out: "bored," "confused," "like slitting my wrists."

James frowned and bent over his notebook, writing furiously. I stared at my blank page for a moment, bent over it to write a single word, and held it up to show him.

Curious.

He smiled more widely and took out a fresh piece of paper, scribbled something quickly, and held it up to me.

Alive.

I put a finger to my lips and shifted my eyes around to look at our classmates.

He laughed, and that's when Reesa walked in. I dragged my gaze away from James to my own paper, but not soon enough. Reesa glared at me when she sat down. She scribbled out a note and tossed it on my desk.

Thought you didn't like him.

I mouthed, "Who?" and gave her the best confused-and-befuddled expression I could muster. A shadow fell over my desk and I looked up to see Mr. Eli hovering there. He plucked the note out of my fingers, tucked it into his shirt pocket, and kept strolling.

Reesa and I exchanged cringes. I stifled a moan. Mr. Eli told everyone to finish up their work and pass their papers up to him. "We'll revisit these at the end of our section on Shakespeare," he said, "and see if anything has changed."

Then he pulled Reesa's note from his pocket and glanced down at it before crinkling it into a tiny ball. "Everything is not as it seems!" he bellowed. "A common theme in Shakespeare's plays, you'll find. Right, Ivy?"

My head snapped up. "Um, right?"

Mr. Eli chuckled, dropping the note on my desk as he walked past. I scooped it up and kept my head down for the rest of the class. When the bell rang, I darted out, avoiding James but not quite fast enough to escape Reesa, who cornered me at the end of the hall.

"You like him."

"No." I shook my head. "I was just being friendly."

Her eyebrows pinched together in the middle. "Promise? Because he's the first guy I've liked in so long. I know this sounds crazy because I've hardly spoken to him but . . . I think I'm falling in love."

I laughed to myself—Reesa was always dramatic. But I took a deep breath and told her what she wanted to hear, because she was my best friend. I couldn't afford to lose her. And the lie was easier than the truth.

"I promise," I said. "He's all yours."

ELEVEN

I'd been without my piano for four days now and I was beginning to feel the effects, my hands shaky with unplayed emotions. So, instead of heading to the cafeteria for lunch, I veered off toward the band room.

It was empty and quiet, except for a set of hi-hat cymbals tinkling against each other as if an invisible drummer had left his foot on the pedal. An upright piano sat facing the wall in the corner, next to the smartboard. I walked to it and let my fingers slide across the keys.

Pressing my thumb to the middle C, I let the sound mingle with the shimmer of the cymbals. I added my middle finger and pinkie, plunked a C chord. The piano was slightly out of tune, but I could feel the soothing vibration all the way up my arm. Playing always calmed me, as long as no one was listening. I slid onto the bench and lifted my left hand to the keys as well and slowly played the ascending chords, key by key, majors then minors. I was drawn to the minor keys today. They matched my mood.

I let my thoughts mingle with the scales, adding syncopation and rhythm to the notes I played. Why did Reesa assume James was wealthy? Just because he drove a nice car? Maybe he'd worked for it, earned it with his own money. Maybe he was the kind of guy who wouldn't care whether a girl lived in a mansion or a shoe.

The notes spilled from my hands, taking me back to the argument between my parents I'd overheard that morning. Low and soft and anxious. Then racing, like my heart had been. Pedaling fast, falling, knocked so numb and senseless, I'd actually been relieved to see Lennie, the fear returning when he sped away, riding shaky and slow—it all came out in a frenzy of sound. Then smiling, a quick and happy note to James and back. A laugh. Alive and curious, two playful melodies coming to an abrupt halt. Then taking it back. My happiness undone.

If anyone knew how to listen properly, they'd hear all my secrets in the song I played.

A calm came over me once I finished dumping my day onto the keyboard. I then played something familiar, comforting—one of the lullabies I'd written for the twins. I sang the melody as softly as I could, so nobody would hear me out in the hall.

"That's nice."

I spun around to see Molly Palmer sitting there, partly hidden by a bass drum, with a clarinet on her lap.

"Sorry," she said. "Didn't mean to scare you or spy on you or anything. I just sat down to practice when you walked in. I thought you saw me, but then you started playing and, well . . ."

"It's okay." I quickly closed the lid of the piano and hurried for the door. I had forgotten Molly even played the clarinet. Her dad was a musician, I remembered. They had a little recording studio in their basement.

"You're good, you know," she said. "I'd love to hear more."

I stopped and looked up at her. We used to tease her for the crazy flowered dresses she wore when we were friends in ninth grade, but there wasn't a flower to be seen on her anymore. She was still quirky, though. Beat-up army boots with tight, faded jeans and a cable sweater so big and baggy it nearly swallowed her knees. She looked like she might have escaped the 1980s.

"No, you wouldn't," I said. "I'm a sheep, remember?"

She smirked. "I said 'Don't *be* a sheep.' That's what happens if you stay friends with Willow Goodwin too long."

"I'm not really her friend. I just play one on TV."

She laughed, a bit too loud. "Well, you don't *sound* like a sheep. You have a beautiful voice. And whatever you were doing on the piano before? That was crazy good, too."

I shook my head. "Not really."

"Uh, yeah," she said. "Really. What *was* that?"

I laughed, a sudden gush of nerves. "I just made that up. It was nothing."

"That was *not* nothing. Seriously. It gave me the chills. I felt like I was somewhere else there for a minute. Or *someone* else."

As a musician, I could never hope to receive a more

meaningful compliment. To create music that was transformative, that changed how people felt *about themselves*?

"Thanks." I took a step toward her. "Nobody ever said that about my music."

"I've never heard anything like it. And I listen to a *lot* of live music."

"Where?" I asked.

"The King Theatre in Belleview. They do an open mic night once a month. I always go."

"To perform?" I was impressed.

"No," she said quickly. "Nobody wants to listen to a lone clarinet squawking away. But if I had a pianist to accompany me . . ." She left the suggestion hanging there.

My throat started to get tight just thinking about it. "I, uh . . . usually only play for myself. By myself, I mean. At home."

"Oh. Sure. I understand." She rolled her eyes and started pulling her clarinet apart to put it back in its case.

"No, really. I get stage fright," I explained. "Really bad. Like completely paralyzed bad."

"Have you tried therapy?"

I shook my head. "I couldn't do that."

"Why not?"

I thought of Brady, the therapy he needed just to deal with normal, everyday stuff like talking and using a pencil. Paying for it had cost us our home. Getting therapy for something as lame as stage fright felt a little self-indulgent.

"The piano is my therapy," I said. "You know when you feel like screaming or crying or laughing really hard? I just do that on the piano." I'd never really explained this to anybody before, and here I was telling Molly Palmer.

"That is awesomely weird," she said. "And I mean that in the best possible way."

I smiled as the bell rang. "Maybe I'll see you next time. We can practice together." The words came out before my brain had a chance to realize what I was saying. Practice together? I *never* did that.

"Sure," she said. "Just don't tell Willow. You'll be banished from the herd."

I nodded and left, feeling more like myself than I had in a while—though I wasn't exactly sure who "myself" was anymore. The thing was, I hadn't told a single lie to Molly. I hadn't worried what she would think or who she would tell. And there was nobody else I could do that with. Not even Reesa.

I started to fantasize about that secret room in the supply closet, about hiding in there all day with James's books. I could read all the notes in the margins of his Shakespeare and nobody would bother me. Maybe James would find me there and we'd sit and talk and ignore the rest of the world. I was thinking about that when Reesa caught me trying to disappear upstairs after last period, and my face went red. I could feel the heat shoot up my neck into my cheeks.

"You're mad at me," she said.

"No." I only wanted to get to my secret room to find out if James had answered my question, and the guilt of lying to Reesa about James was eating at me. "Why would I be mad at you?"

"Because I invited James to New York since you can't go and that is a totally sucky thing for a best friend to do and then I freaked out when you smiled at him or whatever because I'm paranoid and crazy?"

It took a minute to process. "Right. I'm totally mad at you," I said.

"You are?"

"Um . . . no."

Reesa slumped against my arm. "You are the best friend on the planet. Gotta go. I'll call you later."

She ran for the bus. I realized I hadn't asked her how it was without me. We used to sit together, put our backpacks on the seat over the wheel hump, and slouch down in the one behind it. We had an ongoing game of "Guess What's Happening to the People in that House." All it took was a single sighting of a human entering or leaving a house to get us started. The scenarios we imagined usually involved wild affairs with gardeners or mysterious packages being delivered to spies. A woman with luggage? *She's leaving him,* Reesa would say. *She's fed up with his affairs.* Then she'd get quiet and I would know she was thinking about her parents, who were always on the verge of divorce.

I reached the supply room and slipped inside, locking the door. It was easy now to find the switch and the little room. I noticed some paper towels missing, and the mop bucket was in a slightly different place. The secret room, however, was untouched—except for the addition of a book on the shelf.

It rested on top of the Shakespeare. *The Hitchhiker's Guide to the Galaxy.*

I picked it up and smiled. How could you not love a book whose characters had names like Zaphod Beeblebrox and Gag Halfrunt? I flipped open the first page and read the brief note penciled there, presumably for me:

Your turn.

I assumed he was lobbing the question of what he read for fun back to me. But I hadn't brought a book. I'd have to leave something in the morning, though my collection at home was a little sparse at the moment. Most of my books were back at our old house, waiting to be sold off along with everything else.

I flipped through *Hitchhiker's* for a while, then closed up the little room and checked to see if the hall was clear. There was one place I could grab a book. I took the back hallway to avoid Lennie's stairwell. All the English classes were taught there, and Miss Poppy's free book bin sat outside her door. I stopped to peruse. There were eight copies of Homer's *Odyssey*, five of Dante's *Inferno*, one *Wuthering Heights*, and a single cover-missing copy of

Jane Eyre. Maybe nobody else would classify *Jane Eyre* as "fun," but I'd read it three times, and not for any class.

I pulled the book from the bin and hugged it to my chest. There was something about Jane. She was refreshingly uncomplicated amid a complicated life. If only I could be that way.

I rushed back to the secret room with Jane and slipped her onto the shelf, wishing I could take up residence there, too. Jane was in good company. It was more than I could say for myself.

TWELVE

On Thursday morning, I met Reesa by our lockers. Our conversation was a game of dodgeball. It was "James this" and "James that" and all I could think about was whether or not he appreciated *Jane Eyre* and would he leave me another book today.

I managed to avoid smiling at him in AP English, but I worried he'd think I didn't like him as much as I worried that Reesa would think I *did*. He played along, or maybe he didn't care for my smiles after all.

Molly caught my eye in the cafeteria as I sat down at my usual table with Willow. She gave a quick and sympathetic grin but didn't say hi or wave or give any indication that we might be the slightest bit friendly. Her discretion only made me feel like a bigger fraud.

Reesa never mentioned James in front of Willow or Wynn, so I wasn't the only one telling lies of omission. She probably worried they'd swoop in and nab him for themselves. He was a senior, and even though he was taking my junior AP English class to make up some credits, he didn't eat lunch our period.

Willow wouldn't have allowed him at our table, anyway. She had a "no boys" policy, claiming that lunch was reserved for girl talk. I suspected it had more to do with her tendency to grow tired of boyfriends after about five weeks. She didn't want to have to give up *her* table to some guy.

"Mark your calendars, ladies," Willow announced. "Halloween is on a Friday this year, so we're having our party the Saturday *before*." The Goodwins threw a huge bash every year, and it was a terrible faux pas, her mother believed, to host a Halloween party in November.

"Theme?" Wynn asked.

"Mom's still deciding," said Wynn. "It's either the Roaring Twenties or Broadway."

"Flappers or Cats." Reesa held her hands up like claws.

"Ooh," said Wynn. "I want to be a flapper." She mimed holding a long cigarette.

The previous year, we'd all rented elaborate—and expensive—dresses for a medieval theme, with laced-up bodices and flowing sleeves. "I vote Broadway," I said, thinking I could dress as an orphan from *Annie*.

"Your preferences will be taken under advisement," said Willow with exaggerated snootiness. It wasn't that different from her regular voice. "But Mom has her heart set on this jazz band she saw at the Lincoln Center. Her assistant is finding out if they're available."

The party always featured a live band. The Goodwins put up

a circus-sized tent and erected a wood dance floor on their lawn. It was crazy. I couldn't help thinking what our family could do with that party budget. Probably pay our mortgage *and* Brady's therapy for a year.

"So, ladies," said Willow, "if there's anyone special you want on the guest list, speak now or forever hold your peace."

Wynn started rattling off the cutest members of the basketball team, lacrosse team, and soccer team. "Jeremy Dillon, Evan Stans, Andrew Hudson . . ."

Willow held up a hand to interrupt. "Suffice it to say that every cute guy in this school will be invited," she said.

"Even . . ." Reesa started, then snapped her lips shut.

"Even who?" said Willow.

Reesa darted a warning glance my way. She'd almost said James's name but must've remembered she was keeping him a secret from Willow. "Nobody . . . never mind."

"How about Molly Palmer?" I suggested. "We all used to be such good friends. She's—"

Willow nearly choked on her portobello sandwich. "Why the hell would I invite *her*? I heard she lives in Lakeside now. Some trailer park or something. I would *die*."

I glanced at Reesa, our eyes holding the growing number of secrets we kept between us. As for the ones I kept from her, I swallowed them with a gulp of my chocolate milk.

* * *

Following my new routine, I made my way to the tiny room in the supply closet at the end of the day. *Jane Eyre* sat untouched where I had left her on the shelf. I flipped through her pages, front and back. *Nothing*. Maybe he'd gotten bored of the little game we were playing. I left, disappointed, after my required twenty minutes of waiting.

When I pedaled into our neighborhood, Lennie was leaving in his red Jeep. I steeled myself for some kind of harassment, but he just drove by. Didn't even glance my way.

I tucked my bike under the back stairs and trudged up to our apartment, muscles still complaining from my accident the day before. I let myself into our miniature kitchen, rounded the half island with its three stools, and went for the fridge to get a drink. Mom had stuck a note there with a magnet advertising a local pizza joint. In our old house, she never let us stick papers on the Sub-Zero.

> *Ivy—Walk over to the store and get potatoes. See coupon on counter. Six bags, if you can manage it.—Thx, Mom*

I picked up the six dollars she'd left on the counter, and a two-for-one coupon on five-pound bags of Yukon Gold potatoes. How exactly did she think I was going to carry thirty pounds of potatoes? And what was she going to do with that many potatoes, anyway? The store she referred to was not Bensen's, the gourmet market we used to frequent, but the Save-a-Cent on the corner. I could walk it, lug four bags in my backpack and one in each hand, or I could take my bike with its trusty basket.

I left my backpack on the kitchen floor and headed back down the stairs. The Save-a-Cent had a bike rack out front, next to some metal boxes that dispensed newspapers. I rode right past them and parked behind some Dumpsters, then cut through the parking lot before heading to the main entrance.

Yanking a cart free, I spun it around and rolled into the store, ignoring the stacks of ginger snaps and clementines near the entrance. Not in the budget today. My mouth started to water thinking about them, though. They weren't even my favorites, but suddenly they were an extravagance. I headed for the produce department, where I spotted the BUY ONE, GET ONE FREE sign above the potatoes. I dug into the giant mound, counting out six bags. Someone stepped up to pick through the loose baking potatoes beside me. He chose one and dropped it into his handbasket alongside a T-bone steak and a small bunch of fresh green beans. I had this silly urge to start a conversation with "Hello, single-steak guy. I'm crazy potato girl." Then I glanced up and realized, with a gurgly choking sound, that it was him.

James.

He turned, no doubt alerted by the embarrassing noise I'd just made, and spied me standing there with a bag of potatoes clutched in each hand. One of his eyebrows cocked upward.

"Hello," he said.

"Um, hello."

"We've got to stop meeting like this."

"Right. Yeah." A nervous laugh erupted from my throat. I snapped my mouth shut and plopped the potatoes into my cart. "You, uh . . . shop here?"

He lifted his basket to indicate that yes, he did, indeed, shop here.

"Stupid question." I grimaced.

"The prices are good," he said. "I've been comparing."

A bargain shopper? Reesa would be devastated. "Research for a home ec project?" I said, "Or, uh . . . just a hobby?"

The corners of his lips tweaked up a tiny bit. "Trying to save money. That's all."

I glanced toward my haul. "My mother sent me. She's preparing for Armageddon, apparently."

"That's a lot of potatoes." He peered from my cart into his own basket. "My groceries are feeling a little intimidated."

My laugh came out normal this time, and I felt like an almost-regular person for a second. Until a tall, tattooed figure approached. I tried to blink him away but he kept coming.

"Are you following me?" said Lennie. He was wearing a green apron with the Save-a-Cent logo across his broad chest.

"No, I . . . uh, you work here?" Again, my grasp of the obvious was stunning.

"Nah, I just like wearing the uniform." Lennie hitched his thumbs under the straps of his apron, like a farmer tugging on his overalls. "Fetching, isn't it?"

He looked around me and spotted James, wiped his hand on his apron, and reached his tattooed arm out to shake.

"Hi. I'm Lennie."

"James," said James. He took Lennie's hand and pumped it twice.

My heart was thumping double time but my brain seemed to be working in slow motion. I should've noticed the evil grin that came across Lennie's face and hurried out of there. But I wasn't fast enough.

"You want some bananas?" Lennie leaned over my cart and spoke in one of those conspiratorial whispers loud enough to wake the dead. "I got some in the back I'm supposed to trash. They've only got a few brown spots, though."

I shook my head. "No. No thank you."

"You sure?" He was trying to embarrass me in front of James and doing a fine job. "I could set some aside for you. That was your bike I saw parked out behind the Dumpster, wasn't it?"

"I . . . I don't need bananas." I pleaded with my eyes. *Please don't do this to me.*

He glanced at James. "How 'bout you, Jimbo? Bananas?"

I bowed my head in a silent prayer that a trapdoor would appear in the dingy linoleum and swallow me whole. But James responded as if free, overripe produce was offered to him every day. He didn't even flinch at the nickname Lennie had given him.

"Thanks, man," he said. "Another time?"

"You bet," said Lennie. He made a clicking sound and pointed his finger at James like it was a gun, then holstered it in his apron pocket. He sauntered to the double doors at the back of the produce area and pushed them open saloon style.

I exhaled.

"Your friend is . . ." James paused.

"He's not my friend," I blurted. "I hardly know the guy. He's . . . I think he's a drug dealer."

"Oh. Well . . . he seemed cool."

Way to go, Ivy. He probably thought Lennie was a great guy now, and I was a total bitch. I maneuvered my cart to face the exit. "I've gotta go."

"Oh." His voice was soft, almost sad. "Good-bye, then, Ivy Emerson."

My eyes widened at his use of my full name, and the way he said it in that soft, low voice, at the realization that he knew my last name at all. "Bye!" I chirped.

I hurried to the checkout and loaded my potatoes on the conveyor belt. My fingers were shaking when I handed the coupon and six dollars to the cashier. She noticed and looked at me funny. I quickly grabbed my bags and ran out. Lennie was standing by my bike. He started wheeling it toward me.

I stormed over to him, piled the potatoes into the front basket, and snatched the handlebars away from him. All the maybe-he's-not-so-bad feelings I'd been having since he rescued me by the side of the road had completely evaporated. "Are you trying to ruin my life?"

"No, I . . ."

"Can you just leave me alone, please?"

I pedaled off and got about ten feet from where he was standing when one of the bags fell and broke open. Potatoes rolled across the asphalt. I jumped off to pick them up, but my bike didn't have a kickstand and I couldn't lay it down or the rest of the potatoes would spill.

Lennie watched it all without budging. When I whirled to see if he was going to help, he held his hands out by his sides, palms up. "You said to leave you alone."

I got back on my bike, tears stinging my eyes, and rode off—leaving the potatoes scattered across the parking lot.

THIRTEEN

"Where's Mom?" I leaned the bike against the side of the house and lugged the bags of potatoes toward the back stairs, where the twins squatted with their sticks. It was rare to see Brady unsupervised, because wandering off was a constant worry. He'd collected an impressive pile of gravel that had migrated all the way to the backyard.

"Upstairs," said Kaya. She pointed to the first-floor apartment. "Miss Carla is watching us. She went in there."

"Then she's not watching you, is she?" I shifted my lopsided load of potatoes, my shoulders aching under their weight.

Kaya silently mimicked my grumpy remark. I made like I was going to swing an armload of potatoes at her and she ducked.

I hadn't really spoken to Carla since we'd moved in. I knew what kind of underwear she wore, however, because she hung it to dry on a line out back. When she emerged from the house, I was struck by her style, which did *not* scream "Lakeside landlady." She was tall and fit and slender, with dark, spiky hair that shimmered with a hint of deep purple highlights. She wore silver hoops in her ears and a vibrant blue scarf over a simple white blouse, jeans, and black boots.

I looked down at my drab hoodie and jeans and felt underdressed.

"Hello, Ivy." She spoke with the slightest tinge of a Spanish accent. "Did you have a nice day at school?"

I nodded. "Mm-hmm."

She held out a plate. "Cookie?"

"No, thank you." My arms were about to fall off. "I'm just going to put these away."

I climbed the stairs, let myself in our back door, and dropped the potatoes on the kitchen counter. Mom was in the shower, I could tell, thanks to the high-pitched whine that reverberated through the pipes. I peered between the kitchen blinds to make sure Carla wasn't ignoring the twins out there again. She had placed the cookies on a small plastic table and was pouring glasses of a bright-orange liquid from a pitcher. The twins gobbled and gulped, wet orange mustaches curling up around their lips. I had a feeling it wasn't the organic, all-natural juice my mother used to buy for us.

Plopping on the couch, I let my head fall back to stare at the ceiling. It was that kind of ceiling that looked like stucco. It hid cracks and flaws but was impossible to clean. You could see where someone had tried and rubbed off a section of the nubby surface.

My brother and sister were all giggles and chatter outside. The windows were closed, but I could hear every word through the thin walls.

I started thinking how nice it would be to stay on the couch for the rest of the day (the week, the year, my entire life . . .), just slip between the cushions and hide until the movers came and took us back to where we belonged.

Things got quiet outside, so I lifted my head to make sure the twins were still alive. They weren't at the plastic table anymore, and their mud hole was vacant. I heard the music then, and felt it. A dance beat pulsed from below, setting the glassware in the kitchen cabinets vibrating. Our landlady was partying with the twins? I threw open the door and ran down the stairs.

Kaya answered Carla's door when I knocked, a silky purple scarf wrapped around her head. She shimmied to the Latino pop song blaring on the stereo. "*Hola*, Ivy!"

Behind her, Brady danced around in a too-big cowboy hat, with castanets on his fingers.

His eyes sparkled. We'd all been so worried about how he'd adjust to the new place, but I swear he was handling it better than I was.

I looked around Carla's apartment, which was so much nicer than ours. Its hardwood floors were covered with richly colored rugs, not the wall-to-wall beige carpet we had. The couch was a creamy white. A large, rustic wood table took up most of the space, though. It was draped with fabrics, books, and magazines.

I didn't even see Carla sitting there until she jumped up and turned down the music. She was a chameleon blending into her surroundings.

"Come in, come in." She handed me the cookies again and this time I took one.

"So, you're at Vanderbilt High?"

"Yes," I said, biting into the cookie. It was still warm, and a bit gooey—delicious.

"Then you must know Molly Palmer. She lives around the corner. And Lennie, of course." She took a cookie and bit into it, watching Kaya dance in front of a floor-to-ceiling mirror.

So Willow was right about Molly living in Lakeside—though our neighborhood was hardly a trailer park. Maybe some of the houses were trailer-ish, but ours definitely was not. Unless someone had turned a trailer on one end and slapped a roof on the other.

"Has he offered you a ride yet?" Carla was still talking to me, I realized. "Lennie. He said he would. It's silly for you to be riding that bicycle. . . ."

"I'm fine," I said quickly.

She studied me for a moment. "I see. Well, I'm sure he'd be happy to take you if you change your mind. He's a good kid. Smart, too."

"Mm-hmm." I blinked a few times. He clearly had her fooled. And if Lennie was so smart, why wasn't he in any of my AP classes?

"You should get to know him," said Carla.

"Yeah, I don't, uh . . . We're not going to be living here very long, so . . ."

Carla's eyebrows raised upward a hair but she didn't say anything, just kept smiling. Which was infuriating.

"We better go." I scooted the twins out the door. "Thanks for watching them. And for the cookies."

"Oh, sure." She stared at me. "Anytime." She saw us out and leaned in her doorframe with arms crossed as we clambered up the stairs.

"What happened to the sixth bag of potatoes?" Mom barely waited for me to get through the door before she started in on me.

"I dropped it," I said. "It isn't exactly easy to carry thirty pounds of potatoes, you know. Want me to go pick them up off the side of the road?"

She huffed. "No need to be surly about it."

"Whatever," I mumbled, and retreated to my room. I tried to focus on my trig and chemistry homework, but my brain wouldn't cooperate. Half of it wanted to talk to Reesa, tell her about Lennie and the potatoes and James. The other half was considering a lobotomy. It felt like I was playing a board game with the wrong pieces or something. Nobody was matching up to who they were supposed to be or where they were supposed to go. Lennie Lazarski, "a good kid"?

Mom declared it breakfast-for-supper night, Brady's favorite. I came back downstairs, ate my pancakes and scrambled eggs in silence, then retreated back to my room to continue my homework. I heard Dad singing "Blackbird" again and looked at my clock; it was bedtime for the twins. As the melody rose up into the attic, my chest ached. I missed it so bad, singing to them. But I couldn't do it here. This wasn't the right place.

I dug my earbuds out from the depths of my backpack. It was silly to take them to school, since I couldn't exactly walk around listening to music on a phone that was supposed to be lost. Desperate to block everything out, including my own thoughts, I quickly scrolled past my usual homework-friendly choices of Vivaldi and Bach, and blasted Queen. If Freddie Mercury couldn't banish "Blackbird" and Lennie from my brain, I didn't know who could.

Around midnight I closed my books and fell asleep to "Crazy Little Thing Called Love." When I woke an hour later, the music had stopped and the wind was howling in a way I'd never heard before, like wolves in the distance. I scrambled to the head of my bed, reaching for the corner post, but it wasn't there. This wasn't my room . . . *this wasn't my bed.*

I fumbled for my lamp in the darkness but my knuckles knocked up against a wall. *Not my wall.*

Then it all came flooding back to me.

I found the lamp on the wrong side of my bed but didn't turn it on. No need to illuminate what I didn't really want to see. This wasn't the lavender-and-white room I'd grown up in, the room that held all my memories.

What would happen to those memories now?

I felt detached from them, from my old life. From myself. I sank under the covers and turned to the wall, running a finger along a peeling edge of flowered wallpaper. I tried to push it back into place but it kept springing out, farther each time.

I pulled my knees up to my chest and hugged them in the darkness. I just wanted to go back to the way things were.

FOURTEEN

The next morning passed without incident. But then lunch came. After packing for a few days, Mom calculated the expense and decided I should start buying what the cafeteria offered. "I tried for the free lunch program, but we didn't qualify. Still, it's much less expensive to buy something," she declared. "Just make sure you grab whatever fruits and vegetables you can."

When I arrived at the table with my tray, you'd have thought I'd slapped a dead chicken carcass on the table.

"Ew," said Wynn, looking at my chicken patty on hamburger bun with pickle and a side of corn. "That's nasty."

Willow opened her designer lunch bag. "How can you eat that?" She took out her usual portobello and sun-dried tomatoes on focaccia.

I closed my eyes and took a bite. "It's not that bad."

Reesa held her apple out to me. "Trade you for the pickle," she said, nodding at the limp sliver of green on my plate.

"Ew," said Wynn again. There were days when it was the only word in her vocabulary.

"You sure you want it?" I waggled the droopy pickle at Reesa. She nodded, so we made the swap. I snarfed down the apple because it was the only edible thing on my tray. Reesa never touched the pickle.

As I finished eating, Reesa kicked me under the table, her eyes flicking up to someone approaching from behind me. "Incoming," she whispered as Willow and Wynn sneered. I turned slowly, just in time to catch the object Lennie tossed to me.

A potato.

Every ounce of blood in my body raced to my face. I held the potato in my hands like I was cradling a baby chick.

"Good catch," he said. "You dropped that. I can bring the rest of the bag by your . . ."

"No! Uh, no." I was desperate to stop him from revealing my location. That he knew where I lived at all. "That's okay. I don't need them. Thanks."

Lennie's eyes flitted from my face to my friends behind me. I could only imagine the looks they were giving him. He put his hands up. "Whatever, dude. Have it your way. You know where to find me if you change your mind."

There was a moment of silence. Several long moments, really, until he was out of sight. I still had the potato cupped in my hand when I turned back around.

"What. The. Hell?" said Willow. "You know where to find

him? Who does he think he is?"

"He's nobody. He works at the grocery store. I dropped some potatoes. That's all." I tucked the potato into my bag and picked up my chicken sandwich. "He's nobody," I mumbled. No chance I'd be able to swallow anything, but I took a bite, anyway.

"What store? Not Bensen's," said Willow with dismay.

I shook my head. "Some crappy store my mom stopped at the other day. I don't even remember the name of it."

"But where . . ." Willow pressed.

"Who cares where he works?" said Reesa.

Wynn ducked low to the table. "He could be stalking you. Wasn't he bothering you the other day? And you were talking to him. You should never engage with a stalker. It encourages them."

I shook my head. "He's not a stalker."

"You talked to him?" said Reesa.

I wanted to yank my own head off and throw it across the room. "You mean when I thanked him for opening the door for me?"

"You shouldn't encourage him," said Wynn.

I took a few breaths and spoke slowly. "I am *not* encouraging him. Can we please just drop it?"

Reesa tossed the uneaten pickle back onto my tray. "Just stay away from him, Ivy."

I stared at the pickle, trying to figure out what Lennie was up to. If he was trying to be nice, he had a funny way of showing it. He knew the school hierarchy—why would he keep trying to talk to me, especially in front of my friends?

As soon as lunch was over, Reesa shuffled me down the hall and into a corner under the stairs. Her face was red. "Please tell me you are not hanging out with Lennie Lazarski."

"I'm not hanging out with him. He lives in my neighborhood. In the house beside ours."

"Lazarski lives next door to you?"

I shushed her and explained how he offered me a ride and gave me the bike helmet, and what happened at the Save-a-Cent with the potatoes. I left out the part about seeing James.

"And he stopped and helped me when I fell off my bike." It was like a confessional, and I had sinned.

"Great," said Reesa. "So what, you're, like, buddies now?"

"We're neighbors. That's all."

"Look," she said, "I'm trying to cover for you, but if you're going to start hanging out with the scariest guy in the entire school? There's not a whole lot I can do."

"I told you," I said, teeth clenched. "I am not hanging out with him."

"Well, he obviously didn't get the memo." Her nostrils were flaring. "Just tell him to stay away from our lunch table, okay? I don't want to be associated with him . . . and you shouldn't be, either. People will start to think we're dealing drugs."

I watched her storm off, absorbing her anger like a sucker punch. I gasped for breath. How could *she* be mad at *me*? And what exactly was she mad at?

I stumbled up the stairs, away from my locker and my next class. I needed to pull myself together, and the secret room beckoned.

When I got in and shut the door, a sense of quiet calm washed over me. I looked over at the shelf. There were only *Gatsby*, Shakespeare, *Hitchhiker's*, and *Jane Eyre*. But I found a note penciled on the inside flap of *Jane Eyre*.

So serious? Love me some J.E., but what do you read for laughs?

I smiled. I knew just the book to offer in reply. I simply had to steal it back from my sister, who, unlike me, had been smart enough not to leave all her books at our old house.

FIFTEEN

On Monday, nobody said a thing about the potato incident and I was foolish enough to consider it forgotten. Then the cafeteria served mashed potatoes on Tuesday. Jeremy Dillon brought an ice-cream-scooped blob of it to me on a napkin. "I heard you really like potatoes," he said, laying it on my tray while the rest of the basketball team laughed.

Willow and Wynn wasted no time bailing on me and laughed right along with everyone. I turned to Reesa, who wasn't laughing but moved away from me, clearly mortified.

"Uh, no thanks." I handed the napkin of potatoes back to Jeremy.

"Oh, I get it," he shouted to his friends. "She only likes Lazarski's potatoes!"

The entire cafeteria erupted in hoots and the gossip started flying.

"Lazarski gave her a potato?"

"Sure it wasn't a dime bag?"

"Are they dating?"

Willow and Wynn inched away from me now as well, as if I had suddenly contracted a highly contagious disease. I tried not to make eye contact with anyone, until my gaze landed on a familiar face at a distant table. Molly was sitting there smiling at me, in a see-how-it-feels? sort of way.

Molly's banishment had been set off not by her move to Lakeside, but by her saying yes when Trevor Freebery asked her to the Jack Frost dance freshman year. Willow had been planning to go to the dance with Trevor (unbeknownst to Trevor, but that's beside the point). Rumors started circulating about Molly—that her dad was in jail, that she was pregnant with the baby of a guy who was in jail, that she was a cutter, that she was having an affair with a teacher . . . all kinds of crazy stuff. Trevor swore he'd never even invited her to the dance, that she'd made the whole thing up. Then she disappeared from school for a couple of months, and when she came back, she didn't talk to any of us anymore. She sat by herself or with the other outcasts.

Caught in Molly's gaze, all I could think was: *I barely made it a week.*

For the rest of lunch period I kept my eyes on the table in front of me, not even looking at Reesa, who seemed just as uncomfortable as I felt. I finally mumbled some excuse about using the bathroom and left early, shuffling toward my next class upstairs. As I passed the supply closet, I saw a light on under the door.

I had snuck in earlier—before school started—to leave the

book I'd snagged from Kaya's shelf . . . the one book that always made me laugh, no matter what: *The Essential Calvin and Hobbes.* I could skip class, sneak in there and see if James had found it and left a note. He'd barely acknowledged my presence in English, but I had a feeling that had more to do with avoiding Reesa, who kept asking him nosy questions.

"I asked him where he was from, and he said, 'around' all mysterious," she told me after class. "Around where? Why won't he tell me?"

"Maybe he's in a witness protection program," I offered.

"Then he'd have a whole story prepared," she said. "And I don't buy that 'country boy' stuff. He's wearing Diesel jeans. They don't sell those at Walmart."

"How do you know? You've never been to a Walmart."

She shot me a look. "He's too well dressed to be some hick."

It didn't occur to Reesa that maybe James wasn't interested in her, that maybe he was interested in someone else.

I stood outside the supply room door, looking at the slit of light beneath it, and listened for a sound. I knocked quietly, not really thinking what I'd do if someone other than James answered (or if James answered, for that matter). But no one came. So I knocked again, louder. Nothing. I was about to walk away when the light went off. My breath caught as I wrapped my fingers around the knob. I pulled the door open and peered into the darkness.

"Hello?" I waited for an answer, but all I heard was a rustling and a soft click. Somebody was in there. I fumbled for the light switch and slipped inside. The door closed behind me. Slowly, I stepped through the narrow space and into the corridor that went past the secret room. This time, there was a light coming from the other end, around a corner.

I walked toward it. The corridor bent in an L shape to the right and back to the left to another exit. With a sharp intake of breath I opened that door and found myself in a main hallway, the one that ran along the back wall of the school, parallel to where I'd started. There were a few students still straggling into classes, and small clusters gathered around their lockers. Looking past them, I spotted James—his sandy hair, his smooth gait. He turned down the stairwell and disappeared.

I hurried after him, not exactly sure what I'd do if I caught up. At the end of the landing at the top of the stairs were huge windows overlooking the faculty parking lot. I peered out. A lone figure emerged from the exit door located almost directly below where I stood.

James was leaving the building?

He opened his messenger bag and dug through it as he walked, and the trunk of his car popped open. I watched him put the bag inside and slam the lid shut. He moved to the driver's side and got in.

I sighed a heavy breath that steamed the window so I could barely see through it anymore. I was tempted to pound on the pane, call out to him. But it was too late. And I wasn't that brave. I didn't want to cause another scene. I lifted my finger to the glass and wrote in the steam: *W-A-I-T*, knowing he wouldn't see it. Knowing I shouldn't want the boy my best friend wanted, anyway.

I'd never cut school before, but I had an overwhelming urge to disappear. I couldn't face all the gossip about Lennie and that stupid potato. And my bicycle was waiting. I took the stairs leading to the same back entrance James had exited, and pushed open the door, expecting to see an empty space where his car had been.

But it was still there. And so was James.

He stood by the open car door, looking straight at me. He glanced up at the window above, then back down at me. Then crossed his arms over his chest and leaned against the side of the car, as if to say, *I'm waiting.*

The decision should've been harder. I should've hesitated for a second or two at least, to consider Reesa's feelings. I had promised. But I was fresh from the sting of her scorn, and my only thought in that moment was to put Lennie's damned potato and my lunch humiliation behind me. It was all I could do to keep myself from sprinting over to James, and I almost succeeded in walking across the lot like a normal person.

"Ivy Emerson." He did it again. Said my name like it was a work of art, and framed it with the most adorable, shy smile I had ever laid eyes on.

"James Wickerton." It was the first time I'd spoken his name aloud and I loved the sound of it.

"I, uh . . . got your message." He pointed to the window.

"Fortunately, I can read backward."

The letters I'd drawn in the condensation were still faintly visible. *T-I-A-W*. "I didn't . . . I thought you were gone."

"Still here." And still smiling.

"Shall we make our escape?"

"We're escaping?" he said. "What do you need to escape from?"

My presumption that he and I would leave school together now struck me as a bit, well, weird and presumptuous. "Oh, I, uh . . . what I . . . um, that's . . ."

James left me stammering and walked around to the front passenger door, swinging it open with a flourish. "Your chariot awaits. Would you care to ride shotgun?"

I smiled. "Yes. Yes, I would." I slid into the black leather interior, placing my backpack at my feet.

He snapped the door shut gently, ran around to the driver's side, and got in. Then he shifted into gear and pulled out of the lot.

"I wanted to thank you," he said, "for saving me the other day, in English."

He had hardly needed saving, the way he'd read those lines to Mr. Eli. "I wanted to get it over with," I said. "The longer I sit there getting nervous, the worse it is."

"I know the feeling. You did great, though."

"Thanks."

A million questions bounced around in my head: *Are those your books in the supply room? (Or was I flirting with the janitor by mistake?) Did you really read all of Shakespeare's plays? Where did you come from?*

Probably not the best conversation starters.

I looked out my window to stop myself from staring at him. That's when it hit me—I realized I had no idea where I was. I had driven off in the middle of the day with a guy I barely knew. It was exactly the kind of thing my parents had warned me against for years.

"So, where are we going?" The slightest hint of worry had crept into my voice.

He pulled up to an intersection and stopped, looking past me out the window to check for crossing traffic, then back the other way. "One of my favorite places," he said. "I hope you don't mind hanging out with dead people."

SIXTEEN

"Excuse me?" I squeaked.

"Okay, I hope this doesn't creep you out, but there's this cemetery I like to go to sometimes. It's a great place to think, to unwind. Whatever. It's quiet. Nobody bothers you. It has these massive old trees, and . . ."

He glanced over to gauge my reaction. "You . . . don't like trees?"

"Love trees. Trees are good. I'm not so sure how I feel about the graves, though."

"You'll like these graves." He nodded knowingly.

"We'll see," I said.

"You're a skeptic. Not a blind follower, then."

I remembered what Molly had said. "I don't want to be a sheep."

"I always thought sheep should have different names for singular and plural," he mused. "Like, one sheep and two sheepies. Or one shep and two sheep."

"Same with moose," I said. "One moose and two meese."

"Or one moo, two moose."

I laughed again. "I *really* don't want to be a shep or a moo."

"Or a deer," he said, pointing to one of those fake deer standing behind a low hedge in someone's yard. It had been decapitated. "Especially *that* deer."

I laughed. It felt so good to laugh.

We sort of giggled back and forth for the next mile or two. This neighborhood we were driving through was some sort of haven for weirdness. I spotted a tree-shaped sculpture made with sticks and empty wine bottles. Just as we passed that, we saw an all-white house with a single window on the second floor with a bright-yellow frame.

"What do you think?" I asked, nodding toward the house. "Paint job interrupted? Or unusual design choice?"

James stroked his chin as if he had a beard. "Maybe it's a portal to another world, a bright-yellow one. I've been trying to figure it out for a week now."

"You could knock on their front door and ask," I said. "Solve the mystery once and for all."

"Nah. What if it's some lame reason?"

I shrugged. "At least you'd know the truth."

"Truth is overrated," he said. "It's hardly ever as good as what you imagine."

I nodded, keeping my eye on the yellow window until it disappeared from sight. We drove in silence for a few minutes. My relationship with the truth was complicated at the moment, and if James wanted to stick to imagination, I was all in favor.

He pulled into a little strip mall and parked in front of a flower shop. "I'll be right back," he said, jumping out. He returned with a small bouquet of daisies, and for a split second I thought they were for me. But he put them in the backseat.

"I like to bring flowers," he explained.

"Oh! Is someone you know buried there?"

He hesitated, which seemed strange. Either he did or he didn't. But he said no, and explained, "I come here a lot, so they all feel like family, I guess. I just like to leave flowers."

"That's sweet."

He flashed me an embarrassed smile as we turned into the parking lot of a large brick building with a white steeple—the Northbridge Methodist Church. The cemetery was massive, with stone pillars on either side of a black arching gate. James grabbed the daisies and we walked toward it. He lifted the heavy latch and swung the gate open far enough for us to squeeze through. It clanged loudly when he pulled it shut, the noise echoing off the sea of tombstones sprawling out before us.

"This way." He started up a grassy hillside, cutting diagonally across a row of graves dating back to the early 1900s, and glanced over to make sure I was following.

I stepped gently, calculating where the coffins might be buried in relation to the headstones and trying to walk around their edges.

"You can't hurt them, you know. They're already dead. And they like visitors." He waved to some nearby graves as if they were old friends. "Hey, folks. This is Ivy. Ivy, that's, uh . . . Eunice and Gerald."

I pretended to curtsy. "Pleased to meet you."

James laughed. "See? They love you already."

"As long as they don't start talking back."

He leaned down to speak in a hushed voice, as if the tombstones might hear us. "That's why I like it here so much. Nobody talks, nobody tells you what to do, nobody judges. They only listen. That's all they can do."

I smiled. "I think I like this," I said.

"Told you." James beamed at me and stretched out his hand. "Come on."

He pulled me along the rows, zigzagging between stones. *Holding my hand.* This was so much better than sitting in the cafeteria with everyone staring at me.

A twinge of guilt fluttered in my stomach. If Reesa knew where I was and who I was with, she'd kill me. But James had barely spoken to Reesa, I reminded myself. How could she claim to like him so much?

James slowed our pace among the tombstones, swinging my hand in his left hand and the daisies in his right. We took turns reading the names of people who were long gone, imagining who they were and how they had died. There were entire families buried together. One man had a beloved wife on both sides. The first had died young, only twenty-eight. The other had outlived him. James pointed to one who shared his birthday. I couldn't find any with mine. We entered the oldest part of the cemetery, where some of the stones were barely legible. I started to read out the more interesting names: *Adaline, Selinda, Cletus, Bertram.* We saw plenty of men named James, but not a single Ivy.

"There's got to be an Ivy somewhere," I said. "Maybe if we went row by row . . ."

"I've done it," said James. "There aren't any."

"Oh!" I blinked a few times. *He searched the entire cemetery for . . . for a dead woman with my name?*

He noticed my expression and his eyes went wide. "I mean, I've walked all the rows. Lots of times. I would've noticed . . . if I saw . . . I'd remember an Ivy, is all." He swung the daisies nervously from hand to hand but kept strolling.

I walked a bit closer to him, so our arms brushed, and after a bit he took my hand again. This time it wasn't a sudden grab and pull but a gentle slip of his fingers between mine. It sent tingles up my arm. He pointed to the far end of the cemetery, where a giant oak tree stood. The rows of graves fell away from it like folds of a billowing skirt. "That's where we're going."

I had a sudden urge to run, to release all the tension and worry that had been coiled up inside me these past few weeks. And the coffin-width path of grass before me was so inviting.

"Race you."

"Serious?"

"On your mark, get set . . ." I dropped his hand and took off.

"What happened to 'go'?" he called, laughing. I could hear his feet pounding after me.

It was a straight shot for fifty yards or so; then I'd have to cross a few other rows of headstones and run up a hill. I pumped my arms and sprinted, then darted at an angle, weaving between the graves on the final stretch. James appeared in my peripheral vision, leaping over the stones like a gazelle. He surged past me but slowed just before reaching the tree, so we both touched the trunk together, panting.

"You're fast," he said, dropping the daisies to the grass so he could lean both of his hands on his knees.

I shook my head, still trying to catch my breath. I leaned my back against the tree. "You're like a track star."

"I never hurdled dead people before," he said. "Hope they don't mind."

From this vantage point, the tombstones looked like seats in an amphitheater. And we were at center stage. They sat quietly, patiently. Listening.

"I don't think they mind," I said softly.

He leaned his shoulder against the tree, next to me. His face was inches from mine, close enough that I could see the silvery bits that made his pale-blue eyes shine the way they did. As if sensing I wanted a better look at them, he pushed his hair back. It flopped right down again.

"Need a haircut," he murmured.

I shook my head. "No."

James bit his lip as an awkward silence passed between us. Was he going to kiss me, here in the cemetery? I couldn't decide if that would be romantic or creepy. My lips felt dry thinking about it, but if I licked them now, he'd know I was thinking about kissing.

He picked up the daisies instead. "Here."

"For me?"

He smiled. "Or you could pick who we leave them for."

My eyes widened. "Ooh, yes," I said, clasping the daisies to my chest.

He nodded toward the nearest row of tombstones, and I strolled along, reading the names and dates. I stopped in front of a heart-shaped stone that happened to memorialize a man named James and his wife, Clara.

"This one," I said. "James Aloysius Robertson and his wife, Clara Rose."

James had a funny look on his face, like he really *had* seen a ghost.

"Do you know them?" I said.

He shook his head. "No, I . . . uh . . ." He stepped back and sat on the bench in front of their grave. "I always sit here when I come. It's just funny you picked that one."

I squatted in front of the stone and traced my fingers over the dates etched there. They had both passed in September, five years before—Clara on the sixteenth, and James on the twenty-third.

"That's today," I said. "He died exactly five years ago today."

James nodded. "A week after his wife," he said quietly. "Couldn't live without her."

"It's sweet, isn't it? In a sad way," I said.

I laid the flowers in front of the stone and joined James on the bench. We sat quietly, the breeze rustling the leaves above us. A few fluttered to the ground with each gust of wind.

"You were right," I said. "It's nice here. The trees . . ."

"Trees are good," he said, smiling.

I was tempted to ask him if the books in the supply room were his, to be sure. But I liked the secretiveness of it. It got me through each day, anticipating a book or a note, a little treat just for me. If I revealed myself, it wouldn't be the same.

James stood up suddenly. "I have to show you something," he said.

I got to my feet and followed as he led me to the edge of the highest point of the hill overlooking the cemetery. We faced the rows and rows of headstones. Then he said the one word that frightened and excited me more than any other in the English language.

"Sing."

I snapped my head around to face him. How did he know? How could he . . . ?

"Or yell, or shout, or recite poetry, or tap-dance." He held his arms out wide. "Yodel, maybe."

"Yodel?"

He laughed. "Maybe not. Here. I'll show you."

James gently nudged me to the side, turning my shoulders to face him. "No laughing."

I shook my head.

Then he spoke, with a hint of a British accent. "'But, soft! . . . What light through yonder window breaks? It is the east, and Juliet is the sun.'"

He flashed me a quick smile.

I'd never seen or read the play version of *Romeo and Juliet,* but I'd watched a movie version with my mom, the one with a very young Leonardo DiCaprio and Claire Danes. I hadn't understood everything they were saying, but the way they looked at each other was explanation enough.

I lifted my hands to my face, squinting at James through my fingers.

"'See, how she leans her cheek upon her hand! O, that I were a glove upon that hand, that I might touch that cheek!'"

He stopped, backed up as if stepping off the stage, and was James again. "Good timing with the hands," he said. "Now your turn."

I kept my face covered and shook my head. "Uh-uh."

"Come on." He grasped my wrists and pulled them toward his chest, shaking me gently. "It's fun. Dead people make a great audience. You can do anything."

My wrists were still in his hands, and I made no move to take them back. His hands were warm and strong, and I needed all the strength I could get if I was going sing to these tombstones. Or scarier yet, to James.

But then I saw my watch peeking out between his fingers and the time . . . oh, no. "What day is it?"

"Uh, Tuesday?"

"Oh, my gosh. I'm supposed to be home for the twins' school bus. I promised I wouldn't forget." It was already four o'clock, and the bus would be dropping them off in ten minutes. "If I'm not there . . . if my brother . . . Can I use your cell?"

"I don't have one." He patted his empty pockets. "There's a phone back in the church, though."

I started walking. Fast. As we got closer to the gate, James said, "This way," and led me down a little path that emerged between some trees at the edge of the parking lot. Our feet pounded on the asphalt as we sped for the church. James yanked open the massive door and I dashed inside, blind for a moment until my eyes adjusted to the darkness. The scent of candle wax and old Bibles wafted over me.

"In there." James motioned to a vestibule off the entrance area. A black phone hung on the wall, with a sticky note posted above it. "Dial 9 for outside line." I picked up the receiver and punched 9 on the keypad, then stopped. If I called my mother, she'd be furious. I couldn't call Reesa, who was already mad at me for consorting with the enemy, and anyway, she might refuse to drive to Lakeside. For a single, crazy moment I considered

Lennie but quickly shook that awful idea from my head.

"You going to call somebody?" said James.

"Yes, I . . ." It had to be Carla. But I didn't know her number. "I need to look up a number."

James found a phone book on the cloakroom shelf. I flipped through it and found Carla's name and my own address. I dialed quickly and the phone rang three, four, five times. It was ten past four now and the kids would be stepping off the bus any second, locked out of their house and alone. I wasn't even sure the driver would let them off if there wasn't an adult to meet them.

On the sixth ring, Carla answered.

"Carla? This is Ivy. Ivy Emerson, from upstairs."

"Well, hello, Ivy from upstairs."

"I'm running late and the twins'll be home any minute, and Brady . . . I was wondering, if you . . . would you mind . . ." I hadn't been very nice to Carla the other day and I felt weird asking her for help.

"No problem," she said. "I see the bus pulling up right now."

I let out the breath I'd been holding. "Thank you. Thank you so much, Carla. I owe you one."

"I better go out and greet them."

"Yes. Okay. I'll be home soon," I said, staring into the receiver before placing it back in its cradle. I took a deep breath and turned to where James had been waiting, but he was gone.

"James?" I checked the sanctuary, and another room off to the side. I found a piano, but no James.

Then I heard the unmistakable purr of his car engine outside. I was in my seat and buckled in seconds, and he tore out of the parking lot.

SEVENTEEN

"I'll drive you home instead of back to school," said James as we passed the house with the yellow window. "Where do you live?"

I didn't want him to see. *The truth is never as good as what you imagine.* "Actually, it's okay. I need to grab my bike."

"You sure?"

"Yeah. It's fine. I'd never hear the end of it, anyway, if I showed up with a strange boy."

He tossed his hair to the side. "I am *not* a strange boy."

I laughed, for the umpteenth time that afternoon.

"I had a really good time," I said as he pulled into the faculty parking lot. "This was exactly what I needed."

He smiled and said, "Me too."

I headed in the direction of my old neighborhood first, so James wouldn't see me pedaling toward Lakeside. Then I cut down a side street and found my way back to Jackson Boulevard. I was soon rattling down the gravel road toward our house, where I saw four figures in the yard. The two small ones were the twins, and the woman with purplish hair was easy enough to identify. But it wasn't until I'd rolled up close that I recognized the other one.

Lennie.

He was leaning against the front steps, chatting with Carla like they were old pals. I wheeled past them to stow my bike under the back stairs, dropping my helmet to the ground.

I went straight for Carla. "Thanks so much. You saved me."

She waved my gratitude away like a pesky gnat. "That's what neighbors are for." She nodded toward Lazarski. "You know Lennie."

I turned my head slightly but didn't make eye contact with him. "Yes."

Carla crossed her arms and studied us for a moment. "What have you done to her, Leonard?"

"Nothing!" He lifted his hands in mock surrender. "I swear."

I grimaced as Brady ran over to Lennie and tugged on the front of his T-shirt. "Airplane?" My brother stuck out one foot and one arm, nearly toppling over.

"I don't know, Brady—" Instinctively, I reached over to stop them, to protect him. It might make him dizzy. He had a hard enough time with his balance as it was. But Lennie had already grasped him by the ankle and wrist and was lifting him off the ground. Brady let his other arm and leg fly out wide as Lennie spun him around. Just once. But to Brady it was like the ride of a lifetime. He lay on the ground laughing while Kaya took her turn.

Lennie swung her around and around. Carla must've told him about the twins, about Brady's disability. He seemed to know to take it easy on him. I was surprised.

"Again!" Brady said as soon as Lennie was done spinning Kaya.

Lennie wobbled over to Brady. "I need a break, dude."

I hurried over and grabbed the twins by whatever I could get my hands on—the shoulder of Brady's jacket and the strap of a Kaya's jumper—and led them to the back steps. "Anyway, we have to go in now," I said to Carla. "Thank you again for watching them."

"Anytime."

Brady pulled free of my grasp and ran back into the yard. "I play with Lennie." My grip on Kaya loosened and she darted off as well. The three of them stood there staring at me, awaiting my verdict.

"You play with Lennie, too," said Brady, looking up at Lennie. "Can she?"

"Sure," said Lennie, grinning. "Ivy can play with me anytime."

I gritted my teeth. "One more spin, each of you, then inside. And I mean it. Mom'll be home soon." I made my way up the stairs and peeked out the kitchen window to make sure they were okay.

The twins begged him for more but he stopped at one each, actually obeying my edict. They hollered, "Bye, Lennie!" about a million times and finally came in. It took a while to get them settled at either end of the coffee table with a drink and a snack and some coloring books. Fifteen minutes later, I glanced out the window to the backyard. Lennie was lying on the grass, staring skyward. Aside from blinking occasionally, he didn't budge.

I walked downstairs and poked my head out the door. "They're not coming out again. You can go now."

He kept gazing at the sky. I craned my neck to see what he was looking at, but there was nothing but clouds.

I checked the twins once more to make sure they were still okay coloring, then pulled the door closed behind me and stomped down the outside stairs. I circled around him to stand where I could keep an eye on our apartment, my arms crossed.

"What are you doing?"

He shrugged. "Nothing in particular."

"Then would you mind doing it in your own backyard?"

He crossed his legs and laced his fingers behind his head. "Something tells me you didn't appreciate the gift I brought you in the cafeteria on Friday."

"Are you serious? You call that a gift?"

"I did purchase a whole new bag of potatoes for you with my very own money so, yes, technically, that's a gift."

I glared down at him. "No, I did not appreciate it."

He nodded over to where my bike was leaning under the stairs. "That's a spiffy new bike helmet you got there."

I knew the helmet must've come from him, but didn't want *him* to know I knew. "I thought it was . . . someone else. I'll pay you back for it."

"Not necessary," he said. "But a thank-you would be nice."

I glanced up at our kitchen door. It wasn't good to leave Brady alone this long. "Thank you for the helmet," I said quickly. "And the roadside assistance. I didn't ask you to do that." I didn't know why he was being so nice to me, either.

He shrugged. "It was my pleasure."

The way he said *pleasure* made it sound like he'd done something way more stimulating than purchase some protective headgear and fix my bike chain. I should've gone inside then, ignored him, but I couldn't help noticing that his shirt had hiked up a bit to reveal his abs, and they were disturbingly six-packy.

"Stop undressing me with your eyes, Emerson," he said.

I gasped indignantly. "I was not!"

I jumped over him to head home, but he sat up at exactly the wrong moment and my foot accidentally kicked him in the side of the head. I fell to my hands and knees.

"Ow, shit!" Lennie's hand flew to his eye.

"Oh, my God." I crawled to his side. "Are you okay?"

Lennie rocked back and forth holding his left eye.

I reached out to touch him. "I'm so sorry, I didn't mean to—"

He shoved my hand away.

"I'll get you some ice." I started for our back stairs.

"Don't bother." He got to his feet and stalked away, still holding his eye.

"Lennie . . ." I got up and took a few steps toward him but he kept walking. "I'm sorry!" I called after him. "I really am!"

He didn't turn back, and I stood in the yard until I heard the door of his house slam.

"Shit," I said.

Kaya's face was pressed to our living room window above, watching the whole thing with saucer eyes. I knew Carla had probably seen it, too. Or heard it. And Brady . . . I ran upstairs to find him curled up on the floor, bawling.

"Now look what you've done," said Kaya.

I knelt beside him and spoke in the most soothing voice I could muster. "It's okay, Brady. Everything is okay."

He banged his fists to the sides of his head. "You hurt Lennie."

I groaned. "I'm sorry. It was an accident. I said I was sorry."

Kaya gave me a stern look and took over, gently rubbing Brady's back and cooing softly in his ear as I latched the back door so he couldn't escape. I moved next to Brady, who started crying loudly again.

"Just go away," Kaya said.

"Fine." I backed off. "When Mom gets home, tell her I'm in my room."

Feeling like crap, I climbed the two flights of stairs to my attic room, sank into my bed, and pulled the edge of the comforter around me.

EIGHTEEN

It was dark outside when I woke up—seven o'clock, and I had slept through dinner. Without my piano, sleep was my only escape. There was no fear of being found out or humiliated, of losing my best friend or falling for a boy who was too good for me. Or the wrong boy.

There was nothing.

When I went downstairs, everyone was sitting around the coffee table playing Chutes and Ladders, Brady's favorite.

They were all crowded together on our single couch, Kaya and Brady crawling across our parents' laps to take their turns. My father would nudge them to the side or pin them under his elbows when he reached to spin the wheel, and they'd squeal.

Back home, in our real house, we had so much space to spread out. You could get away, to think or read or breathe without the entire family witnessing your every move. Brady's therapists used to come and work with him at our house; now Mom had to take him to their offices.

I sighed. I missed my piano room.

I missed my window-seat bedroom.

I used to sit at my window, surrounded by soft pillows, talking to Reesa on my cell phone. She'd walk over to my house with her phone to her ear and I'd wave to her as she crossed the yard. We'd keep talking until she was in the house and up the stairs and sitting next to me and we'd say bye and hi without skipping a beat.

I missed that so much. Thinking about who had replaced her as my neighbor made my stomach ache.

I picked up the remote to the small television from our old kitchen that now sat in the corner of the living room. A black screen of static blasted me when I turned it on, so I quickly muted and flicked to another channel, and another. Only a few local stations came in, and they were fuzzy. "What's with the TV? We can't get cable here?"

My father slid his player down a chute. "Essentials only, Ives. The less we spend, the quicker we pay off our debts."

"And get the hell out of here?"

"Language." Mom said sternly, snatching the remote out of my hand and turning off the TV. "Come eat some supper."

"I don't want any supper. I want to get out of this stupid place. I want to go home."

"Ivy!" said Mom. "We are home. What's gotten into you?"

"She had a fight with her boyfriend," singsonged Kaya.

"He's not my boyfriend, Kaya." I stomped into the kitchen, which wasn't particularly satisfying as far as dramatic exits go, since it was only three steps away. I climbed onto one of the bar stools with my back toward the living room, and folded my arms on the counter so I could bury my head in them.

Mom heated up a plate of sausage risotto and slid it in front of me. It was my favorite. "You want to talk about it?" she asked.

"No." I picked up a fork and shoved a bite into my mouth.

Mom poured a glass of milk and set it down next to my plate. "Delicious, nutritious, and affordable. Reminds me of when your father and I were first married. We hardly had two nickels to rub together, but we—"

"Can you please stop trying to make it sound like some great adventure? Because it's not. You moved us to the worst possible neighborhood in the district. Brady's got the freaking drug dealer next door for his new best friend, and the entire school is laughing at me. This place sucks, and nothing you say is going to make it suck any less." I pushed my plate away so hard, it accidently fell off the counter and clattered to the floor.

Mom leaped back with a gasp. "You think I wanted this?" She bent down, scooped up a handful of risotto, and splatted it into the sink. "You think I didn't do everything within my power to stop it from happening?"

"How would I know?" I shouted. "You've spent the past year telling me everything was just fine. Nothing to worry about. Nothing at all!"

The expression on my mother's face then made me stop, and she wasn't even looking at me. She was looking at the rest of our family. I spun around to see. Dad had an arm around each twin, hugging them to his chest and covering their ears. Brady was pounding his own hand on top of Dad's, and his mouth was wide open in what appeared to be a silent scream. I'd never seen him do that before.

Mom rushed to them, took Brady's face in her hands. "It's okay, sweetheart. It's okay." She shushed quietly until he stopped pounding and the silent scream turned to hiccupy tears. Dad kept his arms around them all, a big hug of family that didn't include me.

I turned to the risotto mess I'd made and began wiping it up with paper towels. When I'd cleaned most of the goop off the floor, Dad appeared with a bucket and mop and handed them to me.

"Your mother is working very hard to make the best of a difficult situation," he said quietly. "Maybe you could put a little effort into making it easier on her. Not harder. Huh?"

I nodded, feeling like utter crap . . . again. "Okay."

He stepped closer and spoke even lower, so nobody else could hear. His jaw was tight. "I don't ever want to hear you talk to your mother like that again. Understood?"

I nodded again. "Yes, sir."

Daddy went back to Mom and the twins while I mopped the kitchen floor. He and Kaya resumed their game of Chutes and Ladders. Mom held Brady on her lap next to them, still shushing.

I felt my throat tightening. Tears hovered dangerously close to the surface.

Daddy caught my eye. "Join us?"

I shook my head. There wasn't any room for me, anyway. "I've got homework," I mumbled.

After the twins got so upset that first night about missing their favorite toys, Dad had started spending every evening doing something special with them, no matter how tired he was when he got home from work. They played games, or he pushed them on the swing in the park across the street, or they made up silly stories. They played "Would You Rather" and Daddy always asked if they'd rather have cake or ice cream, snowdrifts or sand dunes, kisses or hugs. My own personal version of the game was not so fun: Lakeside or Westside? Embarrassment or total humiliation? Losers or druggies?

I retreated to the attic and opened my laptop, which was the only computer my parents hadn't sold. They agreed I needed it for homework, and I just had to let Mom and the twins use it sometimes. No cable in this joint, but at least we had internet access. A little red circle popped up on my email icon, alerting me to sixteen new messages. I scanned through them, deleting the spam and ignoring Wynn's links to cat videos. That left three from Reesa. They had all had been sent after lunch, while I was racing through the cemetery with James. A pang of guilt rang through me when I saw the subject line of her first email: SORRY. I clicked the window open to find a short message.

Sorry about the idiots at lunch. I dropped some mashed potatoes into Jeremy Dillon's sweatshirt hood after you left, if that makes you feel any better.

I smiled, hoping he'd discovered it by putting his hood on.

The next email was titled YOU MUST DO THIS! It was the ad for the job at her country club. She wrote:

Auditions on Saturday!

I hit DELETE.

Her next email was a link to a Little Invisibles video, a song called "Breathless." I loved this band because the lead singer was a girl, and she played keyboards, right up front in the middle of the stage. She also sang with her eyes closed most of the time, like she was a little afraid to see the audience out there. And I totally got that.

I closed my own eyes and listened, mouthing the words she sang, pouring my frustrations and fear into the silent song.

When I looked up, my mother was standing in the doorway. "Were you singing?"

Was I? I snapped the laptop closed. "No."

"Thinking about it?" She sat on the corner of my bed.

"Just memorizing some lines. For AP English. *The Canterbury Tales.*"

"Hmm." She studied my face. "Reesa's on the phone."

I tensed. "Okay," I said. "I'll be right there."

Mom padded away and I made my way down to the kitchen to take the call. My parents had vacated the living room to put the twins to bed, so I curled up on the couch with the phone to my ear.

"Hey, Reesa."

"*Hey, Reesa?* That's all you have to say to me?"

"Um . . . how are you?"

There was a strangled, growling sound on the other end. "Where *were* you? You were supposed to meet me in the band room after school."

"I was?"

"You didn't get my note?"

Since I'd joined the land of the cell-phoneless, we'd been leaving notes inside each other's lockers. She knew my combination and I knew hers. But I hadn't gone back there when James and I returned from the cemetery.

"Sorry. I went home early. I . . . uh . . . didn't feel well."

Reesa snorted. "That's great. I waited for an hour. Molly Palmer was in there playing her clarinet."

"Did you talk to her?" I was nervous, yet oddly hopeful. If Reesa and Molly became friends again, maybe I could stop sneaking around about everything.

"No, I did not talk to her," Reesa snipped. "She looked at me like she was going to bite my head off if I got too close. I waited in the hall."

"Why were we supposed to meet there, anyway?"

"So you could practice! For the country club thingy. Auditions are next Saturday. I thought . . ."

"Wrong," I said quietly. "You thought wrong."

"But you'd be perfect, and the money . . ."

"It's not happening, Rees." Yes, I needed spending money. It would raise fewer questions if I didn't have to decline every single activity that cost more than five dollars, which was the amount Mom had decided we could spare for my monthly allowance. But . . . no. I couldn't sing for people like that. "Can we talk about something else?"

She huffed, gave me a few seconds of silent treatment, then said, simply, "James."

Not the subject I was hoping for.

"I've been doing some research," she said. "His car has New York tags."

"It does?" I hadn't even noticed that.

"So I focused my search on New York. And I found them. They're loaded."

"Who's loaded?"

"The Wickertons. Ever hear of Wickerton Investments?"

"Uh, no?"

"I hadn't, either. It's some hedge fund or something. The owner is this guy Joseph Wickerton. He's on the list of the richest people in America. Number twenty-nine. Worth like nine billion dollars. I found an article about him in the *New York Times.* He and his wife are big philanthropists. They give all kinds of money to charity."

"So what makes you think they're related to James?"

Reesa sighed. "His name is Wickerton. And he's from New York."

"That's all you got?"

"For your information, Wickerton is not a very common name. They were the only Wickertons I found. Anywhere. They have to be related. Plus, in the article, it said they had a teenage son and a daughter in college. But they didn't mention their names. I'll have to keep digging on that."

A dozen questions came to mind.

"It can't be him," I said. "Why would he live *here*?" Sure, he looked the part. And he was well dressed and charming. But he was my secret and that would all change if he was a bajillionaire. He'd be special and I'd be . . . not. *Please don't let it be him.*

There were muffled sounds on Reesa's end, which I recognized as her shouting to someone while holding her hand over the phone. When she came back, she said, "Mom needs me for some bullshit."

"Okay. See you tomorrow."

"Oh! I didn't even tell you what happened with Lazarski."

"What?" I forced myself not to scream into the phone.

"Coming!" she shouted, and then to me, "Sorry. Tell you

about it tomorrow. You're gonna die."

"Wait . . . what?"

The phone clicked and Reesa was gone. And I was left feeling as helpless as a game piece on the Chutes and Ladders board, never knowing when I'd be sent tumbling downward again.

NINETEEN

In the haze of half sleep and early dawn, I wondered why so many birds had chosen top of our house for their morning perch. And also, why were they tap-dancing? But the sound soon revealed itself as rain thrumming on our roof, a few inches from my head. I bolted upright.

Shit. Rain.

I'd be soaked if I tried to ride my bike to school. The day I'd been dreading was here. *Already*. I was going to have to take the bus. The state pen bus.

My bed thought I should stay, bury myself in its warm folds and forget school. Forget everything. I wanted to listen to it, but ditching school a second day in a row probably wasn't the best idea. Plus I needed to find out what Lennie could've done to earn a you're-gonna-die rating from Reesa.

I selected my favorite ankle boots, a pair of tights, my vintage paisley dress with the short flowy skirt, and a cropped jacket. Might as well go down looking fabulous.

"Can you drive me today?" I gave my mother a pathetic, pleading look as I spooned cereal into my mouth. It was worth a try. "Please? Don't make me take that bus."

"Sorry, Ivy. I've got to get myself ready, see the twins off on their bus, and drop your father at the office, then get to work myself. I'll barely make it on time as it is." The newspaper had offered Mom additional work hours two mornings a week, and this was one of them. "Did something happen on the bus yesterday?"

Sometimes it was hard to keep up with my lies. "Uh, no, nothing."

I zipped my backpack and found an umbrella hanging on the coatrack by the door. It had purple and pink cats and dogs all over it, but at this point, what difference did it make? I carried it down the front steps and pushed the umbrella out the door ahead of me as I opened it into the wind. Maybe the dress wasn't such a brilliant idea. I clutched it tight against my thigh with my left hand while wrangling the cats and dogs with my right. The rain was coming down hard, spraying my legs. The narrow walk that led to the road was mostly puddles. I jumped from the lower step to the first spot of high ground, and another and another until I reached the gravel drive and turned toward the main road where the bus picked up. It was about a thousand puddles away.

I leaped to the middle of the road, which appeared to offer the driest path, and walked slowly.

A car horn beeped and I spun toward the sound. Lennie's Jeep sat there, its low rumble masked by the pounding rain. I puddle-jumped over to the tinted driver's-side window, which he rolled down about an inch to keep from getting drenched. I could barely see him in there.

"Nice umbrella," he said.

"Thanks." Any other day I would've had something far less gracious to say, but I'd been humbled. And he could bring up assault charges against me for what I'd done yesterday.

"Sure you don't want a ride?"

I contemplated my options as water seeped through the seams of my boots. Standing in a puddle is always a nice place to discover your footwear isn't waterproof. A ride with Lennie wouldn't have been my first choice, but it was a clear winner over riding the Lakeside bus. I finally nodded, walked as gracefully as possible to the passenger side and climbed in, dropping my soggy umbrella to the floor. "Thanks," I said again.

His only reply was to push the gearshift roughly into place. The Jeep was warm; he had the heat cranked. I wondered how long he'd been waiting out there.

"I'm so sorry, Len, about kicking you yesterday. It really was an accident. I didn't—"

He held up his hand. "It's okay. I guess I had it coming."

"Still . . ."

Lennie kept his face pointed straight ahead as we drove past a couple of umbrellas with legs waiting for the bus, and rumbled out onto the road. The rain was coming down in torrents, and the

Jeep's wipers couldn't keep up with it. It was almost impossible to see where we were going. He leaned toward the windshield.

"Be careful," I said. "Can you see?"

"Yep."

It was raining so hard, I doubted anyone would look up from their mad dash into the building to notice who had chauffeured me to school, but still I was glad when Lennie parked in a small lot along the side of the building. Less chance of being spotted there. When he cut the engine, I unbuckled my seat belt and shifted to face him, but he kept staring straight ahead.

"Look, I'm sorry," I said. "It's been hard, moving from Westside to Lakeside . . ."

"Must be awful for you." He nodded.

"No offense, it's just . . . not what I'm used to."

"Yeah, we're kind of short on limousines and butlers."

"We didn't have those, either," I said. "I just don't want to make a big deal about it. Okay? The entire planet doesn't need to know that we moved to Lakeside. It's embarrassing."

"You mean I'm embarrassing."

The guy had an amazing bullshit-o-meter. "Okay, fine. You're embarrassing me. You threw a potato at me in front of everybody in the cafeteria. I was embarrassed."

"Come on. If one of your friends had done that, nobody would've blinked."

Was he really going to make me spell this out? "My friends don't have your reputation. Which isn't exactly stellar."

He gasped in feigned shock. "It's not?"

"Might have something to do with the fact that you come to school every morning smelling like a bong."

"I don't smoke pot."

"Okay." I laughed, rolling my eyes. "Sure you don't."

He started to say something, then stopped and continued to stare straight ahead.

We waited for the rain to stop or for somebody to say something else. I wasn't sure which. But we sat and waited and watched others go into the building. The five-minute warning bell rang.

"You go ahead," Lennie finally said. "I'll wait here, so I don't embarrass you or anything."

I sighed. "Whatever."

It was weird, the way he wouldn't look at me. I picked up my wet umbrella and climbed out. Instead of walking toward the school, I rounded the front of the Jeep and approached his window. It was still raining and I couldn't see more than a blur of him sitting there, but I knew he could see me.

I tapped.

He again rolled it down barely far enough to expose the top of his head.

"Roll it down, Lennie. All the way."

He chuckled, in an it's-not-really-that-funny sort of way. The window squeaked down. I knew it was coming but the sight of it made me cringe. The socket of Lennie's left eye was colored a hideous shade of bruise. Purple and yellowish brown. I'd given him a serious shiner. And his eye wasn't open the whole way.

"Here's lookin' at you, kid." He tried winking at me with the bad eye and winced.

"Oh, Len. I'm sorry."

"Stop saying that, would ya?"

I stood on tiptoes and leaned in the window to get a closer look at the damage I'd inflicted. As my head was tilted to the side inspecting his eye, he leaned down and kissed me on the cheek. Soft and gentle. Just like that.

I stepped back and lifted my fingers to my cheek. "I'm sorry," I said again.

He grinned and pulled his head back into the cab. "Don't worry. I'll survive."

TWENTY

My hand trembled as I dialed the combination on my locker. I made a fist, digging my nails into my palms, forcing them to be calm. *Lennie kissed me.* Why? And why had I said, "I'm sorry"? I was sorry I kicked him. I was sorry I'd given him a hideous bruise. *I was sorry I let him kiss me?*

My wet jacket dripped a puddle around my feet. I stripped it off and hung it on the hook in my locker and grabbed the books I'd need for my first two classes. Amid the scramble of students hurrying to beat the bell, I heard the hooflike clomp of four heels, approaching me in purposeful unison. Maybe if I stood perfectly still, they wouldn't . . .

"Ivy." Willow growled my name.

I turned around slowly. She and Wynn crowded up against me. They both had potatoes clutched in their fists and pushed them at me.

"What is with Lazarski and these effing potatoes?" said Wynn.

I stared down at the potatoes I was now hugging to my chest. "W-what?"

"He gave me that potato yesterday after seventh period. He yelled my name in the hall, and when I turned around, he tossed it to me! I'm lucky it didn't hit me in the face. The guy is seriously twisted," said Willow.

"He did the same thing to me," said Wynn. "After school, out in front of the building. What is his deal?"

I shrugged. My mind bounced through the possibilities of what Lennie had been up to. "No idea," I mumbled.

Reesa walked up to us, saw the potatoes in my arms. "He's giving them to all the prettiest girls in school," she said casually. "Bethany Bartell got one, too, and Shawna Evans. He even gave one to Chandra."

Chandra Mandretti was a senior, and the most gorgeous creature ever to walk the planet. Harps played when she passed by, I swear. She had a long, thick, wavy brown mane that belonged on a TV commercial for hair care products. And her body was like a work of art. Toned and curved and shazzam in all the right places. I would kill for that body.

"Chandra?" Willow and Wynn said in unison. They looked stunned, and then . . . I couldn't believe it . . . pleased.

"Yeah." Reesa laughed. "She asked Lazarski what the potato was for, and he told her it was a tradition where he's from to give potatoes to the most beautiful girls in town."

"What?" I screeched.

"That's what I heard. He said it was a rite of passage of sorts, like a bar mitzvah or something. Chandra thought it was really sweet and funny." Her lips curled into an exaggerated pout. "Now I'm kinda pissed I didn't get one."

Willow and Wynn gave Reesa the most ridiculously insincere "poor you" faces and assured her she was stunning. Lazarski simply hadn't gotten to her yet, of course! Then Willow snatched her potato back from me and Wynn did the same. They smiled smugly and clomped off. With Chandra's blessing, Lennie's potatoes were now a coveted symbol of beauty.

I shook my head as they flounced away. "You cannot be serious."

Reesa's face broke into a wide grin. "He did give potatoes to Shawna and Bethany, but I made the rest up."

"Chandra?"

"Total bullshit."

"The tradition of . . ."

"Utter fabrication," said Reesa, clearly pleased with herself. "Someone had to save your ass."

"Thanks." But part of me knew full well it wasn't only my ass she was saving. She didn't want to lose me as a best friend, but she also didn't want to be the best friend of a loser.

I slipped into my homeroom seat as the bell rang, still unnerved by my own bizarre behavior. And Lennie's. The potato thing was . . . weird. When I'd left school with James yesterday, everyone was chattering about Lennie and me and the potato. This morning, it was diffused. Four other girls had received potatoes, so the gossip was no longer focused on me.

Maybe it wasn't Reesa who had saved my ass. Maybe it was Lennie.

But, I reminded myself, Lennie was the one who got my ass in trouble in the first place.

As our homeroom teacher took attendance, the speaker came on with a fuzzy blast and one of the office receptionists said, "Excuse me, Mr. Dalton? Could you please send Ivy Emerson to the office?"

"Okay," said Mr. Dalton. "She's on her way." Everyone made the ooohh-you're-in-trouble sound. My face did its I-am-a-beet impersonation.

The speaker gave another fuzzy blast and then the morning announcements began as I left the room. The Pledge of Allegiance reverberated down the hallway, accompanied by the squeak of my wet boots. I waited outside the office door until the pledge was over, but I could see James sitting in there, studying the floor between his knees.

He didn't smile or nod or lift an eyebrow when I entered, merely held my gaze. Under the fluorescent lights, his eyes seemed dimmer than they had in the cemetery. No reflection of bright-blue sky today. No light from within. I gave him a faltering smile but his face didn't change. He looked like he might be sick.

The assistant principal, Mrs. Lanahan, stepped out of her office and asked us both to follow her. James stood and gestured for me to go first. We took seats facing her desk.

"Ivy. I'm surprised to see you here." Mrs. Lanahan was in charge of discipline and had been for years. She flipped through a manila folder with my name of it. I knew it was filled with honors and perfect attendance. "I'm told you missed your afternoon classes yesterday, but I have no record of an early dismissal. Explain."

"Oh, um, I wasn't feeling well and wanted to go home." I glanced at James. His presence here meant she knew we'd been together. "James offered me a ride."

"I see," she said. "You know you can't simply leave school because you feel like it. Even if you're ill, you must ask to be excused. Why didn't you go to the nurse?"

"I don't know, I needed some air, I guess. . . ." My voice trailed off.

She turned to James. "And you, Mr. Wickerton, are studying here under special circumstances, as a part-time student." She picked up a thinner, blue folder with his name on it. "You are free to leave the premises after your classes. But if I learn that you are transporting other students off the property before their dismissal time . . ."

"It won't happen again."

"I expect it won't," she said, and looked back at me. "Ivy, I'm letting you go with a warning, because of your perfect record.

Next time, you'll be enjoying a stay at camp detention. Got it?"

"Yes, ma'am."

She waved the back of her hand toward the door. "Get a late pass from Miss Bennett. James, stay a moment."

I collected my things and scooted out her door, pulling it closed behind me, then wishing I hadn't. What was she saying to him that she didn't want me to hear? I waited for my pass, straining to catch bits of their conversation. It was all too quiet and muffled until the door opened, and I heard the last bit.

". . . can't hide the truth forever," she said.

The hall was empty as we headed toward class. James walked about as far away from me as he could get and still looked slightly green. I felt like my own skin must've turned a lovely shade of creamed asparagus.

What did she mean, "can't hide the truth"? Surely, my parents had submitted a change of address, maybe even explained our circumstances. If that woman told James anything about it, I would report her for . . . for breach of privacy or confidentiality. Or something.

"Sorry to get you into trouble like that," said James, merging over to my side of the hallway.

"It was my idea. Remember?"

He smiled. "In that case, thanks a lot for getting me in trouble."

I shoved him gently with my elbow. He shoved back.

"So . . . ," I said. "You're part-time? I didn't even know that was allowed."

"Technically, I'm homeschooled." He made little air quotes around the term. "That's the only way they'd let me enroll for just two classes—AP English and art history. But that's all I needed." A guilty expression came over his face, like he couldn't believe he was getting away with it.

"To graduate?"

He nodded. "My last high school was pretty intense."

He didn't elaborate further and I didn't ask. The only schools I knew of like that were private and expensive. There was an all-boys boarding school people said was like the first two years of an Ivy League college. Kids came from as far away as California to go there. Maybe Reesa was right about James and the wealthy Wickertons.

As we started for the stairs, James took my wrist and pulled me into the same corner where Reesa had reamed me out over Lennie the day before.

"I have something for you." He reached into his messenger bag and handed me a piece of notebook paper that was folded into a small rectangle.

I started to unfold it.

"Not now," he said. "It's too embarrassing. Open it later, okay?"

The door at the top of the stairwell swung wide and one of the math teachers came plodding down. He gave us a dirty look. "Passes?"

We pulled ours out and showed them to him.

"Move along," he said.

James motioned for me to go ahead of him. When we reached Mr. Eli's room, he put one hand on the doorknob and the other on the small of my back. It was a simple gesture, but it melted me. He looked into my eyes, opened the door, and poured me into the room.

I quickly wiped the swoon off my face when I realized the entire class was staring at us, including Reesa. Mr. Eli took our passes and even he gave us a funny look. I sat and tried to focus on what he was saying. I gave up after about two minutes and pulled out the paper James had given me, discreetly smoothing it flat inside my notebook.

Then I looked down at it and . . . *Oh, my God.*

It was the most incredible drawing, a crazy collage of our trip to the cemetery. The wine-bottle sculpture was there, and the headless deer, and the giant oak tree and tombstones. And he'd drawn us on the hill as Romeo and Juliet. It actually looked like us, except I wasn't wearing a hoodie for a change. He'd depicted me in a flowing dress with wings—like an angel. It was insanely beautiful. Around the edges of the paper he'd colored in a yellow frame—like the one on the house we'd driven past—our portal to another world.

At the center of it all was a little illustration of an open book, and on its pages a note in old-fashioned cursive handwriting:

Our sweet adventure ended far too soon,
Please meet me in the library at noon.

I had to stifle a laugh. It was like the last two lines of a sonnet! I snapped my notebook shut and looked straight ahead, my face nearly bursting with giddy surprise. I wanted to look at it again, but Reesa was shooting curious eyebrows my way and I *definitely* didn't want Mr. Eli to confiscate this note.

James dropped his pencil then and it rolled under Reesa's chair. He smiled at me over her head when she swooped down to retrieve it for him. I don't know if he did it on purpose, but it distracted her long enough so I could pull myself together.

I refolded the note into a rectangle and slipped it in my pocket.

TWENTY-ONE

My swelling heart dropped into my stomach when I saw Reesa's face after class. She was glowing. "He touched me, right there," she said dreamily, rubbing a knuckle on her right hand. "I'll never wash it."

"Aren't you being a little dramatic?" I mumbled.

She ignored me. "And he said 'thank you.'" She mimicked James's deep whisper. "And his eyes . . . oh, man. His eyes are like . . . like . . . I don't know, like pools of liquid heat. But icy. Icy heat, like . . ."

"Bengay?"

"No. Like a hot angel boy. Or something." Reesa giggled and nudged me down the hall. Any hopes I'd had that she'd lose interest in James were officially dashed. She'd seen into his eyes. Hello, mesmerized.

The illustrated note in my pocket suddenly weighed as much as a brick and was just as bulky.

"Cute hat," I said in a feeble attempt at diversion. "Where'd you get it?"

Reesa's hand went up to the pink ribbed-knit beret that tipped back on her head. "Bloomie's."

"Nice." I almost asked what it cost but knew the answer would only depress me.

"Are you jealous or something?" she said.

I reached into my bag for a roll of mints and slipped one into my mouth. "Of your hat?"

"No." She grabbed my mints and took one for herself. "Of James and me. Because you keep changing the subject whenever I mention him."

I almost choked. "Uhh . . . no. I'm . . . uh . . ."

"I mean, I'd understand," she said. "With him being a super gajillionaire and everything, and your financial situation being what it is. You won't be jealous, will you, if he asks me out?"

"N-no. Of course not." I fingered the paper in my pocket. "You think he, uh . . . likes you?"

She nodded and smiled knowingly. "The way he dropped his pencil right under my desk?"

Though I knew otherwise, her confidence gave me doubts. Reesa was gorgeous, after all. And if James was as wealthy as she said, he'd quite possibly want nothing to do with me when he found out where I lived.

I heard myself say, "I'm sure you'll be very happy together," and it was like tearing my own heart in half. I wanted James for myself but I wanted to keep my promise to Reesa, too. I stopped in the middle of the hallway and just stood there. For a few seconds I couldn't seem to move forward or backward. Literally.

"What's wrong?" said Reesa.

"Nothing, I . . . uh . . . I forgot something." I spun on my heel before she could question me further and went straight for the supply room. Maybe he'd be there. I'd seen him go in there after English that one time a few days ago. We could escape again to the cemetery or even just lock the door to that tiny room and shut out the world.

I was a horrible friend and Reesa would never forgive me but he'd drawn me as Juliet to his Romeo and I had *wings* and I wanted to fly away with him. I turned the knob and cracked open the door enough to slip inside and . . . it was completely, absolutely, totally dark. Nobody was there.

I don't know if it was pent-up anticipation or emotion or the lies on top of secrets, but I felt tears prick at my eyes. I stumbled through the dark to the tiny room. I switched on the lamp and quickly checked the bookshelf. Everyone was there: *Gatsby*. Shakespeare. Beeblebrox. *Eyre*. *Hobbes*. But they were now joined by none other than Ponyboy.

He'd left *The Outsiders*. I smiled and wiped the lone tear off my cheek. If only he knew exactly how appropriate that book was. I was a refugee from the world of the Socials—the Socs—now hiding smack-dab in the middle of greaser territory.

I flipped open the cover to see what he'd written. Like his other notes (though unlike his crazy beautiful drawing), it was brief:

Greaser or Soc?

I loved that I never knew what to expect from James. He was this amazing surprise. The cemetery, the snippet of sonnet, and these cryptic little secret notes. I loved it all.

So I sat in the orange, duct-taped library chair with *The Outsiders* and contemplated my own brief response. If this book was about our school, my friends and I would be the Socs. Lazarski's gang would be greasers. But everyone hated the Socs in that book. They were all bullies, except Cherry. She was the only one who crossed sides. I pulled a pencil out of my backpack and scribbled a single word. Not Soc. Not Greaser.

Cherry.

Reesa caught me leaving the supply closet after second period, when I should've been in chemistry. I had stayed in there until I heard the bell ring so I wouldn't have to walk into class halfway through.

"Is that where you disappeared to? What's in there?" she said, trying to peer around me through the door before I pushed it shut. "And why is your face so red?"

"It is?" I put a hand to my cheek and a guilty lie stammered out.

"I was, uh . . . just looking for a place to practice for that country club audition." It was the first stupid lie that came to mind, and the second those words spilled out of my mouth, I wanted to swallow them back down.

But Reesa's face split into a huge smile and she squeezed my arm. "This is going to be so great! I'll help you. We'll meet in the band room after school. There's a piano. It's no Dr. Steinway, but it's a piano! And I'll help you pick a song. . . ."

She went on like that for a while, suggesting songs and ways to spend the money I would earn, never once questioning why I'd consider practicing in a supply closet. At least it took her mind off James for a while, and I didn't have to listen to her describe his eyes or fantasize about the same lips I was fantasizing about. Off-limit lips.

Maybe that's why my face was so red.

"Okay. After school," she said.

I nodded, but it must not have been the most convincing nod. She held me by my shoulders and made me face her squarely. "Promise?" she said.

I nodded again. "I promise."

TWENTY-TWO

"Costume shopping this weekend, girls!" Willow squealed.

It wasn't even October yet, but that hadn't stopped her from flitting around all day handing out save-the-date cards for her Halloween party. Mrs. Goodwin had succeeded in hiring the jazz band from Lincoln Center and the "Roaring Twenties" theme was official.Wynn was Googling flapper dresses on her phone and kept holding them out for us to see. Their giddy enthusiasm was actually one of the reasons Reesa and I were friends with them. It was easy to get swept up in that kind of excitement—the anticipation of something big.

And if the Halloween bash wasn't enough to push them over the top, Willow and Wynn were still basking in the glow of their ascension to the "fairest of them all" potato club.

I went to my lunch period in the cafeteria at 11:45, though my mind was on James in the library at noon. There was some discussion as to where on earth Lazarski "came from" that had this unusual tradition. Poland? Lithuania, perhaps? Reesa babbled on about how she read somewhere that peasants would bring baskets of crops as a gift to female royalty during medieval times. The fairest of them all received the most.

“That’s how sweet potatoes got their name,” she said.

I gave her a warning look. If she laid it on much thicker, even the *W*’s would realize she was bullshitting them.

“I never knew that,” said Wynn, happy to accept any version of history that ended with her being singled out as pretty or sweet. She had conveniently forgotten that it was Lennie Lazarski who’d given her the stupid potato.

I glanced around the cafeteria, wondering what Lennie thought of the whole thing . . . but he wasn’t there. I hadn’t seen him since I’d walked away from his Jeep that morning. And whenever his bruised eye surfaced in my mind, I pushed it away. That kiss . . . that was just a peck, the kind you might give a friend to say hello or good-bye. *It was nothing*.

I glanced at the clock on the cafeteria wall. It was exactly noon. I clutched my seat to resist the magnetic pull coming from the library. I couldn’t do that to Reesa, not after the way she’d saved me with the whole potato thing. But then I imagined James standing there amid the books, checking his watch. Waiting for me. Thinking I didn’t like him.

Reesa nudged me under the table with her foot. “You okay?”

“Yeah. I . . . uh . . . have to use the bathroom.” Scrambling to my feet, I hurried for the door. Five minutes past twelve. Heel-toe-heel-toe, I fast-walked down the hall. The library wasn’t far.

If he was still there, I would simply explain that it wasn't going to work out. I turned the corner and came to a sliding halt outside the library, took a deep breath, and pulled open the door.

I didn't see him at first. He hadn't mentioned exactly where to meet, so I strolled past the computer workstations and along the shelves, glancing left and right. I finally reached the "quiet study" section. No James. There was one more place I hadn't checked, a little nook where periodicals were kept. I turned the corner and nearly bumped into him.

"I was looking for you," he whispered. "I didn't think you were coming."

I bit my lip. "Neither did I."

James pulled me farther into the nook and frowned. "You didn't like the drawing?"

"I loved the drawing. It isn't that. It's just . . ."

"What?"

"I . . . don't know." I couldn't tell him that Reesa liked him, or that I wasn't who he thought I was. I just stood there, silent. It felt like someone had taken a novel, torn out all the pages, and thrown them back together in the wrong order. I couldn't make sense of anything or anybody. It was all turned upside down. "I could really use that yellow portal right about now. Step into a different world where nobody knows who I am, nobody expects me to be something I'm not."

James tilted his head back, looked up at the ceiling, and laughed. "I know exactly how you feel," he said.

He moved away from me and motioned drawing a big rectangular shape. Then he reached through the imaginary space and held out his hand to me. "Brand-new world," he said. "Come on over."

I took his hand and pretended to step through the window. I glanced around at the periodical room. "Funny, it looks exactly like the library."

"Parallel universe," said James. "Much better than that other one."

I had landed very close to him when I came through the imaginary window, and his face was now inches from mine. We weren't touching, but I was definitely within his gravitational force field. I swallowed. "If you say so."

"I say so," he said. The joking tone I liked so much was gone and his face got serious, but I liked that, too. His gaze went from my eyes to my mouth. And at that moment, everything else disappeared. He leaned in and I closed my eyes and his lips had just barely grazed mine and I was thinking *he's kissing me right here in the library* when we heard someone approaching and quickly separated. I grabbed a magazine and plopped down at the nearest table. *Popular Science.* James snagged an old copy of *Seventeen* with Selena Gomez on the cover. The librarian who peered in at us gave him a funny look but moved along. When he realized what he was reading, his face went red.

"Smooth," he said, shaking his head.

I giggled softly. "I better go."

His shoulders slumped, but he was still smiling. "Can I drive you home today?"

"No!" I blurted, then lowered my voice. "No. My parents . . ." I left this vaguely open, hoping he'd think my parents were simply overprotective. It didn't matter if we fantasized a different world—I was still living in the real one. And I didn't want him to see me there.

"Saturday night, then?"

I nodded. "Sure." *Wait, did I just say yes to a date?*

"Where should I pick you up?"

"I . . . I'll leave you a note." I'd figure out somewhere I could get to on my bike. "In our secret place."

"Which one?" he said.

At first, his question puzzled me . . . it seemed obvious. But now we had two secret places, the supply room and here in the library. Three, actually, if you counted the cemetery. Maybe he was counting the hedge where we first met, where I hid my bicycle.

I gave a playful shrug. "That's for me to know and you to find out."

When the final bell rang that day, I headed to the band room. I didn't want to break another promise to Reesa, but I also had no idea how I was getting home. The band-room doors were decorated with a giant illustration of a snarling tiger, our school mascot. As I approached, its jaws opened and Molly burst out, nearly knocking me over. She held her clarinet in one hand, its case in the other, and had a crumpled pile of music tucked under her arm.

"Hey. Hi," I said.

Her face was red and angry. She brushed past me, dropping sheets of music as she went. I hurried after her, picking them up.

"Molly?"

She stormed off without answering, disappearing around the corner. What the . . . ? I collected her scattered papers and went to find Reesa in the band room.

She was sitting at the piano.

"What happened to Molly? She tore out of here looking supremely pissed off," I said.

"I asked her to leave," said Reesa dismissively. "I mean, why can't she practice in her dad's fancy recording studio?"

"Oh, my God. You didn't say that to her, did you?"

She shrugged, which meant she had.

"Reesa! They don't live there anymore! Remember?"

"Oh. Yeah," she said.

I groaned. "I can't believe you did that."

"Fine. I shouldn't have asked her to leave, but she was acting like she owns the place."

"This is the *band* room, Reesa. She's in the *band*. You're the one acting like you own the place."

Reesa rolled her eyes. "Since when do you care so much about Molly Palmer?"

"Since I remembered we used to be really good friends with her, and we treated her like crap," I shot back.

"Oh, give me a break." Reesa swiveled to face the piano keys, turning her back to me. "What are you now, like the voice of the little people? Standing up for the downtrodden, the po—"

"Excuse me? Are you serious?"

Reesa clunked her head down on the piano keys. "I'm sorry, Ivy. I didn't mean that. You said to make sure nobody was in here, so that's what I did."

"I didn't tell you to be a total bitch about it. You're acting like Willow."

"Ouch."

"Well, you are. And the downtrodden?" I said. "News flash! I *am* one of them now."

"Okay. Sheesh. I'm sorry. I said I was sorry."

"Don't tell me." I pointed toward the door. "Tell Molly."

"What? Right now?"

I plopped down on one of the metal band chairs to wait. "No time like the present."

Reesa huffed and trudged out, returning about ten minutes later with Molly, who was still seething. I gave her the pile of music I'd gathered up. "Here," I said. "Sorry about all that."

She took the music. "Not your fault," she said, shooting a daggered glance at Reesa.

"She means well," I whispered.

Molly snorted, but sat and shuffled the sheets of music into a neat pile.

"I invited her to stay, if that's okay with you," said Reesa, a slightly evil grin coming to her lips. "You really need to get used to performing in front of an audience. And there's no time like the present. Is there?"

I stared at her, my mouth open in a surprised O. Only Reesa could turn a shitty moment into an opportunity.

TWENTY-THREE

Molly slouched on a metal chair near the entrance, arms folded across her chest. Reesa paced next to the piano. The doors were locked. All I had to do was sit myself down and play something, sing a few bars. Complete the lie.

I wiped the sweat from my palms onto the sides of my dress. It didn't matter if I was performing in front of two people or two thousand. My heart still raced, my chest still got tight, my breath still rasped as if someone had been chasing me. I could barely feel my fingers as they hovered over the keys.

"Just pretend we're not here," said Reesa, tiptoeing away.

I closed my eyes and imagined the twins there, just the two of them, waiting for a lullaby. I started to play, and my voice, when it came time to sing the melody, sounded like fingernails on a blackboard.

I kept going, eyes pinched tight, feeling my way across the keys. When I finished, I held my breath until Reesa broke the silence.

"That was amazing," she said.

I didn't believe her, but Molly had shifted from slouching to perching on the edge of her seat. "Really beautiful," she said.

"But you have to sing something receptiony," said Reesa.

"Receptiony? Like, what . . . the Macarena?" The only thing worse than embarrassing myself in a performance would be doing it in the process of singing cheesy wedding songs. "This is a really bad idea."

Reesa started rattling off names of soft-rock pop tunes that made my teeth ache. Molly didn't say anything, but I saw her cringe a few times.

"You want elevator music," I said.

"No!" Reesa sashayed across the room like she was walking a runway while holding a wineglass. "Think, like, classy cocktail party."

Classy cocktail parties were about as far away from my reality as I could get. I fiddled around on the keyboard. Freddie Mercury found his way into my head again, with the song I fell asleep to the other night: "Crazy Little Thing Called Love." But nobody could sing it the way he did, so I decided to go for a bluesy-baroque version. Billie Holiday meets Bach, which sounds weird, but I loved mixing styles. It was part of what made me nervous to perform in front of other people, though, because they might not get it. Kaya and Brady didn't know any better, after all. They'd grown up with my crazy songs.

"Ready?" Reesa waggled her fingers, prompting me to get started.

I nodded and closed my eyes, this time pretending to be in the cemetery with James. And out there, over the top of my piano, nothing but a sea of tombstones. Listening quietly. Not judging.

My fingers danced over the piano keys. I sang. It wasn't too terrible. When I finished, Reesa was smiling like a total goof. "How do you do that?"

"What?"

"This." She held her cell phone out for me to see the video she'd just recorded.

"What did you do? Delete that!" I grabbed the phone from her, and with my thumb hovering over the trashcan icon, I looked and I *heard* myself singing and . . . I couldn't believe it was me.

"See what I mean?" Reesa snatched her phone from my grasp before I could delete it. "You're amazing."

I turned to Molly for her opinion, but she was gone. "Where's Molly?"

She shrugged. "I guess her ride came."

I don't know why her opinion meant so much to me. But now I worried that she hadn't liked what she'd heard and skipped out so she wouldn't have to tell me.

Reesa's phone bleeped as a text came in. "Shit. Mom's outside. I have to go, too." She gathered up her stuff and headed for the door. "You rode your bike, right?"

I shook my head, pointed to the windows. "Too wet."

"Oh." Her face went blank for a minute, clearly trying to figure out a graceful way to not offer me a ride.

"Don't worry. My mom's coming," I lied.

The relief on Reesa's face was easily visible from outer space. "Oh, good. My mom's already pissed that I didn't get the bus home. She'd probably kill me if I made her drive to hell and back."

Whoa. Way to twist that knife, Rees.

"Okay, that came out wrong," she said. "Sorry."

I waved off her apology. "'Hell' is about right."

She rushed over and hugged me tight but didn't linger. "I'll call you."

"Mm-hmm." I closed the lid on the piano keys and reached for my bag. There had to be a pay phone in the school somewhere. They didn't expect everyone to have their own phone, did they? One or two of those old coin-operated thingies must still be hooked up somewhere for the few pathetic students with no other options.

Just as I was about to leave, I heard the clatter of something falling to the floor. It came from the door next to the band director's office. A door that was slightly ajar. A door I assumed to be a closet.

"Is someone there?" I asked. "Molly, is that you?"

Then the door opened and I yelped.

James walked into the band room. "Sorry. It's only me."

"Oh!" I backed away as he stepped slowly toward me.

"I know this looks weird," he said.

Yes. Very weird.

"I was in the library. I heard music coming from a closet. So I followed it." He held open the door so I could see that the closet opened into the library on the other side. Our school was apparently a maze of secret passageways. "Was that you?"

"You heard me? You were listening?" I bumped into a music stand, knocking it over.

He came closer, reaching out to help.

I held my hands up to stop him. "Don't."

"Ivy." He let his arms drop to his sides. "What's going on?"

"It's just . . . I didn't think anyone was listening. We locked the doors and I . . . I . . ." I sounded completely ridiculous and paranoid.

"I shouldn't have snuck up on you like that. I'm sorry."

"It's okay," I said. But it wasn't. If he heard me sing, then he must've heard my conversation with Reesa afterward. He knew I lived in a place even my best friend was afraid to visit. "I have to go."

"Whoa. Wait up," he said. "What's wrong?"

I forced a smile. "Nothing." *Everything.*

He held out a hand but I didn't take it.

"Let me drive you."

"No, that's okay." I kept backing toward the door.

"Look, I'm sorry I heard you singing. I'm sorry I scared you."

"No, it's not that." I shook my head. I couldn't explain why I was so upset. I hardly understood it myself. I just didn't want him there, where I lived. I didn't want him to know. He was an escape from my reality. I didn't want him to *see* my reality.

"I just . . . I have to go." I made it to the door and pushed it open.

"Talk to you tomorrow?" he called after me.

I turned back, gave a quick nod, and rushed out.

It was still raining. The entire planet was pretty much conspiring against me. I headed toward home, my umbrella keeping little more than my face dry. I made no effort to avoid the puddles. My boots were already soaked through. Anyway, it was water.

Water couldn't hurt me.

After about twenty minutes, I heard the familiar *meep-meep* of the red Jeep before I saw him approach. Lennie rolled to a stop beside me, and the passenger door swung open. He surveyed my soggy state from top to bottom but said nothing.

I silently climbed in.

He made a U-turn. "Kaya said you hadn't come home. I thought you might need a ride."

"Thanks." I couldn't figure out why he was being nice to me.

"'S okay."

We drove the few miles to our neighborhood in silence, but he didn't turn down our street. "You mind if we stop at Save-a-Cent? I gotta pick up my paycheck."

"Okay."

Lennie found a spot near the front and hopped out. The rain had let up to a light drizzle, at least for the moment. He walked toward the entrance holding his fingers to his temple, trying to hide the black eye from view. At least the swelling had gone down.

The minutes ticked by. I thought back to James, what he'd said, how crazy I must have seemed. How had things gotten so complicated in such a short time? Mom was always saying things had a way of working themselves out. But they were *not* working themselves out this time. They were working themselves into knots—really tight ones that I would never be able to untie.

Lennie finally came back out, still scratching his forehead so the palm of his hand shielded his eye. He was halfway across the lot when he stopped to talk to someone approaching the store. As he moved to the side, I gasped and dived to the floor of the Jeep.

It was James.

Please don't tell him I'm here please don't please. I waited, tucked under the dash. After another minute, I heard the slap of feet approaching on the wet asphalt. I peeked up from my hiding spot and saw Lennie staring at me through the driver's-side window. He yanked the door open and got in. I steeled myself for whatever wiseass remark he was preparing to make, but he didn't say a thing.

And his silence made me feel small.

I climbed back onto the seat as he pulled out of the shopping center. "Sorry, I didn't want him to see me."

"With me," Lennie said.

"No, it's . . . he . . ."

"Look. You either like me or you don't. You want to be friends, or you want to pretend I don't exist." Lennie stopped at the light and turned to face me with the full force of his bruised eye. "If you could decide which one it is and stick with it, that would be great. Because I really hate being jerked around."

He floored the gas when the light turned green. I fell back against the seat and was tossed to the side when he turned sharply onto our street. I braced against the dashboard as he slammed to a stop in front of my place.

"Len, I . . ."

He reached across my lap for the handle of my door and shoved it open. "Good-bye, Ivy."

I sat rigid for a moment, then slowly collected my backpack and umbrella and got out. I pushed the door closed and watched him drive in reverse the short distance from our house to his. He stayed in the Jeep for a while. I could see him sitting there, leaning on the steering wheel. Finally, his door swung open. I don't know why I kept watching, why I couldn't seem to move. He turned and looked at me looking at him.

Then he spat on the ground, like he was spitting at *me,* and walked into his house.

TWENTY-FOUR

"I'm going to invite him to Willow's party," said Reesa on the way to AP English. "I mean, everyone will be there. We don't want him to feel left out or anything. And if he wants to go, I could ask him for a ride!"

I stayed silent. It was a no-win conversation I didn't want to have.

"Or maybe I should just give him my number," she said. "Do you think that's too forward?"

"I think he'll ask you for your number if he wants it," I said.

She huffed. "Why should I wait for the boy to make the first move?"

"Then ask him for *his* number," I suggested.

"Maybe I will." Her mouth twisted side to side while she pondered her strategy. "Maybe instead of waiting for Willow's party, I could tell him I'm getting some friends together. We could all go to the movies, or that Little Invisibles concert."

"Or maybe we could all fly to Paris for the weekend." I

mimicked her breathless excitement.

"Sorry." She cringed. "I forgot."

"You go ahead," I said. "Just because I can't afford anything doesn't mean you have to take a vow of poverty."

She looped her arm around mine. "Once you get that job at the country club, everything will be back to normal."

"Yeah, normal," I mumbled. I slipped my arm out of hers as we approached Mr. Eli's room. James was standing outside. His eyes followed me through the crowded hallway.

"Now's my chance," Reesa whispered. She bopped ahead of me to talk to James. When I slipped past them, she was saying, "I'm getting some people together this weekend . . ."

They followed me into the classroom. "We might just hang out and watch movies," said Reesa. "You want to join us?"

I sat at my desk and buried my head in my backpack, as if I was having a hard time finding my ginormous Shakespeare textbook.

"I . . . uh . . . have plans Saturday," said James.

"Oh! Oh, well," Reesa chirped. "Maybe next time."

I glanced up at James, but Reesa was blocking my view. Then Mr. Eli called him up to his desk, and while they were talking, Reesa leaned halfway across the aisle between our seats. "Screw him," she whispered. "Saturday is girls' night. My house. Just you and me. 'Kay?"

I couldn't say no. After complaining that I didn't have the money to do anything, I couldn't exactly claim to have other plans. Besides, I missed her. I missed lying on her bed and staring at the glow-in-the-dark stars, talking about everything. Maybe everything would feel normal again at her house.

I smiled. "You and me."

James didn't look at me again during class, but on the way out he shoved a note into my hand. I went to the bathroom and closed myself in a stall to read it.

I'll be your secret if you'll be my girl.
Are we on for Saturday?
Tell me when and where.

I shoved the note into my pocket. At least he'd figured out that I wanted to keep him a secret. But now I had to choose between my best friend and the guy my best friend claimed to be falling in love with. My subconscious must've sensed my need for some piano therapy, because I was pushing the band room doors open before I even realized where I was headed. Molly sat in her usual corner near the drums, putting her clarinet together.

"You want me to leave?" I said.

"No way," she said. "I was hoping you'd show up. Join me?" She nodded toward the piano.

I hesitated. I'd never played with anyone before. "If you want," I said.

She picked up her stuff and came to the piano, scooting a chair next to the bench. I sat down and arched my fingers over the keys.

"Warm up a bit?" she said.

I nodded, and started playing scales. Molly jumped right in, easily transposing from her B-flat instrument to the piano's C. I tried harder and harder keys, with four and five flats or sharps, and she stuck right with me.

"You're good," I said. "How about this?" I made something up then. A few measures of what I was feeling. The crazy of James asking me to be his secret girlfriend. The guilt of it all with Reesa and the weirdness that was now our friendship.

She closed her eyes and played it back for me, adding a couple of trills.

It was like the old movies when one guy would tap-dance something really complicated, a challenge, and the other would tap it back but with extra flourish. We went back and forth for a while.

Molly was winded when we stopped. "That," she said, "was ridiculous."

I swept my fingers from the very top C on the piano to the bottom one, a final glissando. "I didn't get stage-frighty at all," I said. "Weird."

"It's because you're not worried about what I think," said Molly.

"That's not true," I said. "I care what you think."

"Yeah, but you're not *worried* about it. Because nobody else cares what I think." She grinned as if this didn't bother her in the least. "My opinion means very little at this school."

I couldn't argue with the truth of the statement. But it wasn't right. "It means a lot to me."

She twisted around to look at the clock above the door and started putting her clarinet away. "We should do this again. Maybe work on a piece for open mic night. They have one tomorrow, if you want to go." She must have noticed my body stiffen because she quickly added, "Just to listen?"

I knew of the King Theatre but had never been there. The place was supposed to be huge, with a big stage for major concerts and some smaller ones for local acts. Concerts were usually pretty expensive. "I don't know. . . ."

"It's only five bucks." Molly tore a corner of paper out of her notebook and wrote down a phone number. "Friday at eight. Call me if you need a ride."

An idea came to me then, one that would save me from choosing between James and Reesa. I took the stairs to the second floor, and sidled up to the supply closet door. The hall was still full of students getting to their next classes. I waited a moment, made sure nobody was paying attention to me, and slipped inside. The books were still stacked on the shelf in the secret room. I opened *The Outsiders* and found a new note:

Dally: Sexy or rude?

I knew he was referring to the character Dallas Winston, a friend of Ponyboy's and the toughest of the greasers. In the movie, he was played by a young, dark-haired Matt Dillon. But in the book, he had blond hair and icy-blue eyes, just like James.

That's about where the similarities ended. Dally was dangerous. And rude. But, yeah . . .

Sexy.

I wrote the word down hoping James would know I was referring to him as much as Dally. Then I added:

Change of plans:
Meet me Friday, 8:00
King Theatre

I closed the book and laid it back on top of the stack. We were just going to listen, not perform. I could handle that, though the prospect of getting close to a stage still made me nervous. It sprang from a completely unreasonable fear that someone might pull me up there. But practicing with Molly was giving me confidence. With her at my side, and James, too, maybe I could stop caring what anybody else thought.

I laughed to myself. *Yeah, right.*

TWENTY-FIVE

"This whole supper cost less than ten dollars." My mother swept her arm over the serving dishes she'd set out on the kitchen counter. I kept my mouth shut this time.

We ate buffet style, filling our plates and then gathering around the coffee table since the island in the kitchen only seated three. The food may have been cheap, but our dishes were not. Mom had stocked our kitchen cabinets with the antique bone china my father had given her for their fifteenth wedding anniversary. Each blue-and-white flowered dish was rimmed in gold leaf. She'd sold the glassware and silver, though, so our fancy plates were slumming it with plastic cups in assorted colors and a cheap set of cutlery that used to come out only for picnics.

"Looks delicious." Dad picked up the carving knife and sliced into the roasted chicken, while mom poured the gravy into the antique gravy boat. It was the twins' favorite meal, and one of mine, too. Mom was definitely pulling out all the tricks in her bag, trying to make it feel like home.

But it only made me miss my real home that much more.

"Chicken, on sale for only five dollars. The potatoes were a dollar a bag, right, Ives?" She hadn't adjusted her calculation for the missing bag, but I didn't say anything about that. "Carrots, about three dollars. A dollar or so for the herbs, butter, salt . . ."

I held up my glass. "Milk?"

"Oh. I forgot that. Extra for beverages." She knit her brows together. "But still, not bad for a family of five."

Despite my meltdown a few days ago, my parents continued to treat our family's financial disaster like we were starring on some kind of reality show. *Survivor: Poverty Island.* Mom announced every penny she saved as if it was a golden nugget she'd panned herself. Finding chicken on sale at the supermarket? That was the equivalent of hunting down a wild turkey and plucking its feathers with her teeth.

Mom waited until we were halfway through our meal to announce her next big money-saving idea. "We'll go to the food bank on Saturday. That'll really help bring our cost per meal down."

I dropped my fork and it clattered from plate to table. "I'm sorry, what?"

"The food bank," said Mom.

"But . . . that's for . . ."

Poor people.

"It's for people who need a little help providing nutritious food for their families." Mom took a delicate bite from her fork.

"People like us. You don't have to be completely destitute to take advantage of these programs. That's why they're there. To keep people from getting to that point."

I picked up my fork and took another bite, but it didn't go down so well. I couldn't even believe we were in danger of not having enough food.

Kaya made a lake in her mashed potatoes, filled it with gravy, and floated a bit of carrot in the middle. She poked at it a few times, pushing it down and watching it bob to the surface. Then she smashed the side in so her gravy streamed all over her plate.

"Are we slum bums?" she asked.

We all froze and stared at her.

"Did someone call you that?" said Dad.

She nodded. "Sienna Goodwin. I was telling my class how we moved and the houses are real close together and we can play right on the street and walk to the Save-a-Cent. Sienna said that's the slums and that makes us slum bums. Miss Fisher put her in time-out."

I was already sitting on the floor, so it wasn't far to fall when I slumped over sideways and laid my cheek on the carpet. Sienna was Willow's little sister.

"Sit up," Mother hissed at me, then said to Kaya, "You're not a slum bum, sweetie."

"But what is it?" Kaya didn't look particularly upset by the whole thing. Only puzzled.

"It's . . . well, it's . . ." Mom stabbed at her potatoes, as if searching for the answer in their gravied depths. "It's a not-very-nice name for people who are living . . . well, modestly."

"What's modestly?" said Kaya.

I lifted my head from the carpet. "She means poor. And you know what a bum is."

"Someone who smells like pee?"

"Yeah," I said, dropping back to the floor. "Someone who smells like pee."

Mom scowled at me. "Bum is a not-very-nice name for a homeless person," she said. "But we are *not* homeless. We have this very nice apartment, and this is not the slums. It's an affordable housing community."

"Slum bum," said Brady. "Slum bum slum bum slum bum . . ."

Dad got right in front of Brady, to make sure he was paying attention. "No, Brady. We don't say that. It's a bad word. Kaya, do you have a good word for him today?"

We all turned to my sister, the keeper of new words. "He didn't want a word today. He only wanted to say Lennie's name."

Brady's eyes lit up. "Len-nie-Laz-ar-ski," he said perfectly. "Lennie is my friend."

I moaned into the carpet, ignoring my mother's toe-nudging. My mistake, I realized, was in assuming things couldn't get any worse than they already were. Because every time I thought that . . . they did.

***

Friday morning I rode my bike to school with dread hanging around my throat like a too-heavy necklace. If Sienna knew we lived in the slums, it was only a matter of time before Willow found out. I wished I didn't care what she thought, but I did. Molly was right. It wasn't that I couldn't tolerate the bad opinion of one person. It was the multiplier effect. It was the fear of walking down the hall knowing that every single person you pass is laughing at you. Or pitying you.

I slunk to my homeroom, head down. Ashamed of how weak I was. The dread turned to a hard knot in my chest as I walked toward Mr. Eli's room. Every time I saw a blond head, I thought it was Willow. She'd ask if it was true, what Sienna told her. Had we really moved to Lakeside? She'd have that something-smells-bad sneer on her face, like when Lennie tossed the potato to me, before it was "cool." And Reesa wouldn't be able to cover it up with some crazy story this time.

James was leaning against the lockers outside Mr. Eli's room when I got there. He smiled and lifted a finger to his lips, which I took to be a gesture of secret-boyfriendliness.

I smiled back. I tried to say, *Yes, I'll be your secret girlfriend* with my smile. I figured I might as well enjoy the last few hours before the Willow News Network destroyed me.

His grin widened. He mimed wiping sweat from his brow.

Reesa came up next to me. "What's that all about?"

"What?" I hadn't realized she was there. "What's what all about?"

She nodded toward James. His eyes darted quickly away from me; then he waved to someone down the hall behind me. Someone who had no idea who he was.

"Oh," said Reesa. "Never mind."

Willow came stomping over to my locker before lunch, and I thought the moment of truth had come. I even felt kind of relieved, anticipating it. But all she did was thrust an orange envelope into my hand. "Here," she said. "Mother insisted on mailing printed invitations. Yours came back. What's up with that?"

I took the envelope and looked at it. It was addressed to me at our Westside house and stamped NO FORWARDING ADDRESS.

My heart thumped in my ears. Could she hear that? "Weird," I said. "Thanks."

"Did you move?"

"No. Of course not," I said quickly. My mother had forgotten to put in the forwarding order and only realized it when we didn't get a single item of mail for a few days, not even bills.

"Aren't you going to open it?"

"Oh, right. Yeah." She hovered over me as I tore open the envelope and pulled out the invitation. It was beautiful, as expected, with an art deco illustration of a flapper on the front.

"It's going to be amazing. We're all going to that theater rental place on Saturday to pick out our flapper costumes. Meet us there at eleven o'clock. Okay?"

She didn't wait for my answer but continued down the hall to bestow her presence on a pack of admiring sophomore boys.

I sank against the locker wall.

TWENTY-SIX

When I checked the secret room at the end of the day to see if James had gotten my note, the *Outsiders* book was gone.

A nervous feeling nagged at me, like maybe someone else had snuck in there and taken it. But when I got to the parking lot, his car was gone, too, so I retrieved my bike from the hedge and headed home. It was late September and getting cooler. The wind blew through my sweatshirt like it was made of gauze. Then a car passed so close, it sprayed muddy water all over me. I was fairly certain it was a red Jeep.

Cold and shivery, I left my bike in the yard. My fingers fumbled at the lock to the front door, too shaky to line up the key. It dropped on the steps, bounced once, and fell through the wooden slats of the porch to the dirt below.

I got on hands and knees and peered down at it. The crawl space under the stairs was muddy and dark. I'd have to shimmy on my belly to squeeze through the opening. I started to whimper just as Carla opened the door. The aroma of freshly baked cookies wafted out.

"Happens to me all the time," she said. "Come on in. I have extra keys."

"I'm all wet." I stood and held my arms out.

She directed me to a rug inside the door. "I'll get you a towel. What happened?"

"Got hit by a puddle," I said, accepting the towel she handed me. "Can I use your bathroom?"

Carla pointed the way. I cleaned up and made friends with a gray cat that sat next to the sink, batting its paw at drops of water that fell from the leaky faucet. It followed me out to the living room.

"I see you've met Valentino." She handed me a warm mug. "Chamomile okay? I was just making tea."

"Yeah. Thanks." I sat and sipped, letting the warmth seep into my chest.

Valentino hopped onto my lap and dug his paws into my thighs like he was kneading dough. When my lap was sufficiently softened to his satisfaction, he lay down and rested his chin on my knee.

Carla watched the whole thing with amusement while she placed a plate of cookies on the table between us. "You are hereby officially blessed and deemed a worthy human pillow for His Royal Majesty." She bowed her head and rolled her hand in the air, in that universal royal-majesty gesture that seemed unusually popular around here. I'd seen Lennie do it, too.

I rubbed the cat under his chin with one finger, and he purred. "He's not very particular, is he?"

"*Au contraire.*" Carla gave me a long look, perhaps deciding whether or not she agreed with her cat's endorsement. "He's actually a very good judge of character. Used to pee in my ex-husband's shoes all the time."

"Really?"

Carla smiled at Valentino as he stretched on my lap and then curled back up again.

"Bad kitty," I said.

"Actually," said Carla, "I should've listened to Valentino and thrown the guy out with the shoes. It would've saved me a lot of heartache. And *money*."

"Is that how you ended up . . ." I realized before I finished the question that it might be a rude one to ask, so I stopped myself.

"Yes," Carla answered anyway. "That is how I ended up in Lakeside. But it was a choice I made, to live here. We had a house in Westside. I could've stayed there."

"Why didn't you?" I said.

She smiled. "It's complicated."

I hated when adults assumed that teenagers were incapable of understanding their complicated adult lives. Did they not remember high school at all?

"Yeah," I said, nodding. "I've spent the past three weeks pretending I still live in Westside, trying to convince my best friend that I don't like the boy she likes even though I do, and basically hiding who I really am from every single person I know. So I *get* complicated. What I don't get is why someone would choose to live *here* if they didn't have to."

Carla's eyes had widened as I was speaking. "Okaaay," she said. "It's like this. When I was married, my husband made the money and he made a lot of it, but it always felt like what we had was never really *mine.*"

She paused to take a bite of cookie, wiping a bit of gooey chocolate from the corner of her mouth and licking her finger. "We got divorced and I wanted to prove that I could take care of myself. I also never wanted to find myself in a position again where money factored into decisions of the heart. I stayed with my husband a lot longer than I would've because of the money, because of the nice house and the lifestyle we had."

She put her hand to her chest. "I own this house. I paid for it with my own money. It's mine. It's not much, it could use a paint job . . ."

The look on my face apparently revealed my agreement on this point, because Carla laughed. "At least I know if a man falls in love with me, it's not for the money. Or the house. Unless he *really* likes the color brown," she said. "Maybe you can help me pick out a new color. And paint it?"

"I'd love to." I sank back into my chair with exaggerated relief, and she laughed again.

"You and Molly, perhaps. And Lennie."

I looked away from her smiling eyes. Petted the cat.

"Not Lennie?" she said. "So he's not the boy you like who your friend likes, too?"

I nearly choked on the sip of tea I'd just swallowed. "Lennie? God, no. No."

"Oh!" She seemed genuinely surprised. "I thought . . . well, he certainly seems to like *you*."

"Excuse me?"

She lifted an eyebrow. "Don't tell me you haven't noticed."

"I've noticed that he's completely infuriating," I said.

She chuckled. "Of course he is. Because you like him, too."

"Um, no . . . I really don't."

She shrugged and took a sip of her tea. "If you say so."

"He's a total pothead," I said, "and a drug dealer, and . . ."

"Where on earth did you get that idea?"

"That's what everyone at school says. . . ."

"And you believe everything you hear?" Her voice had taken on a slightly harder edge. "Last time I checked, the high school rumor mill wasn't exactly a good source of credible information."

"True," I said. "But I saw him taking money from some guy in the stairwell and giving him a little bag. And people are constantly driving up to his house and handing him money in exchange for little packages. It doesn't take a genius to figure out what's going on."

Her lips pressed into a thin line. "And you know what's inside those little packages?"

"Well, no, but . . ."

She stood and carried our tea mugs to the sink. "I've known Lennie since he was a boy, and I cannot believe he would ever do such a thing."

Or maybe she just didn't want to admit it?

"Maybe you're right," I said, not because I believed it. But she was obviously fond of Lennie and didn't take kindly to me trashing him.

"Not everything is always what it seems to be," she said, sounding just like Mr. Eli. "You should ask him about it."

There was a rumbling in the distance; the twins' school bus approaching. Mom had picked up some more hours at work this afternoon, so I was on Brady duty. I started for the door. "Thanks for the tea."

"Anytime." Carla pulled a key ring from the drawer and followed me out, unlocking the door to our apartment as I ran to meet the bus. The twins hardly stopped to say hi. They dashed right past me to Carla. I watched them circling her legs, telling her about their day. I'll admit it, I was a little jealous. Even with them, it seemed, I was on the outside looking in.

Dad insisted on coming out to meet Molly and give her car a thorough visual inspection when she pulled up out front to pick me up for open mic night. I had asked him to please not grill her about her family or her favorite subjects in school or any of the usual dad stuff, so "that tire looks like it could use a little air," was all he said.

Molly assured him we'd stop at a gas station on the way and top it off. Which we actually did. "Your dad's really nice," she said, then drove in silence the rest of the way to Belleview.

The King Theatre was on a city street that was busy by day, when all the employees from downtown businesses were buzzing around, but almost deserted at night—except for the people coming and going to hear music. We found a parking spot easily—though it took Molly a few attempts to parallel park the car.

"It's a miracle I got my license," she said, attempting to straighten out the tires without bumping into the car in front of us.

I could see the theater from a block away as we approached. It had one of those old-timey half-circle movie marquees out front, all lit up and glowing. My heart pounded at the sight of it. At the box office, we paid our five dollars (finally, something I could afford!) and they directed us to the main stage theater. When we went through the double doors, my breath caught.

It was so beautiful. And so big.

The theater had been abandoned during World War II and sat vacant for decades before someone raised the money to restore it. But rather than make it look all shiny and new, they had left the ornate paintings on the walls—what remained of them—by sealing them with some kind of clear coating. The colors were a little faded and much of the paint had chipped away over the years, but you could see how glorious it must've been in its heyday.

The stage backdrop was a patchwork of textured panels that shimmered in the colored lights. But what really caught my eye was the grand piano at the side of the stage, all shiny and black. I wanted to go up there and stroke its surface, glissando my hands up and down the keys.

Molly reached over and flicked me under the chin. "Catching flies, Emerson."

I snapped my mouth shut and smiled. "This place is amazing," I said. "I don't even care if anybody performs."

She laughed. "The sound is great, too. You'll see."

There was a bar in the back, and Molly went to get us sodas while I excused myself to the bathroom. When I came out, she was getting her arm signed in Sharpie by some kid with a four-inch-high Mohawk. He looked about fifteen years old. "He'll be famous someday," she assured me. "And I'll have a photograph of his autograph on my arm." She pulled her cell phone out of her pocket and took a picture of it.

"I thought you were going to say you'd never wash it," I said, thinking of Reesa when James had touched her hand in class.

"No," said Molly. "I'm not that pathetic."

We stood in the back for a few minutes, searching for a good place to sit. I kept glancing toward the doors, looking for James.

"Waiting for someone?" said Molly.

I hadn't told her I'd invited James, hoping it might seem more like a chance meeting than a date. "I did mention to someone that I'd be here," I said. "I hope you don't mind."

She narrowed her eyes. "It's not Reesa, is it?"

"No." I couldn't blame Molly for disliking Reesa, but I felt guilty talking behind her back, even if I wasn't really saying anything.

"We'll save a spot, then," Molly said. "For your mystery date."

We found three seats in the middle of the front section. "I like to be close enough to see their fingerings on their instruments," Molly explained.

When they lowered the houselights, a flutter of nerves rushed to my throat. I had to remind myself, *It's not you up there, it's not you.* But I couldn't help envisioning myself standing next to the piano. Unable to move.

"You okay?" Molly was looking at me funny.

"Yep!" I pushed the image to the back of my mind and forced a smile, shifting to get more comfortable in my seat.

The first act was a rock band made up of three women—drums, bass, and the lead singer on guitar. They called themselves the Llama Mammas. They sang an original song of their own called "Spinning Free." The bass player twirled around and around, got tangled up in her cord. My heart raced for her. I would've died of embarrassment, but she just laughed and unplugged herself and stepped out of it and plugged back in.

I kept looking back to the entrance so I could wave James over when he came in. But he didn't, and after an hour I began to lose hope. We sat through a bunch of solo performances, people singing with guitars or a cappella. One guy played a bagpipe.

Someone told jokes. Molly applauded and whistled for everyone. It made me wonder if she really thought I was any good or if she was just supportive of music in general.

It was past nine o'clock and still James hadn't shown. Then someone tapped me on the shoulder and said, "Ladies?"

I spun around and there was . . . Lennie.

"What are you doing here?" I snapped.

"I'm supposed to meet someone." He stared at me for a moment, then looked around. "Not sure if she's here, though. It's kind of a blind date."

Molly pointed to the empty seat next to me. "You can sit with us if you want."

I glared at her.

"Or not . . . ," she mumbled.

"That's okay." Lennie grinned crookedly. The bruise around his eye was purple and must've still hurt. "I can see you're waiting for someone special."

The next performer had taken the stage, so I turned to watch. Lennie left, went I-didn't-know-and-I-didn't-care where. The seat next to me remained empty for the rest of the night.

Molly noticed my disappointment. "Sorry about your . . . uh . . . friend."

I shrugged. "The music was great," I said, eager to change the subject. There was such a crazy variety of performers, but the organizers had presented them in a way that flowed just right. It all ended with the most amazing quartet that sang a number from *Les Misérables*. The audience was on its feet before they finished.

I felt both exhilarated and annihilated, wanting to sing like that but knowing I never could. Molly squeezed my arm as if sensing my mood. But she didn't say anything, which was exactly the right thing to say.

TWENTY-SEVEN

Mom shook me awake on Saturday morning. "Time to get up. I want to leave in a half hour. I made you some oatmeal."

I looked at the clock on my little desk. "It's only seven. I thought you said they open at nine."

"Yes," said Mom. "But the lady at the food pantry told me they start lining up at eight. To get the good stuff."

Mom had broken it all down for me the day before, how the food bank collects and sorts all the donated food, then supplies it to the pantries, which dole it out to people at risk of hunger. Mom kept calling them "the hungry."

"We're not hungry," I had said.

"No, we're not." She'd been scrubbing at a stain on the counter that was never going to come out. "Not yet."

I rolled over in bed and groaned. "Do you think we'll see anybody we know?"

"We might." Her voice had that high, tinny sound like when she'd first told me about moving here.

I swung my legs to the floor. "Might as well get this over with."

Mom had already driven Dad and the twins over to Dad's office so he could get some work done while they played with the shredder. He had let them shred some documents once and you'd have thought they'd died and gone to heaven. Now he saved up all his shredding so they could do it for him when he worked on weekends. He'd even purchased a shredder with a special safety device so they couldn't shred their fingers by accident.

Mom called up to me as I was getting dressed. "Wear something, uh . . . not too flashy."

"Dress like a poor person," I mumbled. "Got it."

My hoodie supply was running a little low, so I pulled on the humblest sweater and jeans I could find. Instead of the knee-high leather boots I usually wore with it, I donned my oldest, most beaten-up pair of Chucks. I didn't brush my hair or put makeup on.

"How's this?" I said, twirling around in the kitchen.

"I didn't say you had to look like you'd been attacked by birds," she said. "Go brush your hair."

When we were finally on our way, Mom explained that the pantry was at a church. "It's a choice pantry," she said. "That means we get to choose what kinds of foods we want. Some of them just give you a box that they've preselected."

She kept rambling on about what to expect, but I honestly didn't want to know. I just wanted to get it over with.

We drove out of our neighborhood, passing my school and

heading in the same direction James had gone the day we escaped. We passed the beheaded deer and the wine-bottle tree. My heart started to pound. “Mom? What church is this pantry at?”

Mom fumbled in her purse and pulled out a square of paper. “Northbridge,” she said, passing the note to me. “Northbridge Methodist.”

I groaned. That was James’s church. The cemetery. “Is it okay if I stay in the car?”

“I need your help,” said Mom with a look of despair. “To carry things. I don’t think they have carts.”

We had a pile of canvas shopping bags in the backseat of the station wagon—the Volvo. My parents had sold the Mercedes but the Volvo was already paid for, so that’s the one we kept. Still, when we drove into the church parking lot, it was definitely the nicest car there.

“Oh, my,” Mom said as we circled around to the food pantry entrance. There was a line of about fifty people already waiting. This was “the hungry” she’d been talking about. Not visibly starving like on TV, when they show children with distended bellies and skeletal limbs. These people seemed tough, like hunger was the least of their problems. It was the rough ones who stood out to me first. The guy with wiry muscles and a face etched with lines, smoking a cigarette. A woman who looked like she’d beat me up if I so much as blinked in her direction. They glared at us as we drove past. Did they think we were going to take their food?

“Oh, my,” Mom said again.

"We don't belong here," I said. "Let's go."

Mom drove all the way around the church and pulled into a spot facing a car that looked perfectly respectable, except for the passenger window was cracked and held together with clear plastic tape. It had a handicapped tag hanging from the rearview mirror.

We stayed in the car and watched more people arrive and get in line. One family drove up in an RV, which I assumed was their home. I noticed quite a few handicapped tags, and a number of people with walkers or canes. They weren't so tough. More weary. After a few more minutes, a man came out of the church and handed plastic laminated numbers to those in line, and everyone dispersed a bit, going back to their cars or sitting on a grassy embankment.

"Let's go in now," said Mom, though she didn't actually make a move.

I wasn't ready. "Not yet," I said.

A car pulled into the spot next to ours. I turned to look at the driver. It was Chandra Mandretti. My eyes went wide, and hers narrowed. We both looked away. Oh. My. God. *Chandra Mandretti went to the food pantry.*

I sucked in my breath.

Mom gave me a quizzical look but was too busy working up the nerve to go inside to ask what I was gasping about. She turned off the ignition and studied her reflection in the rearview mirror. Even in her not-too-flashy clothes, she could've been dressed for lunch at the country club. Although I was wearing my rattiest sneakers, I had forgotten and put my leather jacket on.

We did not look needy of free food.

Mom took her earrings off and dropped them in her purse. They were the small diamond studs that Dad had given her for a birthday a few years ago. "I forgot I had these on," she said apologetically.

"I thought you said we didn't have to be destitute to come here."

"We don't. We're being silly." She reached into the backseat for the canvas bags we'd brought. "Come on."

I glanced at Chandra as I got out of the car, but she had her elbow propped in the window to hide her face. Her mother had gotten out and gone to collect a number by herself. But I couldn't do that to Mom. Not this first time.

When we got to the door, a man with a brigh-orange VOLUNTEER tag handed us the number sixty-seven.

"We're new," said Mom, as if we were joining a social club. "I understand there's some paperwork we need to fill out?"

He took us inside to a lady volunteer who gave Mom a form with questions about our name and address and monthly income and how many people were in our family. She also offered us some literature on SNAP benefits. "That's what they call food stamps now," the lady explained.

"Food stamps?" I hissed in Mom's ear. "Seriously?"

Mom just kept this smile plastered to her face and wrote her answers in the little blocks. She added up her hours of work for the past two weeks and doubled it, calculating a monthly income, and wrote the figure down.

"What about Dad's income?" I asked.

"Nothing to report," she said.

"Family income, it says. You need to put Dad's down, too."

She tapped the pencil on the paper and leaned toward my ear. "Your father is not bringing home an income at the moment, Ivy. Everything he earns is going toward the bank debt on his business."

"What?" I glanced back down at the dollar amount Mom had written, what she brought home from her part-time job at the newspaper. "Seriously? How are we paying for Brady's therapy?" I asked.

"We'll talk about that later," she whispered.

The orange-badged volunteer reviewed our form and seemed satisfied that we were as poor as we said we were. She waited with us until a man with a microphone called out "up to number seventy!"

We shuffled into line with the other hungry. The realization that we were really and truly one of them came on much the way the sensation of hunger does, with a dull ache in the stomach. Only this one felt a bit more like a sucker punch. How did things get so bad, so fast? I wanted to bend over and lean my hands on my knees to catch my breath, but that would only make it worse. People were already staring at us.

When we got to the front of the line, Mom tried to give our number to the man, but he explained that we should hand it in at the end. There were different sections for different kinds of foods. Our volunteer lady pointed out the canned stuff, like fruit and veggies and tuna, boxes of pasta and rice, cookies, and crackers. She called them "shelf-stable products." There was a center section for fresh fruits and vegetables, and another for bread and muffins and other baked goods. "The refrigerated items are in the back," she said. "Meat, eggs, yogurt, milk, cheese."

Hanging on every shelf was a sign that indicated how many of each item you were allowed to take, based on the size of your family. Mom kept reading them aloud, as if I couldn't understand the simple system. Or maybe she didn't want the others to think we were claiming more than our share. "We're a family of five, so we take three boxes of cereal," she said. A family of two was allowed to take one.

"Two pounds of ground beef." She pulled them from the refrigerator. A smaller family could take only one.

"You don't have to announce it," I murmured in her ear.

We stopped to watch a little cooking demonstration going on, teaching people how to prepare a nutritious meal from groceries that were available. They were making a chicken Caesar salad.

Mom kept saying things like, "Oh, look, they have Cheerios!" and "It's just like the market!" But it was *not* just like the market. People didn't snake through the aisles single file like this at the market. They didn't get excited about two pounds of ground beef. And the market never ran out of groceries. By ten o'clock when we finished our shopping, the shelves were almost bare. And people were still showing up.

"Should we give them some of ours?" I asked Mom as we hauled our bags to the car.

She paused and considered, resting her bags on the pavement for a moment. "No," she said firmly, snatching them back up. "I'm sorry. I can't worry about everyone else. I have to worry about us."

We got in the car, and Mom put her earrings back on. Her hands were shaking, but I didn't say anything about that. I turned and saw Chandra still sitting in the car parked next to us. She looked at me again and nodded, before turning away.

As we drove toward the exit, I saw a car I recognized. Its front bumper was held together by duct tape. Leaning against the passenger door was Rigby Jones, one of Lennie's friends. I might've pretended I didn't see him, but he raised a fist and bumped it toward me. I smiled and bumped back.

"Who was that?" said Mom.

"Kid from school." I twisted back around to wave good-bye. That's when I noticed the orange badge. Rigby wasn't using the food pantry—he was a volunteer.

"Everything is not as it seems," I mumbled.

Once we were a few miles away from the church, Mom let out a huge sigh, as if she'd been holding her breath that whole time. "I'll make that Mexican rice and beans with chicken that your father likes," she said, "and the chicken Caesar. That's a good idea. A meat loaf, or maybe a meat sauce . . ."

She was over the challenge of getting the food. Now she had to find a way to stretch it, because at our income level we were only allowed to visit the pantry once every three weeks. I wondered what poor looked like for the people who could shop there every single week.

"You were going to tell me," I said, "how we're paying for Brady's therapy."

Mom didn't reply right away. She probably didn't want to tell me, only said she would to shut me up earlier. "I don't want you to worry about it."

"Mom." This was getting ridiculous. I was worried about it. If I'd known, I would have been looking harder for a job.

"Okay, okay." She fidgeted at the steering wheel. "Insurance pays for some of it. And all the money we made from selling the furniture, jewelry, appliances. That'll pay for the rest. For a while."

"Then what?" I asked.

Mom took a deep breath. "We'll figure something out."

I looked out the window as we headed home, newly determined to find a job.

TWENTY-EIGHT

Later that day, I headed over to the used-book shop, but the elderly woman working there laughed when I asked if she was hiring. "Barely make enough to pay myself, dear," she said.

So I went into the Save-a-Cent. The man working behind the customer service counter gave me a little clipboard with an application to fill out. When I handed it back to him, he said, "We'll let you know if there's an opening."

"You don't have anything?"

"There's a waiting list," he said. "And I'll be honest. A lot of the applicants are older and have families."

"I have a family," I said.

"Are they relying on you to put food on the table or are you just looking for some extra spending money?"

I shrugged. I didn't want to admit that I might need to help my parents buy food. "Extra money, I guess."

"We'll let you know," he said, shoving my application into the back of the folder.

I started to walk out, then turned back around. "I've seen other kids my age working here. Do they support their families?"

"Actually, yes," he said, nodding. "Some do."

"Oh," I muttered, turning and walking out. Maybe I should've considered that country club job, but it was too late. The auditions had started an hour ago.

Brady was on the front lawn when I got home, throwing his gravel into the road. Kaya was sitting on the porch with a coloring book.

"Where's Mom?" I asked.

"Upstairs talking to Daddy," said Kaya.

I looked around for Carla, but she was nowhere to be seen. "Who's watching Brady, then?"

She sat up very straight. "I am!"

"What if something happens? You're six years old."

"If Brady leaves the yard, I'm s'posed to holler as loud as I can. Like this . . ." She took a huge breath.

"No!" I stopped her. "I get it." Had Mom forgotten that Brady would have a total freak-out if Kaya yelled like that?

I went over to my brother and took his arm. "Brady, come with me. We're going inside."

He yanked his arm away and went back to his rocks. "You go," he said.

"You need to come with me," I said. "Now."

He scooped up a pile of rocks and kept throwing them, one by one.

I batted the gravel out of his hand and seized his wrist. "Enough with the rocks, Brady! You can't put them all back. You'll never put them back!"

He dropped them then, and his hands went to his ears. Pounding. He started that silent-screaming thing again.

Kaya rushed over to us. She pushed me in the stomach. *Hard.* "You ruin everything," she said. "Leave him alone."

I stumbled away from them, almost falling over the bike I'd left in the yard yesterday. Mom and Dad hadn't even asked me about it. They were too busy worrying about money to pay attention to me or even Brady.

I ran up the back stairs to get them, but when I reached the top, the door was ajar and I could heard them arguing.

"What about unemployment? Can't you get that?" my mother said.

"I'm not unemployed, Susan."

"You should've been there, Mark. Those people were poor, and not because their multimillion-dollar businesses were failing. I felt like a fraud."

Dad slammed something on the counter. "I'm doing the best I can. You want me to give it all up? Go begging for a job at Sheffley's?" That was Dad's competition, and the biggest printing company in the state. They weren't known for treating their employees particularly well.

"No," said Mom. "I just hope it turns around soon. I don't know how long I can keep this up."

"It's not that bad, Susan. We have a roof over our heads, we have food, we have clothing. The kids are in their same schools. Brady is thriving here. He's—"

"He's playing in the gravel by the side of the road! He's palling around with the neighborhood thug!"

Ah, so she didn't think so highly of Lennie after all.

"That boy is no thug. His only crime is living in a poor neighborhood," he said. "Don't be such a snob, Susan."

Mom gasped. "A snob? Now I'm a snob because I want something better for my mentally disabled child? For all my children?"

"*Our* children," Dad corrected, his voice louder. "They're *our* children and *we* made this decision together. It's not going to kill them to learn that everything in life doesn't come to them on a *goddamned* silver platter."

My hand flew to my mouth as if I was the one who'd cursed. My dad *never* swore. He *never* raised his voice at Mom, either.

Their voices got lower then, and I heard Dad saying, "I'm sorry. I'm doing the best I can." It sounded like he might cry.

I pushed the kitchen door open then. Dad was sitting on one of the kitchen stools, and Mom had her arms wrapped around him. They were sort of rocking back and forth. They looked up when I stepped inside and realized I must've heard the entire argument. Or maybe they just didn't have the energy to put on their everything's-just-fine faces anymore.

"I'll get a job," I said. "I just put an application in at Save-a-Cent."

Dad's whole body slumped even farther than it already was. "You don't have to do that, Ivy."

"If they don't have anything, I can try some other places. And there's . . ." I took a deep breath, for courage. "There's this job at the Morgans' country club. . . ."

"It's too far," said Mom. "I'm already driving your father to work and myself to work and Brady to therapy and . . ."

"Okay then, I'll find something around here that I can walk to," I said, relieved that the country club option was out. "I could give piano lessons, maybe . . ."

Dad sighed and Mom stroked his back, and we all just stood there not saying anything for a few minutes. We could hear Brady's gravel landing in the road, one tiny fistful at a time.

Kaya could take care of him just fine, apparently, and I ruined everything. I climbed the two flights to my room and sat by the attic window, looking down on my neighbors. Looking down *at* my neighbors, that is. I couldn't exactly look down on them anymore, could I?

TWENTY-NINE

Reesa called around four o'clock. "How'd it go?" she asked, all breathless.

"Oh . . ." I hesitated, deciding whether to lie and tell her I'd bombed the audition or confess that I hadn't gone.

"You bailed, didn't you?" Her voice had that steady, I-am-pissed-off-but-trying-not-to-show-it tone.

"Yeah," I said. "It was too far away, anyway." I paused, waiting for her rant, but it didn't come. She only sighed. "Are we still on for tonight?" I asked.

"Yeah," she said. "Get over here already. I have something to show you."

I yanked my hair into a ponytail and splashed water on my face, threw some clothes and my toothbrush in an overnight bag, and went down to the kitchen. Mom looked me up and down. "That's what you're wearing?" I had the same clothes on I'd worn to the food pantry.

"Since when do you care what I wear to Reesa's?"

She had put on a nicer outfit just to drive me over there, maybe expecting Reesa's mom would invite her in. But Mrs. Morgan didn't even come out to say hello.

"I'll pick you up in the morning. Ten o'clock," Mom snipped.

I couldn't believe Reesa's mom would've brushed her off on purpose, but she was right there in the kitchen when I went inside. She smiled like she was posing for someone who was taking too long to snap the photo.

Reesa dragged me upstairs. "Wait till you see what I found."

I was expecting an amazing dress, maybe a couple of great flapper costumes from her mother's closet. But she opened her laptop, clicked on a browser window, and stood back.

"There," she said. "The Wickertons of New York."

I leaned in. It was a fuzzy photo of some people standing at the bottom of a big staircase.

"It's from a few years ago, but look," she pointed to a boy. "Same hair, only shorter. It's got to be him."

I looked at the caption, which identified the boy as Robbie Wickerton. "Wrong name," I said.

"Maybe it's a nickname. Because that kid looks exactly like James. You can't tell me that's not him."

I looked closer at the boy named Robbie. There was definitely a resemblance, but I refused to agree with her.

"Please. It doesn't look anything like him," I said.

"It looks *exactly* like him," Reesa insisted. But she put the photo away and didn't bring up James or his family's obscene wealth again after that. I hadn't told her about the trip to the food pantry or my failed attempts at getting a job, but even Reesa was perceptive enough to notice that something was bothering me.

"What you need," she said, "is some Reesa therapy."

She pulled out her nail polishes and gave me a manicure while we listened to music, taking turns choosing songs. Determined to cheer me up, she pulled out the big guns: her 1980s playlist. For every "Raspberry Beret" and "Girls Just Wanna Have Fun" she blasted, I countered with an "Over the Rainbow" or "I Dreamed a Dream." It was Madonna versus *Evita*, Wham! versus Wagner, Joan Jett versus *Phantom of the Opera*.

"You are not giving Reesa therapy a chance," she said, as her latest selection, "Jessie's Girl," started to play. "The first step is admitting you have a problem."

I nodded. "I definitely have a problem. But I don't think Rick Springfield is going to fix it."

She pulled me up from the bed to dance with her. I tried, really I did, but "Jessie" started with a *J*, like James, and it only reminded me that he'd stood me up at open mic night. It appeared he didn't want me to be his girl, after all.

I flopped onto Reesa's bed and flipped through her huge stack of celebrity magazines. She played with my hair, twisting it into ringlets, then teasing it so it stood straight out like a giant afro. It was hard not to feel at least a tiny bit better.

After dinner (take-out sushi from our favorite sushi place), Reesa grabbed our coats and led me out back to the deck. I could see our old house from there, the window of my bedroom. It was dark. Empty.

"Here." She pulled a key from her pocket and handed it to me. "I found this."

I turned it over in my palm. "A key. To what?"

"Your house, silly."

"Um, thanks. I guess my mom can give it to the bank people, or the Realtor or whatever." I slipped it in my pocket.

"No, dummy. It's for you. To get inside. Hello?" She wiggled her fingers like she was playing a piano. "It's still there, right?"

It was. My piano hadn't been sold yet.

"I know you miss it," said Reesa. "I thought you might want to go back and play it one more time."

I stared at the key in my hand. "But . . ." I missed everything about home—my old life—so badly. How did she know it was the piano I missed the most? "What if they changed the locks?"

Reesa shrugged. "Guess we'll find out."

She took my hand and we walked the short distance from her house to mine, slinking through the shadows.

"I feel like a burglar," I said.

"It's not like we're going to steal anything," said Reesa. "We're only visiting, and it's your house, anyway."

I pulled out the key as we approached the back door. We hadn't been gone that long, but everything seemed so different. The yard was sprawling, the patio immense. The flower beds so . . . so trimmed and mulched.

The key slid into the slot and turned easily. When I pushed the door open, the alarm sounded, which I expected. It was just a little tiny beep, a reminder to disarm it. I punched in the code, the last four digits of our phone number, and pressed ENTER.

It went silent. *I was home.*

We stepped inside and pulled the door closed. It was dark in the house, and cold. I knew the heat was turned off, or set very low. But there must be electricity since the alarm was working. Reesa flipped one of the six switches by the kitchen door. The recessed lighting above us flickered on.

I breathed in the smell of home. But it wasn't quite what I remembered. Whatever combination of odors made home smell like home—the cooking, the furniture, the soap Mom used and Dad's cologne, Kaya's rescued frogs and Brady's bouquets of dandelions—it was already dissipating.

I crossed the kitchen to the back stairs that led up to my room. Reesa followed me, turning on lights as we went. Everything was so big and so painfully empty. None of our furniture remained. I knew it was being sold off, but didn't realize they'd take it all so quickly. The hardwood floors were bare. Our footsteps echoed through the house. I entered my room, stared at the spot where my four-poster bed used to stand. No more desk, no dresser, no vanity, no rocking chair. It was all gone. Only the window seat remained. I walked to it and sat in my usual spot, where I used to watch Reesa crossing our yard on the way to my house. I wondered if Reesa remembered how we used to talk on our cell phones until she made it all the way up the stairs and sat down across from me.

She plopped herself down there now and put her hand up to her ear and mouth like a phone. "Bye. Hi."

She remembered.

"Bye. Hi," I whispered.

Reesa dropped her hand to her lap. "It's weird in here. Like a ghost town."

I nodded. Nothing was the same, and now that I was here, I knew we'd never be back. I just hadn't expected everything to be so . . . gone.

"You want me to stay?" said Reesa.

"I think I'd like to be alone, if that's okay."

She nodded and scooted out into the hall. I waited until I heard the kitchen door close before making my way to the piano room, tears pricking at my eyes. Everything was so different. I couldn't believe I'd lived here less than a month ago. It felt like a lifetime. And seeing the piano there, all by itself in the moonlight in the middle of the room, reminded me of a line in the nursery rhyme song, "The cheese stands alone." I plunked out the simple melody on the keys, and sang along. "Heigh-ho, the derry-o, the cheese stands alone. . . ."

I nudged the piano seat out and sat down, played one of the lullabies I'd made up for the twins. It sounded hollow.

Just rusty, I told myself. I tried again, grasping for something deep inside that would bring the song to life. Came up empty.

It didn't feel right here. No furniture, no rugs, no family . . . nothing but cold, bare floors. Only memories remained, and they were lonely here, too. I closed the lid on the piano keys, slid my hand over its smooth wood surface. Every sound I made was magnified, eerie.

I thought I heard a noise downstairs and checked my watch. Only seven thirty, not time to go. I tiptoed to the door, listened. Footsteps crossed the kitchen and started up the steps. I clung to the wall.

"Ivy?" Reesa waltzed into the room. "Where are you?"

My shoulders relaxed. "Rees, you scared the crap out of me."

She turned to see me huddling by the door. "Your mom just called." She thrust her cell phone into my hand, a pinched look on her face. "You need to call her back."

I couldn't figure out why Reesa seemed angry. "Is everything okay?"

"You have a visitor."

"A visitor?" I ran through a mental list of people who knew where we lived and might pop by unexpectedly, and came up with . . . nobody. "Who?"

Reesa put both hands on her hips. "Apparently, James Wickerton is at your house, waiting to see you."

THIRTY

I followed Reesa out of my old house, turning lights off as we went. She didn't speak to me the whole way, just stomped a few paces ahead of me. It gave me a moment to be: A, scared that this was the end of me and Reesa; and B, mortified that James was in my apartment. When we got to her yard, I called Mom.

"It's me," I said.

She had her we've-got-company voice on. "There's a young man here to see you. His name is James. He says you have a date."

"A date?"

Reesa glared at me.

"Would you like to speak to him?" said Mom.

"No, no. I, um . . ." I glanced at Reesa with pathetic, help-me eyes.

She grabbed the phone and put it to her ear. "Hi, Mrs. Emerson. It's Reesa. Why don't you ask James if he wants to pick Ivy up here at my house."

She shoved the phone back into my hand and plopped down

on one of their deck chairs, arms crossed firmly over her chest. There was some discussion in the background on Mom's end.

"He says that's fine," said Mom. "We're giving him the address."

"Thanks, Mom. Sorry about the, uh . . . confusion."

"Just be home by eleven. Here, at the apartment," she specified. "Not Reesa's."

I pushed the button to end the call and handed the phone back to Reesa. She snatched it and walked away from me into the yard.

"Reesa," I called after her. "I was going to tell you. . . ."

She spun around. "That you're dating the guy I've been pining over for weeks? You didn't think it might be appropriate to mention that he already has a girlfriend, and that girlfriend happens to be YOU?"

"I'm sorry." I put my face in my hands.

"You *promised*," said Reesa. "I asked you if you liked him and you looked me right in the eye and you promised me you didn't. And, shit . . . that day in the hall? When he was making hand signals at you? You were totally lying to me!"

I shook my head, knowing it was true but not wanting it to be. "It just happened. I didn't think he liked me that much. I was pretty sure he'd bail the second he found out where I live."

Reesa let out a sharp burst of laughter. "You really think highly of him, don't you? Must be a real catch. I guess I should thank you for saving me from the guy."

"I was wrong, okay? I'm sorry."

She brushed past me to go inside.

"It's not like I stole him from you." I followed behind her. "He never showed any . . ." Oohhh . . . I could tell that was the wrong thing to say before I even finished saying it.

She wheeled around. "I get it, Ivy! He didn't like me. He never liked me! That hurts, but it's nothing compared to my best friend lying to my face for three weeks. I guess I know now why you insisted he wasn't my type."

"I thought you'd be mad," I said. "I was afraid you'd tell everyone about . . . about my move, and . . ."

"Fantastic! I'm delusional *and* I'm a shitty friend. Thanks a lot. I feel so much better now."

She stormed into the house, and I trailed behind her, pleading. "Reesa, I'm sorry. Please."

She grabbed my stuff from her room, threw it at my feet, and slammed the door. I picked up my bag and went into the hallway bathroom to do something about my hair. It was still teased into a ridiculous Afro. I dug through my bag for a brush and dragged it over my hair until it was straight enough to braid. When I was finished, I looked like some kind of crazed Heidi.

I changed into my extra clothes—a cute skirt and boots I'd brought in case Reesa wanted to go out. I paused outside her door, but the music was blasting and she didn't answer my knock. I whispered, "I'm sorry," then hurried downstairs and outside. James was just driving up when I reached the Morgans' gate. He looked incredibly hot and thoroughly confused.

"Hey," he said.

I hopped into his car without a word and he drove off. I had no idea where we were going but didn't really care. I was pretty sure I'd just lost my best friend. Losing James, too, would be a perfect icing on the cake of my increasingly miserable life.

"You didn't get my note, did you?" I said. "About meeting at the King last night?"

"No," he said. "I looked everywhere. Where did you leave it?"

"Right on the shelf."

He shook his head. "Didn't find it. Then I thought maybe you left it at the cemetery, so I went there this morning and searched all over the place."

I groaned. "I'm sorry."

"So you thought I stood you up?"

I nodded. "How did you find me?"

"I waited at the Save-a-Cent until your friend"—he cleared his throat—"excuse me, not-your-friend Lennie came along, so I could ask him where you live."

"You didn't," I cringed.

"Yeah, and he wouldn't tell me at first. He said if you wanted me to know where you lived, you would've told me yourself."

"Well, that's kind of true."

He took his eyes off the road long enough to throw me a thoroughly exasperated look. "Why wouldn't you want me to know where you live?"

I sank down in my seat a bit. "You've seen it, haven't you? I live in the worst neighborhood in the district."

"And . . . you think I care about that?"

"I don't know," I said meekly. "You drive such a nice car. . . ."

He pulled up to a red light and squared his shoulders to face me. "Is that why you like me? Because I drive a nice car?"

"No." I bent over and buried my face in my knees. I took a deep breath, hoping the words would come out right, and flopped back on the seat. "That day when we went to the cemetery, you said truth is never as good as what you imagine. I was afraid I wouldn't live up to . . . you know, whatever you imagined."

The light turned green and he drove on. I stared at the road in front of us until he pulled to the side and stopped the car.

"All I imagined was a girl who makes me feel special," he said. "Who likes me for who I am, not for where I live, or who my family is, or what kind of car I drive. You could live in a cardboard box for all I care."

"Well, it might come to that," I said.

"Don't care," he said.

"I can't afford to go places, like into the city. Or to concerts. I can't even rent a stupid costume for Willow's Halloween party."

"*Really* don't care about any of that."

"You say that now," I said. "But when everybody else is doing something fabulous and I can't?"

"You're all the fabulous I need."

I sighed. "Stop saying the right thing."

He laughed. "I'm not trying to."

A reluctant smile came to my lips. "Stop being nice without even trying."

"I'll, uh . . . try to, um, not try?"

We both laughed, and he took one of my braids in his fingers and tugged it until my lips were close enough to kiss. And then he did, he kissed me until it felt like he was my oxygen and I was his. Cars zoomed by in the darkness, their head beams hitting us with bursts of light—like fireworks ignited by the heat of our kisses.

When we finally pulled apart, I looked into his icy-blue-warm eyes, and said, "You need to not try more often."

He threw his head back in a silent laugh and shifted the car into gear, and we sped off into the night—my lips tingling and heart singing.

THIRTY-ONE

We ended up at my favorite burger joint, the Charcoal Hut. It had mini jukeboxes at each booth, with a selection of mostly old songs. James threatened to play "Stairway to Heaven." And he insisted on ordering for me in a British accent. I couldn't help thinking how much Reesa would've loved that, if she was on this date instead of me.

"The lady will have the cheeseburger deluxe, hold the onion. And I shall have the same. A basket of fried potatoes, as well."

The waitress rolled her eyes and scribbled it down. "Anything to drink?"

"Just water for me," I said, realizing the five dollars I had in my pocket might not even cover my cheeseburger.

James leaned toward me across the table, holding the menu up to hide our faces from the waitress's view. "My treat. Don't worry."

"See? This is exactly what I was afraid of. I don't want you paying for me all the time."

"It isn't all the time. It's one time. And *I* asked *you* out. You can pay the next time."

"That's just it. I can't pay the next time. I can't pay *any* of the times."

The waitress shifted her weight from one hip to another, tapping her pencil on her order pad.

James peered over the menu at her. "Could you give us a minute? We're still deciding."

She rolled her eyes and walked away.

James laid the menu down and crossed his arms on the table, leaning toward me again. "So we'll do things that don't cost money. We'll go to the library or the park or the cemetery or watch TV or . . ."

"We don't get cable. We can't even watch real TV at my house."

"Whatever." He gave an exasperated sigh but paired it with a mischievous smile. "I wasn't actually planning to *watch* the TV."

I felt my face go red.

"I really don't care where we go or what we do or how much it costs," he said softly. "Every single other girl I've ever dated has . . ."

He stopped abruptly and looked down, fiddling with the corner of the menu.

"Has what?" I whispered.

"Cared more about money than they have about me," he said.

I lowered my face to catch his downcast eyes. "How is that

even possible?" I said. "You're so much better than anything money could buy."

He smiled, chin still tipped downward. "Stop saying the right thing."

I laughed. "I almost *never* say the right thing. You should seriously be savoring the moment."

"I am." He looked up at me out of the top of his eyes, through the sweep of hair across his brow. "There's just one thing that would make this moment even better."

I felt the blood rush to my face, sure he was going to ask me to kiss him. Right in the middle of the Charcoal Hut. But he opened the menu instead.

"Please share a milk shake with me," he said in a pleading voice. "I've been thinking about it all day. Two straws."

"All right." I smiled.

He opened the menu again. "Chocolate okay?"

I nodded and he sat back to look for the waitress. When she finally sauntered back to our table, he struck up the British accent again. "Chocolate milk shake. Two straws, if you please."

"Anything else, Your Highness?" She was begrudgingly enjoying herself.

"That will be all, kind lady."

Our milk shake arrived and we slurped away at it quietly, laughing each time our foreheads touched.

"So," he said. "Your parents seemed nice—a little confused when I showed up—"

"Sorry about that." I took another sip of milk shake.

"You're, uh . . . new to Lakeside?"

I paused, and then everything I'd been holding in or hiding from, pretending wasn't there . . . it all started tumbling out. What happened with our house, my dad's struggling business, Brady's disability and needing the money for his therapy. Even the trip to the food pantry at the church that morning.

"I've seen people lined up there before," he said.

"It was scary. I mean, the volunteers were nice and everything but the people . . ." I didn't want to act like I was any better than they were, but some of them had genuinely frightened me—the hardness of their gaze and the way their struggles seemed to be etched into their faces. "They made me feel like a fraud, I guess—"

"Like you hadn't suffered enough to be there?" he said.

"Yeah. Exactly." I felt lighter, like I'd been wearing a heavy cloak and had finally managed to shrug it off. "Now you know all my secrets," I said playfully, "You have to tell me yours."

He shifted uncomfortably in his seat. "What makes you think I have secrets?"

I shrugged. "Everyone has secrets."

"I'm pretty boring," he said, stirring his straw in the bottom of the glass to break up a chunk of ice cream. "At least I'm not a secret from Reesa anymore. Am I?"

I shook my head. That heavy feeling I'd just shed was starting to come back. "Could we talk about something else?"

We both leaned in to sip from the shake and our foreheads

touched. "What do you want to talk about?" he said in a voice so low, it sent a tingle up my spine.

I pulled back a few inches. "Um, I . . . uh . . . how about Shakespeare?"

He smiled and sat back, too. "You want to talk about Shakespeare?"

"Okay, no. But I do have a new appreciation for *Romeo and Juliet.*"

"I totally butchered it," he said. "We should go see it onstage sometime, with real actors. . . ."

It was yet another thing I couldn't afford to do. I looked down at the plate the waitress had just slid in front of me, the juicy burger and mound of steaming French fries. I'd never realized how much money ruled our lives, every activity, every conversation. It was impossible to avoid.

"They have free performances in the park sometimes," James said quietly. "Or we can go back to the cemetery and read the lines to each other. Or . . ." He paused, a slow grin lifting the corners of his mouth. "I read the lines, you sing them."

"Uh-uh." I shook my head. "No way."

"Come on." He shook the ketchup bottle and squirted a blob onto his plate. "I want to hear you sing again."

"I can't."

"Why not?"

I dipped a fry into the ketchup and took a bite. "I'm afraid."

"Of me?"

"No. Of *me*."

It was a ridiculous thing to say, but James didn't laugh at me or joke about it. He seemed to understand or, at least, he didn't *mis*understand.

"It's hard to explain," I said.

He had stopped eating and was watching me, listening to me.

I stared into his pale-blue eyes. "There was this talent show when I was in the fifth grade, not just for the fifth grade though," I said. "It was a big deal, the whole school district was involved, kids a lot older than me performing—it was held at a huge auditorium. I wrote a song and I practiced for months. I imagined it every night before bed, how I'd get up there and play perfectly and sing perfectly and everyone would applaud and I'd take bow after bow.

"But I tripped on my way onstage, just a little bit. Probably nobody even noticed, but I started thinking how I'd already messed up. It wouldn't be perfect. Then I saw everybody staring at me and I felt nervous and I never felt that way when I practiced. It wasn't how I imagined it. And I thought, 'Now I've really ruined it.' And the longer I stood there, the worse it was. I really *had* ruined it then. I completely froze onstage. I could hardly breathe. Some kid had to lead me away."

"But you were little," said James.

"I know that, but I can't get rid of it," I said. "The stage and the audience—that's just what sets it off. The rest happens in here." I tapped the side of my head. "It's my own brain. It's *me*. My throat closes up. I can't even sing to the twins at bedtime anymore because someone might hear me through our walls."

"You sang in the band room that day, in front of Reesa, and . . . you know"—he lowered his voice—"that creepy guy in the closet."

I tried to a smile. "Yes, but I didn't know you were there. And I've known Reesa my whole life."

"But you did it."

"Barely. And I had to pretend. . . ." I hesitated, not sure I should trust him with the full magnitude of my weirdness.

He reached across the table to rub his thumb across the back of my hand. "Pretend what?"

"I had to imagine myself in your cemetery," I said. "Singing to the tombstones."

He grinned madly. "My tombstone trick worked?"

"Yeah," I mumbled. "But I don't know if I can trick myself like that again. And now my friend Molly wants me to perform something with her at open mic night."

"Ah," he said. "That's why you were there?"

I nodded.

"And the audience was scary?"

"No," I said. "They were pretty supportive, actually."

"And you still think perfection is a requirement at open mic night?"

I shrugged. It wasn't something I required of anybody else, but I expected it from myself. I don't know why.

James leaned across the table, bent low. "Okay, so here's the plan. You go to open mic night. You don't have to tell anybody. Just show up and sing to the tombstones. Write a song about imperfection, and then mess it all the hell up. Do it for yourself."

I shook my head. "I don't know. I'll think about it."

He took another slurp from the milk shake, and I leaned in, and our noses almost touched. His hair fell across his eyes and he pushed it back. "Seriously," he said. "If the last sound I ever hear is you singing, I'll die happy."

I didn't know how to respond to that. My family and Reesa had been telling me for years, and now Molly, too. Maybe I could start believing it was true. I looked away so he couldn't see that my eyes were watering.

"Too much?"

"Nope," I said. "Just right."

THIRTY-TWO

I went to sleep Saturday night nearly delirious over my date with James, but Sunday morning the joy was gone. Reesa hated me. I kept picking up the phone to call her, to apologize again, but what more could I say? I *had* lied to her. She had every right to be mad.

I took a walk around the neighborhood after breakfast and found Molly sitting on the stoop of her house, which was small but cute. The yard was neatly trimmed, and flower boxes hung below the windows. She smiled as I approached. "Hiya, neighbor."

"Hey," I said. "I think I can see your house from my bedroom." I pointed toward my attic window, which peeked out above the squat houses. Molly had picked me up on Friday night, so I hadn't been sure which house was hers until now.

She craned her neck sideways to see my window. "Ah. Cool."

"Lennie calls it 'Turd Tower.'" I crinkled my nose.

She smiled. "At least you have a view."

"Luxurious Lakeside penthouse with spectacular view," I said with exaggerated enthusiasm, like I was reading a real estate advertisement. "Extra-brown exterior hides the dirt!"

Molly swept her hand to the side to present her own house. "Charming mobile home poorly disguised to *not* look like it belongs in a trailer park!"

I laughed. "It doesn't! Not at all."

"Yeah?" she said, standing and motioning me to follow her. "Wait till you see the lavish interior."

We went in, and it was nicely decorated but there was no hiding that it was a trailer once you stepped inside. It was long and narrow. Molly's room was on one end. We walked through the living room, kitchen, and bathroom as she led me to her room, and my mouth fell open as I stood in the middle of it and looked around. Unlike the drab décor of my attic, which clearly evoked that I had no intentions of staying long, Molly's was a work of art. She had painted a collage of images and words directly onto the walls. There were poems, quotes, lines from books. It was a cocoon of self-expression, of grief and joy and everything in between.

"Wow. This is amazing." My eyes scanned the walls, reading quotes by Mark Twain and Dr. Seuss, Emily Dickinson, and Charlie Brown. I pointed to one that had no attribution:

Reality is for people who lack imagination.

"Who said that?"

"Anonymous," said Molly. "Anonymous has a lot to say."

Some of the quotes were scribbled with pencil or marker, others were applied neatly with stencils. There were colorful designs twined through and around them, like a complicated dance of snakes and vines and fireworks.

"This is my current favorite." She pointed to one scripted beautifully in purple ink.

It was by Picasso. "I'd like to live as a poor man with lots of money," I read.

"When I first saw that, I was like, huh? Who would live like this if they didn't have to? But then I thought about all the stuff that's actually kind of cool about this place."

I gave her a skeptical glance. "Seriously?"

"I can scribble on my bedroom walls and nobody pitches a hissy fit," she said.

"You can eat supper on the living room floor," I said. "You can talk to somebody at the other end of the house without getting up."

She laughed. "Nobody cares if your lawn isn't mowed just so, or what kind of car you drive, or if you have the right clothes or the right friends or . . . you know. All that crap."

Or if you shop at a food pantry, or let your disabled brother play in the road, or . . .

"Money does come in handy now and then," I said. "For, like, food and stuff."

"Yeah. There's that." She grinned.

"Speaking of which. I looked for a job yesterday," I said.

"Where?"

"A used-book store. And Save-a-Cent."

"Any luck?"

I shook my head. "Do you have one?"

"Nah. My mom wants me to focus on school, get a scholarship if I can."

I hadn't even asked what had become of my college plans. There was supposed to be a fund for that, but I didn't know if it was still there.

"I don't know what I want to be when I grow up," I said.

"Me neither. It's impossible to think that far ahead," said Molly. "I hardly know what I want to be *tomorrow*."

I lay back on her bed. "Why did we ever stop being friends?"

"I was ousted. Remember?" The slightest edge came to her voice. "Queen Willow didn't want me in her court anymore."

I kept staring at her ceiling, not sure what to say to that. I'd been a member of that court. I still *was*. I had felt horrible about what had happened at the time but I hadn't *done* anything. I hadn't questioned Willow's version of the truth. I hadn't said anything about my suspicions that Willow was the one starting all the terrible rumors about Molly.

I swallowed. "I wasn't a very good friend to you. I—"

"Don't." She held up a hand to stop me. "It's done. I don't blame you."

"But I should've stuck up for you. I just went along, like a sheep."

"It's okay," she said. "I got off the ride and you stayed on."

I watched her spinning on the chair and realized that was exactly how I felt—like I was spinning around and around on a ride that was moving too fast to get off. I'd been hanging on and trying not to fall, or at least not vomit. Keeping up appearances, being the girl they thought I was . . . it was dizzying.

"I really need to get off that ride," I said. "I can't take it anymore."

Molly smiled. "So do it."

"Just jump off?"

"Walk away. Don't look back," she said. "That's what I did."

"But, they're my friends—I . . ."

Molly stretched her arm out to tap her finger on one of the wall quotes:

A friend is someone
who knows all about you
and still loves you.

I leaned closer to see who said it, which was written smaller. "Elbert Hubbard," I said. "Who's that?"

"Writer, philosopher. Died, like, a hundred years ago. Smart dude."

"So I should just tell them everything." That about-to-vomit feeling started to come back.

"Or not." Molly shrugged. "Do you even care what they think? What Willow and Wynn say?"

I bit my lip, afraid to tell her that I *did* care what they thought. At least what Reesa thought. Maybe I shouldn't, but I did. I lay back on her bed while she doodled at her desk. What was the worst thing that could happen if I told everyone about the move to Lakeside, the food bank? James didn't care. Molly certainly didn't care. I was faking it for the wrong reasons, for the wrong people. It was too much work. I could see what it was doing to my parents, pretending everything was okay when it wasn't. It would've been easier if they'd told us all along.

When I got up from Molly's bed, I still felt a little dizzy, but I knew what to do. "I'm going to ride the bus tomorrow," I said.

She twirled her chair around to face me. "You want to sit with me?"

I shook my head. "No, actually. I want to try and face it on my own. Is that weird?"

"Nah," she said. "But I'll be there if you need me."

Monday morning, before I left for the bus stop, I checked myself in the full-length mirror Mom had hung on the inside of our front door. She would've considered that garish at our old house, but her standards were different now. I looked okay. My hair was still slightly damp so it was behaving itself. Skirt, tights, boots, jacket . . . all good. Since I wasn't riding my bicycle, I traded my backpack for an oversized tote bag I'd bought at Bloomingdale's a couple of years ago and used maybe once.

Molly was waiting at the bus stop, swinging her clarinet case, when I arrived.

"Hey," she said. "Nice bag."

"Thanks." I started to say where I'd gotten it but stopped myself.

Lennie drove past us in his Jeep. He was very intently not looking at me, but he did slow down and ask Molly if she wanted a ride. He looked at *her* and said only *her* name, to make it perfectly clear I was not invited. "No thanks," she hollered, and he continued on.

"I'm cultivating a reputation as a badass," she told me, "and the state pen bus is a key part of my strategy."

"Is it as awful as they say?"

"Nah," said Molly. "Most of these tough guys are just big talkers. Talk back and they usually leave you alone."

She kicked at the gravel a bit. A few pieces went into the grass. *Brady will get those later,* I thought.

Our bus, number thirteen, rumbled up and we climbed on. The so-called "cool kids" were sitting in the back, the ones who were afraid of them in the front. I found an empty seat in the middle. Molly sat across from me diagonally and slumped down, propping her knees on the back of the seat in front of her.

I tried to assume an equally relaxed pose, but it was a little more difficult to accomplish in a skirt. The bus wasn't crowded, so nobody bothered me for my seat. Then this guy got on who looked like he should've graduated three years ago. He strolled down the aisle, giving a couple of the kids in front a less-than-playful shove. I kept my eyes focused on the dark-green faux-leather seat back in front of me and waited until he passed to let out the breath I'd been holding.

Too soon.

He stepped backward and sat right next to me. "Mind if I join you?"

He angled his body toward me with one arm draped over the back of the seat. I could feel his hand grazing my shoulder. "I'm Mick," he said. "What's your name?"

Turning my head slowly, I considered a fake name. But I'd had enough of the lies. "Ivy."

"Where you from?"

"I live here in Lakeside." Time to own it.

"I didn't ask where you lived," he said. "I asked where you're from. 'Cause you sure ain't from Lakeside."

Someone in the back of the bus yelled, "She's one of those snobby Westside bitches."

"Thought so." Mick grinned, looking me up and down. "Aww, what happened? Lose your trust fund, sweetheart?"

"Get lost," I said.

"Now, don't be like that." He slid his thumb down my arm.

I jerked away from him, and he laughed but pressed even

closer. His knee jabbed into my thigh. I felt a surge of anger, like everything I'd been holding in these weeks was about to explode. In one swift movement, I scooped my hands under his leg, lifted it off the seat and shoved him away. I may or may not have let out one of those tennis-player grunts in the process.

He fell backward, his arms flailing but unable to grasp anything. The surprise on his face was matched by my own. I had toppled the guy. He landed with a loud *thwack* in the aisle, his arms and legs sticking upward.

"Hey!" He scrambled to right himself and lunged for me, but another set of hands came out of nowhere and pushed him back down.

"You heard her," said Molly. "Beat it, asshole."

"What the . . ." Mick's face reddened, whether in anger or embarrassment I couldn't tell.

Molly leaned into him before he could regain his balance. "Back off," she snarled. If she hadn't been saving my ass at the moment, I would've been more scared of her than Mick.

He ambled away, trying to salvage his tough-guy image. There was a smattering of "nice try" and "don't take that shit" remarks from the back of the bus. Molly reached her hand out and said, "C'mon," and led me to her seat.

"Thanks." I slid toward the window, strangely calm now that my anger had found an outlet.

"He did the same thing to me when I moved here. The jerkoff." She plopped down, flushed and breathing heavily.

"How long ago was that?" I said.

"Last fall."

Beginning of sophomore year. Months after Willow had ousted her from our circle, which explained why I hadn't known about it at the time.

"Did one of your parents lose their job or something?"

She didn't answer right away, and I thought perhaps I'd gotten too nosy. "Sorry, none of my business," I said quickly.

"No, it's not that." Molly looked down at her hand and began tracing the lines of her palm with a finger. "My dad died."

I closed my eyes. "God, Molly. I didn't know. I'm so sorry."

"Thanks." She sighed. "Anyway, we couldn't afford the house in Westside after that."

"We lost our house, too," I said.

"Sucks," said Molly.

I nodded. "The worst part is losing my piano. That's why I went to the band room to practice that day."

"I can't practice at home either." She drummed her fingers on the clarinet case sitting in her lap. "Mom works nights, sleeps days. It's too loud."

"Sucks," I said back to her, and we both laughed.

Having someone to talk to—and laugh with—was helping, but not enough to completely calm my anxiety about stepping off that state pen bus in front of everyone. When we pulled up to the school, I was surprised that nobody seemed to notice I even existed. Molly nudged me with her elbow. "It's really not that bad.

You think everybody's watching you, but they really only care about themselves."

I looked around as we walked into the school, at the girls smoothing their sweaters and skirts and hair from the rumpling of the bus. At the guys shoving each other in the arm, nervously glancing at the girls derumpling their sweaters and skirts and hair. At kids who laughed a bit too loud. Or rolled their eyes at the kids who were laughing too loud. Everyone was pretending to be something—cool, aloof, carefree. Something they weren't. I was so tired of pretending.

Willow and Wynn were already taking out their containers of organic vegetables and finger sandwiches when I got to our lunch table later that day. Jenna Watson was there, too. She sat with us when she was between boyfriends. But Reesa was nowhere in sight. She had sat in stony silence through AP English and had breezed past me and James when we stopped to talk after class. I kept trying to catch her in the hall, but she kept disappearing. I never got a chance to tell her what I planned to do at lunch.

I sat down at our table with the apple I'd brought from home and a carton of chocolate milk. There was no way Taco Surprise would make it down my throat today.

"Did you see that skirt Chandra Mandretti is wearing today? Sooo cute. Must be vintage," said Willow.

Wynn's eyes lit up. "She probably went into the city. There are some amazing vintage shops in Manhattan."

"Remember that Pucci dress I found last summer?" said Willow.

Wynn mewed appreciatively, but Jenna stayed quiet. Did she know Chandra was more likely shopping at the Goodwill or Salvation Army these days? She caught me watching her and looked down at her uneaten sandwich, pushing it back into its wrapper.

Reesa finally appeared and sat in her usual spot across from me, but she refused to meet my eye. Her silent treatment further weakened my already-dwindling courage, so my voice came out in barely a whisper. "I have something to tell you all."

Nobody but Reesa even noticed I said anything. She kicked me under the table, gave me a warning shake of her head. At least she cared enough to do *that*.

I cleared my throat and spoke louder. "I have something to tell you. All of you."

Wynn's head snapped in my direction. "Ohmygod, you're pregnant."

"What? No! Why would you think that?"

"She's not even dating anyone," said Willow. "Please."

"You got a car," Wynn declared.

"Did she ask you to guess? Stop guessing!" Willow scolded, turning a patronizingly patient face toward me. "What's the big news, Ivy? I hope it explains why you didn't show up Saturday to shop for our costumes for the Halloween party."

A guilty expression came to Reesa's face briefly. So she'd gone without me, without *telling* me. "So much for honesty," I muttered.

She looked down at her lunch and I turned my attention back to the other girls. "I just wanted to tell you that we moved. My family. We moved to a new place."

My announcement was met with a chorus of surprise. "I didn't know you were moving!" "Why did you move?" "But you have the best house!" "Where?"

I took a bite of my apple to buy some extra time while I formulated my next sentence. Every coherent thought seemed to evaporate from my mind. I chewed thoroughly, took a sip of chocolate milk. And a deep breath.

"My parents decided we needed to downsize, because of the shaky economy and all that." I decided not to get into the part about the foreclosure and the expense of Brady's therapy. "We're renting a place. It's out past Jackson Boulevard," I said, waving my hand in that general direction.

"Oh. My. God," said Willow. Her eyes were huge. "It's in Lakeside, isn't it? My sister came home last week rambling on about Kaya living in the slums and I did not believe her. Are you serious?"

"Yeah," I said as breezily as I could manage. "No biggie. It's not that bad. It's temporary, anyway."

"Oh, my God," said Wynn.

They didn't laugh, but the looks they gave me were far worse. It was a horror-disgust-pity combo of facial expressions that made me want to crawl out of my skin and under the table. Then Reesa opened her mouth. Maybe she thought she was coming to my rescue, or maybe she was trying to throw me under the bus.

She said, "Aren't you going to tell them about your billionaire boyfriend?"

Willow and Wynn and Jenna and everyone else within earshot swiveled their heads to hear more, and Reesa delivered. "The guy's loaded, and he doesn't care where she lives. Apparently."

I shrank at her mention of his wealth. I didn't care if he was loaded, and we didn't know that for sure.

"Who are you talking about?" said Willow. "I didn't even know you had a boyfriend."

"We just started dating," I mumbled. "His name is James Wickerton."

"Does he go here?" said Wynn. "Why haven't we met him?"

Reesa crunched a carrot stick and waved it as she spoke. "He's in our AP English class. Really cute."

They were clearly finding it hard to believe a cute, rich guy had been roaming our halls undetected. "He's homeschooling part-time," I explained. "He only takes two classes. That's probably why you haven't seen him."

"I've never heard of anybody doing that." Willow turned to Reesa. "Have you ever heard of anybody doing that?"

Reesa looked to me for an explanation, but I had none. I hadn't questioned it. And when we'd gotten in trouble for ditching, Mrs. Lanahan had been aware of his part-time status. She'd referred to it as unusual, but clearly he was attending our school. As dreamy as he was, I was pretty sure I hadn't conjured him entirely.

"He got special permission to take AP English and art history. That's all I know." I slurped my chocolate milk.

Willow wouldn't let up. "Do you have a picture of him?"

I shook my head.

"I do," said Reesa, pulling her phone from her bag. "Snapped it in class the other day when he wasn't looking."

She scrolled through her images until she found the one of James and turned it toward Willow, who leaned in to get a better look.

Her face lit up. "That guy?" she said, a wide smile spreading across her face. "I've seen that guy. And believe me, he's no billionaire."

I didn't care if James was a billionaire, but Willow's bait was too tempting not to rise to it. "How would you know?"

"I've *seen* him," she said, "doing things that . . . let's just say no billionaire would ever do."

"Like what?" I tipped my chin up. "His own grocery shopping?"

"Oh, no." She batted her eyelashes. "It's much worse than that. You really need to see for yourself. How about I pick you up at Reesa's house after school. We'll all go on a little field trip."

"Just tell me," I said.

She pinched her lips together and motioned turning a key and throwing it away over her shoulder.

"I have to be home by four," I said.

"No worries," Willow said, smiling as she nibbled her sandwich. "It won't take long."

After school, I got on my old bus to Westside Falls with Reesa. She begrudgingly let me sit next to her.

"Do you know what this is all about?" I asked.

She shrugged, still not talking to me.

As the bus pulled out and circled around to the exit, I found myself gazing longingly at the state pen bus. I should've gone home with Molly.

"Why am I doing this?" I muttered.

Reesa sighed. Said nothing.

"I didn't care if he was a billionaire, you know. I don't care."

She rolled her eyes.

"Honestly, I was hoping he wasn't, because it would only make me feel poorer than I am."

She stared straight ahead. I was clearly having a conversation with myself, so I stopped talking. We got off the bus when it pulled up to her gate, the ornate letter M flaunting her family's wealth in my face. I used to love that sculpted gate, but now it seemed over-the-top.

Reesa punched her code in the keypad by the little foot entrance at the side, and it clicked open.

"Aren't we waiting here for Willow? She's supposed to pick us up any minute." She had driven her Miata to school that day and had to switch to a bigger car.

Reesa stood at the little gate like she was about to shut it in my face. "I'm not going," she said, and then she did. She shut the gate in my face.

"But—"

"I'm not interested in Willow's little field trip, and I don't care what she thinks of James Wickerton," she said. "Maybe he's a billionaire, maybe he's not. I really do not have the slightest interest in wasting one more minute of my life on James Wickerton."

"Because he might not be filthy rich? You were obsessed with him when you thought he was."

"I was obsessed with him when I thought he might like me, but that clearly isn't the case," she snapped. "I was just curious. I mean, what's this billionaire kid from New York doing here, anyway?"

"Come along then." I really didn't want to do this without her. "Please? Don't make me go with them by myself."

She shook her head. "I'm sure they'll tell me all about it tomorrow. You have fun now." She wiggled her fingers good-bye and turned, walking up her driveway without another word.

I didn't have to wait long before Willow pulled up in her mother's Lexus, with Wynn riding shotgun, the music blaring.

I climbed in the back.

"Where's Reesa?" said Willow.

"Not coming. Can you just drive me home?"

"Oh, come on. It'll only take a few," she said. "Besides, I need a latte."

"Me too," said Wynn. "Tall, with a shot of caramel."

"Where are we going?" I asked.

"You'll see," Willow singsonged.

A few minutes later she pulled up in front of Bensen's, the gourmet market. "If you're stopping here for lattes then just take me home after. I really have to be there by . . ."

"Four o'clock. I know," said Willow. "This is our final destination, anyway. So chill."

She turned off the ignition. I followed them into the little coffee bar, where they ordered their lattes. While the barista was making them, Willow took me by the wrist and led me around the corner to the produce section. She stopped by the onions and pointed across the store where the fresh-squeezed juices were.

"There's your billionaire," she said.

His back was turned to me, but I could tell it was James. He was wearing an apron. Not bright green like Lennie's. It was light blue, same as the walls and the shopping carts at Bensen's. As I slowly walked toward him, he dipped a mop into a bucket and pushed down on a lever to squeeze it out, then slapped it to the floor. He was oblivious to the small audience behind him—Wynn had joined us with a latte in each hand. A white cord ran from his ear to his pocket. He was mopping to the beat.

I had walked slowly closer, and when he finally turned, there was surprise, even delight in his eyes, at seeing me. He pulled the earbuds out.

"Ivy. What are you doing here?"

"Wh-what are *you* doing here?" I stammered.

"Uh . . . mopping?" His gaze flicked to where Willow and Wynn stood sipping their drinks, then nervously back to me. "Someone dropped one of those half-gallon containers of OJ. Didn't even tell anyone, so it got stepped in and carts rolling it all over the place. Big mess."

He leaned on the mop pole.

"So, you, um . . . work here?" I said. "As a janitor?"

He pushed the mop away and looked at it, like it had magically appeared in his hand and he had no idea how it got there. "No." He laughed. "Not a janitor. More like an errand boy. Stacking shelves, unloading trucks, carrying groceries to cars. Occasional mopping."

"Oh," I said. It all sounded perfectly reasonable, except that he'd never mentioned it before.

"No food prep, though," he said. "I absolutely draw the line at wearing a hairnet."

He was trying to be funny, and I wanted desperately to laugh or smile but I couldn't seem to make the muscles of my face move. Not with Willow and Wynn watching and judging and . . . I tried to swallow but couldn't. It was like being onstage again and I froze. An audience of two—two miserable, horrible friends I didn't even care about—and I couldn't speak, I couldn't budge.

I dropped my gaze to the pocket of his apron. There, stitched in white, was the name JIM.

I didn't hear them walk up beside me until Willow's hand was on my shoulder. "You'll have to excuse our friend," she said to James. "She may be in a state of shock. She thought you were a multibillionaire!"

"You really had her fooled," said Wynn.

I stood paralyzed, like someone was shining a giant spotlight on me. I kept opening my mouth to say something but nothing came out.

I could only stare at the stitching on his pocket: JIM, JIM, JIM, JIM. What had Lennie called him? *Jimbo*. The janitor? No—errand boy. Stacker of shelves. Why hadn't he told me? He knew everything about me. I hadn't held anything back.

"Ivy?" James stepped toward me.

Willow pulled me away. "Maybe you should leave her alone now. You've done enough damage."

James let the mop clatter to the floor and stepped over it, coming closer as Willow continued to pull me away. "You thought I was a billionaire?" he said. "That's why you liked me?"

It felt like I'd been slapped. I shook my head. "No, that's not . . ."

"After all you went through with your family—" He tore his apron off. "I thought you were different," he said.

I watched him turn and storm away from me, my vision closing in like a tunnel. Then I was in Willow's car again and she was gunning the engine, tearing out of the parking lot. She and Wynn were talking over each other. ". . . mopping . . . what a loser . . . can't believe . . . who does he think . . . poor Ivy . . ."

Then Wynn was shaking me. "Where do you live? We have no idea how to get there."

I pointed, and said "turn here" a couple of times. When I saw the Save-a-Cent coming up, I told Willow to stop. "This is good," I said.

"You live *here*?"

I didn't answer, just pushed myself out of the car and stumbled across the parking lot toward the wooded area next to our neighborhood. I couldn't find the walking path that cut through it, though. So I just pushed my way into the brush. Branches scraped my bare arms, but I didn't care. I didn't . . . Where was my jacket? I stopped and dug around in my bag, but I must've left it in Willow's car.

"Shit," I said, then laughed at myself.

Losing my stupid jacket is what I can finally speak up about? *Brilliant, Ivy. Just brilliant.* Stand there like a fucking idiot in front of James and let him think you care if he's rich and don't say a fucking word and fuck fuck fuck fuck *fuck*.

I mouthed the word, repeating it soundlessly because as pissed off at myself as I was, I still wasn't the girl who said "fuck" out loud. And that *really* made me laugh. Everything that had happened—losing my house and my piano and my best friend and my boyfriend, my parents fighting and the food bank and . . . and . . . I was still going to watch my language?

My mind darted and swirled around the frantic conversation in my head as the tree branches tore at my arms and clothes. The strap of my bag got caught and I couldn't get it unstuck so I shoved it from my shoulder and left it there. I stumbled and fell forward, my hands and knees slamming into the ground. I cried out from the pain and then I . . . I just rocked back onto my heels, then sat and cried.

Tears ran down my face, and my body convulsed with shuddery gasps. I didn't remember ever crying like this before, so out of control. I couldn't make it stop as I replayed the past few weeks—had my life really fallen apart so thoroughly in that little bit of time?

My hysterics finally turned into minisobs and hiccups, and I stood up, wiping my hands on my skirt and my nose on my sleeve. My bottom was soaked and my knees were stinging. The skin exposed through my torn tights was scraped and bleeding.

I searched the ground for my bag and finally found it hung up in a tree directly behind me. About three feet away from where I stood was the path.

I've totally lost my mind.

I stepped onto the path and started walking toward home, and that's when I heard it: the distinctive rumble of a school bus.

The twins' school bus.

Four o'clock, oh, my God, I was supposed to be home at four o'clock. I pulled my not-a-phone out of my bag to check the time. It said 4:12. Ohmygod ohmygod *ohmygod.* I ran as fast as I could, tearing down the path and bursting from the woods onto the playground. There were kids on the swings—kids who rode Brady and Kaya's bus!

I ran toward then, shouting. "Did Brady and Kaya get off the bus? Did the driver let them off?"

They stared up at me like startled little fawns stuck in a car's headlights. Nobody answered so I shouted again. "Brady and Kaya Emerson? We live over there." I pointed to Turd Tower. "Did they get off the bus?"

One of the boys shook his head nervously. "I . . . I don't think so," he said. "They can't get off without a grown-up 'cause that kid's retarded."

"He's not . . ." I started to correct the boy, to explain that we don't use that word anymore. That he's mentally disabled. That he's special and wonderful and . . . I just shook my head and ran from them, sprinting for the road, my feet pounding on the gravel until I reached the bus stop, crying and gasping and . . . *there was no bus*. I ran up Jackson Boulevard, hoping the driver might be lingering at the next bus stop, or the next. But it was gone. The bus was gone.

I limped back to the house and pounded on Carla's door, hoping maybe she'd seen the bus arrive and had the kids with her. But the windows of her apartment were dark and she didn't answer. I looked toward Lennie's house. His Jeep wasn't there.

The bus driver probably wouldn't have handed the kids over to him, anyway.

I was really crying now, not for myself but for Brady, who must be so scared. And for Kaya, who would be scared, too, and mad. She would never forgive me for this, for ruining everything once again.

I let myself in the back door as the phone rang in the kitchen. I lunged for it. "Hello?"

"You're there?" It was Mom. "I just got a call from transportation. They said nobody was there for the bus!"

"I wasn't here. . . . I was late. . . . I . . ."

"Ivy!" Mom said sharply. "The bus driver had to take them back to school. I'm leaving work now to pick them up. And you better hope this hasn't scarred your brother so badly he'll never ride the damn bus again, because I don't know what I'm going to do if that happens."

"Mom, I . . . I . . ."

"One simple thing, Ivy. That's all I asked, and you couldn't even do that?"

I stammered to answer her, but I couldn't find any words—only the shuddery hiccups that remained from my cry. Then I heard a *click* on Mom's end and a few seconds later, a dial tone.

My mother had hung up on me.

I returned the phone to its cradle and walked toward the front stairs so I could be waiting for them when they got home. Then I caught a glimpse of myself in the full-length mirror on the door. Scraped arms, torn tights, muddy skirt. I couldn't let Brady see me like this.

I watched out the window from my parents' bedroom, which was in the front of our apartment. When our car pulled up, Mom and Kaya got out, but Brady wouldn't. I heard Mom pleading with him. "Come on, buddy, it's okay. It's safe." The bus driver must've said it wasn't safe, and he thought that meant it was *never* safe here. Mom turned and looked up toward the apartment. It was one of those all-hands-on-deck moments, and my hands were inexplicably absent.

Lennie drove up then, parking his Jeep along the road in front of his house. He got out and waved and Kaya rushed over to him, and then he and Mom were talking low and . . . Lennie leaned into our car. Like *that* was going to help.

Then I couldn't believe it. Brady got out of the car. He was smiling and holding his arms out to Lennie. Lennie lifted him up, then sat him in the grass and took him by one hand and one foot and . . . gave him an airplane ride. Once around, so he wouldn't get too dizzy.

But I did. I got dizzy, watching Lennie save the day, while I sat there helpless and pathetic and wrong, wrong, *wrong* about everything. And *everyone*.

THIRTY-THREE

Mom found me asleep on top of her bed in my mud-caked skirt. She shook me awake, a look of horror on her face.

"Mom." My voice was raw. "What's wrong?" I'd forgotten for a moment what I must look like.

"What happened to you?" Then a more panicked expression came to her eyes.

"No . . . I . . ." How could I explain my breakdown? "I fell, in the woods . . . I . . ."

"Oh, sweetie." She gathered me in her arms. Everything hurt when she touched me, but I didn't want her to let go. I just wanted to cry on my mother's shoulder and let her take care of me.

And she did. "Come on, let's get you cleaned up."

She led me down to the bathroom and filled the tub, helped me peel off my clothes without taking too much skin along with them, and gently washed the dirt from my wounds. She spoke in the soothing tone I remembered from before the move, not the sharper more harried one that had replaced it lately.

"So what happened?" she asked softly.

"I just, I got home late—my ride left me by the Save-a-Cent, and I walked through the park. Only I couldn't find the path and I got tangled and fell, and . . . and then I heard the bus, and . . ." I started to cry again.

"I'm so sorry I yelled at you. I was on a deadline at work. . . . If I'd known . . ." Her own eyes filled with tears and she reached for the corner of a towel to wipe them away. "Look at us. We're a mess."

I cry-laughed, nodding. "We really are."

"Okay, finish cleaning up. I need to check on Brady and Kaya. They're still outside with Lennie." She got up. "You know, maybe we were wrong about that boy. The twins adore him."

When the bus unloaded in front of the school the next morning, I pushed against the flow of students going in to head the other way—toward the back parking lot. I stood where James always parked his car, waiting until the first-period bell rang. But he didn't show. I waited again outside Mr. Eli's room.

Reesa must've thought I was waiting for *her,* because she stopped halfway down the hall and pretended to tie her shoe. When she looked up and I was still there, she dug around in her backpack for a while. Wow. She *really* did not want to talk to me. Join the club. Reesa, James, even Lennie . . . nobody could stand being around me. I was like poison. *Poison Ivy.*

I snorted at my own joke and went into class. Reesa finally came in a second before the bell rang, so there wasn't a moment to talk to her even if I wanted to. Instead, I spent most of my morning classes drafting a letter to James, in case he showed up but refused to speak to me. At least I could shove it into his hand and hope he'd read it. I tried to explain everything—how Reesa thought he must be a member of this wealthy Wickerton family from New York that she found online. How I didn't care. How I was glad he wasn't. How I didn't want a boyfriend who could go places and do things that I couldn't do. I was just surprised that he'd never mentioned a job. I would've felt better about my own circumstances if I'd known about his.

But I never had a chance to give him the letter. There was no sign of James all day, not even in our secret room, where I'd left an especially long note after English class. I started to worry that he was gone for good, not just the day. But his books were still there. He wouldn't leave without his Shakespeare, would he?

At home after school, I searched my room for the Charcoal Hut receipt James had written his home phone number on. I took the phone to my room and pressed my shaky fingers to the buttons. It rang nine times, and I was about to hang up when someone finally answered.

"Hello?" An elderly woman's voice.

"May I speak to James, please?"

Silence.

"Ma'am?"

"May I ask who's calling?" she said.

"It's Ivy Emerson."

There was a muffled sound on the other end, like her hand was covering the phone as she spoke to someone. It had to be him. She wouldn't have asked my name if it was a wrong number. Right?

She came back on. "I'm sorry. He's not available at the moment."

"Oh. Um, could you please tell him . . ."

Click.

I stared at the dead phone. My first instinct was to call back. I pressed my finger to the redial button, but let it go and placed the receiver in its cradle.

It rang almost immediately.

I swooped the phone to my ear. "James?"

"No. It's me." *Mom.* "I'm picking the twins up from school today and taking them directly to Brady's therapy appointment, okay?"

"Oh, yeah, okay."

She rattled off some instructions for me, something about starting supper, and I heard her but I wasn't listening, because all I could think about was that James was at home. The woman who answered the phone had spoken to someone before telling me he wasn't there. That he wasn't *available.* I flipped open my laptop while Mom was still talking, and typed the phone number I'd just called into the search window. Wasn't there some kind of reverse directory where you could put in a phone number and find the name or the address?

"Ivy? Did you hear a word I just said?"

"Yeah, Mom. I'm just doing some . . ." I caught myself before another lie came out. "I'm just searching for something online, for an address," I said.

She let me go as I hit the RETURN key and the name IDA MCDANIELS popped up with a Belleview address. I typed her name into another search window and found an obituary, not for Ida but for a man named James A. Robertson

Then everything started falling into place. The cemetery. The tombstone where James and I sat on the bench. *James Aloysius Robertson.* And J.A.R. . . . from the Shakespeare book. I searched the obituary for any mention of James. It noted grandchildren but didn't name them. Just a sister, Ida McDaniels, and a daughter—

Sheila Wickerton.

I went back to the listing that showed Ida's address: 845 Clayton Street. I quickly mapped it, hoping it wasn't too far to get to on my bike. When the directions popped up, I scrolled down to see the total distance. Seven miles.

I scribbled the directions on the back of my hand, grabbed the letter I'd written to James, and ran for my bike.

THIRTY-FOUR

I pedaled faster than ever, ignoring honks of the early evening-rush-hour drivers. My legs were on fire and my hair wet with sweat when by the time I rolled onto Clayton Street. It was the kind of neighborhood I had hoped we might move to, with nice two-story houses lined up next to each other. Brick, not brownstone, with cute little porches and sidewalks and cars lining the street. I bicycled as close to the parked cars as I could get without bumping into their rearview mirrors and slowed as the house numbers got closer to 845. A sleek red sports car with New York plates turned in front of me and zipped into an empty spot . . . right behind a black BMW. I steered to the opposite side of the street and pulled onto the sidewalk beside an SUV. Unbuckling my helmet, panting, I heard a familiar voice.

"What are you doing here?" snarled James.

The tone surprised me and I turned immediately, a pit in my stomach. But he wasn't talking to me. He strode toward the girl who emerged from the red car like she was stepping off a fashion runway. She had sandy blond, wavy hair and a straight, delicate nose. I ducked farther behind the SUV so I was mostly hidden but could still see them through the windows.

"Nice to see you, too," she said. "No hug? No kiss?"

James took a few steps forward and gave her a stiff hug, followed by a quick peck on both cheeks. It made me think of Wynn, who kissed that way, too.

"What are you doing here?" he asked her again.

"Came to see how the other half lives." She gestured toward the houses along the block, as if there was something unseemly about them. "Aren't you tired of slumming it?"

"Staying with Aunt Ida is hardly slumming it."

"Fine. But working as a stock boy in a grocery store? Come on," she said. "You could've gotten a dozen other jobs that easily paid more. You're only doing it to annoy Daddy."

James shrugged. "Think what you want. I told Dad I could take care of myself, and I have. How I do it is my business."

She stepped back and leaned against her car, crossing her arms under her chest. "Fine. You've proven your point. Now it's time to come home. Hopefully, it's not too late for Daddy to pull some strings and get you into one of the Ivies. I'm sure the academy will fudge those two credits you're missing, with the proper incentive. A nice donation—"

"I don't want him to pull strings for me or buy off my school, Rebecca. That's the whole point," said James, his voice rising. "People look at us and all they see are dollar signs. Don't you ever wonder if anybody would give a fuck about you if they didn't know who your daddy was?"

She laughed. "Yeah, Robbie. Life's rough all over."

Robbie?

James turned his back on her and marched into the house. The girl—Rebecca—remained leaning against her car, inspecting her manicure. My legs were so shaky I was afraid to move—afraid I'd fall flat on my face if I did—so I stayed behind the SUV. Then James emerged from the house carrying a large duffel bag. He strode to his car, popped the trunk, and shoved it in.

"I was leaving anyway," he said, slamming the trunk closed. "Happy?"

Rebecca shrugged. "I'm just sick of all the yelling and crying and . . ."

James whirled around. "Who's crying? Mom?"

"Well, it certainly isn't Dad."

Something seemed to collapse in James, his defeat evident in the slump of his shoulders and the sag of his head. I don't know why I didn't run to him then, stop him and explain myself and—and . . . ask him what the hell was going on. But I hesitated, and before I could blink, he got behind the wheel of his car and drove away.

Rebecca got into her red car, too, and zoomed off after him. When I finally stumbled out from behind the SUV, all I could do was stare at the spot where they had stood arguing, stunned that James was gone.

A gray-haired woman emerged from the house—Aunt Ida, I

presumed. She offered me a sympathetic smile. "You're the one who called?"

"Yes."

She nodded slowly, arms folded around her middle, then turned to go back inside.

"Wait!" The note I'd written to James was clutched in my hand. I ran up to the porch and held it out to her. "Can you get this to him?"

She took the folded paper and tucked it into the pocket of her dress. "Can't make any promises," she said. "But I'll try."

It was dark by the time I got home, and Mom was furious. She followed me up to the attic, scolding me as quietly as her anger would allow so as not to upset Brady. "You were supposed to start supper. Where have you been?" she hissed.

"I screwed something up, Mom, and I was trying to fix it. It's a long story," I said, hugging a pillow to my chest.

"Well, I don't have time for a long story right now, because I have to make supper," she started down the stairs, then turned back. "You're grounded, by the way. Until further notice."

I wasn't even upset about that. It made sense, at least, when nothing else did—like whatever I'd witnessed between James and his sister. *Robbie.* Reesa was right all along. But James had left home, apparently, to fend for himself? To prove something to their father? My chest ached when I remembered the worst part, what he'd said about wanting to see if anybody would care about him if he didn't have money.

I lay down and stared at the ceiling, aching for my piano. I needed to get this horrible feeling out of my chest and put it to music.

The ukulele I'd retrieved from our old house sat dusty and unused in the corner next to my dresser. I got up, took it in my hands, and strummed, cringing at how off-key it was. I fiddled with the tuning pegs. Strummed again. Better.

But it was a ukulele, and it sounded too happy for my mood.

I closed my eyes and let my voice take over. I don't even remember what I sang, if there were words involved or just sound—moaning or humming or bellowing open vowels of agony. I didn't care if someone out there heard me. I just had to get it out.

When I stopped and looked up, Brady was standing in my doorway. His little face was twisted into a question mark as he struggled to assess the situation.

"It's okay," I said quickly. "I was just . . . I was singing."

His eyes lit up. "Sing for Brady?"

I nodded as he shuffled to the bed and sat next to me, his legs dangling off the edge. I wrapped my arms around him and held tight. After what I'd just seen, the way Rebecca talked to James, so cold and uncaring . . . I craved the warmth of a good hug.

We sat close with the ukulele on my lap. "What kind of song do you want?" I asked.

"La-la," he said, and I smiled.

"Okay," I said. "One la-la lullaby coming right up."

I strummed and plucked until a tune came tumbling out. It started a bit slow and mournful, but Brady's la-las were too exuberant to be satisfied by a sad song. I picked up the pace and let the music cheer me up.

"You know what? I think we need Kaya," I said to Brady.

Brady smiled and shouted, "Kaya!" at the top of his lungs. I did the same. "Kaya! Kaya!"

She bounded up the stairs. "What are you doing?"

"We're singing la-las," I said.

She grinned and threw herself at me, a laughing tackle-hug onto the bed. "You're back," she said.

I paused, realizing she didn't mean I was back from my bike ride. She meant I was *back*. Back to myself. Back to being part of my family. "Yeah," I said. "I'm back."

THIRTY-FIVE

The next few days at school were quiet. At lunch I started sitting with Molly and Rigby, the friend of Lennie's who had air-fist-bumped me at the food pantry. I didn't see the point in subjecting myself to more torture at the hands of Willow and Wynn, and Reesa's ongoing silent treatment was unbearable. Molly slid her tray over and made a spot for me, no questions asked.

On Saturday, Mom lifted my grounding, and I immediately went back to Clayton Street. When Ida saw me standing on her front porch, she gave a big, weary sigh and held the door open. I stepped inside and followed her to the front room. The house was beautiful, with its hardwood floors and Oriental rugs and lamps with fringed fabric shades. There was a quiet, fragile feeling to her home, like an antique shop. The only sound was the tick of a clock coming from another room.

"Have a seat," said Ida. "Can I get you something to drink?"

"No thank you," I said. "I can't stay long."

She lowered herself slowly into a flowered chair that seemed to hug itself around her as she sat. There was a table next to it, with books and reading glasses. I wondered if James had sat here, too, on this same couch when they talked.

"So, you're Ivy," she said.

"Oh, sorry . . . yes," I stammered. "Ivy Emerson."

"Well, I've always been partial to three-letter names that start with *I*." She winked and held out her hand, its knuckles swollen with arthritis. "I'm Ida McDaniels."

I closed my fingers gently around hers. "Nice to meet you."

We settled back into our respective seats and I tried to find the right question, the right thing to say.

She rescued me. "You're wondering about Robbie."

It was hard for me to think of him that way. "Was that his real name? Robert?"

"Middle name. Robertson, actually. James Robertson Wickerton, named after my brother, his grandfather."

"James Aloysius Robertson. He's buried at the Methodist cemetery, isn't he?" I said. "With his wife, Clara. They died a week apart."

Ida smiled. "Robbie took you there? He was very close to his grandfather." She pointed to the fireplace mantel, which was lined with framed photos. "There they are."

I walked over to see the picture. It was a young James, maybe five years old, in bare feet. His grandparents stood on either side, each holding one of his hands while he swung like a monkey between them. He was grinning like crazy.

"He spent a week here every summer. They let him really be a kid. Not like . . ." She let her voice trail off.

I smiled at the boy in the photo. "James didn't tell me they were his grandparents. He didn't tell me . . . a lot."

"Well," said Ida, returning to her chair. "I'll leave him to explain why he left home, what happened with his father and all, because that's his business not mine. But I took him in. This was his grandparents' house, and he's always welcome here. I called my friend Olivia Lanahan—Mrs. Lanahan to you—and got him enrolled at the school so he could finish high school. And the rest, as they say, is history."

"Why didn't he tell anybody who he was?"

"He wanted to start with a blank slate—no money, no status, none of that—and see if people would treat him differently."

"So I was an experiment?"

"Not you specifically. People in general, I suppose," she said. "But he liked you. He came home that one night and told me, 'She didn't even want me to pay for her milk shake!' The girls at his school all expected him to pay for that and a lot more."

A pang of guilt caught in my throat. I had been drawn to James before I'd known anything about him. But had Reesa's speculation about his wealth played a role as well? I couldn't deny the possibility. He had everything I'd lost, and more. If I'd thought, from the very beginning, that James worked mopping grocery store floors, would I have ever gotten into his car that first time? Or would I have treated him like I'd treated Lennie?

I sat the photo back on the mantel. "Have you heard anything from him? Did he . . . did you give him my note?"

"I mailed it to him, but I haven't spoken to him since he left. I tried calling, but that snooty butler of theirs kept telling me he was unavailable." She chuckled in a humorless way.

"Could you give me his phone number? An email address?"

"I don't use email, so I don't know if he has one of those," she said, reaching to her table for a piece of paper and pen. "But I can give you his mailing address and phone number. Can't promise you'll get through."

"Thank you," I said, the thought of James believing nobody would ever like him for himself gnawing at my stomach. "I have to try."

I sat on my bed with the phone cradled in my lap. I had dialed his number eight times now, always chickening out at the last minute and slamming it down before anyone answered. What if he hung up on me?

My hands trembled as I punched in the number Ida had given me once more, then lifted it to my ear.

On the fourth ring, a deep, male voice answered. "Hello?"

I'd expected something fancier, and it set me off to a bad start. "I . . . um, could I speak to James . . . uh . . . Robbie . . . Wickerton?"

"May I ask who's calling?"

"Ivy Emerson?" I immediately cringed at how ridiculous I

sounded, like I was guessing at my own name.

"One moment," the man said. They had hold music. Classical. Chopin's Nocturne in C-sharp for piano, to be exact. I knew it, because I'd played it. So *there*, snobby butler guy, who was taking way longer than "one moment." It was at least ten minutes before the man came back. "I'm sorry, but Mr. Wickerton is not available at this time."

He didn't offer to take a message, but I gave him my name and phone number, anyway.

THIRTY-SIX

After my failed attempt to call James, I gravel-kicked my way down to Molly's house. She held a finger to her lips when she answered the door and motioned me into her room.

"Mom's sleeping," she said, quietly closing her door. "What's wrong?"

"Life sucks." I flopped backward on her bed and gazed up at the new additions to her wall. "You can quote me on that."

She pointed to a far corner. I could barely make out where she'd written in pencil:

Life sucks.—Me.

I snorted. "See? My life even sucks at sucking. It's a rerun of somebody else's sucky life."

Molly tapped her finger to yet another quote, this one a clipping from a magazine:

Been there, done that.

Moping around at Molly's was my new favorite pastime, but it made me miss Reesa. She never let me mope. Not for long, at least. She always came up with the plan to fix whatever needed fixing. A completely insane plan, usually. But a plan.

I turned on my side and bent my arm to prop up my head. "What do you do when a guy—the guy you like—won't even acknowledge that you're alive?"

"Which guy?" said Molly. She didn't know about me and James. Hardly anybody did, since I'd kept it such a secret. It was like it had never happened.

"Any guy," I said. "Hypothetical Guy."

She twirled slowly on her desk chair. "Is Hypothetical Guy dating someone else?"

"Not that I know of," I said.

"Does he know you're trying to get his attention?"

Had James gotten my letter or my phone message? "Hypothetical Girl is uncertain."

"Ahhhh." Molly spun back around to face her desk and bent over her journal. She collected quotes there, including random things she overheard people saying during the course of her day. I had a feeling I'd just been quoted. She clicked her pen a few times. "You could throw a party."

"A party."

"You know, one of those things where people gather and

dance and drink and talk and laugh?"

"Yes, I know what a party is."

"So, you throw a party and you invite Hypothetical Guy. But it's not a date. If he comes, awesome. If he doesn't, it's a party. You're still having fun."

Considering I was presently estranged from most of my friends, throwing a party sounded like a great way to make a complete fool of myself. But heck, I was on a roll.

"Halloween," I said. "We could invite all the people who weren't invited to Willow's bash."

"We?" Molly raised her eyebrows.

"Well, yeah. It was your idea."

An hour later we had decided on a theme for the party: "Come as you are." And not as in "I'm too lame to figure out a costume" but rather, "This is who I really am." Our invitation would encourage guests to let it all hang out, reveal their hidden identities, show their true selves. I didn't know how I'd get James there, but after what happened between us, maybe this theme would hit home. I just hoped I could get through to him.

Walking back to my place from Molly's, I was nearly sideswiped by a souped-up truck that stopped in front of Lennie's place. I slowed my pace to witness the transaction. Lennie came out with a small paper bag, handed it to the guy, took his money, thank you, good-bye, the guy drove off. Carla's advice came back to me:

Ask him about it.

Lennie disappeared around the back of his house, into the shed. I hurried across the gravel road and followed him. The small wood-and-metal structure was windowless. I stood at its door, my imagination conjuring visions of pot plants and grow lights.

Before I could change my mind and retreat, Lennie burst out and nearly crashed into me. We both jumped.

"Whoa. Hey." His hands went to my shoulders, to steady me. Then he quickly dropped them to his sides. "Didn't see you there. What are you doing?"

"Yeah, I . . . uh . . . just . . ." I tried to peer into the shed but his shoulders were blocking my view. "Wanted to thank you for helping out with Brady the other day. I royally messed up, and you seem to always swoop in and save the day when it comes to Brady. So, uh, thanks."

"He's a great kid," he said. "I like him a lot."

"Yeah." I smiled nervously. "He really likes you, too."

Lennie kicked at the dirt with his boot. We hadn't spoken in a while, since open mic night, and I hadn't exactly been friendly to him then.

"You, um, want to come in?" He motioned with his thumb inside the shed.

"Oh . . . okay." I nodded.

"You've probably been wondering what I do in here, anyway . . ."

"No, I . . . well, yes." I gave a nervous laugh. "People are always driving up and buying something from you, so . . ."

"It's not drugs, if that's what you're thinking."

"No, I . . ."

Lennie smirked, reached back, and pushed open the shed door. "Welcome to my den of iniquity."

I stepped gently into the small space, which was lined with shelves, each one about six inches deep. Covering the shelves were gears and chains and mechanical-looking pieces I couldn't begin to identify. In the corner, on a plywood workbench, sat a computer—a brand-new desktop Mac. And in the middle of it all, a table with a postage meter, and some packing tape, scissors, and boxes. Everything was super neat and organized.

I strolled around the table, browsing the bits and pieces on the shelves. "What is all this?"

"Small engine parts, out-of-stock stuff mostly," he said. "I take them off junkers, put them up on my website, people order them for old cars they're fixing up, stuff like that."

"You have a website?"

He walked over to the computer and hit the space bar. The screen lit up. Across the top it read, LAZO'S ENGINE PARTS. The artwork was similar to Lennie's tattoo.

"Lazo?"

He shrugged. "Better than Lazarski. I didn't want my business to get confused with my dad's. He used to have a body shop."

I took the computer mouse in my hand and scrolled around

the site. There was a section for automotive parts, and another one for other types of engines—lawn mowers, chain saws, washer/dryers. You could order an item to be shipped or pick it up. Voilà.

Not a drug dealer, then, but a budding entrepreneur? "Did your dad teach you all this?"

"Some." He picked up a part that was lying on the desk and placed it next to a similar one on a nearby shelf.

"You said he had a body shop. . . ."

"Yep." Lennie ducked down to search for something in one of the boxes beneath the counter. "Messed up his back when a car fell on him a few years ago. So now he mostly sits around smoking weed." Lennie found the part he was looking for and stood up to face me. "Medicinal purposes."

I stepped back. "So your dad's the pot smoker?"

"Didn't see that one coming, did ya?"

I swallowed hard. "I'm sorry."

He shrugged. "Not your fault."

"I mean, I'm sorry about what I said, before. About you smelling like a bong. I thought you were a total pothead."

He snorted. "Guess you were mistaken."

It'd been happening to me a lot lately.

"Why didn't you say something?"

"I don't know," he said. "I figured you'd decided who I was, and nothing I said was going to change it."

"Not being totally freaking scary might've changed it," I said.

He laughed. "I'm not that scary."

"Seriously? That first day when we moved in? You and that guy with the scar?"

"That's my cousin Frankie. He's such a bonehead."

"Well, he's a scary bonehead. He called me a Westside bitch. He didn't even know me."

Lennie leaned back against the workbench, arms folded across his chest. "And what do your friends call me? They don't know me, either, but I'm pretty sure they don't think very highly of me."

All the words we'd ever used to describe Lennie's crew ran through my head. *Druggie. Stoner. Lowlife. Loser.* But I didn't say them out loud.

"That's because you hang out in a pack, like you're part of a gang—"

"And you don't?" he interrupted, coughing like he'd just swallowed something the wrong way. "Your friends are a *way* scarier pack than mine are. I mean, that day I brought you the potato? I was just trying to be funny, and Willow Goodwin nearly sliced me open with her *eyes.* That bitch is scary."

"Yeah, okay. I see your point. But your friends have *tattoos,* and they, I don't know . . . they *snarl.*"

Lennie bent and unbent his elbow in my direction so show off his tattoo of gears and chains. "Oooh. Scaaary," he said, then gave me his best snarl. "Like this?"

"Yeah, like that." I smiled, then stepped closer and pointed to his tattoo. "Can I see it?" I had been curious, but didn't want him to think I was staring before.

"Sure," he said, pulling his sleeve up over his shoulder. His arm was more muscular than I would've thought, since he was so tall and lean, but I pretended not to notice. I focused instead on the intricate gears on his elbow and shoulder, and the chain that wound around them. I wanted to trace it with my fingers, the way it bulged across his biceps.

"Stop flexing," I said.

He laughed. "I'm not. I'm just naturally buff."

"Right." I gave his shoulder a gentle shove.

I suddenly heard Mom calling for me from the side yard, looking up toward our kitchen. I stuck my head out the shed door. "Over here, Mom."

"Oh!" She spun around, surprised to see me with Lennie. Or maybe it was the way he was pulling his sleeve back down over his tattoo. "We're home from therapy," she said. "Can you watch Brady for a bit?" She pointed to where he was gathering his stones out front.

"Sure," I said, then turned to Lennie. "I have to go throw gravel now. Thanks for giving Brady a new hobby, by the way."

He laughed. "No problem."

THIRTY-SEVEN

"Does this answering machine work?" I held up the ancient device and shook it against my ear, to see if anything rattled. Mom had resurrected it from a cardboard box in our Westside basement so we could cancel the answering service through the phone company and save money on our phone bill. "Has anyone actually received any messages?"

Mom pulled it out of my hands. "Yes, it works." She pressed the PLAY button. Molly's voice blasted our kitchen, "So, about the Halloween party. I can only fit three people in my house and you can probably fit about seven. Can we have it in your yard? Do you think Carla will mind? Call me!"

"Party?" My mom looked at me and raised her eyebrows.

I grinned sheepishly. "Oh, right." That's how my parents learned that we were hosting a Halloween party. Once Molly and I assured them our costs would be minimal—we'd make lemonade and serve chips—they agreed to it. Honestly, I think they were just happy I'd made a friend here and was no longer begging to leave.

But it had been more than a week since James had left and still no call. I'd sent him a paper invitation and countless letters. I phoned Ida to see if she'd heard anything, but her answer was always the same: "Nothing, dear. I'm sorry."

Molly had made the invitation to our party, cutting words out of magazines and taping them together like a ransom note. Then she snuck into the office at school and made photocopies on that hideous orange-yellow copy paper they use for notices they don't want parents to ignore.

"Goldenrod," Molly clarified. "It was the Halloweeniest color I could find."

"Weeniest," Rigby said, snickering.

Molly handed us each our allotment. Rigby was an honorary cohost of the party. "Don't invite any douche bags," she said to him.

I took one and wrote in the margin above the COME AS YOU ARE heading:

> *I don't care who you are.*
> *I just want to see you.*
> *—Yours, Ivy*

I addressed it to James in New York and dropped it in the big blue mailbox at the entrance to our neighborhood. I mailed one invite every day, in different kinds of envelopes. I always included my email address so he could reply more quickly. But I was careful not to print a return mailing address on the outer envelope. Maybe one of them would get through.

On my way back from the mailbox one day, I saw a woman with salt-and-pepper hair come out of Lennie's front door with a blanket wrapped around her shoulders. She fast-walked toward an old Honda Civic that was parked in the grass on the other side of their house, ducked into the backseat, and shut herself in. Her head dipped to the side and she disappeared from sight. I slowed my pace to see who would follow, if Lennie or his dad would come out and drive her away.

But nobody came.

Then I noticed that the car had a flat tire and one of the taillights was out. I walked along the hedges between our houses and knocked on the door to Lennie's shed. He opened it a crack and peeked out.

"Hey." He smiled and nudged the door wider when he saw it was me. "Come on in."

I stayed outside and gestured toward the Honda. "No thanks. I just . . . There's a woman hiding in that car. Do you know her?"

He sighed and his shoulders dropped a bit. "That's my mom."

"Oh." I looked toward the Honda again. "Is she okay?"

He wiped some grease from his hands with a rag. "Probably just hiding."

"Oh," I said again.

Lennie held up a finger. "Wait here."

He strode over to the car and tapped on the back window. The woman sat up and rolled it down. I couldn't hear what they said, but she reached a hand out and stroked his cheek. He nodded and turned back to me.

"Is everything okay?"

"Sorry," he said. "Can we talk later? I—"

"Yeah, sure. No problem." I backed away toward my house, lifting my hand in a little wave. "See you later."

"Thanks." He locked up the shed and went in the back door to his house.

I found my mom in our kitchen, chopping onions. "Have you met Mrs. Lazarski?" I asked.

"Couple times," she said. "She's very quiet."

I hadn't even thought about Lennie having a mother, to be honest. I'd never seen her before. "What does she do?"

Mom shrugged. "Takes care of her husband, I guess. Why don't you ask Lennie?"

"I will," I said.

The tenderness between Lennie and his mom made me wonder about James and his mother. Rebecca had been all "Daddy this" and "Daddy that," barely mentioning their mom. But James had looked like he'd been punched in the gut when he'd heard she'd been crying.

I opened the obituary of his grandfather on my computer again and stared at his mother's name. *Sheila Wickerton.* She'd grown up here, in a family that went fishing and bowling. Had she turned her back on that long ago, immersed in her high-society life? All

I had to go on was a hunch that she had a soft spot for this place, and for James. I took out a sheet of paper and wrote *her* a letter.

I told her how James and I met, how we'd gone to the cemetery and left daisies on her parents' grave. I told her how much I liked her son, that there'd been a misunderstanding and if she could give him a message for me . . . I very much wished he would call.

When I carried the letter to the mailbox fifteen minutes later, Lennie's house was still quiet. I hoped everything was okay in there.

THIRTY-EIGHT

I knocked on Lennie's shed door after school the next day. I'd been half expecting to see an ambulance or a hearse drive up, as quiet as it had been around his house. There hadn't even been any customers.

Lennie opened the shed door and pulled out his earbuds. "Hey, come in. Sorry about yesterday—my mom and all," he said as I shut the door. He moved back to the far counter and fiddled with a pile of bolts.

"What happened?" I'd been worrying about it more than I cared to admit.

"Ah, nothing, really. My dad was having a bad day. Mom needed a little break is all."

"Oh." We stood in awkward silence for a few seconds. I noticed a little section of his shelves that had books instead of engine parts, so I went to peruse. They were mostly automotive manuals, but also some paperbacks. A thesaurus and a Spanish-English dictionary, a copy of *The Great Gatsby*. I pointed to it and said, "Summer reading?"

He nodded.

He had all the same books that used to sit on my shelf, from English class. The books that made you look like you were serious about literature. *The Bell Jar* by Sylvia Plath. *Howl* by Allen Ginsberg. There were copies of *Jane Eyre* and *The Outsiders*. I stroked its spine. Couldn't seem to get away from reminders of James.

I hadn't been to our secret room for a few weeks now. What was the point? James was gone, my secret of living in Lakeside was out. But looking at these books made me miss it a little. I shook my head and turned, nodding toward Lennie's iPod. "What were you listening to?"

He stepped closer and held the earbuds out. I put one of them in and handed the other back to him.

"So you don't totally blast me out," I said.

We had to stand really close to share the earbuds, shoulder to shoulder. He glanced sideways at me. "You might not like this."

"You'd be surprised."

He smiled and tapped PLAY. The song started out in Latin, with eerie church choir voices, and I quickly realized the lyrics were all words for Satan. ". . . Behemoth, Beelzebub . . . Satanas, Lucifer . . ."

My eyes widened. "Oh, my God. What is that?"

Lennie just bobbed his head to the beat as drums and electric guitars came in. Then he grinned. "Swedish metal band, Ghost. Cool, huh?"

"I guess . . ." I gave him a wary look. The music was cool, actually, though I didn't usually get into metal. Or Satan.

He laughed. "Don't worry. I'm not a Satan worshipper . . ."

"You just play one on TV?"

"Gotta keep up appearances." He flexed his tattooed arm and gave me the badass scowl I recognized from the old days, before we ever met. Just as quickly, he shrugged it off and turned back into the kinder, gentler Lennie I was getting to know. "They're not really Satanists. The band. It's just their shtick. The lead singer dresses like a cardinal, with skeleton makeup. They all wear hoods and capes and their concerts are like a horror show."

"You've seen them in concert?"

He nodded. "In Philly once."

"Nice."

We started talking about bands we'd seen live, or wanted to. He played a song from another favorite group. I recognized it immediately, because I'd been totally obsessed with them for a few months last year. I loved the way they mixed piano and symphony and choral music into a hard rock sound.

"I'm teaching Brady how to play the ukulele," I said.

Lennie scanned his music and pulled up a ukulele recording. "Jake Shimabukuro. You know him?"

I shook my head and listened for a moment. "Is that 'Bohemian Rhapsody'?"

"Yep," said Lennie. "Dude is amazing."

"I always thought of the ukulele as a wimp of an instrument, something to use in a pinch if you didn't have anything more substantial. But I love it now. And this guy really is amazing."

Lennie smiled and let me scroll through his music selection while he went back to work sorting through a box of odd parts. I played a few more Shimabukuru tunes. ("Ave Maria" on ukulele? Bach's Invention No. 4 in D minor? Crazy.) I found lots of heavy metal, too, but also stuff like the Beatles and Bob Dylan. Then I saw something that really surprised me.

"No way." I bit my lip so I wouldn't laugh.

"What?" He tried to grab the iPod from me but I held it out of his reach.

"The sound track to *Titanic*?" I said through giggles. "Céline Dion?"

Lennie groaned. "She only sings one song. The rest is instrumental. You know in the movie when the musicians are performing right up to last moment before the ship sinks? That stuff is on there, and . . ."

I held up my hand. "It's okay, Lennie. I won't tell anyone about you and Céline."

He shook his head, smiling. "I hate you."

"Trust me. You're not alone," I mumbled.

He narrowed his eyes at me for a second, then went back to his gadgets. He was photographing each of them on a white background. I offered to help, and soon we had a rhythm going where I stood behind the camera and took the pictures while he positioned one item after another.

It was nice, comfortable. I didn't think about Reesa or James. We just played music and worked in silence. After a few minutes he said, "I don't really hate you."

I looked up and smiled. "I know."

We continued to work for another hour, logging the parts I had just photographed into his online inventory. He read off model numbers and descriptions and I keyed them in.

"I should pay you something," he said.

"It's okay." I could use the money, but didn't feel right taking it from Lennie.

"Why not? You're cutting my workload in half. At least."

I shrugged. "I like doing it. It takes my mind off . . . other things."

He finished labeling a gear and slid it onto the shelf. "Like that guy James?"

I stayed quiet. I never did find out what James had said to convince Lennie to give him my address.

"He, uh . . . seemed to like you a lot," said Lennie. "Whatever happened to him?"

That achy feeling that came to my chest whenever I thought about James started to flare up again. It got worse with each day he didn't call or email. I was starting to lose hope.

But I didn't want Lennie to know how thoroughly I'd been dumped. "He's visiting his father," I said. "In New York."

"Oh." Lennie looked down at the label he was marking and put the item on a shelf.

"He should be back soon," I said. "Any day now." I'd given up lying, but was it really a lie if I sincerely hoped it to be true?

Lennie held my gaze for an awkwardly long time. "That's great," he finally said.

He read the model number of a tractor gasket, and I keyed it in. When I looked up for the next item, his face was dead serious. "Ivy," he said, "I have a confession to make."

I swallowed hard. "About what?"

His voice dropped to a whisper. "Promise you won't tell?"

"I promise," I whispered back. My heart started racing.

"I lied to you. About Céline Dion." He broke into a crooked grin. "I love that song." He put his hand to his chest in that pained-heartbreak sort of way and started belting it out. Really, really off-key.

I almost peed myself laughing.

We kept working and laughing, and every time my giggles subsided, he'd sing another little bit of a Céline Dion song he knew. It was horrible.

And wonderful.

THIRTY-NINE

An envelope.

In the mailbox.

Addressed to me.

The handwriting looked familiar. Not the cursive James had used to write the snippet of a sonnet on the drawing he made for me, but his printing—the way he'd jotted notes in the books in our secret room.

I tore it open, my hopes lifted at the prospect of a message at last. Please, please, *please* don't hate me anymore.

But it wasn't a letter. It was a flyer for another open mic night at the King Theatre. Whoever sent it had circled the part where it said, SHARE YOUR TALENT! But there was no note. Not even a scribble in the margin.

There was, however, a little starburst shape in the bottom corner announcing a cash prize to be awarded to the winner of this month's event. It didn't say how much, but there were four dollar signs and a couple of exclamation marks. So it had to be more than a few dollars. Maybe fifty or a hundred? It was *something*, though. A trip to the grocery store. New shoes for the twins.

"What's that?" Mom stood at the top of the attic stairs, holding freshly laundered sheets.

"Nothing." I shoved it into my backpack.

I had told James about open mic night, how Molly wanted me to do it with her. And he'd encouraged me. *Show up and sing to the tombstones,* he had said. *Do it for yourself.* And a cash prize? That was an even better incentive, since my job hunt wasn't going so well. I started to fantasize that maybe it was even more than a hundred dollars. Maybe two hundred. Two fifty. Five hundred? Mom wouldn't have to worry about day-to-day expenses for a week or two.

"Everything okay?" Mom dropped the sheets on my desk chair.

I smiled, my heart racing. "Sure. Everything's great."

She flicked a quick glance toward my backpack, then reached over to strip my bed. Mom had employed a maid when we lived in Westside. Now she held a job and did all the housework, too. The apartment was small, but I swear she cleaned it three times as much as our old house. Or maybe I just noticed it now. It was surprising how much I hadn't noticed before.

I took an edge of the clean sheet.

"Thanks, sweetie," she said.

When we finished (she insisted on hospital corners), I waited for her to disappear down the stairs before retrieving the flyer.

Maybe Molly had sent it. But why would she be so secretive? We'd talked about working on a song together, maybe trying our back-and-forth duel between piano and clarinet. She had no reason to send an anonymous flyer. She would've just walked down the road and shoved it into my hand.

It had to be James.

I folded and unfolded the ad, tracing my fingers over the words he'd circled: SHARE YOUR TALENT! Would he be there? Or watching somehow? If this was the way to reach him, if it would prove to him that I cared, there was only one thing to do.

It just happened to be the one thing that terrified me most.

I went to the secret room first thing Friday morning and opened my copy of *Jane Eyre,* almost expecting to find the page blank—that I'd imagined the whole thing. But the note was still there.

So serious? Love me some J.E., but what do you read for laughs?

I pulled out the envelope that the flyer had come in, set it next to the note from James. There was no mistaking they were written by the same person.

I slumped into the old library chair and stared at the flyer again. I couldn't do this. I couldn't get up and sing in front of all those people.

But I had to. Not only for James, but the prize money . . . I had to do this.

The next open mic night was less than a week away. Next Thursday. A crazy assortment of songs raced through my mind, tumbling over each other. I needed to pick one that would speak to him. Or maybe . . .

I pulled out a notebook.

Ours wasn't a love song. Not yet. It was a song of finding him when I needed someone. Of making mistakes. Realizing I didn't have to fake it anymore. He'd been there for me, and I'd let him down.

I got up and peeked into the outer supply closet, to make sure nobody was there. Then I locked myself in the secret room.

It wasn't easy without my piano. I thought about the moment James and I first met by the hedges, tried putting it into words. *"Caught by surprise, leaves in my hair . . ."*

I wrote it down. More lyrics came. And along with it, a melody. I bent over my notebook and scribbled, singing along. *". . . Rusty bicycle, you didn't care . . ."*

Soon, my pencil could barely keep up. The song fell out of nowhere onto my lips. It didn't come out perfectly. Words didn't always rhyme where they should, but the message was there. *"All I knew was a mistake, my world a lie, my life a fake . . ."*

I wrote and erased and wrote some more. I tried to imagine the piano accompaniment. Moody and slow, eerie almost, then building faster and louder like thunder before a final calm. I couldn't wait to lay my hands on a piano. When I'd done as much as I could with paper and pencil, I gathered my notebook and bag and ran for the band room.

The band was in there.

I laughed at myself, how making music made me oblivious to everything around me sometimes. Like the fact that school was in session.

It was nearly eleven. I'd missed my first two classes, so I scurried to my third-period trigonometry class. Took my seat in front of Reesa. She didn't say anything but tapped my shoulder. When I twisted around, she handed me a sheet of paper.

It was an assignment from English.

"Thanks," I said.

She nodded. It wasn't much, but it was a start. We still were not officially talking. Our communication had advanced from icy glares to the occasional grunt or nod. I caught her watching me with Molly and Rigby, and she caught me watching her with Willow and Wynn.

I'm pretty sure I'd landed in the happier place. She kind of looked like a kidnap victim afraid to risk an escape from her captors.

* * *

Molly and I sat on the curb outside her house Friday after school, soaking up the last few rays of Indian summer sunshine. We were trying to make a playlist of music for the party.

"No Lucinda Williams," I said. "Too depressing."

"Yeah, but if I hear that song 'Happy' one more time, I'm going to scream. It's like the song that will never die."

"Don't forget, Rigby is making a song list, too." I glanced sideways at Molly and we both started laughing. Rigby had turned out to have eclectic taste in music.

"I love that kid," said Molly, "but what was that drum-circle thing he was playing the other day?"

"I liked it," I said, still laughing. "It felt very, I don't know . . . primitive."

"If you're into that sort of thing," said Molly. "Personally, I've never been a fan of the didgeridoo."

We played songs back and forth until Lennie's Jeep drove up to the corner. He beeped his horn and waved for us to come over.

"I'll go see what he wants," I said.

I jogged to the road and leaned on the open passenger-side window. "What's up?"

"I'm making a trip to the junkyard," he said. "Wanna come? Now's your big chance." He waggled his eyebrows like it was the most tempting invitation imaginable.

Lennie had promised, or rather dared me to go with him engine-surfing (his term) at the junkyard. Once a week or so, he scoured the new arrivals for parts. I made the mistake of saying it sounded like fun, and he went on and on about the thrill of the hunt. When I busted up laughing and told him I was kidding, he said I definitely had to go. He would prove how much fun it was.

"Sounds like a blast, Len," I said. "Really. But I promised Molly we'd get a song list ready for the party. You're coming, aren't you?"

"You mean to the party in my own backyard?" he said. "Yeah, I'll probably be there."

"I'm glad," I said.

Lennie gave me a thumbs-up and threw Molly a salute.

I skipped back to the curb in front of her house and sat down.

"Call me crazy," she said, "but I'd say Hypothetical Guy is plenty aware that you exist."

"Huh?"

"Lennie. He's Hypothetical Guy, right?"

"What? No! Why would you think that?"

"Oh." Molly looked away with a pursed-lip smile. "No reason."

"He's not," I said. "Absolutely, totally not."

FORTY

Mom woke me early on Saturday for our second food pantry run. We knew what to expect this time, but that only made us dread it more. We needed the food, though. Mom had served a meal she called "mixed steamed grill" the night before. It was basically little bowls of whatever we had leftover from the last few nights, and some mashed potatoes she whipped up with an egg and fried.

We pulled into the parking lot of the Northbridge Methodist Church. Again, we sat and watched for a while, working up the nerve to get in line for our number. I recognized some of the people we'd seen last month. But I didn't see Chandra or Rigby anywhere.

"I don't know that I'll ever get used to this." Mom let out a sigh. "Let's go."

We got in line.

As the door opened, the same man from last month started handing out numbers. We were seventy-five.

Mom said, "Any idea how long it will be?" Like we were in line for a table at a restaurant.

"Thirty, maybe forty minutes," he said.

She nodded. "Let's wait in the car." Mom started to walk away, but I turned back to the man.

"Is the church open?" I asked. I remembered there was a piano, when James and I were here last. And I hadn't had a chance to play the song I'd written yet. This was the perfect opportunity.

He nodded. "Around front. Sanctuary's straight ahead."

"I'll meet you back here," I called to Mom, and bolted around the corner before she could argue.

But I didn't go inside right away. I looped around to the side that faced the cemetery. Crossing the church parking lot, I followed the path James and I had taken to the giant oak tree. I even sprinted to the top of the hill to recapture the breathless intensity of that day, to remember how he'd made me feel. To remember *him.* We'd been apart now longer than we'd been together.

Was I hanging on to nothing? It didn't matter.

I dropped onto the bench that overlooked the cemetery. Something was lying in the grass in front of the Robertsons' tombstone. I went over to get a closer look.

Daisies. Fresh cut.

I spun around, searching for him. "James?" I called.

It was a cloudy day, and the sound of my voice seemed to disappear into the gray.

The only other soul in the cemetery was an elderly man.

He stood in front of a stone for several minutes with his hands clasped in front of him, then turned and hobbled slowly away.

I was alone.

I made my way back to the church and went in the same doors that James and I had entered to find a telephone. I peered into the sanctuary. It was empty, and so was the room to the side where I'd seen the piano that day.

"Anybody here?" I called out.

James told me the pastor kept it all open so people would feel free to come and go as they pleased. So I went in. The piano sat in the corner, past a long table filled with artificial flower centerpieces. I looked toward the doorway to make sure nobody was there, lifted the lid from the piano keys, and sat down to play.

It came out mostly as I'd imagined, with a few surprises from today's visit to the cemetery. An intricate, somewhat frenzied bit was my heart racing, searching for him. Then it calmed and ended sweetly. The happy ending I hoped for.

I sat motionless, breathless, for a few minutes.

Clap, clap, clap.

I gasped, turning to the sound of a single pair of hands, applauding from a dark corner.

"Beautiful," said a faint voice. A figure stepped into the light. It was the elderly man from the cemetery. "This is why I leave the church open."

"I'm sorry," I said. "I tried to find someone to ask . . ."

He hushed my apology. "Come again. Whenever you like.

Maybe you can perform for our congregation someday."

I bit back my usual reaction to dismiss such a suggestion as ludicrous, and smiled instead. "Someday," I said.

Running around to the food pantry entrance, I heard the man announcing "Up to eighty!" on his microphone, and saw Mom walking in.

"Mom!" I called.

She turned, looking peeved. "Where—"

"There was a piano inside," I said breathlessly.

That's all I had to say.

FORTY-ONE

The days leading up to open mic night and our Halloween party spilled together, an abstract painting of my rising panic. I hadn't told anyone I was planning to perform, since it was scary enough knowing James might be in the audience. I didn't want a hoard of friends and family showing up. But keeping it secret was only making me more nervous.

If Reesa hadn't been mad at me, I would've told her, but . . .

"Hey!" Molly snapped me out of my wishful thinking. I'm not sure how long she'd been sitting there across the lunch table. "Where *were* you just now?"

I smiled. I had to tell someone. "Open mic night. Onstage. Scared shitless."

"Seriously?" Her eyes widened. "You're going to do it?"

I looked around, made sure nobody was listening. Swallowed. "Yeah," I said. "Don't tell anybody. Can you come? I might need someone to drag me off the stage if I freeze up."

Molly grinned. "First of all, you're not going to do that.

You're going to be awesome. And second of all, I wouldn't miss it. Friday?"

"No," I said. "It's Thursday."

"I'll be there. Do you need a ride? I . . . wait." She opened her bag and pulled out the little agenda she used to keep track of homework assignments. "Shit. I can't go."

"Why not?" My voice was suddenly all whiny and pleading. I hadn't realized how badly I wanted someone to be there with me. To get me through it.

"It's my dad's birthday," she said.

Her dead father's birthday. "Oh."

"Not a good night to leave Mom home alone," she said. "We're going to my dad's favorite restaurant. There will be crying involved."

"I understand," I said.

"I'm hoping it gets easier. Last year was a bitch." She returned to her sandwich until she realized I wasn't eating. "You want me to help you rehearse? You look like you need a fix."

I smiled. "I do. But the band room is occupied by the jazz band. So annoying."

She snort-laughed. "How rude of them. You could always use the piano in the choir room."

"There's a piano in the choir room?"

She looked at me like I was an idiot. "You're kidding."

I skipped lunch that day and again Thursday so I could practice. But the song changed every time I played it. I was so distracted, obsessing over how to fix it. Reesa would've noticed something was wrong. But Molly was busy with everyone who kept running over to RSVP for our party.

"What if all these people actually come?" She held up the list she was keeping in her Trig notebook.

"Maybe we should decorate or something," I said. "I think my mom has some Christmas lights we could drape around the trees."

Molly nodded toward Willow, who was racing up and down the halls like a lunatic. Our party was getting all the buzz, and it was sending Willow over the top of crazy. She kept reminding people about the amazing band her mom hired, and the caterer. Don't forget the caterer! All this time I thought people cared about that stuff. But somehow, our promise of a bag of chips and maybe some dip was going head to head with her beef tenderloin wraps and stuffed mushrooms. And we weren't losing.

It was Halloween, after all, and Lakeside was a helluva lot scarier than Willow Goodwin's well-appointed living room. Our "come as you are" theme was appealing, too. Guys were not interested in dressing like it was the Roaring Twenties. They had no idea *how* to dress for the 1920s.

Willow was putting the full-court press on everybody she knew, collecting RSVPs like votes in an election. "Can I count on you?" "I'm counting on you!"

Molly and Rigby and I watched it all like the circus it was. We just wanted our little party of outcasts to have fun.

"You haven't told me what you're wearing," said Molly. For a second I thought she was talking about open mic night, and almost described the shimmery purple dress Dad had rescued from our old house. I had snuck it out of Mom's closet, along with a pair of black heels. But what to wear for Halloween?

"I have no idea," I said.

"Come on. You're just not telling me."

I smiled, wishing that was the case.

"Fine." She crossed her arms. "I'm not telling, either."

The morning of open mic night I spotted Reesa standing in front of her locker—staring into its depths. She'd been doing a lot of that lately. Then she'd sort of "wake up" and look around and almost catch me watching her—just as I kept almost catching her watching me. Even Molly had noticed it. She said, "Talk to her. She clearly wants you to."

I wanted to tell her about open mic night. I wanted her to *be* there. But every time I thought to approach her, I'd remember how she'd slammed the gate to her driveway in my face that day. I don't think I could take it if I told her about my performance and she didn't show up. Not with her knowing how scary it was for me.

But the Halloween party wasn't a big deal. If I invited her and she didn't show, I'd live. So when I saw her standing there alone, and the party only two days away, I knew I might not get another chance. I opened my bag and pulled out my last invitation. She didn't even notice me until I was inches away.

"Here." I thrust the invitation into her hands. My heart was in my throat, waiting to see if she'd crumple it up or throw it at my feet. But she took it and scanned the text.

"Come as you are?" She did a pretty good job of pretending she hadn't heard about the party.

"Uh-huh."

"How very Kurt Cobain of you."

I shrugged. I hadn't thought of the Nirvana tune when we came up with the theme, but she wasn't the first to mention it. Lennie kept singing it when we were working in his shed. He had the perfect raspy voice for it. "Anyway. I hope you can come."

"It's the same night as Willow's party," she said.

"Yeah, well . . ." *Willow and I don't have the same friends anymore,* I almost said. I felt tears coming to my eyes so I blinked a few times, really fast.

"I'm late for class," Reesa said quickly, then turned and walked away.

"I can't imagine having a party without you," I said, but I don't think she heard me.

FORTY-TWO

I told my parents I'd be spending the evening at Molly's, not catching a cab into downtown Belleview to perform an original song in front of a crowd of strangers. The fewer people who knew I'd be there, the fewer people who'd witness my humiliation if I froze again onstage. After this, I told myself, no more secrets.

What I hadn't anticipated, however, was finding a note from my mother under the Buddha paperweight on my desk in place of the money for cab fare I'd put there.

Borrowed some cash for groceries.
IOU $40, will pay you back in the a.m. Hope you don't mind. Thanks, sweetie!
–Mom

I threw my room upside down on the odd chance I'd forgotten about some hidden cash. Then I sat on the top step to the attic, nearly hyperventilating, and dropped my head between my knees. I would simply ask Dad for the money when he got home. If he got home in time. He'd been working late the last few days on a big job he said might turn things around for us. I could ask . . . *Who could I ask?* Molly and her mother were broke. I certainly couldn't ask Reesa or any of my old friends. There was nobody. Except . . .

I jumped up and looked out the tiny attic window at Lennie's shed. There was a sliver of light beneath the door, so I ran down our three flights of stairs and into his yard, and knocked. The door wasn't latched and pushed open slightly at my touch.

Lennie turned in his computer chair and saw me. "Come on in," he said, swiveling back to face his work.

I took a couple of steps toward him. "I, uh . . . have a favor to ask." I paused. "Remember when you offered to pay me for my help, and I wouldn't take it? Well, I need some money now and I was wondering if, maybe . . . if you could loan me forty dollars."

He spun slowly around to face me again. "For . . ."

I opened my eyes wide. "None of your business."

"Okay." He returned to his keyboard. "Then no. I'm not giving you forty dollars."

"I didn't ask you to give it to me. It would be a loan."

"Not until you tell me what it's for."

"Why do you even care?" I stomped over to where he sat. "Fine. It's for a dress. I need to buy a dress for . . . homecoming."

I cringed at the lie, the pathetic breaking of my promise to stop telling them.

He shook his head. "Uh-uh. First of all, where are you going to find a nice dress for forty bucks? Lame-ass lie, Emerson. And you wouldn't come begging at my door for dress money, anyhow."

"I'm not begging. You said you'd pay me."

"And you said you didn't want to be paid. But now you do. So what gives?"

"Nothing gives. I just . . . need . . . forty dollars!" I sucked in a shuddering breath and started to cry, which surprised me as much as Lennie. I buried my face in my hands.

"Whoa," he said. "What are you doing?"

"What does it look like I'm doing?" I grabbed for a roll of paper towels he kept on the counter and tore off a few sheets to bury my face in. Once the tap was open, I couldn't stop until it ran dry.

Lennie backed away from me at first, like he was afraid I might explode, then stepped closer and closer until his shoulder was aligned with my nose. He put his arms gently around my back and pulled me into a hug. I let my head fall against him, my body relax.

"Sheesh," he said. "I'll give you the forty bucks already."

"It's not for a dress," I said, still sniffling.

"You don't have to explain, really. I—"

"It's for cab fare into Belleview and back, to the King. That's all. I'm performing at open mic night tonight. Nobody knows."

His brows knit together. "What time do you have to be there?"

"Seven."

He smiled. "I'll take you myself."

FORTY-THREE

It was six thirty in the evening when Lennie pulled his Jeep around the corner near Molly's house, so my parents wouldn't see me leaving with him. I jumped in, tucking my bag with Mom's purple dress on the floor between us. He threw the Jeep into gear and we lurched forward.

As my eyes adjusted to the dimming evening light, I noticed he wasn't wearing his usual tan work boots but a black pair instead, with dark jeans. And he'd traded his flannel shirt and concert tee for a charcoal-gray button-up and black leather jacket.

He pushed his hair back and it fell forward, brushing his jawline. No ponytail, and the scraggly ends were gone.

"Did you cut your hair?"

He tipped his head down, as if to hide behind what remained. "Carla did it," he mumbled.

"Looks . . . nice."

He smiled. "Didn't want to embarrass you or anything."

I punched his arm lightly. "I can do that all by myself, thank you very much."

We rode in silence for a while, watching the headlights and taillights go by. It struck me suddenly that I was about to see James. Finally. But instead of being happy and excited about it, I was terrified. Why hadn't he just called, let me explain? This performance felt like some kind of weird test. Did I have to risk total humiliation to prove my sincerity?

"You'll do great." Lennie reached out to stop my knee from bouncing up and down like a jackhammer. "Don't worry."

He'd misread my jitters about James for nerves about singing, which only reminded me how nervous I was about singing.

"You're pretty confident, considering you've never heard me sing," I said.

He pinched his lips into a smirk, a decidedly guilty one.

"Have you?"

"Eight thirty lullaby. Best concert in town."

"Lennie!"

"What? I was over at Carla's one night and heard you singing. You can really sing."

I shook my head. "But I can't. Not in front of people. That's the problem. I freeze up. What if I do that tonight? I've done it before."

"That was a long time ago," he said. "You were only a kid."

Wait a minute. "How do you know? You weren't there."

Ignoring me, he reached for the radio to turn it on and dial past one fuzzy station after another until he found a song he liked. "This okay?"

"Lennie. Were you there? The district talent show?"

He turned to me and held my gaze longer than he probably should've while driving on a major highway. "You don't remember."

"Remember what?"

He turned back to watch the road. "Nothing," he said, turning the volume lower. "Hey, I haven't seen Brady for a few days. How's he doing?"

"You were, weren't you? At the talent show."

He took a deep breath and let it out slowly. "Fine. Yeah. I was there."

"Why didn't you say so?"

"What difference does it make? I was there. I saw you." He shot me a glance and a quick smile. "You don't want to think about that tonight, anyway. You want to think about getting on that stage and blowing everyone away."

"Right," I said.

But I couldn't stop thinking about it, and I guess Lennie couldn't, either, because then he said, "You were really beautiful that night, in your butterfly wings, you know."

His Jeep seemed so quiet then, like all the sounds of the road and the motor had completely disappeared. "Thank you," I whispered.

He flashed me a quick grin, then reached for the radio and

turned the music up louder. "So, how's Brady doing?"

I swallowed the lump in my throat. "He's . . . uh. . . he's having a lot of therapy after school. And, uh, learning to speak in full sentences, dress himself, stuff like that."

"Must be hard," said Lennie.

I didn't know if he meant to ask if it was hard on Brady, or me, or my parents, or Kaya, but in any case, the answer was yes. My mom always said it was okay to admit to that.

"Sometimes I wonder what things would be like if Brady were . . . if he didn't have his disability. Especially since we moved, I imagine it a lot. We wouldn't have lost our house. I'd still have my piano." I paused. This was something I never told anyone. I didn't even want to admit it to myself. "I'm sorry. I don't really mean that. I love Brady just the way he is."

Lennie didn't react right away, and I figured he was contemplating what a horrible person I was, maybe wishing he'd never agreed to take me to this show.

He reached over and squeezed my hand. "How would you want things to be different?"

I bit my lip, not wanting to say more, but the words kept forcing themselves out. "Maybe everything wouldn't be about Brady, about how everything affects Brady. We wouldn't have to be constantly watching him and worrying, and spending all our money on his therapy." I shook my head. "I'm a horrible person."

Lennie chuckled. "You know how many times I've wondered

what would've happened if my dad had been killed when that car fell on him?"

I sucked in my breath. "I don't want Brady to die."

"I'm just saying everyone thinks about how their life might've been different under different circumstances," Lennie said quietly. "It doesn't mean you're a bad person."

We drove in silence for another minute. My nerves had disappeared, for the moment at least. I felt lighter, saying that stuff about Brady. I'd been holding it in, like water against a dam. Releasing it was a relief.

Then Lennie pointed toward a sign looming ahead and said, "Here's our exit." And my nerves came rushing back.

A woman clutching a clipboard guarded the door as musicians arrived with their guitar cases and amps and drum kits. As Lennie and I approached, the woman asked the guy in front of us for his name. She scanned her clipboard and checked him off. "You'll be on first, so go ahead and set up."

I froze. We had to sign up? I thought the whole idea of an open mic night was that the mic was open. Lennie took my arm and pulled me toward the woman.

"Name?" She peered at me over a pair of purple reading glasses.

"I, uh . . ."

"It's Ivy Emerson." Lennie reached over her clipboard and pointed to a name on the list. "Right there."

I was right there?

"Looks like you're our finale tonight. We'll have you do a quick sound check before we start, though. Why don't you head up there now? Piano is stage left."

I nodded and let Lennie lead me toward the stage. James had signed me up? My already-pounding heart did a few extra leaps. Sending the flyer was one thing, but signing me up? I started looking for him, expecting to see him leaning against a wall, thumbs hooked through his belt loops. But nobody in the place was standing still. There was a frenzy of activity—people climbing ladders, adjusting lights, stringing wires, or wheeling things around.

I made my way to the grand piano, catching my reflection in the shiny black top that was propped open. Lennie watched me from backstage. His hands pushed the air in front of him as if physically urging me forward. Seeing him there, in the folds of the curtain, suddenly reminded me of a boy who'd stepped out from the curtains to help me once before.

A boy I remembered only as having dark hair, as pulling me to safety—off the stage that swirled around me. I sucked in a breath.

Lennie?

The memory rolled over me now, how he'd coaxed me to go on, to play. His hands pushing the air forward like they did now. But when I couldn't, he came to my rescue. *You don't remember?* It *was* Lennie. He was the one who'd led me off the stage that horrible time at the talent show, when I'd frozen solid. In my butterfly wings.

I made it through the sound check, barely plunking out a few bars on the piano and a single line of my song before a voice from the darkness said, "We're good, thanks."

I waited on a metal folding chair backstage as the first act prepared to go on. The other performers were peeking out to see the audience filling the theater. I didn't need to torture myself like that. The sound was enough, rumbling louder and louder, like a thunderstorm approaching. Slipping into the dressing room, I pulled the purple dress from my bag and slid it over my head. Amazing how a garment could convey something on the outside so completely opposite to what was inside. I looked smooth, slick, shimmery. I felt rough, sick, shaky. I attempted to tame my hair, dabbed some charcoal eyeliner along my lashes and gave my lips a swipe of gloss. The illusion was complete. Now, if I could only fool myself into believing it.

Lennie had disappeared after my sound check, though I glimpsed him pacing outside when someone had the loading-dock doors open. One hand held his cell phone to his ear and the other kept pushing his hair back. He didn't see me watching him, though.

Before the show began, a man walked onto the stage and tapped on the microphone. The audience hushed and he cleared his throat. "I have an exciting announcement to make, and this is the first time our performers are hearing about it as well."

Everyone backstage moved closer to the edges of the curtains, if they weren't already there, and a buzz of murmurs went through the crowd.

The man cleared his throat again. "As you know, open mic night is something we hold once a month. It is an opportunity for amateur musicians to share their talent. We don't pay the performers, and we don't sell tickets. But tonight, thanks to an anonymous donor, we'll be awarding a cash prize to one lucky performer." He paused as we all nearly burst from holding our breath. "And the amount of that prize is . . . five thousand dollars."

A roar went up backstage and in the audience. My heart, already pounding, thumped harder. *Five thousand dollars?* The man was introducing some people seated in the front row, who would be the judges. I could see them standing and waving but I didn't hear any of it. All I could hear was the scream in my brain. *Five thousand dollars!*

I bent over so my head was between my knees and tried to breathe slowly. In seconds, Lennie was kneeling next to me, his soft voice in my ears. "Don't think about that," he was saying, his hand moving in slow circles on my back. "You can do this. It's just you and your music. Nothing else. Nobody else. Okay?"

I sat up and whispered, "I can't, you know I can't. You were there, Lennie. It was you backstage. I remember now. It was you . . . all this time."

He came around so he was squatting right in front of me, his face level with mine. "I'm right here if you need me. Okay? But you're not going to need me. You're going to blow them out of their seats."

I laughed, then whimpered. *Five thousand dollars.*

Lennie grabbed my hands. "Just you and the music."

He looked into my eyes, and I don't know if it was the stage lights reflecting off my purple gown or if I simply hadn't been paying attention all this time, but Lennie's eyes . . . they were like dark gems that sparkled with a million colors when the light hit them just right.

"You'll be here, right?" I said. "You're not going anywhere?"

He steadied his sparkly eyes on mine. "I'm not going anywhere."

"Okay." I nodded. "I'm good now."

He gave my hands a final squeeze and slipped away. The show began and I lost myself in the other performances, even the bad ones. Anything was better than focusing on what I was about to do. From backstage I caught a glimpse of a sliver of the audience, and for a second, I thought I saw Reesa. Then someone called my name.

What happened next was like an out-of-body experience. I watched the woman who no longer held a clipboard shuttle me into place. A man with a microphone held his hand out to me. I saw myself walk to him, the purple dress shimmering in the lights as I returned his smile, took his hand. He led me to the piano.

"... my pleasure to introduce Ivy Emerson, who will be performing her own original composition, 'There for Me' ..."

Everything was fine until my brain reunited with my body and saw the audience out there ... rows and rows of people. Clapping at first, now waiting ... murmuring.

I sat at the piano, hands on my lap. Heart in my throat. Not moving.

"Ladies and gentlemen, Ivy Emerson ...," the man prompted again.

A smattering of nervous applause, then a tiny voice called out, "You can do it, Ivy!"

Brady?

Everyone laughed. My brother was here? My family? I searched for them among the sea of faces, but everyone looked the same from here. Then I remembered the cemetery, and what James had told me about how the dead don't judge, they just listen quietly. And one by one, I transformed the entire audience into tombstones. Patient, nonjudging, silent tombstones.

And I started to play.

The piano was clear and bright and strong beneath my fingers. When it came time to add my voice, I tried to imagine James out there in the cemetery, and I sang.

I sang about how he was there for me, accepting me for who I was, when everything else in my world had turned into a lie.... I sang about his eyes, his laugh ...

And as I sang, I wondered if it was still James I was singing about. If he was still there for me.

I continued playing beyond the lyrics, and the song took on a life of its own. My fingers melted into the keys, becoming part of the instrument. The piano became my voice. It breathed for me, it gasped and held its breath. It laughed. It *flew*, like a butterfly. It wasn't scared anymore. I was the piano, and I was doing it. I was playing for them. For the boy who *was* there for me.

I don't know how long I played. It was like a beautiful, musical trance. And when I snapped out of it, I played the last chord, and my fingers had stopped but were resting on the piano keys. Shaking. Nobody made a sound at first and I thought I'd dreamed the whole thing. But when I turned, the tombstones came alive, standing and clapping and cheering. The roar of their applause shook me. I clutched the edge of the piano to stand, to bow.

The house lights came up and I could suddenly see the audience. Brady and Kaya jumped around like a pair of pogo sticks. My parents hugged. Carla was there, too, smiling. But Lennie . . . I couldn't find him. I searched, suddenly desperate to know that he was there.

FORTY-FOUR

School the next day was beyond surreal. I kept thinking I had something on my face, the way everyone stared at me. And I wasn't just being paranoid. A group of kids would be huddled around someone's phone, then they'd all look up at me when I passed. And I kept hearing people say, "Five thousand dollars!" So, news of the cash prize had definitely circulated.

I still couldn't believe I had won. I'd given the check directly to my mother. "For food. For bills. Whatever." She'd taken it and slipped it into her purse, but promised the first thing we'd buy was an electric piano for my room. I didn't argue.

Amid the happiness of winning, there was a disappointment also. James hadn't shown. I'd looked for him everywhere, but he wasn't in the theater. I couldn't figure out why he'd gone to the trouble of sending me that flyer if he wasn't going to be there.

***

I walked into English class, where everyone had gathered around Mr. Eli's computer. I peeked between their heads, then quickly backed away when I saw what they were all looking at—me. Someone had videotaped my performance. It was right there on YouTube.

"Nice job, Ivy," Mr. Eli said when he spotted me.

My classmates buzzed around me, full of congratulations and—let's be honest—a bit of shock and disbelief. Their voices blended together into one long stream of praise. "I had no idea . . . so amazing . . . your voice . . . made me cry . . . that song . . . so good . . . where did you learn to play like that?" I nodded and smiled and thank you, thank you, thank you'd.

I looked toward Reesa, the one person I would've enjoyed celebrating this moment with. She sat primly in her chair, a secret smile on her lips.

I sat down next to her.

"Congratulations," she said, not looking at me.

"Thanks," I said back.

That was the extent of our conversation, which left an ache in my heart amid all its leaping and fluttering.

People I'd never met were shouting and whooping at me. I wanted to dig a very deep hole and swan-dive into it. Molly came running up to me just as I was about to take shelter in the bathroom.

"If I'd known you were going to do *that*, I would've convinced my mother to celebrate Dad's birthday at the King," she said. "He would've loved it."

"Aw, thanks," I said as a few of the basketball players came along and high-fived me. "This is so embarrassing."

"It's your fifteen minutes of fame," said Molly. "Might as well enjoy it. And you are totally playing something with me the next time. Some crazy-ass clarinet-piano mind-blowing shit."

"Definitely," I said. "Ours will be the craziest-ass clarinet-piano duet in history. Also possibly the first."

She hugged me, laughing. Over her shoulder, I saw Reesa watching us. I wanted to go to her and make peace. She'd been encouraging me to do something like this for so long. But the moment I caught her eye, she turned and walked away.

"So can we use some of that five thousand dollars to pimp out our party?" Molly asked. "Maybe hire a DJ or something?"

I shook my head. "I gave it to my parents. For stuff like food and shelter. You know."

Molly grinned, "Yeah, that's cool. Our lack of professional entertainment and catering doesn't seem to be affecting the turnout, anyway."

She pulled out a list of guests. "The party's getting a little big," she said. "And these are only the people who told me they're coming. What if the entire school shows up?"

"They know we're not serving beer or anything, right?" I said. "And my parents will be there."

Molly shrugged. "I told 'em. Maybe they're all planning to get loaded before they come."

I cringed. "Oh, God."

"Well," she said, "Lennie's friends will be there in case anything gets out of hand."

"They're the ones I'm worried about," I mumbled.

I couldn't face the cafeteria at lunch, for the polar opposite of the reason I used to fear it. They wanted me today. They wanted to soak in my moment of celebrity, as brief and fleeting as it surely was. All this time I'd been so worried about being cast out, only to discover that being wanted was sometimes harder.

So I went to the secret room. I flipped through the books, hoping I'd missed something, a hidden note. But they were just as I'd left them. No more James. No more notes. I shoved the books into my backpack. I could mail the Shakespeare back to him, at least. He couldn't have meant to leave something so treasured behind.

When I switched off the lamp and closed the door to the secret room, it felt like I had finished the final chapter of a favorite book. I always observed a little period of mourning for the characters I wouldn't be spending time with anymore. Their stories were over. They had walked off the page and into my life, then disappeared. Like James. It wasn't fair. I hated not knowing what happened to him next.

I bumped into someone on the way to my next class and didn't even realize it was Lennie until he offered to carry my backpack.

"What have you got in here?" he said, throwing it over a shoulder.

"Books," I said.

"What kind of books?"

My heart felt like a brick. "Ancient history."

Lennie didn't ask any more questions. He walked me to my locker and set my backpack on the floor.

"Thanks," I said.

His eyes were still gemlike and shimmering—with no stage lights to reflect. No purple dress. I was having a hard time looking away. "See you later?" I said.

"I told Molly I'd take her to pick up some sodas at Save-a-Cent. With my discount," he said. "Meet us out front?"

I hesitated for just a second, distracted by his eyes and the weight of those books in my backpack and the party I was throwing the next day and how James had never responded to all those invitations and . . .

"Unless you're afraid to be seen with me," Lennie was saying.

"Sorry, I . . . what?"

He just shook his head. "You planning to float home or you want a ride?"

I smiled. "Both, I think."

He smiled back, and I forgot about everything else and just wondered, how did I not see how beautiful he was before?

FORTY-FIVE

Molly and I started decorating for the party early Saturday afternoon. We set up chairs that Molly had collected from the neighborhood. And my mother unpacked some strings of white lights she had stashed under the bed, a small fraction of what we used to decorate our old house for the holidays but enough to drape around and illuminate the backyard. Kaya spent the day cutting ghosts and bats and spiders out of construction paper and attaching them to tree branches or recruiting Lennie to hang them from higher limbs. Brady mostly ran around, so excited he could hardly say anything except "Boo!"

Things felt different between Lennie and me. Ever since open mic night when he'd held my hands backstage—my hands felt empty without his. And every time I looked up, Lennie's eyes would find mine. It seemed like he was afraid I'd disappear.

I helped Carla in her kitchen for a while and was stealing a taste of the *pan de huevo* she was making, with chocolate, vanilla, and coconut toppings, when my mother called to me from the screen door, waving a little slip of paper in her hand.

"There's a message for you on the machine," she said as I walked out of Carla's apartment. "From yesterday. I forgot to check until now. It's James."

Lennie looked over from the tub he was filling with ice and sodas he'd brought from the Save-a-Cent.

This was the moment I'd been waiting for, hoping for . . . for weeks. Checking messages every day. Ever since James left, my first and last thought of the day had been of him.

Until I saw Lennie backstage . . .

"What did he say?" I hurried up the back stairs to meet her at our kitchen door.

"He said he's coming to the party," she said, too loud, before glancing over my shoulder and realizing Lennie could hear her. "I saved the message."

The machine was blinking like crazy. I pushed the button to rewind. The first voice I heard was Lennie's: "Mrs. Emerson? This is Lennie Lazarski. I'm with Ivy, at the King Theatre and . . ."

My mom had told me the night before about Lennie calling, telling them all about my performance so they wouldn't miss it. I hit the button to skip to the next message. Lennie again. Then one from Carla. Then my dad looking for Mom. Lennie once more. And finally, the soft, low voice I'd been missing all these weeks.

I held my breath as the recording began to play. "Hi, it's James . . . uh, James Wickerton, calling for Ivy. Ivy? I, uh . . . got your invitation. I'll be there, okay? I'm sorry I haven't been in touch. I can't wait to see you."

I played it back and listened again. He hadn't mentioned open mic night, or the song, but he knew about the party so one of my letters must've gotten through. And he was coming!

That's what I wanted, right?

I listened to the message again and again, and once more before going back outside, where I found Molly icing the sodas alone.

"Where's Lennie?" I said.

She blinked at me a few times. "Went home on the third playback of the message, I'd say, or maybe it was the fourth."

"You could hear that?"

She pointed toward our kitchen. The window above the sink, the one right next to the answering machine, was open.

"I should go talk to him," I mumbled as I started toward Lennie's shed.

Molly stopped me. "Might want to leave him alone for a while."

"But . . ."

"Seriously." Her voice was sharp. "You invite some other guy to the party we're having and you don't think he's going to be pissed?"

"I didn't . . . it's not like that, I . . ."

"Look, it's none of my business. Just stop torturing him, okay?" She started opening folding chairs, a little more vigorously than necessary.

I wasn't sure what to do with myself, now painfully aware of the absence of Lennie's eyes on me. My hands still felt empty and now my heart did, too. Carla's back screen door creaked open and she leaned out, her face tender with understanding. She must've heard it all.

"Can I do anything?" she asked.

I sighed. "Actually, could you help me with my costume?" I said. "I finally figured out what I want to be."

She nodded and let me in. I sketched my idea on paper and we found the perfect gauzy fabric in her bins of leftovers, as well as colorful bits of chiffon. We untwisted some wire hangers and bent them into shape; then Carla sewed and I glued. While it was all drying, I went upstairs and picked out a pair of black boots and black leggings and a stretchy black top with long sleeves. I pulled my hair up with one of those giant black binder clips, the one Lennie had made fun of that day (which seemed like a thousand years ago but also just yesterday).

Then I went back downstairs to Carla's and put on my butterfly wings.

"Gorgeous," she said, motioning for me to spin around so she could appraise our handiwork. "If I do say so myself."

"Thank you so much."

"Why a butterfly?" she asked. "Is that who you *really* are?"

I wasn't prepared to explain it, how the butterfly wings were my way of showing Lennie I *was* the girl he thought I was—a girl who wanted to fly, who wanted fly with *him*. "It's who I want to be," I finally said.

When it was time for the party to start, Molly and I stood out front—me in my butterfly wings and her in an all-white outfit with horizontal lines drawn across the front and back. "A story yet to be written," she explained.

I glanced at Lennie's house as guests began to arrive, but he didn't come out. There were assorted superheroes, as I predicted, and one girl came dressed in full-on princess garb, tiara and everything. The guy Molly liked had simply hung a compass around his neck and declared himself an explorer. Rigby showed up with a bunch of newspaper articles taped to his shirt, all with horrible news about car accidents, fires, earthquakes, unemployment.

"What are you?" I asked.

He flashed a mischievous grin. "Bad news. Get it?"

I groaned, then laughed.

Rigby looked past my shoulder. "What's up, man?"

I turned to see Lennie approaching. He wasn't wearing a costume, just a black T-shirt and black jeans. He folded his arms over his chest when he reached us, his tattoo flexing.

"Let me guess," said Rigby. "Batman? No, a hipster?" He stroked his chin. "Really need a goatee for that. How about . . ."

Lennie didn't answer. He barely acknowledged Rigby's presence. He was too busy staring at me in my butterfly wings, as surprised as if I'd just flown in on them and landed right in front of him.

"Yeah, uh . . . I'll just . . . get myself a drink," said Rigby, flashing me a quick glance. "You okay, Ivy?"

I nodded. "I'm good."

I stepped closer to Lennie and laid my hand on his chest. On his heart. "Who are you?" I whispered.

"Me?" He looked down at my hand. "I'm nobody. Nobody at all."

"That's not true," I said.

"Sure it is." He smirked. "You said so yourself."

"When?"

"Plenty of times," he said. "To your friends. To yourself . . ."

I opened my mouth to protest but he was right. I had said it. "That was before I knew you. I don't think that anymore."

"What *do* you think?" His dark eyes sank into mine, and I didn't look away. I'd done this for him, this costume. Now I was going to have to tell him why.

"What I think is . . ." I took a deep breath. "I think you're the only one who ever really saw me. Like *this*." I lifted my arms so my fingertips could brush the edges of my wings. "You're the only one who thought I could fly."

He took a step toward me, put a hand to my waist. "Now I'm just afraid you will."

My lips parted to tell him I wouldn't, that I wasn't going anywhere. But Brady ran up and squeezed right between us in his pirate suit. Lennie stepped back.

"What are you?" asked Brady, poking his plastic sword at Lennie's chest.

"He's not wearing a costume," I explained.

Brady looked thoroughly troubled by this news. We had told him everyone would have a costume, that it was a costume party. Not having a costume was a *problem.*

Lennie seemed to sense it, too. "Maybe you could find one for me," he said quickly to Brady. "An extra sword or something?"

My brother's face got very serious and he marched back into the house.

"You are in serious trouble now," I said.

Lennie smiled, gazed down at my costume again, and said, "I sure am."

I gave him a playful shove. More guests were arriving, and I soon got caught up with hellos and pointing people to the drinks and giving Rigby a thumbs-up on the music he was playing. When I danced my butterfly wings back over to Lennie, he was kneeling down in front of Brady by the hedge that separated our yards. There was a bundle of red-and-blue cloth in Brady's arms.

"Costume for you," he was saying to Lennie.

I bit my lip, trying not to laugh at the Superman pajamas he held up. "This is great, little dude," said Lennie. "But I don't think it'll fit me."

"Here." I stepped in and separated the red cape from the rest of it. "This is just your size."

Lennie sighed but didn't argue. He let me tie it around his neck. Then he zoomed around Brady like he was flying. My brother clapped, he was so happy. Then he dug something else out of his pocket and held it out to us. Lennie took it and his eyes went wide. He showed it to me.

It was a Wonder Woman Band-Aid.

"Oohh," I said, laughing now. "This is just what Lennie needs, Brady. Very nice."

My brother beamed and ran off, satisfied that his mission was complete. Lennie handed me the Band-Aid. "Would you like to do the honors?"

I unwrapped the package and held the sticky part of the bandage toward him. "Where do you want it?"

He tapped his chest, right over his heart. "This spot could use a little mending."

I swallowed. "Did I do that?"

He shrugged. "It's a recurring injury."

I stepped very close and pressed the bandage to his shirt, rubbing it against his chest with my thumbs to make sure it would stick. "All better now."

"If you say so," he whispered, cupping his hand over mine and pressing it to his chest. He took a few small steps backward into the shadow of the hedge, pulling me with him.

I literally had his heart in the palm of my hand, and it was pounding hard. My thumb slid up to the base of his throat and caressed the hollow spot there. I hardly knew what I was doing. It was as if my body had rebelled against my brain, and my brain wasn't putting up much of a fight.

"Len," I whispered as his lips brushed my jaw. "I . . ."

He inhaled my unspoken words with a kiss so soft and so warm, it made me want to fly. My whole body sighed into his.

When we pulled apart moments later, he smiled at first, his mouth pink from my lip gloss. Then his eyes flickered past me to the party now in full swing, and his body tensed. His hands dropped away from me.

I turned and saw James standing in front of our house, searching the crowd. He was wearing his apron from Bensen's grocery. I took a step farther into the darkness, but Lennie pushed me back. "Don't jerk the guy around," he said. "He doesn't deserve it any more than I do."

"But . . ."

"Your prince awaits," he said as he slipped behind the hedge and disappeared.

FORTY-SIX

I straightened my costume and walked into the midst of the party—friends and strangers dancing and laughing all around. James didn't notice me until I was standing right in front of him.

"Hey, Ivy." He took in my costume, his eyes widening. "Wow. Those wings. You're . . . Juliet, aren't you? From my drawing."

I looked back over my own shoulder to the shape of my wings. I hadn't even thought of it when I'd sketched them for Carla, but they *were* just like the ones James had drawn. He'd snuck into my subconscious somehow, which made me wonder if a part of me still wanted to be his Juliet. "I . . . uh . . . something like that," I mumbled.

"And I almost dressed as Romeo," he said. "That would've been perfect."

What little composure I had pulled together after kissing Lennie was starting to unravel. "We should talk," I said, pointing toward the playground, away from the noise of the party.

"Lead the way, fair maiden," said James, bowing like a Shakespearean actor. He was doing everything that had charmed me before, but all I felt now was confusion and hurt bubbling up in my chest. After disappearing without a word, he thought he could just come back and things would be the same? That we could pick up where we'd left off?

James seemed to sense the tension in the air between us, because he didn't say anything more until we reached the playground. He stood next to the monkey bars while I sat on one of the swings, careful not to knock my wings off.

"I don't know where to start," he said.

"Well, your aunt kind of filled me in."

"I heard." He looked at his feet, kicking at the dirt around the ladder.

I had imagined the moment of James's return a hundred times with a hundred different scripts. And none of them started out with us shuffling awkwardly around my neighborhood, mumbling at each other.

It probably didn't help that Lennie was in my head, the tingle of his kiss still on my lips.

"You got my invitation," I started.

He smiled. "All twelve of them."

"Sorry about that. Your aunt said they might not get through."

"They didn't," he said. "Until my mom got your letter."

I had poured my heart out in that letter, told her how much I liked her son. How he'd taken me to the cemetery that day. How sorry I was . . .

"She showed it to you?"

He nodded. "And we found the other letters. Dad's assistant had been *sorting* my mail." He made air quotes around "sorting" with his fingers.

"Was he *reading* them?" I tried to remember if I'd written anything I should be embarrassed about.

"No," he said. "But my mom was pissed. And they had a big fight. Mom convinced Dad to let me come back if I want. Make my own decisions. I'm eighteen now, so . . ."

"You're coming back?" I shouldn't have been surprised by the news; it was exactly what I'd been hoping for all this time. But it still caught me off guard. I wasn't ready.

James shoved his hands in his pockets, teetering backward on his heels. "Do you want me to? Come back?"

I couldn't believe the answer to that question might be no. But open mic night had changed everything. I didn't answer, only scuffed my feet beneath the swing.

"When I heard from Reesa," he continued, "I assumed . . ."

My head snapped up. "You heard from Reesa?"

"She sent me a message through Mrs. Lanahan. To make sure I saw the video of your performance."

"Oh. So you saw it."

He lifted an eyebrow. "You didn't want me to?"

"No, I did. I wanted you to *be* there. You sent me the flyer and then—"

"What flyer?" he said.

"The flyer about open mic night? 'Share your talent'?" I motioned circling the words with a pen. "The handwriting on the envelope was just like yours, and . . . I thought . . . "

He shook his head. "It wasn't me," he said. "I mean, I knew open mic was that night, and I thought you might do it. I hoped you would. Sing to the tombstones and everything." He was pacing the grass in front of the swings now. "I really wish I could've been there."

"Why weren't you?" I asked quietly.

He shrugged. "My dad made me go to some charity thing with him. He funded this women's shelter—it's . . . Anyway, I couldn't get out of it. I'm sorry."

I sat there in numb silence for a minute. "So Reesa told you about the video?"

"She must've run home and posted it right after your performance."

I stopped the swing from swaying. Reesa took the video? My heart raced. Reesa didn't hate me. *She didn't hate me!* I stood up, my wings snagging the chains of the swing. I wanted to run to the house and call her. I wanted to tell Lennie!

"Reesa said you wrote that song for me," James was saying.

I realized in that moment that the song really wasn't his anymore. Or maybe I knew it even before I sang it. Because Lennie was the one I wanted to run to with my happy news. It was a gut reaction, nothing I could control even if I wanted to.

I walked over to James. "I did write the song for you," I said. "But . . . everything's changed."

His pale eyes searched mine and I wondered what he'd find there. I wasn't sure myself. "Changed . . . how?

"I . . . I'm just different now. These last couple of weeks have been . . . eye-opening."

"So you didn't mean what you said in your letters?" he said. "Were you messing with me?"

"No. I meant every word. I liked you so much. I still do."

He took my hands in his. "So, be with me. I'm here now. It'll be just like it was before. I'll move in with Aunt Ida again. . . ."

I shook my head. "You can't. That's not who you are." I tapped the JIM embroidered on his apron. "Not you."

"Fine, so I'll get a different job." He tore off the apron and threw it to the ground. He wore jeans and a dark shirt, the kind that looked casual and effortless but undoubtedly cost hundreds of dollars. "Would you rather I work at the Save-a-Cent with your friend Larry?"

"Lennie," I said. "His name is Lennie."

"Right." He paused and looked at me. "And he's not your friend."

"He's . . ." My face grew hot. "Actually, he's . . ."

James's eyebrows shot up. "Hold on. Lennie? He's the reason your feelings have changed?"

I lowered my gaze and nodded.

"I thought you said he was a drug dealer."

"I was wrong about that. About a lot of things."

James stepped close and looked at me with his pale-blue eyes. Then he leaned in and kissed me softly. Just once.

"Were you wrong about that?" His smile was hopeful.

I missed that smile.

"I wasn't wrong about you," I said. "I like you so much. It's just . . . this is all make-believe for you, James. It's not real."

"My feelings are real." His voice broke. "You're more real to me than any girl I've ever known."

"But you've been hiding from your real life," I said. "We both have."

He shook his head. "I didn't choose that life any more than you chose this one. So why can't I pick a different one?"

"Because it's a *lie*, James. Pretending to be poor when you're not? It feels like, I don't know, an insult to people who don't have any other choice, who are scraping to get by and would give anything to have what you have."

"But I don't want it!" He clawed his fingers through his hair. "My last girlfriend called me 'twenty-nine' behind my back. You know why?" His voice was full of anger and hurt.

I shook my head. "No."

"Because that's what number my dad is on the Forbes list of the wealthiest Americans."

"I . . . I didn't know."

"Exactly," he said. "You didn't know. You didn't care. I thought you actually liked me for *me*."

"I did," I said. "I do like you for you."

"But you like him better." He nodded toward Lennie's Jeep, parked in front of his house.

"It's not about liking him better," I said. "It's about wanting someone who understands what I'm going through, who isn't going to disappear the minute I screw up. Because, believe me—I screw up a *lot*."

James got very still. "I'm sorry, Ivy. About disappearing. I—"

"You were gone for weeks. Without a word. You listened to Willow and Wynn, but you wouldn't listen to *me*."

He shook his head. "I didn't want you to know who I was."

I sighed. It sounded all too familiar. "I just don't think it'll work," I said. "One of us would always be pretending, and I can't do that anymore."

He walked over to where he'd thrown his grocery apron and picked it up with a sigh. "I actually liked this job. Being normal . . ." He rolled the apron into a ball. "Walk me to my car?"

I nodded and reached for his hand. As we approached the house, he started swinging our hands between us, like we had that day in the cemetery. The day of Romeo. It reminded me of his Shakespeare book. "Hold on," I said. "I have something of yours inside."

I ran in to get it, taking the steps two at a time. I grabbed his *Hitchhiker's Guide*, too. He was waiting on the porch when I came down.

"Here," I said, breathless, handing the books to him. "Your Shakespeare. And your *Hitchhiker's Guide to the Galaxy.* I don't know what happened to *The Outsiders.*"

James's eyes opened wide with surprise. He flipped open the cover of the Shakespeare. "I've been looking for this everywhere," he said. "Where did you find it?"

I laughed nervously. "You know where."

He spotted the note I'd written on the inside and read it aloud. "*And what do you read for fun?* Did you write that?"

All the air went out of my lungs. I lowered myself to sit on the porch steps. "You didn't leave that for me, in the little room off the supply closet? The one on the second floor near the girls' bathroom?"

"Uh . . . no." He handed the *Hitchhikers* back to me. "And that one isn't mine."

I swallowed. "What about *The Outsiders?* Dallas Winston?"

He shook his head slowly. "I've, uh . . . read it. But . . ."

"You never went into that supply room on the second floor, down from Mr. Eli's room?"

"Oh!" he said, recognition finally lighting his face. "I did go in there to find paper clips once. Mr. Eli told me there was a box of them on a shelf in there, and . . . is that where I left it?" He smacked his palm to his head. "I'm such an idiot."

"So you didn't leave *any* books for me in there? With notes in them?"

James slowly shook his head.

It all came into focus. Lennie, hanging out at the end of the hallway that day. He must've seen me go into the supply room. "That's where I left the note," I said, talking as much to myself now as I was to James. "To meet me at the King that Friday. On the shelf."

"I thought you meant the shelves in the library," said James. "The periodical shelf."

I shook my head. Had I been trading notes with Lennie all that time? Which meant the handwriting on the flyer, it was his handwriting. And the girl he was looking for at the King that night—that was *me*.

"I am sooo stupid," I said.

He gave a breathy snort. "It seems to be going around."

I stood and James took my hand again, and when we got to the car I kissed him on the cheek. He slid into the driver's seat and started the car.

When I lifted my hand to wave good-bye, he rolled down the window. "I knew you'd win it," he said.

I leaned closer. "Win what?"

"Open mic," he said. "I knew the judges would love you. Nobody sings like you do."

I stepped back and he drove off, a secret sort of smile on his face. And as I watched him go, I thought, *How did he even know there were judges?* Because there never were, normally. It wasn't meant to be a contest. It was only because of the anonymous donor. . . .

I sank down and sat on the grass. Had my prize money come

from James? I didn't want it to be so. But something told me it had to be. I knew then I'd made the right decision, because I couldn't be with someone who would always be resisting the urge to pay my way. Or to solve my problems with money. I wanted someone who was there for me—but not like that.

I wanted Lennie.

FORTY-SEVEN

Lennie was precisely where I expected him to be: in his shed, wiping the grease off some parts with a shop rag. His face was washed clean of my lipstick, and he'd changed back into his flannel shirt.

He didn't look up when I entered.

"Come to say good-bye?" he said.

I walked straight to his little collection of books and tipped the top edge of *The Outsiders* down. "Not just yet," I said, snatching the book off the shelf and flipping the cover open.

Lennie spun around in his chair. "What . . . ?"

"'Greaser or Soc,' huh?" I read from the exchange we'd written. "You wanted to know if I think Dally is sexy or rude? I should've known it was you."

He scratched his head. "I thought you did."

"No, you didn't."

The party music pulsed on the other side of his shed door, accented by occasional bursts of laughter and conversation.

"At first I did." Lennie leaned back in his chair. "I thought you were messing with me or maybe liked me but didn't want anybody to know. So I played along. Until I showed up to meet you at the King that Friday and, yeah . . ."

"I wasn't playing with you. I thought I was leaving notes for—"

He held up his hand to stop me. "James. I know."

"Why didn't you say something?" I paced angrily around his workshop. "Why did you let me keep thinking it was him?"

"Because that's who you wanted it to be."

"But if I'd known . . . if you had told me . . ."

"Ivy, I gave you a bike helmet," he said. "I picked you up off the side of the fucking road. You still acted like I was a leper."

"I was scared!" I sucked in a shuddery breath. "I didn't know you!"

He twisted and untwisted the greasy rag he was holding. "You didn't *want* to know me."

Maybe I didn't at first, but everything had changed. *I* had changed. Why couldn't he see that? "I just wish people would tell me the truth for a change."

He looked up. "Fine. The truth is you never thought I was good enough for you."

"That's not true."

"Come on, Ivy. At least admit that much."

"It's just . . . we came from two different places and . . ."

"And yours was way better than mine," he finished. "You *never* would've talked to me if you hadn't been forced into this situation. And don't give me this crap about being scared of what your friends would think. It's what *you* thought that mattered. And you thought I was the scum of the earth. Not because I was scary or had a tattoo. Because I live *here*."

I inhaled a sharp breath, wanting to deny it. But the truth of his words stung me. I stumbled to the door, my wings knocking something off the shelf. It clattered to the floor. Lennie stepped over it, reaching me in a single stride. He leaned his arm against the door so I couldn't open it.

"Don't go," he said.

I pulled at the handle. "Let me out, Lennie. Please."

"I'm sorry," he said. "I didn't mean it."

"No. You're absolutely right. I don't belong here. I don't belong *anywhere*." I could feel the tears starting and didn't want Lennie to see me cry again. I grabbed the door handle again, looking down at my hands on it. "Please."

He paused for a moment, then dropped his arm and I flew out, diving through the sea of costumed bodies bouncing to the music. Thank God Molly had the volume way too loud. Nobody had heard our fight, though a few people turned and watched the crying girl run by, butterfly wings askew.

The back stairs to our apartment were full of people coming and going to the bathroom, so I ran to the front porch. I stumbled up the steps and past a girl in a dog costume. She grabbed my arm and spun me around.

"Oh, my God. Ivy. What's the matter?" she said.

"Reesa?"

She nodded.

"Reesa!" I threw my arms around her, squeezing her so tight. "I'm so glad you're here." I held on to her, sobbing and laughing at the same time.

"Hey, it's okay," she said, patting my back as I clung to her. When we finally pulled apart, she lifted one of her fuzzy paws and wiped my face with it. "I leave you alone for a few weeks and look at you. You're a mess."

I nodded. "And you're . . . a dog?"

"Female dog." She smirked. "A bitch. That's what I am."

"No, you're not." I shook my head.

"I am. I was." Her puppy-dog eyes matched her costume perfectly. "And I'm sorry."

"It's not your fault. Everything was so messed up."

"Still," she said. "Major BFF fail."

"I should never have lied to you about James. I don't know why I did that."

"Maybe because I was acting like a complete lunatic? About a guy who barely even said hi to me?"

I smiled through my tears. "I was so afraid of losing you, and then I pretty much did everything I could to make that happen. I was such an idiot."

"Me too," she said.

"I've missed you so much." I sniffled, then started full-on crying again.

She wrapped her arms around me. "I missed you, too. Willow nearly drove me insane these last few weeks."

I stood back with a gasp. "You're missing her party! She'll never speak to you again."

Reesa shrugged. "She's going to have very few people to talk to then, because it looks like her entire guest list is *here*."

I had been so focused on James, Lennie, and now Reesa, I'd hardly noticed how massive the party had become. Our tiny yard was packed, and the overflow had spread across the street to the playground. My dad was chatting with a neighbor by the gravel road, probably wondering when the police would show up and send everyone home.

I turned back to Reesa. "And you were at open mic night. You took that video."

She nodded. "I was so proud of you. You know how hard it was not to run up on that stage and hug you?"

"How did you even know I was performing?"

"Molly told me."

"Molly?" I shook my head. My friends had been rallying around me, and I didn't even know.

I hugged Reesa again, still crying, and dragged her up toward my attic room. Mom had brought the twins in for bed and was trying to convince them to get their pajamas on. Brady started clapping when he saw Reesa. I couldn't believe he still remembered how she'd helped him learn how to clap. She clapped back and gave him a hug, and Kaya, too.

It only made me cry more.

I took her arm and led her up to my room, and she twirled around in the little bit of space in the center. "I love it. You're like Rapunzel, up here in your tower."

I pouted. "More like Cinderella."

"All you need is a prince."

My laugh came out a sob. I hugged her some more and we fell onto the bed.

"Tell me everything. Who did this to you." She motioned to my blubbering face.

"That's the thing," I said with a hiccupy sniffle. "I think I did it to myself."

"Tell me," she said.

I took a deep breath and filled her in on what had happened between James, me, and Lennie. After ten minutes of detailing everything, Reesa stared at me, her mouth gaping a bit. She shook her head. "Wow."

"And I haven't had anyone to talk to about it."

She pulled my head to her furry shoulder. "What about Molly?"

"Molly's great. But she's not you."

Reesa smiled. "Well, I'm here now," she said. "And I'm not going anywhere."

She patted my shoulder and rocked us side to side, saying "there, there" every now and then, like a mom. My shuddery sniffles quieted.

I stood up and looked out the dormer window at the light beneath the door of Lennie's shed. "I don't know what to do."

"So." She sighed. "Lazarski, huh?"

I nodded.

"And James?"

"I really like him, too. He's just . . ." I paced circles around my tiny rug. It wasn't that he'd done anything wrong. If he'd never gone away and I hadn't discovered the fascinating puzzle that was Lennie, I'd probably be trying to sneak behind the hedges with him right now.

"He's good-looking and sweet and funny and perfect in every way," said Reesa. And she was right. He *was.* "He's that guy on dating shows who everyone's rooting for and they can't figure out how the stupid bachelorette could possibly let him go."

I nodded. "But she falls for the one nobody expects her to fall for. The one *she* never expected to fall for."

"The hot, sexy bad boy."

My mouth fell open a little bit. "You think Lennie's hot and sexy?"

Reesa rolled her eyes. "Please. I may be a snob, but I'm not blind."

My mother hollered up the steps then that people were looking for me and I wasn't being a very good hostess, disappearing from my own party.

"Coming!" I hugged Reesa again and let her fix my makeup and hair, then led her to the drinks, where we found Jenna and

Rigby and Molly and her explorer dude. I think his name was Seth. One of Seth's friends, whose geek costume of thick black glasses and a button-up shirt didn't hide how cute he actually was, asked Reesa what she was supposed to be.

Reesa blanched. "I'm, uh . . ."

"The best friend ever," I said. "Loyal, faithful . . . all that."

Geek guy smiled. "I'm Reese."

Reesa and I burst out laughing.

"What?" said Reese. "What's so funny?"

"It's just . . . I'm Reesa."

Reese's laugh was more of a guffaw, which only made Reesa giggle harder. The two of them quickly forgot I existed. I wandered the party, never stopping long enough for anyone to realize I wasn't paying attention to a word they said. Molly dragged me over to dance with her and Seth and company, but didn't notice when I wiggled out of the circle and into the shadows.

I stood at the edge of our yard, watching everyone, Lennie's shed behind me. I could feel it there, though, like warm breath on my neck. When I couldn't stand it anymore, I turned toward it. Toward *him*.

FORTY-EIGHT

On my way to Lennie's shed, I cut through a dance line that was snaking around the backyard. He didn't answer the door or even say anything, but I went in, anyway. He was still twirling around slowly in his chair. I pulled my arms through the straps of my butterfly wings and laid them on the counter, then walked around the workbench to where he was sitting. He still didn't look up, so I stood between his knees and pushed his shoulders back. When his eyes finally met mine, they were red.

"I'm sorry," I said. "Can you forgive me?"

He lifted his hands to my waist and pulled me toward him, so his face pressed into my stomach. He inhaled a deep breath and let it shudder out.

I wrapped my arms around him, holding him tighter, then slid onto his lap. His arms moved slowly up my back and into my hair, lowering my face to his.

"What are you doing with a loser like me?" His voice was low, a bass note that vibrated through me.

"You're not a loser."

He let out a single snort of laughter. "Said nobody ever."

"Said me. Am I nobody?"

He smiled. "You're somebody."

I lifted Brady's red Superman cape that sat crumpled on the counter next to Lennie's chair. "You're a hero."

He grinned. "They don't call me Wonder Woman for nothing."

I laughed. "I'm sorry I looked down on you before, on this place. I don't anymore. And you aren't who I thought you were. Not at all."

He inhaled a slow breath. "What changed your mind?"

I couldn't hold his gaze, so I studied the collar of his shirt instead. "The way you are with Brady," I whispered. "And with your mom."

"Ah," he said. "Nothing to do with you and me, then. . . ."

I shook my head, a shy smile coming to my lips. "Nope."

There was no way I could admit that his touch practically made me forget my own name—the way he was tracing my face with his eyes, the heat of his legs under mine. If he didn't kiss me soon, I was going to explode.

He stood abruptly and I nearly fell to the floor. "Hey!"

"Sorry," he said, not sounding very sorry. He turned his back to me and leaned over his computer. "I just think we're too young to be together because you think I'm nice to children and my mother. If that's all you got, then . . ."

I grabbed the collar I'd been staring at a moment ago and

spun him crashing into me.

"Whoa," he said.

I stood on tiptoes, my whole body leaning into him, and kissed him hard.

"I changed my mind about you," I said angrily, my arms still locked around him, "because you do this to me, you big jerk."

"This?" He kissed me back hard, one hand tangled in my hair and the other holding me so tightly against him I could barely breathe.

"Yes," I said when we broke apart, panting and laughing. "That."

He grinned his crooked grin. "But I've never kissed you like that before."

"Let's not get hung up on technicalities, shall we?" I wasn't about to confess that I'd imagined him kissing me like that quite a few times. And the reality was way better.

He sat down and pulled me to his lap, and I sank right into him like he was custom-carved to fit. We may or may not have kissed for a really long time before we heard a faint knocking at the door.

"Who is it?" Lennie called out.

No one answered, but the knocking continued.

"Brady," I gasped. "It's Brady." I don't know how I knew. But I did. I untangled myself from Lennie and lunged for the door.

The moment I swung it open, Brady dived past me, crying, and wrapped himself around Lennie's leg. I rushed forward with soothing sounds, shushing softly in Brady's ear.

"He must've gotten lost in the dark," I said.

Lennie gently pried my brother off his leg and scooped him up. "I got ya, buddy. You're okay."

Brady clung to Lennie's neck.

My mother ran up then, in a panic. "Oh, thank God. You found him. I tucked him into bed and then he . . . he disappeared." She held her hands out to take Brady, but he only burrowed deeper into Lennie.

Mom looked to me with wide eyes.

I shrugged.

"Hey, little dude." Lennie spoke softly into Brady's ear. "You want to dance with me and Ivy?"

My brother pulled his face from Lennie's shoulder and smiled.

Lennie carried him to the yard as I pulled my butterfly wings back on, and we danced around and around with Brady hugged between us.

Reesa and Reese joined us, and Molly and her explorer dude. Soon my dad came and took Brady up to bed. Lennie slid his arms around my waist, beneath my wings. He pulled me close and the music pulsed through us, and everything else seemed to disappear. It was just me and Lennie, and as his shimmery eyes smiled into mine, I finally knew where I belonged. And it felt like home.

ACKNOWLEDGMENTS

Where to start? So many people have helped me achieve this goal of writing a novel and—even more challenging—getting it published! Perhaps the best place to begin is where the dream ultimately came true: with HarperTeen and my wonderful editor—Karen Chaplin. I wouldn't be writing this sentence if she hadn't pulled Ivy from her pile and helped me bring this story to life. Thanks to everyone at HarperCollins who played a part in making *Between the Notes* a real, live book, and to my agent, Steven Chudney, for his patience and expertise along the way.

There are many others I want to thank, and hope I don't miss anyone: To author Mary Kennedy, who was the first to say "go for it" when I shared my wish to write a novel; to Annie Norman and Patty Langley at the Delaware Division of Libraries and to Janet Hughes for asking me to work with them on the Delaware Book Festival, where I was inspired by authors like Laurie Halse Anderson and Jon Scieszka; to Stacey Burr for all the brainstorming and for not telling me how terrible those very first chapters I ever wrote truly were; to Rhe De Ville for the twist on a kernel of an idea that got this story rolling; to my fabulous writing friends and critique partners—Tamara Girardi, Joy McCullough-Carranza, and Hilary T. Smith—for suffering through early drafts (and revision after revision) and for always being there when I need you, as well as readers Sarah and Cate Kastringer; and to the fabulous YA writing community, especially the TeenLitAuthors group and Fearless Fifteeners . . . thank you all so much! I am also indebted to Renee Bowers and Aaron Fichtelberg and their twins, Theo and Oliver, for giving me a glimpse into their very special life; to Little Invisibles' singer-songwriter-pianist Gina Degnars and singer-songwriter Leah Awitan for insights on songwriting and stage fright; and to so many other friends and family members who have been cheering me on and anxiously awaiting the publication of this novel!

Finally, thanks, Mom, for the lessons in persistence, and Dad, for showing me that hard work pays off. Rich, I'm so glad you were totally on board with my decision to quit PR and start writing fiction. This novel probably won't get us that house in France you've been wanting, but I'll keep at it. Maybe someday . . .

And to Sebastian and Anna—thank you for inspiring me, believing in me, and always being eager to read my books. I hope there will be many more to come!

P9-CWD-637

This is Not a
WereWolf
Story

ATHENEUM BOOKS FOR YOUNG READERS
New York London Toronto Sydney New Delhi

atheneum
ATHENEUM BOOKS FOR YOUNG READERS
An imprint of Simon & Schuster Children's Publishing Division
1230 Avenue of the Americas, New York, New York 10020

For information about special discounts for bulk purchases, please contact Simon & Schuster Special Sales at
1-866-506-1949 or business@simonandschuster.com.
The Simon & Schuster Speakers Bureau can bring authors to your live event. For more information or to book an event, contact the Simon & Schuster Speakers Bureau at 1-866-248-3049 or visit our website at www.simonspeakers.com.
Book design by Debra Sfetsios-Conover
The text for this book was set in Garamond 3 LT Std.
Manufactured in the United States of America
0616 FFG
First Edition
10 9 8 7 6 5 4 3 2 1
Library of Congress Cataloging-in-Publication Data
Names: Evans, Sandra, 1970- author.
Title: This is not a werewolf story / Sandra Evans.
Description: First edition. | New York : Atheneum Books for Young Readers, 2016. | Summary: "This is the story of boarding school student Raul, who waits for sunset—and the mysterious, marvelous phenomenon that allows him to go home"—Provided by publisher.
Identifiers: LCCN 2015025074
ISBN 978-1-4814-4480-4 (hardcover)
ISBN 978-1-4814-4482-8 (eBook)
Subjects: | CYAC: Shapeshifting—Fiction. | Wolves—Fiction. | Werewolves—Fiction. | Boarding schools—Fiction. | Schools—Fiction. | Families—Fiction. | BISAC: JUVENILE FICTION / Animals / Wolves & Coyotes. | JUVENILE FICTION / Legends, Myths, Fables / General. | JUVENILE FICTION / Social Issues / Friendship.
Classification: LCC PZ7.1.E93 Th 2016 | DDC [Fic]—dc23
LC record available at http://lccn.loc.gov/2015025074

To Mac and Mike

Nature shows us only the tail of the lion.

—ALBERT EINSTEIN

Chapter 1

THIS IS THE CHAPTER WHERE THE NEW KID RUNS SO FAST, RAUL DECIDES TO TALK

New kid. New kid. The words fly around the showers and sinks. I can almost see them, flying up like chickadees startled from the holly tree in the woods.

All the boys are in the big bathroom on the second floor, washing up before breakfast. The littlest kids stand on tiptoe to peek out the windows that look onto the circle driveway.

I pick Sparrow up and hold him so he can see. He's the littlest of the littles, but the kid is dense—like a ton of bricks.

I can't believe my eyes. No kid has ever come to the school on the back of a Harley. Not in all the years I've been here, and I've been here longer than anyone. The driver spins the back wheel, and a bunch of gravel flies up.

The new kid is holding on to the waist of the driver. He must have a pretty good grip, because the driver looks over his shoulder and tries to peel the kid's fingers away one by one. Then the driver takes off his helmet.

We all gasp, because it turns out the driver is a lady with long straight black hair.

Next to me Mean Jack whistles. "What a doll!"

Mean Jack thinks he's a mobster. A made man, that's what he calls himself. I call him a numbskull, but not out loud.

The pretty lady turns her head again and says something. The new kid folds his arms over his chest. He just sits there with his helmet on, waiting for her to roar them back down the hill to the freeway and freedom. His black leather jacket is way too big for him. Pretty Lady keeps talking. She looks angry the way moms look when they're doing something they don't want to do but think that they have to. The kid's helmet jiggles left to right. *No,* he's saying. *No. No. No. No.*

That's how I felt when my dad brought me here. My chest hurts just thinking about it, and Sparrow starts to weigh as much as a blue whale. I hoist him up onto my shoulders. Sparrow reaches down and pulls on my ears. "Fanks," he says.

Sometimes Sparrow makes an "f" sound when he should make a "th" sound. You can't try to explain it to him because it makes him sad. The last thing I want is for Sparrow to be sad.

I can feel Mean Jack getting ready to say something rude, so I shoot him a warning look that says something even ruder.

Nobody teases Sparrow about the way he talks when I'm around, but Jack's the kind of kid who forgets what's good for him.

While I'm making sure Jack remembers, everyone starts to shout and cheer.

The new boy is making a break for it.

He's jumped off the bike and is racing toward the edge of the cliff. We all run to the windows on the other side of the bathroom to watch. The grown-ups below freeze, but a second later they come running around the corner to watch too.

"Come back here!" The words float out and pop in the grass. It must be Ms. Tern. When she yells, you can tell she knows you're not ever going to do what she wants.

Ms. Tern's bubble-yell is gas in the new kid's tank. His knees and elbows crank and turn. It's like watching a plane just before liftoff.

My heart soars. It really does. I read that saying the other night, and when I see the new boy run I remember it. Now I know what it means—your heart ruffles and beats like a pair of wings. I feel like I'm flying beside him, racing away.

And where he's heading and how fast he's running, man, that kid even has half a chance.

The school sits on a cliff that looks like the letter *M*. See how it has two points at the top, a left one and a right one? Well, the school is at the tip of the left point, about three hundred feet above the beach. Between the left and right points, the cliff drops straight down to sharp rocks and water. Even if you could swim across the ravine to where the other point juts back out of the sea and scale the cliff, you'd get to the top and find yourself at the far end of White Deer Woods. Let me tell you, because I know it for a fact, no new kid would survive in there for more than an hour.

But the new kid is heading to the left of the left tip of the *M*. *That* side slopes gently down to the water. There's a zigzag path that leads to the beach. You're wondering what happens once he hits the sand, right? Well, there's only one way to go—left, along the water's edge to Fort Casey. And Fort Casey is just what it sounds like—an old military fort. There are tons of barracks and guns and tunnels built into the cliff. It's a big park now. All the new kid will have to do is walk into any one of the fifty tunnels and just sit tight. If he doesn't mind killing time in the dark, chances are good he'll be able to hide from everyone.

Well, at least until the grown-ups find some flashlights and get a search going. Then it's all over for him. He'll meet his fate here like the rest of us. But until then, the race is on.

The girls, whose bathroom is on the other side of the building, must have heard the commotion. They all come out onto the grass to watch.

The kid is running like he's never heard of Consequences.

"Go, kid, go! Go, kid, go!" everyone starts chanting.

I don't say it out loud along with them, but I'm thinking it so hard it's like I'm praying for him.

Then, right before the new kid hits the zigzag path, Mr. Tuffman runs out the side door that leads from the gym.

He's hauling toward that new kid like a Bugatti Veyron (the fastest street-legal car in the world, if you didn't know). Mr. Tuffman was in the Olympics. Three times. He didn't break any records, and it was a long time ago.

But still.

He was in the Olympics. Three times.

We all groan. Jack says a bad word. I set Sparrow down. My back is killing me.

Here they come. Consequences, kid. Nobody wants to find out about them from Tuffman. Mean Jack says Tuffman lost his last coaching job because kids kept disappearing during the 5K runs. I always wonder. When they say "disappear," do they mean the kids got lost but showed up at school later? Or do they mean disappear like never seen again?

I can't look away. It's all over for the new kid.

But then it's not.

"What the—?" Jack says first.

We all look. The kid's legs have started moving so fast that they're a blur. They look like the spokes on a bicycle wheel. He's flying, practically, and he's halfway down the path. Everyone's yelling again.

"Go, kid, go!" the chant starts up again. My skin gets little bumps, and we're all pumping our fists and jumping for him.

But I know Tuffman. And I can tell by the way he's running with his back perfectly straight that he has a lot more juice in him. See, now he's just chugging along. It hurts because of some old spinal injury, but he can go a lot faster. The pain just makes him meaner once he gets you.

And once they're both on the sand, he'll catch the new kid in under a minute.

In fact, just now, I notice Tuffman lean forward from the waist. Oh yeah. He's putting on the speed. I'm gonna hate this part.

Then the back of my neck tingles. The hair on my head stands straight up. Something is about to happen—a magic kind of something that only happens in White Deer Woods. Not hocus-pocus magic with witchy-poo hats and green fizzy drinks, all right? We're not talking werewolves and vampires, either. When it happens it makes you notice things that must have been there all the time. And once it's happened to you, you can never stop noticing.

Tuffman's sprinting. New kid's flying, or just about.

From nowhere a crow darts down and zips right in front of Tuffman.

Right. In. Front.

I see, plain as day, one of its wings slap up and down against Tuffman's face. Slap slap. That was no accident. Crows don't sucker punch Olympic athletes. I move my eyes a little to the left, then a little to the right. Nobody else noticed. A crow just homed in on the gym teacher like a heat-seeking missile and nobody noticed. It wheels around and taps Tuffman's neck with its beak.

Tuffman goes down. Splat, face in the dirt. A huge cheer goes up from the boys in the bathroom. Tuffman's toupee soars through the air and ends up sitting on a round little huckleberry bush. The crow with the attitude swoops down and takes a peck or two at it. Okay, *everyone* notices that.

We all hoot, we're laughing so hard. Some boys are on the floor, bent over, so happy it hurts. Tuffman has made every one of us puke, blush, or run out of gym with a bellyful of sad.

"Who's the punk *now*?" Mean Jack keeps saying.

It's still happening.

From the corner of my eye I see a dark cloud outside the windows across the room. At the far end of the circle driveway a bunch of crows—a "murder" is what you call a group of them—flap up from the old oak tree, clapping their wings.

I watch the crows swarm. I've got what's called "qualms." It means I'm worried about what just happened and what's coming next. Not because Tuffman's eating dirt. I *should* have qualms about that. We're all gonna pay in a big way once he stands up, spits a mud loogie, and starts picking the bird lice out of his toupee.

No, if I've got qualms, it's because those crows and the way they're acting remind me of White Deer Woods magic. Woods magic belongs in the woods. Not in the real world. I don't want my two worlds running into each other, even if it means seeing crusty-shorts Tuffman get some feathers stuck in his teeth.

The new kid jumps from the path onto the driftwood pile. The sky is filled with long low slices of white clouds. A skeleton sky is what I call it.

The crows circle above him, muttering and tumbling on the wind.

Oh, I've got qualms all right.

In the bathroom the boys keep cheering. But I feel very still inside. Scared, but excited, too. For the first time since I found the magic in White Deer Woods, I feel the power of it here at school, in the beat of the black wings against the bone-shaped clouds.

What if everyone found out about the woods magic?

What if everyone found out the truth about me?

I watch the grown-ups below. Not one of them notices the crows.

Then the new kid looks up and raises a fist like he knows we're up here. We all shake our fists back at him and yank the windows up so we're sure he can hear us.

"Go, kid, go!" The chant booms out across the driveway and over the field and down the zigzag path. I'm part of it. This time I'm yelling too.

It's happening.

Maybe the woods magic is everywhere all the time. Maybe it'd be good if everyone knew. Maybe everyone would like me more if they knew.

The grown-ups look up at us now. But we don't stop yelling, even when we see the dean shove his hands in his pockets and start to walk back to the main entrance. He thinks he's gonna come up here and shut us up, but *nothing* will.

Now the new kid stretches both arms above his head and laces his fingers together like a champ taking in the applause from his fans.

And that's when the security guard from Fort Casey rushes at him from behind and tackles him.

We all stop cheering. The new kid is face down in the sand. I know what my dad would say about that. I can hear his voice in my head still. The new kid made the fatal error of celebrating victory before it was his.

The dean must have phoned the Fort Casey Visitors' Center and asked them to send one of their guards in our direction.

Jack swears and points to the path. Tuffman is walking the rest of the way down to the beach, holding his hair in one hand and wiping the blood from his nose with the other. He picks the kid out of the sand and starts marching him up the path back to the school.

Even from here we can see that the kid is crying. Not just a few tears either. He's bawling his eyes out, bent over at the middle. He's sobbing, sniveling, blubbering, driveling. Halfway up, Tuffman stops, squats down, and shakes a finger in his face.

A shiver goes through the room, up and down every spine.

I don't want to go to PE today.

I look up, but the crows have gone back to the woods. The woods magic has left the real world.

It's over.

"Loser," Mean Jack says. Then he remembers his mobster act. *"Mortadella,"* he sneers in his thug voice.

Pretty soon, all the boys who had been cheering the new kid on are calling him a jerk and a poser, a show-off, and, worst of all . . .

"What a crybaby," says Little John.

Little John is one to talk. He cries when a crayon breaks. I've seen every boy in this room cry, and me too, and not just in PE when Tuffman "accidentally" sends the baseball smack into your front teeth.

But I've never seen one of them outrun Tuffman the way that kid just did.

"Shut up," I say.

The room goes totally silent. Not a boy moves. I guess you could say that I'm not a big talker. In fact, I don't think I've said a word to anybody in a month or more.

"Shut up," I repeat. "If I hear even one of you make fun of the new kid for crying, you'll be crying yourself. I guarantee it."

I pat Sparrow on the head and walk out of the bathroom, slamming the door behind me.

In the main hallway on the second floor I cross paths with the dean. He's breathing pretty hard.

"They got him," I say.

The dean stops dead in his tracks and just stares at me. Then he smiles. He wipes a trickle of sweat from the side of his face and leans toward me.

"Thank you, Raul. Thank you for informing me." He talks real quiet, the way you do when you're trying to get a rabbit to come out of the blackberry bush and eat the lettuce in your hand.

I keep walking toward my room. I'm glad me talking makes him so happy, but I'm not gonna do it again just because I like him. Talking is useless. One minute everyone says they love you and the next minute they forget all about you. Nobody listens, and everybody lies.

The only truth is in the woods, and nobody will believe it anyway. Look how they can stand under a sky full of crows on a mission and not even notice.

After a second I hear the dean panting behind me, trying to catch up. *Huff, huff, huff.* The dean needs to take a few laps with Tuffman, if you know what I mean.

"Raul," he says. He sounds like he's had an idea. "I'd like you to take the new boy under your wing. I think you may have a lot in common. Will you help him settle in?" The dean's eyes bug out even when he's not excited about something, but when he is, they look like two big marbles.

I know what he's thinking. He doesn't think I'm gonna help the new kid. He thinks the new kid is gonna help me.

But I nod, mainly so that he'll stop looking at me like that.

"Wonderful!" he says with a huge smile.

He doesn't stop. Now his eyes are the size of alien moons. It's freaking me out. What if they pop?

I'm about to open the fire door to the boys' wing when I hear Dean Swift say something that makes *my* eyes pop. I have pretty good hearing. Once, after she took the headphones off me and stopped fiddling with the dials, the nurse told me she thought I could hear sounds from a mile away. She kind of whispered that like it scared her. But I heard her.

So I can hear the Dean even though he's halfway down the hall. Now, usually when Dean Swift is talking to himself, it's about the refraction of light or bioluminescent fungi or mapping the human genome. So I don't listen too closely because no matter how well I hear it, I don't understand it.

"I wonder. Birds of a feather flock together," Dean Swift is saying to himself.

That gets my attention. Didn't he say I could take the new boy *under my wing*? Why's he talking about birds again?

Did he notice the crows? The thought paralyzes me.

"They will be the best of friends. There is strong evidence that the new one has secrets too." Dean Swift's key turns in the lock.

I push through the fire doors and walk down the hall to my room, chewing on his words like a dog with a bone. I wonder about the new kid's secrets.

Did he say "too"? Does that mean Dean Swift knows what the woods magic does to me?

And if he does, why isn't he afraid of me?

And if he's not afraid of me, could he help me?

Chapter 2

HERE'S WHERE YOU FIND OUT ABOUT THE BONE IN THE BLACKOUT TUNNEL

I remember how it felt when I was the new kid here. I felt like the only one of my kind, and all around me were the other kids in their groups like herds of wildebeests and prides of lions and crashes of rhinos and unkindnesses of ravens and leaps of leopards and wrecks of sea hawks. Remembering makes it hard to breathe, like huge hairy hands have grabbed my heart and lungs and squeezed. (Not *werewolf* hands, if that's what you're thinking, because I'm too old to believe in monsters.)

I sit on my bed and wait until the big hairy paws let me breathe again. On my nightstand is a headband my mom used to wear in her hair. I pick it up and hold it to my face for a second. It doesn't smell like her anymore, but that's okay because I know I'm the one who sniffed the scent away.

The new kid is somewhere in the building. He's probably stopped bawling by now, but I bet he's got a big hard lump in his throat. I bet he feels lost. I'm still the only one of my kind here. But I don't feel lost anymore.

If I *was* gonna show the new kid around, I'd tell him how easy it is to figure out where everything is. *See,* I could say to him, *from the outside the building looks like a castle with turrets and windows and fancy stone carvings. It* looks *like the kind of place where you'll get lost. But don't let the outside fool you. The outside of anything almost never tells you what's inside. The building's a rectangle with a wing at each end. Ignore the wings on the third floor because that's where the girls are. Ignore the turrets because they're full of stuff nobody uses anymore, and the doors to them are always locked. Classrooms are on the main hallways of each floor, and if you can't find one then you just end up missing twenty minutes of listening to the teacher blab, and is that really so bad?*

Here's all you need to know. First floor, dining hall. Got it? Okay. Second floor, boys' rooms in the north wing and boys' bathroom in the south wing.

Eat, sleep, shower—what else is there to do?

And if you forget to shower a few days or weeks, you're a boy, so it's only expected.

And then, if I liked the look of him, I'd tell him the truth. *The woods are all that matter, kid.* That's what I'd say. I wouldn't mention woods magic. I wouldn't tell him that the woods are alive with secrets. I wouldn't tell him that you'll find everything you've ever lost and everything that has ever lost you in them.

I'd just point him in the right direction.

~~~

My stomach informs me that food would be welcome. *Now*. My dad says only a fool argues with his vital organs.

On my way to the dining hall I hear the sound of breaking glass coming from the animal care room. *Sparrow.* If you hear something breaking in this place, nine out of ten times, Sparrow is involved. Then I hear screams. If you hear someone screaming in this place, ten out of ten times, Mean Jack is involved.

I trot over and look through the window set into the top half of the door.

Mean Jack is chasing Sparrow around the room with the business end of a pencil. Barking, squeaking, flapping, hissing—the animals are going wild. As I put my hand on the doorknob to go in and rescue him, Sparrow jumps up on a high table where the aquarium sits, with its fifty tropical fish.

"Do ya feel lucky?" Mean Jack snarls, jabbing the pencil at Sparrow's feet. "Well, do ya, punk?"

Sparrow jumps. Mean Jack misses. Water sloshes out of the top of the tank. A red swordtail goes over the rim, flops on the table, and hits the floor. Gandalf the cat swallows and then stretches. Forty-nine fish.

Sparrow jumps again, and this time he grabs on to the pipe that runs along the ceiling.

Mr. Baggins the hamster is running in his wheel, tossing little looks over his shoulder at me. *Get in here,*
~~~

man, he's saying. *Get in here and shut this crazy kid down.*

I like to let Sparrow fight his own fights sometimes. I'll go in when he needs me.

Then, as Sparrow's swinging along the ceiling, one of his feet catches the latch on Gollum's cage. Snake loose. His other foot rams Mean Jack in the nose, and the mobster takes the mouse tank to the floor with him. Ten little mice scamper toward freedom . . . and the fangs of Gollum.

I predict a bloodbath.

I'm turning the doorknob, when I smell cinnamon and honey. *Mary Anne.* She pushes me aside and opens the door.

"Put down the pencil, Jack. That's a one-way ticket to juvie," she says.

Mean Jack drops the pencil and puts his hands up. Sparrow lands on the high table with the aquarium. A rainbow fish flops over the rim and into Gandalf's mouth. Forty-eight.

Mary Anne's the same age as me and Mean Jack, but she has amazing power. I've never heard her say, "I'm telling." She doesn't need a teacher.

She pulls me into the room, shuts the door, and drops the blind over the window so that nobody can see in.

"Get to work," she says.

I give her the *What, me?* look, and she says, "You too. Sometimes you must choose to observe and sometimes you must choose to act. *You* made the wrong choice."

My stomach is growling, but I start sweeping sawdust and grabbing mice. I give Mean Jack a little shove every time I come near him. Mean Jack doesn't mess with me. Nobody does.

Then Bobo the German Shepherd growls, low in her throat.

Tuffman opens the door. We all freeze.

He's combed his toupee out pretty good, but there's still one spot in the back that looks a little mangled.

I don't think I'll point that out to him, though.

Mary Anne looks at each of us and shakes her head slightly. *Do not be a rat.* We don't need the warning. At One of Our Kind Boarding School we don't tattle. We don't point fingers. We. Don't. Rat. It's the single most important rule. Dean Swift calls it solidarity. Mean Jack punches his palm with his fist and calls it Stitches for Snitches. I call it keeping my mouth shut, and for me it's pretty much SOP (standard operating procedure).

"Got a problem?" Tuffman asks.

"No problem," Sparrow squeaks. "I'm cleaning the cages since it's my week for pet care, and my friends are helping."

Good cover, I think. It's actually Mean Jack's week for pet care, and he was obviously trying to force Sparrow, at pencil point, to do the work for him. If he'd just turn that graphite tip toward a piece of paper instead of some kid's eyeball, Mean Jack could write a book on it: *A Practical Guide to Extortion for Kids.*

"No problemo, you say? Well, you lost one, pip-squeak." Tuffman pulls a mouse from his pocket and dangles it by the tail.

Sparrow grabs the mouse. He strokes its head and says softly, "You gonna be okay now, little guy."

"You didn't say 'thank you,' short stuff," says Tuffman.

"Fank you, Mr. Tuffman," Sparrow says with big eyes.

"No *fanks* to you, that's what Mr. Mousie says."

Sparrow puts the mouse back in its cage.

"I'm still talking to you, so look at me. Look at me when I'm talking to you," Tuffman says.

Sparrow's lower lip starts to wiggle.

"When you clean these cages, it's your duty to protect these animals. Do you understand the word 'duty'? Do you? Answer me."

Sparrow can't say a word. He's shaking, and I want to grab Tuffman by the throat and make him shake too.

If I met him one weekend in White Deer Woods—when the woods magic was happening to me—I could scare him pretty good. He wouldn't even know it was me.

The idea of me pouncing on him in the woods must have made me smile a little.

"You hear something funny, weirdo?" he asks me.

His eyes paralyze me.

"Nothing about this is funny. I don't like to see

animals in cages. It ain't natural. But you kids want your pets. You make an animal helpless, then you darn well better help it. You turned it into a baby. You're its parents now."

The room is so quiet.

"I can see why a kid like you wouldn't understand." His voice gets meaner.

My face burns.

"How could you understand how parents are supposed to act? What kind of mother walks out on her kid? And your dad sticking around was hardly better. I read your file." He digs a finger in his ear. "Parental neglect. That's what the state social worker called it. It says she found you eating on the floor like a dog. It says you didn't know what soap was."

I'm not going to cry. That's all I can think. *I'm not going to cry in front of Mary Anne.* I pay attention to my mouth. As long as you keep your mouth straight, nobody can tell you're sad.

"Is your old man still forgetting to come get you on weekends?"

"His dad comes." Sparrow sticks up for me.

From the corner of my eye I see Mean Jack yank Sparrow back. "Let it go," Mean Jack says in a low voice.

"That was a real pain for the dean, you know? All the other parents remember to get their kids on the weekends. Except your dad. How can a father *abandon* his son? That's what the dean would say."

It's funny. Words are air and spit. But they can hit you harder than any fist or belt or slap. They leave bruises in your belly and on your heart and in your mind that will never turn yellow and purple and fade. That will ache every time you remember them.

And he's lying about the dean. I know he is.

"What kind of kid can parents like that make? You tell me, Raul. What kind of kid did your mom make?"

He's not going to stop until I talk or cry. My mouth slips.

"We understand," Mary Anne says. She steps in front of Tuffman so that me and Sparrow end up behind her. She looks him straight in the eye. "I know you'll agree that we ought to finish our task here. If we were all to miss breakfast, I'm sure Dean Swift would expect a faithful account of every deed and every *word*."

Tuffman's eye twitches. Mary Anne's playing hardball. Dean Swift wouldn't like it if he knew someone was telling stories about my parents like that. Especially since they're true.

Tuffman opens the door to leave and then turns back.

"Sparrow," he says, "do you know what a loser is? A loser is someone who loses things. Things like games, or races, or mice. Try harder. Try harder not to be such a loser."

The door slams. The room moves again. Mr. Baggins's wheel squeaks. Gandalf stretches.

Mean Jack looks from me to Sparrow. "Forget about it, you two. The guy's a schmuck, don't know his head from his—"

The door opens again and slams shut. Before any of us can stop him, Sparrow has flown out of the room, sobbing.

Tuffman made Sparrow cry.

All my sad turns to mad. I must look like I'm about to charge after Tuffman and drop him. Mary Anne grabs my arm and pulls it down, like it's a leash on a lunging dog.

"Whatever you do will just make it worse," she says.

She keeps her hand on my arm, and I know she's trying to say she feels bad about what Tuffman said to me. The tears jump from my throat to my eyes.

"Yo. Forget about the jockstrap. He's just trying to get under your skin," Mean Jack says. "We got bigger fish to fry here. Has anyone seen the snake?"

Mary Anne's face goes white.

Mean Jack takes charge. "Me and Mary'll finish up spring cleaning here. Raul, you go collar Sparrow. Last thing we need is this story getting back to the authorities."

Last thing *you* need, you mean. But it's hard to hate a kid who just saved you from bawling in front of your crush. And he's right. Forget about Tuffman. It's my fault anyway. I let him get under my skin. I let him see what I was thinking. I have to be careful. Words aren't the only thing that can give my secrets away.

"Come on, Bobo," I say.

She stands up and stretches. I hear her joints crack. As we head out the door, she puts her nose in my hand. *Thank you,* she's saying. You always know what a dog really means. Did you ever think of that? A dog *can't* lie.

There's a drawer in my mind where I put things I don't like. I shove everything Tuffman just said in it.

I know where Sparrow is, and I'm not gonna let him sit there and cry all alone in the dark.

When Sparrow feels bad he runs to Fort Casey. He's stealthy. Nobody but me ever sees him go. He dashes across the big field in the middle of the fort and heads for a bunker built into the hillside. The Blackout Tunnel is the darkest, blackest, scariest place you can imagine. If by some freak occurrence a prehistoric man-eating, bone-gnawing dinosaur survived the asteroid, then *that's* where it'd be living. Put your hand in front of your face. Now bring it so close that it's almost touching your nose but isn't. If you were in the Blackout Tunnel, you wouldn't be able to see that hand.

I head out the front door. I take the path the new kid took, but nobody is going to call security on me because

1) I'm not what they call a "flight risk"—meaning I've never tried to run away—and 2) Dean Swift believes in what he calls "personal liberty"—which as far as I can tell is a fancy way of saying that kids should play outside a lot and grown-ups shouldn't bug them much. Over the front door he had me carve a sign that says *Silva Curat!* which is Latin for *The forest heals!*

I'm warning you. Do *not* ask him about the forest and its wondrous ability to Heal children. His eyes will pop up round as boiled egg yolks, and he'll talk until your ears bleed.

I agree with him, though. Only, I would've carved something different. I would've carved *The forest has secrets.* I should write Mary Anne a note and ask how to say that in Latin. But then she'd want to know the secrets.

I look around, remembering the feeling I had earlier this morning when the crows gathered. It's gone but I know it's near. Today's Thursday. Woods magic happens Friday at sunset. Everyone likes the weekend. But I like it most of all.

Bobo lopes up ahead. The path drops off and she jumps down onto the driftwood pile. Her hind legs give way and I wince for her. She forgets how old she is. But a second later she's at the water's edge, barking at the waves.

A gleam down near Bobo catches my eye. It's black and shiny. As I get closer I see it's a helmet. It must have gotten knocked off the kid's head when he got tackled.

I pick it up. Bobo sniffs it. Her eyes ask, *Good to eat?* I scratch her ears. *You'll break every one of your last five teeth on it, dog.*

I set the helmet on a driftwood log so I remember to grab it on the way back.

Sparrow doesn't want to come out of the Blackout Tunnel.

"Come on!" I yell. Even if I didn't have Bobo, I wouldn't go in there. It reeks. My nose sniffs. I don't want to but I do, because that's how my nose works. I smell wet cat, reptile cage, park toilet, and something else—something familiar. After a few more sniffs I smile.

"Get out already, Sparrow," I yell. "It smells like Tuffman's breath in there!"

Sparrow's sputter of a laugh echoes off the walls and pings toward me like a bouncy ball. That's all it takes with Sparrow. Make him laugh and his worries are over.

He races out, drops to his knees. and throws his arms around Bobo. She licks his face like it's the most important thing she'll do all day long.

"What took you so long?" he asks.

All the way back to the school he won't stop talking. It turns out it wasn't just my joke that got him to come out. He'd also found an awesome bone.

"Is it human?" he asks me for the fiftieth time as we head down from the fort to the beach. "I fink it's someone's pinkie finger bone. Maybe the monster ate all of someone but was too full for the pinkie. This is all that's left. Poor guy. In heaven with no pinkie." He looks at me and grins. "It's a monster that only eats PE teachers."

We could use a monster like that around here.

I think it's the jawbone of a raccoon that a coyote must have dragged in there, but I let him ramble on and on about the very exclusive diet of his monster.

Why burst his bubble? I've seen some things in White Deer Woods that nobody would believe.

In fact, *I* am something that nobody would believe.

I shake that thought away. It's best to keep my worlds separate, even in my head. Look what happened with Tuffman. Just thinking about woods magic can get me in trouble.

On the way up the zigzag path Sparrow wears the new kid's helmet. He's so small, it covers his head and rests on his shoulders.

"I'm Darth Vader," he says. He holds the bone like a lightsaber and waves it in front of me. "Raul," he says in a gravelly voice. "I am your father."

I smile but I must look sad, because he takes the helmet off.

"You wanna hold the bone?" he asks after a second.

I nod. Of course I wanna hold the bone.

Chapter 3

WHERE YOU DISCOVER PART OF THE FIRST SECRET AND LEARN ABOUT LOVE

After I drop Sparrow off at the dean's office to find out about the bone, I look at my watch. Twenty minutes left before the dining hall stops serving hot food.

But to get to the dining hall you have to walk by the wood shop. Every day I do the same thing. I take one step into the wood shop, just to breathe in the smell of sawdust, and I'm hooked. I get busy carving or sanding, and before I know it an hour has slipped by.

Dean Swift told me once about the scientific method.

"Everything you need to know is in front of you, Raul," he said. "You have to figure out the design. When a scientist wants to come up with a theory and prove it, he reads and wonders and observes. The truth is there all along, sitting hidden in the facts."

It's the same with a carving. The carving is in the wood, waiting for my knife to free it.

The fishing pole I'm making for Sparrow is almost done. This is my favorite part, where I take the fine-grain sandpaper and rub the birch wood until it's soft as sugar.

My mom's hands felt that way when she would rub my back before I fell asleep. I miss her. It makes me feel bad to say that. I bet it makes you feel bad to read it. I don't want my story to make anyone sad.

So I'll tell you part of my secret: I miss her a whole lot less now than when I first got here.

Tuffman can talk all he likes. They all can. The words burn, but they're smoke, not fire—just the ashes of the truth, just what's left of it.

The truth about my mom is beyond words.

I finish sanding Sparrow's new pole. It's a beauty, way better than the last one I made for him. He broke the last one using it as a drumstick.

Do you want to know what the other drumstick was?

A lightbulb.

Did I mention I was hungry? I am ravenous, famished, voracious. *Give me food, woman,* I feel like yelling, except the cook is Patsy and she is very nice.

"Hey, Raul," she says as I grab my breakfast tray, "will you give me a smile if I give you this?" That's Cook Patsy's favorite joke.

Usually, though, it's more like "Hey, Raul, will you give me a smile if I give you a bowl Little John didn't sneeze into?" Or "Hey, Raul, will you give me a smile if I give you a spoon the chemistry teacher didn't use to mix sulfuric acid?"

Of course I always give her a smile, but today I give her a word, too. Because today she hands me a mini flashlight she found in the bottom of a box of my favorite cereal.

"Thanks!" I say, because I was not raised by wolves. That means I have good manners.

"For your nighttime, after-Lights-Out, reading emergencies," she says.

I click it on and off. It's red. Very small but powerful. And LED so the bulb will never die. I wonder how she knows about my midnight reading emergencies.

I smile at her again and slip the flashlight into my pocket. Sometimes I think Cook Patsy is looking out for me a little, the way I look out for Sparrow. It makes my throat tight, like I might cry, except it would be stupid to cry because someone is *nice* to you, wouldn't it?

Dean Swift is showing the new kid and his mom around the dining hall.

"Now," he says in the voice he uses for the parents, "boys and girls are together during mealtimes and some of our advanced classes. Our youngest residents, the Cubs, sit closest to the food service area. The older girls—the Wolverines—sit at the round tables, and the older boys—the Pack—sit at the picnic tables."

The new kid stares at the floor, driving the toe of his shoe into a crack in the linoleum. Every time I hear him sniff up his tears, I look over to make sure Mean Jack and his wake of buzzards keep their yaps shut.

Mean Jack catches my eye once and that's all it takes for him to get the message. I was grateful to Jack for a split second after Tuffman yelled at me. But now everything's back to normal. In my age group there's the boys in the Pack and then there's me.

I walk to my usual stool at the counter. The counter is at the far end of the cafeteria, set against a window that takes up the entire wall. I sit with my back to the room, looking out at Admiralty Inlet. All I can see is sky and water, and today they are the same color.

Dean Swift, Pretty Lady, and the new kid come over and stand behind me.

My stomach feels hollow. Will Dean Swift introduce me? I wish he hadn't said anything about me helping. It's not really doing the guy a favor, is it? Here, new kid, here's the boy who's been here the longest and who fits in the least. Why don't we have him show you around?

In the end the kid will join the Pack. They'll tease him. Mean Jack'll take a little of his allowance every week and all of his brownie on Mondays. But if he puts up with it and doesn't snitch, then Mean Jack'll call him a stand-up guy and that'll be that. Once you're in with the Pack, you're never out.

The stool next to me scrapes, and Mary Anne sits

down. Now my stomach feels like a trampoline with thirty kangaroos on it.

Mary Anne's a shifter, that's what I call her. Not in the way I am, though. She shifts between groups of people. *Everyone* listens to her. *Everyone* likes her.

Everyone. Including me. Most of all.

She has long hair that hangs in curls that look like the tops of small waves right before they break on the sand. If I carved a mermaid, I'd make it look like her. *Blech.* Mary Anne makes me as sappy as a pine tree. If it hasn't happened to you yet, it will. One day you'll look up and see someone who makes your heart feel like hot pudding and your mouth feel like the Sahara Desert.

Right now her face is pale. "We didn't find the snake," she says.

Prison break. Gollum at large. Mildly venomous snake on the lam. The words run through my mind, but I don't say any of them. I just nod.

"And who sits here?" I hear the new kid's mom ask.

I look back out the window. Straight ahead. *Please don't introduce me now. Please. Not in front of Mary Anne.*

"Children of all ages sit here; it's a question of temperament."

What he means is that the weirdos sit here. We're the ones who look at the water.

Most mornings it's silver and blue like the moonlight that has just said good-bye to it.

We don't mind being called weirdos. Nobody says it mean, except Tuffman. Everyone calls us that, even Dean Swift, who a second later, says, "*Freedom* from constant adult supervision, the bane of the modern child's existence! *That* is the soul balm we offer these broken winged babes: personal liberty, independence, the wonders of the forest. Because our property extends into White Deer Woods, students can fish and explore as much as they like, which makes even the weirdos here at the counter happy."

The new kid's mom gasps. "The last thing any child needs is to be labeled a *weirdo*," she says. Her voice is so sharp it hurts my ears. "This is precisely the kind of bullying we dealt with in the public schools."

From the corner of my eye I see the new kid shake his head. For a second I hate him. I'd give my teeth—all of them—to hear my mom chew someone out for me.

I hear the dean gulp. I wait for one of his lies. They are always so unbelievable that whoever he's lying to usually feels sorry for him and pretends to believe him. It's what I used to do whenever he'd try to explain to me why my dad wasn't coming to get me for the weekend.

"I didn't say 'weirdos,'" Dean Swift finally says.

I give him points for using a very hurt voice. Nice touch, Dean.

"I said 'Werewolves' because that is what the students who sit here call themselves. They are wandering wonderers and wondering wanderers with a future in the sciences."

Mary Anne covers her giggle with her hand. I don't think it's funny, though. The dean can call me pretty much anything he likes, just not that. I'm no werewolf.

Dean Swift walks toward the back of the dining hall. "I'd like to show you the kitchen, where our residents help with meal preparation."

"Come on, Mom." The new kid turns to follow the dean.

Pretty Lady steps toward the window. She looks like she's about to cry. My mom would have hated leaving me here too.

I don't want this lady to think it's true.

I'm not a werewolf. I've read about them. Werewolves are humans who got cursed. I'm not cursed. They have unibrows, and if you cut their skin you'll see fur, not blood. Two fingertips fit between my eyebrows. I bleed. Werewolves attack people in the woods and eat them. I wouldn't do that. Not even to Tuffman, and not just because he'd taste like old cheese and toe jam. Werewolves run with two feet and one hand and push their other hand back like a tail. That's just awkward.

So I turn around on my stool and shake my head at Pretty Lady. I mouth the words to her, "I am not a werewolf." I am not a monster.

She swallows and walks away fast, pretending like

she's afraid of getting left behind and not afraid of me.

Mary Anne lets out the laugh she's been holding back. "You *petrified* her. She's abandoning her child here and she has the gall to take Dean Swift to task over a *word*." She makes a *humph* sound and lifts an eyebrow. "You sure can make your eyes look scary."

My cheeks feel hot. I don't understand 95 percent of what Mary Anne says on any given day, but I think that was a compliment. *You have scary eyes*—the nicest thing a girl has ever said to me. Pathetic. But I'll take it. Beggars can't be choosers, right? Another one from my dad.

I shift around on my stool so Mary Anne doesn't see me blush.

My spine tingles. Gollum's in here. Don't ask me how I know it, but I know it. Mary Anne would like me even better if I put that snake back in its cage. Word would get to the new kid too. *Yeah,* they'd say, *the kid over there with the shaggy hair. He caught a loose snake and saved the day.* I scan the dining room.

Sparrow is at the Cubs' table. When he catches my eye, he lifts something up in the air.

"Raul!" he shouts across the room. "Dean Swift says I can keep the bone!"

I give him a thumbs-up.

Mary Anne smiles. I feel proud. I'm glad she can see that the little kids like me, at least.

"Tell them," Sparrow hollers. He waggles his hand at the boys sitting with him. "They don't believe me. Tell them it's a monster that eats PE teachers. Tell them how all I found was some tennis shoes and a whistle," he says. "And a bone."

"A *human* bone?" Little John tilts his head and looks from me to Sparrow.

Sparrows nods solemnly but says, "No. Dean Swift says it was a dog bone."

Sparrow doesn't lie. He embellishes. "And, it is very stinky in that tunnel. Like the cat box at my granma's house." He crinkles his nose. "Ask Raul. He was there. He said it smells like Mr. Tuffman's breath."

The Cubs love it. They laugh and laugh.

Little John points at me. "You should talk more. You're funny."

Mary Anne has been following the whole crazy conversation. "Yeah," she says. "You *should* talk more."

I'm so happy, I can't even smile. Mary Anne wants more words from me. *Mary Anne.*

But then I freeze. I feel someone looking at me. And I know who it is before I even see him. When I check, he's staring at me. Mr. Tuffman.

Maybe he didn't hear?

His jaw moves. His eyes are small. He didn't miss a word. And Mr. Tuffman doesn't want any more of them.

He starts walking toward me. Silence ripples across the room as everyone realizes that Mr. Tuffman heard what Sparrow said I said.

I'm so scared I forget how to breathe. Coming from a kid who never talks, my ideas are getting me in trouble a lot today.

At just that moment Dean Swift pushes open the swinging doors that lead from the kitchen. New kid and Pretty Lady are close behind.

I glance over at Tuffman. His eyes get even smaller, but he stops dead in his tracks.

"Ah. Yes. This is our PE teacher," Dean Swift says.

The new kid looks left and right and everywhere but at Tuffman.

But Pretty Lady puts her hand out to shake Mr. Tuffman's. "I'm so sorry about earlier," she says. "I hope you didn't get hurt when you fell." She stares at his hair the whole time she's talking.

Tuffman's neck gets red, and then it spreads up his face in blotches.

I almost feel bad for him. Nobody wants a pretty lady to have seen his hair sitting on a huckleberry bush without his head in it.

"Mr. Tuffman was in the Olympics," Dean Swift says. "It still amazes me that an athlete of his caliber would forsake fame and fortune to join us here at the corner of nowhere and never-never land."

Dean Swift is starstruck. When he looks at Mr. Tuffman, all he sees is the Olympian.

Mr. Tuffman stands taller. His chest puffs out. He holds on to Pretty Lady's hand and smiles down at her. But she keeps squinting at his mangled toupee. Her mouth drops open and her eyes get bigger.

Is she really that rude?

My eyes follow hers. What I see is awful. I'm so surprised, I can't remember the word, so I point. Mr. Tuffman sees me. He thinks I'm pointing at his toupee. He shifts like he's about to pounce on me. He's going to kill me and he doesn't care who sees it.

"Snake!" Sparrow shouts.

That's the word I was looking for.

Everyone looks up and screams.

Gollum dangles from one of the hanging lights, stretching down toward Tuffman's head.

Tuffman screeches. The sound is so sharp my knees buckle. My skin pricks. Woods magic. It starts to happen again.

Gollum lands on his shoulder and skitters to the floor. She's a long black streak, but Tuffman's quick. He sprints after Gollum. Everyone stops screaming. Tuffman to the rescue.

Then, at the exact same moment, we all notice the hunting knife in Tuffman's hand. It's huge. Everyone starts screaming again.

"No," Dean Swift shouts. "Don't kill her! She's not that venomous."

Tuffman doesn't hear. Gollum darts under chairs and tables, racing for the door.

"Don't kill her!" Sparrow shouts. "She's our *baby*, remember?"

The door to the dining hall bangs open. The reading teacher, Ms. Tern, walks in with her head down and an open book in her hand. Gale-force winds couldn't make that lady pull her head out of a book. Gollum heads in her direction. Tuffman is in pursuit.

"Watch out, Nicolette!" Dean Swift yells.

Ms. Tern looks up just as Gollum slides past her foot into the hallway and freedom, just as Mr. Tuffman lunges and raises the knife.

We all shout. I like Ms. Tern and her mouse-colored hair and her soap-bubble yells and her reading and walking. I don't want to see her get hurt. But I can't look away.

Ms. Tern drops her book. Her left hand flies into the air and catches Mr. Tuffman's right arm by the wrist. The knife clatters onto the floor. What a grip!

With her other hand she punches him in the gut so hard that he grunts and falls to his knees.

The room is so quiet I hear Gollum slither down a vent in the hallway. Tuffman gets back on his feet. He stands there, a little bent at the waist, rubbing his wrist, staring at Ms. Tern.

Ms. Tern shoves her glasses up higher on her nose. "Crikey. Are you very hurt?" she asks. Her British accent makes each word trip to the next.

She looks out at all of us and explains sadly, "I only just finished reading a self-defense manual. I'm afraid I took rather careful notes."

She picks up her book and walks toward the kitchen, her nose down, her fingers flipping pages as she looks for her lost place.

And then, as she walks by me, it happens. Ms. Tern smiles.

I don't think it's the book. I can see the title. *Fifty Unsolved Crimes Against Endangered Species.* Not exactly the kind of reading that's gonna crack you up.

Ms. Tern is smiling because she knocked Tuffman to his knees.

The bell rings for class. I bend down to grab my backpack. I glance to see if anyone's looking at me.

Then I smile too.

Chapter 4

WHERE RAUL LEARNS THE WRONG WAY TO WRESTLE

Nobody can stop talking about Ms. Tern and Mr. Tuffman. Has he been packing a six-inch blade all along? Can you really get a death grip and a right hook out of a how-to book? Who knew her first name was Nicolette?

Then, as we're all heading to class, Little John finds some gross stuff on the bathroom floor under the ceiling fan. He comes running out in the hall saying that Gollum got herself killed.

Sparrow starts to sob. "It's all your fault!" he screams at Mean Jack. "Your! Fault!"

"I didn't want that snake to get whacked," Mean Jack says, and he looks sad, like he means it.

"Look," Mary Anne whispers in my ear. "Even mobsters experience remorse."

I smile like a fool.

Mary Anne and the girls gather in the hall while the boys pile into the bathroom. We make a circle around the mess on the floor. It doesn't look like dead snake to me. I'm not going to write what I think it is because I don't want this book to be banned.

I touch Sparrow's arm and shake my head.

It's not enough. The tears stream down. I hug him.

"It's not her," I whisper. "I promise."

Here's the thing. When you don't talk much, sometimes your words really matter. Sparrow wipes the backs of his hands over his eyes.

"Little John," he says in a scolding voice, "that does *not* smell like snake guts."

Everyone backs away slowly.

Whack. Another one down. It's Whack-A-Mole at school today. One creepy smiling critter of a problem after another.

But my feet have little puffs of air under them. Mary Anne noticed me. She likes my scary eyes. She laughed at my joke. She wants me to talk.

I'm a fool for Mary Anne. I grin like one until I get to my first class.

My first class is PE, so I stop grinning pretty quick. This could be bad. Mr. Tuffman and I have already spent a lot of time together this morning. And he did not enjoy my company.

The new kid is sitting on the bottom bench of the bleachers. He has a brochure about the school in his hand. The dean must have dumped him here while his mom fills out paperwork.

I gotta question the Dean's judgment here. First row seats to the Tuffman Torture Hour are *not* going to make this kid any happier about living here. Just further proof that when it comes to Tuffman, the dean only sees the word "Olympian." Not "soulless psychopath," like the rest of us.

First Tuffman makes us run lines until half the class throws up. There's actually a trough under the bleachers for that.

His bad mood seems worse when he's near me. He runs next to me, calling me a wuss and a wimp. Those are his usual insults, and I don't like it, but it's not personal.

"Sneak," he hisses at me when I touch the half court line.

Sneak? Now *that's* personal. I don't understand it, but I know it's personal.

I look back at the bleachers. I catch the new kid looking away. He must have been watching me and Tuffman.

"You takin' heat from some crumb, Coach?" Mean Jack asks all of a sudden in his big voice.

Tuffman cocks his head. We all stop running and stand there, gasping for breath, grateful for Mean Jack's special skill at distracting teachers.

"You got some serious injuries there on your neck, sir. Want me to settle the score?" Mean Jack punches his fist into his palm.

Tuffman rubs his neck. When he pulls his hand away, I see what Mean Jack saw. Huge puncture wounds barely scabbed over. They look like what would happen if a wolf decided to see how good you'd taste for lunch.

My neck juts forward. I can't look away from those bite marks. I feel weird—like those injuries have something to do with me. I can't explain it. But I feel like I'm involved. Woods magic. I try to push the feeling down. It just gets me in trouble.

I am staring too hard. Tuffman senses it.

"Get a good enough look, weirdo?" he asks.

I stare back at him longer than I should. I don't know why. Maybe it's because of what he said about my mom in front of Mary Anne and Mean Jack. Maybe it's because he made Sparrow cry. Maybe it's because he ran at Gollum with a knife.

Whatever it is, I'm in that kind of mood. The kind of mood where I don't look away.

He turns away first and I get a little surge of energy, like I won some secret game.

Then he pulls down the wrestling mats.

He calls me over. That good feeling goes away.

"Let's see if you can take down an Olympian, Raul." He's circling me, his arms wide and curved like he's holding a huge beach ball. "After my injury they told me I could stay on and coach the Olympic team. Did you know that? Big money, kids, that's what I walked away from. I came here. And you know why? Because it's my mission to teach you how to find your place in this big bad world—how to claim it and how to defend it."

My nose twitches the way it does when I smell a lie. Why would he leave everything for nowhere?

"Crouch, Raul, crouch and circle. I know you've got it in you. Every boy has a predator in him. How fierce is yours?"

Then he lunges at me. All six feet, three inches, two hundred fifty pounds of him. A big gulp of air comes out of my mouth. I think it's my courage escaping.

It's about the time when Tuffman is holding me up in the air to show everyone a wrestling hold called "the fireman's carry" that I begin to wonder if this is how the kids at his old school disappeared.

"I've got my eye on you, Raul," Tuffman breathes into my face as he puts me in a half nelson. "No sneaking around. Got it? You stay out of my territory. It stinks anyway, right?"

"What territory?" Apparently terror makes me talkative. "What sneaking?" I ask.

He twists my arm back. I hear the watching kids gasp. From the corner of my eye I see the new kid stand up and take a step toward me.

Behind me, Jason says in a very thoughtful voice, "I didn't know your elbow could go that direction."

The new kid cringes and sits down.

The pain is terrible. Like someone holding a hot iron to my bone.

"See?" Tuffman calls over his shoulder to the rest of the class. His voice is really upbeat. "Now he can't move, not an inch, or he'll break his own arm. Consequences, kiddos." He tweaks my arm a tiny bit more, and I swear my bone *bends*.

He leans down over me so that only I can hear. "One wrong move, Raul, that's all. Just remember your place. Be the boy you are. You're not powerful enough to challenge me. So don't go trying to change things," he says. "Least of all yourself."

He pushes my face into the mat as he gets up off of me.

"See?" he says to the boys.

I'm splayed out like roadkill. My body feels jumbled, like a box full of puzzle pieces. So does my brain. Everything he says has two meanings. The one he wants everyone to hear and the one just for me. There's a picture here, but right now it's just a pile of pieces.

"All I had to do was stake out my space, my *territory*," he says to the class. "That's all there is to wrestling, kids. That's all there is to life. Mark what's yours. Defend it to the death."

Death? See, now *that* I get. That only means one thing.

I decide to lie on the mat until everyone has left. Especially the new kid. I can't look him in the eye. I wanted to make an impression on him, but this wasn't the one I had in mind.

Finally I hear them open the ball cage. Everyone heads out to the field. I look at the bleachers. I'm alone. I might have a cold. My head is stuffy and my nose feels runny and my eyes are all watery.

Am I about to cry?

I head to my room to change. Why did Tuffman have to do that in front of the new kid? Why didn't he demonstrate that hold on Mean Jack? Mean Jack would find it useful for his future career as a crime boss.

It makes me feel sick. I shouldn't have let Dean Swift and his dumb idea get me all excited. Some of us are born loners.

Tuffman's voice rings in my head. What did he mean when he called me a sneak? That joke I made about his breath smelling like the Blackout Tunnel was disrespectful, not sneaky.

And what does he mean when he says not to change? Does he mean puberty? Do I have facial hair? I rub my chin, but it's smooth.

I'm the same as I was when Tuffman got here. He showed up a year and a half ago, in the fall. It was just about the time my dad stopped coming to get me on the weekends and the woods magic started happening and I decided to stop talking. I was as much a weirdo then as I am now.

Then a scary idea pops up. For a second the puzzle pieces start to make a picture.

I blink at myself in the mirror above my dresser. Does he mean the other way I change?

There is a window next to my mirror. I look out of it. On the far side of the ravine a deer and her fawn nibble on the short grass at the edge of the cliff. The cliff is red and brown and black, and tree roots stick out of it here and there. Every time it rains, chunks of it fall to the beach below, and the colors of the cliff change. The cliff changes every day and nobody notices.

How could Tuffman know my secret? I'm like the cliff. Nobody notices me.

I take a big breath. This calls for the scientific method. I organize the facts in my scientific journal. I use my most scientific handwriting.

Phenomenon (that means unusual event): Tuffman is picking on me and it's personal.

Duration (that means for how long): Targeting began during animal care and increased during PE.

Observations: How was today different than yesterday?

Item 1: Tuffman chased new kid, toupee mashed

Item 2: Tuffman made Sparrow hide in the Blackout Tunnel

Item 3: Tuffman overheard my joke during breakfast

It would make sense if he was trying to get back at me for the crack about his breath. But he didn't mention that. All he talked about was territory and changing and sneaking. I stare at the page for a long time. Then I write down the most rational explanation.

Theory: Tuffman is a jerk.

It doesn't make my arm throb any less or the embarrassed feeling go away, but it does make me smile. Maybe he's just a jerk. Jerks don't have to have good reasons for being jerks, that's what my dad used to say.

Chapter 5

WHERE RAUL MAKES FRIENDS

I decide to wait until the free period after lunch to go up to the new kid's room. After the Trauma With Tuffman I need a little sustenance.

"Pizza cut in triangles," Cook Patsy says when I walk up with my tray.

My favorite. How did she know?

I take two slices.

Then she pulls my tray toward her and puts a little book on it. *Crack Any Code!* it says on the front.

"What are the odds?" she asks. "Two prizes in one day."

"Thank you," I say. I pick it up and flip through it. On every page it tells you how to decipher a different kind of code. This is very useful. I can already see myself showing it to the new kid. An icebreaker, that's what you'd call it.

Cook Patsy holds on to the tray and looks at me for a second.

"I heard Tuffman was pretty harsh on you in gym

this morning. I know you're no snitch, Raul, but can I tell the dean about it? It seems like something he ought to know."

I shake my head. It's strange, but the whole "don't be a rat" rule applies to teachers, too. If a teacher is too mean, then the kids find a way to settle the score without getting the authorities involved. "Poetic justice" is a term we just learned about from Ms. Tern, but we've been doing it here forever. It means the punishment fits the crime. Take the last reading teacher—the one Ms. Tern replaced. He made Mark, the kid who wears the weighted vest, bend over and stand on his fingers in the corner for a whole class period. Yeah. Think about that. Now try it. Really, try it. How do your fingers feel?

Next morning that teacher picked up his coffee mug and couldn't let go of it again. Superglue. It was hard for him to pack up his desk with only one hand, but Mary Anne helped. She gave him lots of suggestions for ways he could make the most of a mug hand. *It'll be great when you stand on the street corner and ask for spare change.* And, *If anyone tries to break into your car while you're sleeping in it, you can just whack him in the side of the head.*

But I'm not the kind of kid who needs a grown-up or anyone else to fix my problems. Grown-ups are the ones who cause all the problems anyway, so I don't know why they think they're so great at teaching kids how to solve them.

Cook Patsy is watching me. She's still holding one side of my tray so I can't leave. "Well," she says, "if he bugs you again, you come to me. I can take care of Tuffman pretty quick for you." She lets go of my tray and flexes her arms down low, like a wrestler on TV before a match.

I gulp. Cook Patsy is what Mean Jack calls "ripped." She winks and picks up her spatula.

"I got your back," she says as I head to the counter.

The last of the bad feeling starts to go away, but for some reason my eyes sting like I'm going to cry.

The view from the stool is gray. A seagull the color of rain and cloud flies by and looks in at me, its beak wide open like it thinks I'm gonna toss in my last piece of pepperoni. Dream on, bird.

I wonder if the new kid ate lunch alone in his room.

Birds of a feather flock together. That means when you have something in common with someone, it's easier to make friends. We've got one thing in common, at least. We both got pummeled by Tuffman today.

And another thing—we've both got problems.

My problem is that my mom disappeared one day when I was five. My dad couldn't take care of me. I think he was too sad. He forgot to take me to school sometimes. Some days he would get me in the car and get me buckled in and then he'd rest his head on the steering wheel. Someone came over to the apartment one day to see how we were getting by, a "social worker," she was called. She saw that for breakfast he put my bowl of Cheerios on the kitchen floor. She said that was bad and that a kid should eat at a table. She said I needed a haircut and a bath and that my pants were two sizes too small. She gave him the name of this school and said it was the best solution until he started to feel better. She said I would be happy and he would visit me on the weekends.

So that's my problem. What about the new kid?

Only runaways live on the top floor, so that's one clue.

But running away is never the problem, is it? The problem is the thing that makes the boy run.

There are just a few rooms in the north wing of the fourth floor, and it's easy to tell which is his because the door is half open.

"Help! Help!" I hear a voice inside the room. It's kind of a whisper and kind of a scream.

I open the door, and the new boy is huddled on top of his desk, shaking. A long black line darts into the hall. I turn and see Gollum slip under another door.

"Should we call the dean?" the new kid asks, peeking around his door. "You know, to tell him which room it's in now?"

I shake my head. Snakes like to be with their own kind, right? And that's Mean Jack's room, so I'm sure they'll get along just fine.

"Man, it's stuffy up here," the new kid says. He walks to the window and yanks at it. He's still trembling from Gollum's welcome party.

The window sticks shut.

I tap him on the shoulder and tip my chin up so he knows I want to give it a try. He steps back and looks at me funny, and I see myself as he must see me: skinny, with my hair hanging in my eyes.

How is this kid gonna do it, when I can't? That's what he's thinking.

The window makes a popping sound and slides up. Freaky strong, that's what Mean Jack calls me.

The new kid nods like he just figured something out.

"So *that's* why Tuffman was messing with you," he says. "You must be the strongest kid here."

All my embarrassment about Tuffman tossing me around like a ragdoll disappears.

"Yeah," he says. "Jerk jocks always pick on the kids like us 'cause we're the ones who threaten them the most." He says it with a sneer, like he knows all about it and it's happened to him a million times.

Did he say "like us"?

"You got the craziest teachers here I've ever seen," he

says. His eyes are shiny. I can tell he laughs a lot. "Do they wave knives around and punch each other every morning?"

I smile so big I cover my mouth with my hand. The older kids here used to call me Dog Boy, because my teeth are so pointed. Most of them have gone back to live with their moms and dads by now, but I still hide my teeth.

With a quick twitch of his shoulders, the new boy sticks his head and as much of his body as he can out the window.

He's tall and thin, with glossy black hair and a sharp, long nose. At first he keeps his hands on the window-sill, but when a gust of wind comes up off the water, I see him lift his hands and flutter them gently, the way a bird ruffles its feather before it takes flight.

My stomach feels empty and my palms are damp. It would be good to have a friend my own age. I'm pretty popular with the Cubs, since I take them fishing every Friday. And maybe—my heart flops like a trout hooked on a line—maybe Mary Anne likes me. A little.

But I see the other Pack boys. They talk about video games and sports. They chase each other and laugh and play games and sometimes they even fight. Not me. As soon as I walk up—and I don't, not anymore—but as soon as I'd walk up, they'd look away like they hadn't seen me. Then they'd stop talking and slowly move away.

Nobody is mean to me. But nobody is nice, either.

"Do you like the woods?" I make the words come out.

The boy pulls himself back in the window.

"Are there trails back in there?" he asks. "I race dirt bikes. I'm a champion in my class. Did the dean tell you that already? My mom says she'll bring me my bike if I'm good."

His window is on the same side of the building as the dining hall and faces the water. He points to the ravine. "Is that where the school property ends?" he asks.

He must already be thinking about how to get away once that dirt bike comes. "Yeah," I say, "that ravine cuts all the way back to the road that leads to the school. You can't climb down it—it's way too steep." I decide to keep talking. I can tell he's really listening. He's worth the words. "There's a way around it, though. I'll show you one day, if you want. And you can pretty much walk out of this place any time. There's no fence keeping you here. Just the Terror of Getting Lost in the Dark Woods." I say the last sentence in a spooky voice.

He smiles at my little joke. "My name is Vincent. You're Raul, right? That boy across the hall said you're a weirdo. But you don't look like one to me."

I forget about my weird teeth. I smile again, really big.

"You have wicked cool teeth, man!"

My elbow hurts when I bend it, but I feel good inside as I head into science.

First off, because I think I might have a friend. And second, because Advanced Science is the one class I have with Mary Anne. So it's safe to say that I'd feel happy right now even if I knew Tuffman would be waiting after class, ready to yank me into a Bavarian pretzel and sprinkle me with rock salt.

Some kids think science is boring, but that's because they don't have Dean Swift for a teacher. And they don't have Dean Swift for a teacher because he won't let any kid who thinks science is boring into his class.

This year he only let four of us into the class. He teaches it in his office. There aren't any desks. We can sit on the soft carpet or lie on our stomachs or, if we get there early, flop in one of the big leather armchairs.

Lately Dean Swift's been talking about the human body. We're studying cells and how every part of your body is made of them. There are skin cells and heart cells and eyeball cells. Mean Jack must have gotten extra fist cells. Tuffman got extra rude cells. Mary Anne must have gotten extra pretty cells. I must have gotten some extra weirdo cells.

But then Dean Swift says something so interesting that I forget about Mary Anne and Tuffman. I don't forget about the extra weirdo cells, though, because from what the dean says, I might be on to something.

"The center of each cell is called the nucleus. Now, in the nucleus of every cell, you will find your DNA. DNA is a code telling your body how you should look, and even how you should act. Have you ever seen a recipe in a cookbook? That is like your DNA," he says. "And it is different for each human. Half of it comes from your mother and half of it comes from your father. It is the recipe for *you*."

I like how he always gives us a picture idea. I think of the cards in my mom's old recipe box. I haven't opened the box since we all lived together. But I imagine a million copies of one of those recipes, written out in her handwriting, floating around everywhere in me. *Kid-Kebab. Raul Stew.*

"Scientists have begun to map the human genome. It will take many generations to fully understand. It's a bit like cracking a secret code."

Then he stops talking. He sits there with his mouth open and no words coming out.

When Dean Swift stops talking, it means that in a minute or two he is going to tell us something he didn't mean to tell us. It's something he doesn't know yet but is trying to understand. It has nothing to do with the learning target. And it's always the most interesting thing anyone will say to me all day long.

"I wonder. Do you know there is another kind of DNA?" he says slowly. "It's a DNA we get only from our mothers. It's in each cell but outside the nucleus. It's a shorter code than the DNA inside the nucleus. It's a special recipe that tells your cells how to turn the food you eat into energy." He writes *mtDNA* on the board. "It's called mitochondrial DNA, but we write it like that. And you only get it from your mother."

He stands and walks to the window that looks out over the ravine. I get a shiver, the kind I usually get when I'm deep in White Deer Woods and I'm me but not myself. My spine sparks like it does when I change.

"This kind of DNA you get from your mother has to do with your body's growth and development," he says. "Sometimes there are mutations. That means changes." He turns around and looks right at me—or right through me. "They only happen very rarely. That mutation will be handed down from mother to child. We know about the problems such mutations might cause. They affect vision and hearing, muscles, and the heart in particular." He pauses and shakes his head. "But we don't know if there are mutations that cause *improvements* in hearing and vision, greater muscle strength, or a heart that beats harder and stronger and longer. We don't know about that because there are no documented studies on that. Not yet, anyhow."

He sits down and looks at me. This time I'm sure he sees me. "Scientists don't really know what gifts our mothers have given us. Only we do."

Dean Swift really has a way with words sometimes.

I look down, because my eyes are saying too much. Maybe Dean Swift guessed how much the new kid coming today reminds me of the first day I came here and how sad and lost I felt. He wants me to know my mom is everywhere inside me all of the time. That it's not just words; it's science.

The bell rings and we pick up our stuff to leave.

Mary Anne holds out her hand for the dean to shake. "Dean Swift," she says in her most grown-up voice, "you soar high above the knowledgeable but pedestrian scientist when you weld wisdom to feeling."

I get the gist of what she's saying. But for me there's a lot more to it than feeling.

Vision, hearing, heart—these all have to do with my secret.

Maybe *that's* why the secret came to me. The secret was my mom's first. Or her grandma's grandma's grandma's. Each mom gave it to her child until it got to my mom. Then she gave it to me.

You can call it magic or you can call it science. I think it's a little of both.

Chapter 6

WHERE YOU HEAR ABOUT WHITE DEER FOR THE FIRST TIME

When I wake up, the first thing I think is, *What's Vincent's class schedule?* And the second is, *It's Friday.*

I hurry to get ready. Maybe Vincent will sit next to me at the counter.

But as I'm going in to breakfast, Vincent is coming out. He's telling a story to Mean Jack and Jason, and the two dimwits are laughing so hard they can't breathe.

So that's that. I know it's dumb, but it feels like someone has taken a rake and dragged it back and forth over my lungs. Vincent is already part of the Pack—the pack I'm not part of.

But Vincent stops when he sees me.

"Raul, my man," he says. He grabs my hand and shakes it. With a flick of his chin he tells the other two to go on without him. "I was waiting for you. Save me a seat at lunch, okay?"

It's crazy how relieved I feel. But I wonder. How long will it last? How long will he be able to be friends with me and with them? A week, I bet.

"I can hardly understand what those two are saying," he says. "It's like they speak their own language. Don't throw me to the wolves like that again, okay?"

He doesn't even know how funny that last comment was.

Fishing Friday. It's my job here. Every Friday after lunch and before parent pick-up I take the Cubs fishing at the lake at the edge of White Deer Woods.

Today Dean Swift joins me at the counter for a quick meeting.

"No sign of Gollum?" he asks.

I shake my head.

Dean Swift exhales. His shoulders drop. "Very unfortunate. But we have another small crisis that is slightly more pressing. Remember the bone Sparrow found in the Blackout Tunnel?" he asks.

I nod.

"The bone undoubtedly belonged to a dog. Last night I explored the Blackout Tunnel myself. It appears that over the winter an animal used it as a den." Dean Swift stares out the window like he's thinking. "That new housing development they put near the ferry terminal has been a catastrophe for so many of our animal friends. I believe we are dealing with a predator—most probably a coyote—that has been displaced from its territory." He shakes his head sadly. A second later, his spine straightens, his elbows jut out a little, and he begins a Lecture.

"In packs, coyotes have been known to attack humans. However, the animal that has claimed the Blackout Tunnel appears to be a loner. And if his territory is centered around the Blackout Tunnel, I doubt you would encounter him so far north as the lake. Especially in the middle of the day. I believe that suspending our normal activities would teach a lesson of fear to our young Cubs. Fishing Friday is their sacred hour free from adult supervision and in the tutelage of that divine preceptor, Mother Nature. But I'm counting on you to keep your eyes open today. Bobo must go with you, as usual. She will function as an early warning system."

Coyotes don't scare me. But I know what he means when he talks about the new housing development. It borders the far side of White Deer Woods, and coyotes aren't the only predators the new human families are making nervous.

After breakfast the Cubs all follow me out of the dining hall and line up in front of the equipment room so I can hand out their poles.

If the dean only knew how Fishing Friday normally goes down, he wouldn't waste his breath warning me about a coyote.

Six times Jane has hooked me, not a fish. Four times Tim has eaten deer poop. Now, the little turds *do* look like berries, but after the first three times you'd think he'd make a mental note of it. Three times I lost one of them for more than an hour, and we all had to fan out in a long line and form a search party. Twice Little John was sure he saw a witch and got so scared he wet his pants. I keep telling him that yes, there is magic in those woods, but no witches.

Before we leave, I line them up and hand out the equipment—poles, hooks, and bait.

Sixty times someone's pole has floated away to the middle of the lake.

When it's Sparrow's turn, I hold his brand-new pole out to him and then jerk it back a little as he grabs for it.

He laughs. "I won't bust it up, I promise," he says.

I hand it to him and squeeze the back of his neck lightly. His hair is soft and wispy.

He flips the pole over in his hand and then looks up at me with his face really still. I can tell he's too happy for words when he gets that look. He traces a finger along the design I carved. It's of two wolves, and they're running around the bottom, tail to mouth. It's the best carving I've ever done. And he gets what it means, he knows what I'm saying to him. I'm saying, *Hey, Sparrow, you're no cub, you're no weak runt, you're a wolf. You're in my pack.*

Five times Sparrow has slipped his hand in mine while we walk back to school from the lake.

You know what Sparrow's problem is? It's so bad it's hard for me to tell it. When he first came here he always had a couple of bruises on his cheek or his arm. Over the week they would fade and turn into yellow smears. Then Friday night he'd go home with his mom.

When he came back on Sundays he'd run to his room, open the door, and chuck in his duffel bag. Then, quick like a bunny, he'd head down to Fort Casey all by himself. But every single time, Sparrow would come back with more bruises. He'd tell the dean that he'd fallen on the stairs at the fort, or that he'd stood up under the cannon and gotten a lump on his head.

I had a bad feeling about it. How can one kid get hurt so much and so bad?

So one Sunday afternoon after his mom dropped him off, I decided to find out. First, he ran to his room and put his bag away. He came back out wearing a too-big baseball cap, and I followed him over to Fort Casey. You know where he went. To the Blackout Tunnel.

Before he stepped into the tunnel he looked back, like he wanted to make sure nobody was watching. He lifted his head up, and for the first time I saw what the baseball hat hid. A huge bruise under his eye.

He stayed in the tunnel for a while and then came out. When he got back to the school he ran up to the dean and said, "Dean Swift, a little boy playing on the field at the fort hit a baseball right into my eye."

Dean Swift clucked a few times, put an arm around him, and took him to the nurse.

I was confused. *Nothing* had hit him at the fort.

My gut told me that Sparrow shouldn't go home on the weekends. But I kept my mouth shut, because I didn't know who to tell or even really what to say. It was just a feeling, that's all.

It turned out Sparrow's mom was hitting him—not because he was bad but because *she* was. I heard the dean telling Cook Patsy one day when they forgot I was in the kitchen. I couldn't see his face, since I was chopping up onions and had to keep wiping my eyes, but I've never heard his voice so furious. Those were the worst onions I've ever chopped.

The dean had found out that Sparrow was lying about getting hurt at the fort because he didn't want his mom to get in trouble. I think he was just sitting in the Blackout Tunnel feeling sad and trying to imagine accidents that would match the bruises his mom gave him.

Now his grandma picks him up for the weekend, and he *never* has bruises anymore.

So I take special care of Sparrow. I should have told the dean what I saw that day at the fort—even though I didn't understand it. It took another month before the dean figured it out. How many more times did Sparrow's mom hit him in that month?

Dean Swift says we have to forgive ourselves when we make mistakes. He has a funny reason for it too. He says if you don't forgive yourself for making a mistake, then you get so that you never want to admit that you made one.

I'm still chewing on that one.

Today Vincent is coming fishing with us, even though he's not one of the little kids. It was the dean's idea—to give the new kid a chance to have some fun.

"If he has a great day today, it will make it easier for him to return on Sunday night," he said.

Here's the thing about Dean Swift. He lies, sure, but only because sometimes it's easier than explaining everything. He's disorganized, but that's because he's always thinking. Studying the natural light phenomena of the island is a big job.

But the main thing is, he's kind. And that's all that matters, isn't it? To us, anyway, to the ones who got left on the edge of an island with nothing but a suitcase full of clothes and a head full of trouble.

No kid here is lucky, but we're all lucky to be here.

When it's Vincent's turn for equipment, I hold up a fishing pole in one hand and a slingshot in the other. Then I shrug a little so he knows he can choose one or the other. Some kids think fishing's boring. But everyone loves a slingshot.

Twenty times I've been hit so hard with a rock in the back of the shin or the private parts that I almost fainted.

Vincent looks from one to the other. "Can I just hang out and watch?" he asks.

I nod. Vincent's not a little kid, but I've seen lots of little kids act like this. As far as I can tell it's just that they're afraid of messing up. So when Vincent says he wants to sit and watch us all have fun, I make sure he sees that I'm packing the slingshot. In case once we're out there in the woods, he changes his mind and decides to try something new.

The dean opens the door for us and hands me the walkie-talkie to use in case of emergency. To him a scraped knee is an emergency.

That man has *no idea* what happens in those woods.

We walk single file in the weeds along the roadside. Bobo leads the way. No traffic on this road, since it only leads from Highway 20 to the school. The lake is ten minutes away, halfway between the highway and the school.

While we walk, I think about my problem. The counselor says I have "trust issues." He says it's because the people I relied on most—my mom and dad—have not been able to take care of me. He says that's why I don't like to talk very much.

Wrong, is what I want to say to him—but not enough to say it. The reason I don't talk is because I can tell nobody is really listening. What I have to say doesn't really matter.

The things that matter happen in the woods. The things that matter don't need words.

Today is Friday. So tonight matters.

Once we step off the road and into the woods, we all breathe in deep to smell the trees and dirt.

Bobo runs off on a scent. There's nothing I'd like more than to drop to all fours and follow her.

I point up into the fork of an old oak tree.

Vincent follows my finger. "A bike! How did that get there?"

It's a rusted red ten-speed. In five places, where the branches of the oak have grown around it, the bike has become part of the tree. It'll be there until that oak falls, and by that time, a boy walking by the trunk won't even know the bike is in there—the oak will have swallowed it up like a snake does a mouse.

Sparrow answers, "Raul put it there."

Vincent laughs like it's the coolest thing ever.

My dad gave me that bike. It was way too big for me. He pushed me around on it a lot the Friday afternoon he brought it up here. Put on a good show for the other parents. When he stopped coming, I decided to give the bike to the tree. It's just as likely to learn to ride it as I am.

We keep walking; we're at the end of the path. The lake is in front of us. On the other side of the lake the trees are so close together and the blackberries scrape and the nettles sting so sharp that nobody has ever gone beyond them. Nobody but me, anyway.

"What's that?" Vincent asks in a whisper.

Pin pricks in my fingers and on my head. For a second I wonder if I'm going to look where he's pointing and see the secret that changed my life.

I follow his finger with my eyes. He's pointing to the straw man that I nailed to a huge cedar last year after Tuffman tackled Sparrow during touch football.

We use it for target practice. It's wearing Tuffman's favorite sweatshirt that says *3X Olympian*. I stole it from the laundry room. He turned the whole school upside down looking for that shirt. Not one of the Cubs ratted me out though, not even when Tuffman leaned in and hit them with his foul breath and a deadly speech about honesty and thieving and the awful punishment you get for stealing a man's clothes.

On the head of the straw man I nailed an old crow's nest that looks like Tuffman's toupee. Cracks me up every time I see it.

I pull my sling out of my back pocket. It's a little harder to use than a slingshot, but it's my weapon of choice.

I walk over to the straw man and point to the feet, the chest, and the shoulders.

"Five points," Sparrow yells out.

Then I point to the knees, and Little John shouts, "Twenty points." A runner's knees are valuable. I can see by Vincent's nod that he gets that.

I point to you-know-where on the shorts.

"Fifty points." I have to say it myself because all the kids are laughing to bust a gut.

I walk back to Vincent. I reach down and scoop up a smooth stone, the perfect shape.

A sling has two cords attached to a leather pouch in the middle. I set the stone in the center of the pouch. I hold the ends of the cords with the fingers and thumb of my right hand. I look at Vincent to make sure he's watching.

I start to spin it above my head. Vincent's eyes follow it. The Cubs whoop as the sling arcs faster and faster. For a minute I just swing and stare at the straw man, finding my rhythm.

I can't help but show off. I close my eyes.

I let the end of one cord go. The stone flies out of the pouch and makes a straight line toward the old cedar.

Thwack. I hear the kids shout and I open my eyes. I look at Sparrow.

"Fifty points," he informs me, and reaches out to shake my hand like a gentleman.

Vincent shakes his head. The look in his eyes means more than any compliment.

I'm about to hand him the sling, but then I think better of it. I want him to do something he can be good at right away. I pull the slingshot out of the knapsack.

It's a lot easier to learn how to use than the sling. And it's a lot safer while you learn. You let go of that sling a little too soon and some kid has a rock between the eyes.

I hand him the slingshot. I show him how to hold the Y-shaped piece of wood and where to put the rock, but I can tell he already kind of knows. I leave him alone to practice and go help the little kids bait their hooks. *Whiz.* I hear Vincent's rock sail by the cedar tree. *Thump.* It falls on something soft, like a big mushroom. *Whiz.* Another one. *Fwip.* A leaf on a branch. Progress.

Whiz. Thwack.

Now *that* hit straw.

I turn back and give him a thumbs up. He stands taller, throwing back his shoulders like a major league pitcher on the mound.

Thwack, thwack, thwack, the sound follows me all the way to where the little kids are squatting over their hooks.

One problem down, another pops up.

Little John is bawling. Tears are streaking through the dirt on his face and snot is running from each nostril like two yellow slugs. He looks at me and sobs, "Wahoul, I don't wanna kill Mr. Wormie."

"It's just a worm," Sparrow says to him. He stabs three of those suckers onto his hook.

I lead Little John by the hand to the edge of the lake.

"Look," I say. I point to the pollywogs swimming around the shiny smooth rocks. I scoop up a bunch and let them wriggle in the palm of my hand.

Little John bends down to look. He stops crying. He starts petting the pollywogs. Nothing like the life cycle of amphibians to get a boy's mind off his troubles.

Before I can stop him, he pops four of them into his mouth. He swallows. A huge gulp. "They're good," he says, rubbing his tummy.

"Oh man," I say. I'm gonna zuke.

Then my scalp tingles.

Something in me says to look up. Woods magic.

I look up.

I look up and see a glowing ball of blue-green fire floating across the lake. Will-o'-the-wisp. I mouth the words but no sound comes out. I've seen it once before—when I first noticed the woods-world. And it takes the breath from my lungs this time too.

Will-o'-the-wisps are one of the light phenomena that Dean Swift studies. *Ignes fatui* it's called in Latin, and that means "foolish fire." People have been seeing it for centuries, but it's still a mystery. Dean Swift says most scientists think it's some kind of chemical reaction caused by a bunch of dead stuff breaking down. He says it with bigger words, but you get it.

When I researched it on my own, I found out that a long time ago people thought will-o'-the-wisps would lead you to treasure or to a secret doorway where you could get in and out of heaven and see people you loved that you had lost.

They were on to something.

I watch the ball of light skip above the water. Tonight I'll go again to the place the will-o'-the-wisp led me a year ago, and I will feel like I am home, and I will find what I have lost.

My breath comes calm and slow like it does when I'm deep in the woods with her.

Little John looks up, his cheeks bulging and a little trickle of slime in the corner of his mouth. He doesn't see what I see.

Then I hear Vincent shouting behind us. "You guys won't believe what I just saw!"

The coyote! I jump up. I can see Sparrow by the lake, but where's Bobo?

Everyone runs toward Vincent. As I hurry to catch up, I notice that they've all dropped their poles. Six poles are floating in the water, heading slowly toward the middle of the lake. I change the count—sixty-six poles have gone adrift. I'm about to say one of those bad words Jack is always saying, when I see a shadow by the big hemlock. It's Sparrow. He's got his new pole in his hand and he's setting it on a thick bed of pine needles far from the water's edge. He looks up and sees me. "I told you I'd take care of it," he calls to me. Then he lopes over, and we head toward the old cedar and the straw man.

Six times he's put his hand in mine.

The kids are all gathered around Vincent. I let out a little puff of air when I see Bobo behind him, her ears flat. Her tail is tucked as far up under her body as it can get.

"It was over there," Vincent says, pointing to the other side of the lake, where White Deer Woods begins. On that side, the water comes right up to blackberry brambles and trees. It takes four legs to find the rabbit and deer paths in that tangle of branches, needles, and thorns.

"What?" I ask. "What did you see?" My heart pounds, *keblam, keblam, keblam.*

My fingertips tingle. I can feel my ears stretching the way they do when the woods magic happens.

Something tells me Vincent's not going to say "coyote."

"I saw a white deer with huge black antlers," Vincent whispers.

"Did it talk to you?" I put my hand over my mouth too late. That was not a question I should have asked. Obviously.

"Did it *talk* to me? No, it didn't talk to me." Vincent's voice sounds strange.

I clear my throat. "I said did it *walk* to you." And that, kids, is called taking a play from Dean Swift's book.

"It looked like it was going to walk across the lake toward me."

"And nobody else saw it?" I ask.

"No. I heard a noise like a jet engine. They ran over when I shouted." Vincent points to Beth, Maggie, Peter, and Paul. "We were all looking at the same spot there, but I was the only one who saw it. It was huge." He hops from foot to foot.

The truth hits me.

Two times now White Deer has come to the far edge of the lake.

Three times and it'll be science, right?

Vincent is staring at me. Bobo is staring at me. The Cubs are staring at me. Am I changing? I lick my teeth, but they feel the same. I realize that they're probably all just surprised at my talking so much.

"My grandma's eyes play tricks on her when she's tired," Sparrow says all of a sudden.

Everyone looks at him instead.

We pack up to leave pretty quick after that. As we step from the path onto the paved road, Vincent grabs my arm.

"I was lying," he blurts. "When I said it didn't talk."

I had a feeling. But why?

He answers my question before I ask it. "I didn't want everyone thinking I'm crazy. But it did. It *talked* to me. It kept saying the word 'raven.' *Am* I crazy?" he asks.

We hear a blaring honk.

It's Sparrow's grandma tearing up the road in her huge blue pickup, coming to get him for the weekend. All we can see of her as she rips by us is her curly white hair and the top rims of her enormous glasses. I'm not sure that lady should be driving.

"Trickster," I say after the dust settles. "The raven is a sweet-talkin' trickster."

Vincent looks at me like I'm speaking gibberish. Maybe I am. But all of a sudden my mind fills with black feathers. Remember the murder of crows swarming over Vincent when he made his wild run for freedom? Woods magic. The crows flew to him the way the wolves once ran with me.

I step closer to him. I want to ask him if he saw the will-o'-the-wisp too. If its light pulled at him so he had to follow. I want to tell him that it will take him to the lighthouse so deep in the woods only the light knows the way in and out. I'm about to tell him everything about my mom and my dad and the wolves in the woods. Then I stop myself. Because I see him shaking his head. A little at first and then a lot.

"Nah," he says, licking his lips. "That's just crazy. Crazy like talking to your cereal crazy. Crazy like riding your bike on the freeway crazy. I'm just tired, like Sparrow's granny says."

He looks confused. "But I didn't want to lie to you. My mom says I have to stop lying before I can come back home."

We walk the last few yards to the circle driveway, scuffing our shoes in the dirt.

I like him for telling me the truth, even if he did lie at first. I like him even more for keeping his promise to Pretty Lady. But I don't think I'll try to explain to him about the magic in the woods and the way it works for me. Because if White Deer couldn't get through to him, how could I?

Chapter 7

HOW RAUL FIRST FOUND THE LIGHTHOUSE

After fishing, we all wash up and eat lunch. Two hours of class. Snack. Doors slam, dresser drawers creak open and shut, the zippers and Velcro on overnight bags zip and rip, tennis shoes squeak up and down the stairs as kids remember stuff they almost forgot. Then motors chug up the driveway, with Pretty Lady's Harley roaring above them all. Hugs and kisses and moms asking in worried chirpy voices, *How are you? Did you have a good week?* and dads crabby from the long drive, grumbling, *It's time to get on the road, Let's try to beat some of that ferry traffic,* and *We're going to hit Seattle at exactly the wrong time.*

Vincent jumps from the bottom step into his mother's arms. She's crying. That's how happy she is to see him, and they've only been apart one day.

It only makes me a little sad before I remember to be happy for him.

"Look!" Mary Anne is next to me, pointing at the sky.

The crows are wheeling and tumbling, blackening

the sky with their wings, swooping over the Harley. The hair on my arms stands straight up.

"His name is Vincent, isn't it?" she asks.

I nod.

"What an amazing coincidence!" she says. "St. Vincent of Saragossa, renowned for his eloquence, is the patron saint of ravens. After he was martyred by Roman soldiers, ravens guarded his body from marauding animals. To this day the site of his tomb is famous for the multitude of ravens that flock there. And here we have these crows, such close relatives of the raven, offering a fitting farewell to our own Vincent."

Vincent and his mom roar away.

My mouth is dry. The coincidence isn't amazing—it's magical. Mary Anne's story happened a really long time ago. But White Deer called Vincent "raven" just a few hours ago. Is the woods magic everywhere and in all times?

She pats my arm to get my attention. "Your name means 'wolf' in Old Norse. Did you know that?"

I shake my head. My stomach wobbles like a rock rolling down a hill. No, I didn't know names were part of the woods magic. Do our names call the animal? Or are we named for the animal we call?

"I guess we don't really want a pack of wolves escorting you off school grounds, though, do we?" she says.

I grin. She's funnier than she thinks. Running off

with a pack of wolves for the weekend isn't as bad as it sounds.

Mary Anne's parents pull up in the circle driveway and honk their horn. She gives me a little wave and runs down the steps. I watch her leave. The trunk pops open. She sets her bag in and slams the trunk.

Her parents drive away.

I'm serious. They go almost all the way around the circle before they jam on their brakes so hard the back of the car rocks up. Mary Anne walks very, very slowly to the car. Even from the window I can see that her face is bright pink. *You shouldn't be embarrassed,* I want to shout. *They should be.*

Mean Jack brushes by me. "See you later, weirdo," he says.

I just grin. Because as he walks away I see something black and shiny, long and reptilian, wiggling out of the half-closed zipper of his bulging overnight bag.

That's gonna be a real fun car ride, isn't it?

One by one all the kids get picked up. And then it's me and Dean Swift standing in the room we call the parlor, looking at the empty driveway.

"Can I drop you off at the bottom of the hill?" The dean asks me the same question he asks me every Friday afternoon.

I shake my head. I don't want Dean Swift anywhere around when my dad picks me up, because my dad stopped coming to pick me up a year ago and nobody knows it but me and him.

Here's how it happened, or like they say in the cop shows, here's how it went down.

At first my dad came every weekend for a long time. We took the Mukilteo ferry and drove to his apartment in Seattle. Saturday mornings we had breakfast at the Sound View Café in the Pike Place Market. He had an omelet and I had a bagel with cream cheese and lox. Lunch was a meat bun from the hum bao stand. Dinner was a can of soup in front of the TV. Sundays we ate at the French bakery. He had coffee and a little loaf of bread. I had three cream puffs, an éclair, and orange juice. That gave me a stomachache that lasted until we got in the car and drove to the ferry to go back to school.

Usually at the ferry we'd run into one of my classmates.

"Would you mind driving Raul in?" my dad would ask. He'd shove his hands in his pockets and look at the ground like he was doing something wrong but couldn't help it.

I don't know if I had fun with my dad or not on those weekends. But I was glad to be with him. And I hated leaving him. I knew that when I was with him he thought about my mom more, but when I wasn't with him, he missed her more.

Then one weekend about a year ago he didn't show up. We waited. It got dark. The dean went to his office and made a call.

"Your dad's car broke down on the way to the ferry, so I'm afraid he won't be able to make it," he said when he came back into the parlor.

I cried, right there sitting on the blue sofa.

The dean sat next to me.

When I could get the words out, I asked, "If my dad can't come, then will my mom?" I don't know why I asked that. I hadn't seen her in years.

Dean Swift swallowed and shook his head.

"Is she dead?" I asked. It was the first time I asked that question out loud. Nobody ever talked to me about her.

Dean Swift's mouth made a long line. "No," he said. "She's not dead. There is no evidence to indicate that. But she's not here. I'm sure that she would be if she could."

He looked right into my eyes. "I don't know where she is. Nobody does."

I don't know why, exactly, but that made me feel better. Sad still, but better. I was glad I had asked that question. And I was glad that he didn't lie to me. Another point for the dean.

The next weekend my dad showed up. He had presents for me and a bottle of wine for the dean.

Then it happened again. All the kids were gone. The sun went down. The night came. The dean called. That time I waited to cry until I got to my bedroom. I cried until the muscles in my throat hurt and my nose was stuffed up and I felt like I had a really bad cold.

The third time it happened, I was mad.

And what was the dean supposed to do with me? See, normally he shuts the place up for the weekend and sends the staff home. He lives in Coupeville, a tiny town a few miles from the school. But if I was stuck at school, then so was he. "I can't leave you here all alone, now, can I?" he said to me with a big laugh the first time, like it was no big deal. We ate beans straight from the can and made sardine and peanut butter sandwiches. I think he had as much fun as I did. But the second and the third weekends? He was missing his family too.

So then Dean Swift took me home with him. He lives in a house painted pink. Victorian style is what he calls it. His wife called me poor little runt the whole time. I did not like her, and, strange thing is, I don't think the dean does either. But he has three teenage daughters. I'm going to marry one of them one day—unless, of course, things work out with Mary Anne. But Mary Anne is a real long shot.

Dean Swift's youngest daughter, June, is a cheerleader, and that weekend she walked around everywhere in her cheerleading uniform even though there wasn't a game. The skirt was very short and so was the top. The Dean kept walking up to her and tugging the skirt down. This made more of her tummy show, so then he'd put his head in his hands and walk away very sadly. I thought she looked like a movie star. She let me curl her hair with the curling iron. I only got a little burned.

May, the middle daughter, took me for a ride on her moped. "You don't need a helmet," she said. "Like, that's totally for sissies." That made the dean upset too, when he saw us come riding back with my hair all wild from the wind, but it was the best hour of my life.

Then April, the oldest, took me to the movies with her. The dean about exploded on Sunday morning when he found out which one we saw. I guess that movie was not for children. There were a lot of parts I didn't understand, but I really thought the party scene was funny. Maybe the actors and actresses should have had on more clothes.

One thing I know is that when I get my license, I'll drive like May taught me—speed up into the corners and turn your headlights off when you're going down hills on country roads at night. The goal, she told me, is to leave part of your tires on the road. Burning out, she called it. *Totally* an adrenaline rush, she said.

Anyway. The dean apologized to me all the way

back to the school Sunday afternoon. It was the greatest weekend of my life, so I don't know what he was so sorry about, but I could tell I wouldn't be going home with him again. Which was too bad, since April told me she'd teach me how to use her rifle next time, and May said there was a beach party with a bonfire and she'd let me use her lighter and some gasoline to get the fire going.

The next Friday, when the dean took me into his office and said my dad couldn't make it because the car was at the garage, I had some hard thoughts. *They don't want to talk about the one thing that matters the most to me?* I thought. *Fine, then. I'm not talking about it anymore either.* I was done waiting for the grown-ups to decide what to do with me.

Later that afternoon I called the dean from the phone in the hallway of the top floor. I pretended to be my dad.

"Oliver," I said, because that's the name the parents call him, "the car is running good. It can't make it up that big hill to the front door, though. Please have Raul wait for me at the bottom of the hill, by the turnoff from Highway Twenty." Then I hung up.

I knew the dean would be easy to fool. I knew he'd be too tired to walk the two miles down the hill to the highway. Plus, people are happy to be tricked if they're getting what they really want from it. And the dean really wanted to spend the weekend with his family.

So when the other kids were jumping into their cars to go home, I went to the dean and shook his hand and thanked him for watching out for me the last few weekends. "I think my dad has figured some things out," I said, then swung my backpack over my shoulder and headed down that hill.

Really, I was the one who had figured it out. I decided right then and there, as my feet hit the asphalt and I looked up at the thin strip of blue sky above the tops of the cedars and pines that lined the road, I was on my own. One day I'd find my mom, and maybe one day my dad would come back with an excuse better than one the dean could think of. But until then, I'd take care of myself.

I had a plan. First, walk to the highway. From there, take the footpath Tuffman makes us run through the woods. Then wait near the lake, and when everyone was gone, climb up the madrona and into my room through my unlocked window.

As I walked down the hill, cars zoomed by me in both directions. Parents coming and going with their kids. The road twists and turns pretty good, and at some point I got worried the drivers might not see me. Becoming roadkill was not part of my plan.

So I cut into the woods sooner. There was no path. The dirt was squishy and dark and covered with pine needles and cones. The woods smelled alive. I was happy to be me, to be there, to have a weekend to do whatever I wanted, whenever I wanted.

Then my skin prickled. My ears stretched like they do when you're in bed alone in a pitch-black room and you hear a sound that only something alive could make. Something alive that's *not you*. I looked behind me and saw a flash of white fur. Maybe it was just a ray of sunlight streaming down through the cedars. I stuck my chin out. I squinted. Eyes stared back at me through the low, bending branches of the cedar.

Animal eyes. I was so scared, my stomach tumbled and my mind lost every thought.

I stood very still. When I looked again, the eyes were gone but the branches were swaying. I started to step away. I sensed it watching me. I walked more quickly. I didn't know which direction to go to get out of the woods. I couldn't think.

I heard a snuffle and a hard crack.

I ran. I ran so hard my lungs burned. I ran so hard I didn't see where I was going.

Branches slapped my face, and blackberry brambles scraped my arms. Whatever it was, it was running on the other side of the trees beside me. I couldn't tell if there was one or more than one. I couldn't tell if it was chasing me or running with me. Was I part of a hunting pack or was I being hunted?

I ran until I ran out of island. One minute I was in the middle of cedars as tall as a mountain, and the next I wasn't. I was in a narrow meadow twenty feet from the cliff's edge.

I looked back a hundred times. Nothing followed me out from the cedars. My breath was so ragged and jagged, it scraped my throat and I tasted blood.

At the end of the little meadow the cliff dropped straight down to a pile of driftwood and then a strip of sand and then the blue, blue water of Puget Sound.

I started to shiver. It was almost dark. Sometimes all your choices seem bad. Was I going to spend the night on the edge of a cliff with a pack of animals watching from the trees, or run back into the forest and try to get home before whatever chased me here caught me?

If I went left, I was pretty sure I'd end up in sight of the school, but not within reach, because of the ravine.

I looked right. Farther down, the trees circled the meadow and came up to the cliff. I stared into the trees. There was a building nestled among them. I walked closer.

It was a lighthouse.

Nobody had been near it for years. Animals maybe, but no humans. The tower was as tall as the tallest trees around it, and its white paint was dappled with a pale green lichen on the landward side that helped hide it in the cedar fronds. At its base was a small cabin with a red roof. Blackberry and huckleberry and ferns and waist-high fir trees surrounded it. I pushed back the ivy covering the door.

I heard the click of little paws scamper across the stone floor as I stepped inside. It was cold and dark and musty. The first thing I thought was how I'd show it to my dad next time he came. The next thing I thought was how stupid can a kid be.

I shut the door behind me and shoved an old wooden chest in front of it.

Something out there was watching me. I could feel its eyes.

As soon as I saw the stairs, I ran up them. The lighthouse light was gone. The windows were cracked and broken and missing, and the edge of the ceiling was packed with the mud nests of swallows. The wind smelled like cedar and salt and wet wood. It was the most magical place I had ever seen.

I spent the night up there, with the moon coming in through the paneless windows. Before I fell asleep, I made a sling from an old leather belt I found in a chest, and gathered up as many rocks as I could.

In the morning I walked back through the woods, my sling in one hand and a rock in the other. No eyes watched me from behind the shaggy trunks of cedar.

There was a big surprise when I got back to the school: Bobo. I wasn't the only one who had been forgotten. Whichever kid was supposed to take her home for the weekend hadn't.

Boy, was she glad to see me. She charged out the door to pee and then charged right back to knock me down and lick me. She was very thorough. I never knew how happy it'd make me to have slimy sandpaper rubbed over my face.

The rest of that weekend went more or less as planned. During the day I wandered through the woods, but I made sure Bobo was trotting along at my heels. I stayed in sight of the road to the school, and before dark I was in the parlor, parked in front of the TV with Bobo for a pillow.

I found out canned pumpkin tastes really good straight from the can. In one of the chem lab closets, I found out what happened to all the crickets from that science experiment we never finished. I found out dead bugs really stink if you get enough of them piled up in an aquarium.

Turns out a German shepherd will eat those dead bugs if you forget to cover the garbage can.

Turns out cleaning up dead cricket barf will make a boy barf.

Best weekend ever.

Later the next week I called my dad one night when I was sure everybody in the whole school was sleeping.

I told my dad not to worry about me for the next few weekends because I'd be going home with different friends. He told me to take the time I needed, whatever that means.

When the next Friday rolled around, I felt a lot better knowing exactly what was going to happen. It felt good to be in charge. I told the dean my dad would pick me up at the bottom of the hill again. He asked if I would like a ride down. I said no.

I only had to call my dad that one time. He never came again. That's the bad part of the phone call. Finding out how happy and relieved he was not to have to be with me.

The good part is that's how the whole adventure, and all the magic that made it, got started. Because my dad stopped coming to get me. Because the dean didn't know what to do with me. Because a pack found me and ran alongside me. Because I got tired of being pushed around.

Don't be like dandelion fluff, shining bright but getting tossed around by the wind.

If people won't take care of you, then guess what? You gotta take care of yourself.

And in the end, I *made* the magic happen.

Chapter 8

WHERE YOU LEARN THE REST OF THE SECRET

Since then, I've found out there's a lot more at the lighthouse than swallows' nests and broken windows.

And so tonight, like every Friday night, I leave Dean Swift at the door with a smile and a wave.

I start down the road. At first I think about the other kids and what their weekends will be like. It's Mary Anne's turn to take Bobo home and I wonder if her mom will be mad about the dog hair on her car upholstery. I wonder if Sparrow's grandma lets him crack the eggs this time when they make brownies. I should write her a letter and tell her not to worry so much about salmonella. That's what soap and water are for, lady! I think about the Venn diagram Vincent made showing me how he was going to prank his stepdad. A flow chart would have been more effective.

I wonder what will happen when Mean Jack sticks a hand in his bag for a clean pair of socks and comes up with Gollum. Man, I'd like to hear that mobster yelp.

Then I notice how the brown branches of the cherry trees have green buds.

The winter months are the hardest. It's cold and the snow hurts my hands and feet when I walk. The woods get dark too early, and there is a lonesome sound in the wind.

In the spring, though, the wind talks to the new leaves. And the birds answer back, each with its own song. I'm always part of the conversation there. The sound of my breath when I run hard tells the woods I'm alive too, and so does the thump of my feet as I skim across the forest floor and the howl of my voice as I seek and find the moon and my mother.

But wait. This afternoon there's a big problem. As I'm walking down the road, I feel someone watching me. I stop. I turn around. The road behind me is empty. I keep walking. But the feeling won't go away. I stop again. I look into the trees. And up into the branches.

Tuffman.

He's sitting in the forked branches of an ash tree, and he's watching me. I catch most of my scream but not all of it. He drops to the ground. It must be twenty feet or more. He lands on both feet, his knees slightly bent. Like it's *nothing* to jump out of a tree and land on your feet and not break every bone in your legs.

"Hiya, Raul," he says.

All the hairs stand up on the back of my neck. His

voice sounds like the voice of a bad guy in a movie. Friendly, but like he wants to hurt you.

"You headin' down to meet your dad?" he asks.

My chest feels empty and my head is too full to think.

"It's funny how he never comes to the door like the other parents," he says.

I shrug.

"You ever hear of natural law? It's the way of the woods. Big things chase little things chase littler things," he says. "You're not safe alone. Not in these woods."

You know how sometimes you get a tiny voice whispering to you to get out of a bad situation? Right about now my tiny voice gets a megaphone. *Get away from this guy.*

I start walking again. Quickly. But something in me thinks that if I run, he'll chase.

He follows along, a step behind me.

We pass the point where I usually duck into the woods and head toward the lighthouse. Every step I take, my stomach feels emptier, my hands wetter, my pulse quicker.

Why won't he go away? I don't want to miss sunset. The secret only happens at sunset. Will it work if I get there after? If I miss a weekend, will it work the next one?

Here's the problem with magic. What if it's like baking bread? Cook Patsy told me that flour, water, sugar, salt, and yeast will only make bread if you use the exact right amounts and the exact right temperatures. What if the magic of White Deer Woods only works when every step is exactly right?

We can see the highway. I don't know what to do. Will he wait for my dad with me? When my dad doesn't come, will he make me go back to school? Will he make me climb the rope and run lines in the gym all weekend and drink protein shakes that taste like barf and chalk?

The wind comes down the hill from the water behind us. My nose twitches. There's a bad smell somewhere in it. On top of the smell of pine needles there's a kitty litter reptile smell I know from somewhere.

When I look back, Tuffman is staring at me.

"You worried about that coyote living in the Blackout Tunnel?" he asks.

Bingo. It's the Blackout Tunnel smell. For a second I feel relieved, like you do when you figure something out. Then it terrifies me. Because it means his nose is as sharp as mine.

"The area has too many predators already, doesn't it?" he asks. "I'm curious, Raul." He takes a long stride and then swings around and stops in front of me. "I'm curious," he repeats. "Dean Swift tells all the teachers that you're the expert on White Deer Woods."

Dean Swift talks about me to the teachers?

"Tell me, Raul."

The proud feeling shrivels up. I don't like how he keeps saying my name.

"Tell me about the woods. What kinds of predators have you come across out there, Raul?"

Tuffman's eyes are so intense, they paralyze me. For a second I don't see anything but the yellow rings around his pupils.

I feel like I have to answer his question.

He stares at me. "Anything bigger than a coyote out there, Raul?"

I open my mouth. The secret is about to fall out.

We both hear the engine coming down the hill at the same time. My mouth shuts. Tuffman glances back over his shoulder.

When he looks away from me, I blink. I've been keeping this secret for a year. Did I almost tell it to Tuffman just now? I cross my arms over my chest. I'm cold.

He turns back to me. "You should stay out of the Blackout Tunnel, Raul."

I nod. I'm trying not to look at him, but when he says my name I can't help it.

"Coyote'd make a meal of a loner like you. I guarantee it. You go back to that tunnel and you'll be sorry."

A car passes us slowly. It stops and backs up. Dean Swift rolls down the window. I'm so happy to see him that if he reached over and unlocked the door, I'd jump in.

"Is everything okay?" he asks.

"Raul and I were having a chat about the natural order, about the way there can only be one predator in a territory," Tuffman says.

Is *that* what we were talking about?

Dean Swift tilts his head and looks at me. His eyes pop a little. I must look as freaked out as I feel.

"I thought you left hours ago, Mr. Tuffman," the dean says.

Now it's Tuffman's turn to blink and look a little nervous. "I forgot something," he says. "So I came back for it. I forgot the key to my house, can you believe it?"

Dean Swift looks like he can tell Tuffman is lying. Then he looks at me like he's trying to figure out what the heck is going on here, exactly. He gives me a quick smile. I take another breath. I can tell it'll be all right. Somehow I'll get to the lighthouse by sunset.

"So," Dean Swift says finally. "Did you get it?"

"What?" Tuffman asks.

"Your key? Did you get it?"

"No."

"So where are you going now, Tuffman," Dean Swift says really slowly. It's a question, but he doesn't make it sound like one.

Tuffman's face is bright red. "To get the key," he says with a big gulp.

Dean Swift nods. "Hop in. I'll give you a ride back.

Unless you think you left your house key in the middle of this road."

Tuffman ducks his head. He lopes over and gets in.

Dean Swift starts to put the car in reverse and then looks out the window again. "You need anything, Raul?" he asks.

I give him a huge smile. "No, Dean Swift, I think I'm okay. My dad'll be here any minute."

Dean Swift nods at me. *Okay,* his face says to me. *You go meet your dad.*

I keep walking. I feel Tuffman watching me in the side-view mirror as the car turns around and heads back up the hill. I turn slightly and then stop myself. It's a woods instinct alive in me. Don't look back at an animal who is stalking you.

My mind focuses. My muscles tense.

The truth is sitting hidden in the facts, like Dean Swift says.

I'm not the only one of my kind. I'm not the only one with the secret.

Didn't White Deer call Vincent this morning? And the swarming crows? And his *name*! Isn't that proof? Woods magic happens to other people too.

Maybe it happened to Tuffman.

Okay, now you *need* to know what happens in the woods.

Remember how I found the lighthouse? There's more.

Two weekends later I was fishing in the lake. It was a Friday right before dusk.

First the woods went silent. Every warm body covered in fur or feather went still. Every bird twitter, every frog croak, every cricket thrum, every bee buzz, every leaf flutter, every rabbit nose twitch, every pebble click, every water lap—every living noise stopped.

Then in the middle of that silence there was a *BOOM* so loud that I thought someone had fired one of the old cannons hidden in the cliffs.

I looked across the lake in the direction of the sound.

From behind the low, swinging branches of a red cedar appeared a big white deer with antlers as black as a newly paved road.

It walked toward me and it spoke to me. It told me what to do so that someone I had lost could return to me. I listened so hard I forgot to breathe.

What would you do to see your mom if you had lost her? Would you go hungry? Would you run for miles and miles? Would you walk in the snow barefoot or under a boiling sun in a fur coat? Yes. Yes. Yes, you would.

I can't tell you the exact words White Deer said. That will always be a secret that I must keep. All I can say is that White Deer told me the light of the woods had spoken to my mother and told her where to find me. That she had been lost to me but that I could never be lost to her.

I put my pole down. Dandelion fluff floated everywhere. I walked out into the water, the twirling seeds catching the last of the day's light and dancing all around me. I dunked my head three times and said the things White Deer told me to say.

Then the woods were illuminated, but not from the sky above. It was from under and inside every dark, damp place. I saw light everywhere. Glowing hunks of green gold in the crevices where logs rotted to the forest floor. Foxfire. Then I saw the will-o'-the-wisp. Over the lake it bounced and shimmered, reaching back to me and hurrying ahead of me, drawing me forward.

As the sun slipped back and away behind the sea, I followed a path of light to the old lighthouse. I felt something watching me and running beside me again, and this time, because of White Deer, I knew who it was and my face was dripping with tears. I wasn't bawling. It was just like water flowing down a river. It was my whole heart in that river of tears, and I was happy.

When I came to the clearing on the cliff, the lighthouse was lit up. The light wasn't coming from inside it, though. The lichen on the tower glowed pale green like water breaking on sand in the morning.

On the threshold, the flowers called bleeding hearts bloomed. I pushed aside the red-green-gold ivy that covered the door. The soft leaves bent toward me and then away. They whispered to me in the language of leaves.

I walked into the lighthouse.

I took off my damp clothes, folded them, and tucked them into the iron stove like White Deer said.

Wings beat in the lantern room above, and I remembered the swallows and wondered if they had come home too.

Then the change came. I can't tell you how it happens. It doesn't hurt. My spine sparks. My skin prickles; it feels warm like it does when you stretch out in the cool grass under a summer sun. My ears pull up, my nose twitches, and my teeth sharpen. The pads of my fingers and toes press against the broken-up linoleum floor of the lighthouse. Do you know how good it feels to have a tail? Humans were meant to have tails. You don't know until you have one just how much you've missed it. You can't imagine what I smell—clover, dirt, bee pollen, frog spit, moss, bunny-rabbit breath, blackberry leaves, water. You can't imagine what I hear—worms sliming, bats hanging, leaves fluttering to the ground, tree trunks heating in the sun.

It's true. Every Friday night at dusk, I become a wolf.

Not a werewolf, don't say a werewolf.

A werewolf is a story someone made up to scare little kids. It's a monster that's half man and half wolf *at the same time*.

Me, when I'm a wolf, I'm a wolf. When I'm a boy, I'm a boy. Do you get it? It's not all mixed up. I'm one and then I'm the other. I change and I change back. I'm not some knuckle-dragging, hairy-faced monster who eats people.

A werewolf changes when he sees the full moon. He can't help it; he has no control over how he acts—it's why he's always gonna be alone. You never know if he's gonna feed you or eat you.

But for me it's a choice. White Deer told me the recipe, but I choose to follow it.

And when I'm a wolf, I'm never alone.

A white wolf meets me as I come out of the lighthouse door. She licks my face and my fur. In her throat she makes happy sounds, and in my throat the same sounds purr and rumble. Together we go to the woods on the side of the lake that nobody knows. We howl at the moon and we chase rabbits. When we walk through the woods together, the other animals fall back into the shrubs and leap under the fallen trees. Our shoulders touch as we sway along, our tails flick the wind.

We don't speak, of course not, don't be silly. We have calls that mean only true things. Not like words.

I have one that means *Where are you?*

She has one that means *I'm waiting right here.*

We have ones that mean *Watch out* and *There's a rabbit nearby, don't look but he's there in the blackberry leaves* and *I'm hungry* and *I'm tired* and *The sun feels good* and *This water is cold and fresh* and the one I hate that means *It's time for us to say good-bye.*

On Sunday mornings I become a boy again. I forget a lot of what happens when I'm in my wolf skin. But I remember enough.

When I'm tired I sleep, curled into her flank, and she watches over me, making soft music in her throat.

She's my wolf mother. She's my mother.

She followed me here all those years ago. She's been waiting for me to find a way to be with her. The lights in the woods told her. White Deer helped her. Those things I know because those are the things she doesn't need words to tell me. The important things, right? The things that matter.

I don't know why the change happened to her in the first place, or why she can't change back and be a human during the week like me. Maybe she forgot the recipe. It's why I'm always so careful to do everything the same way every single time. It's like with bread. If you forget the yeast, then the dough won't rise. Only with magic, when the recipe is wrong, what you get is a lot worse than crackers instead of bread.

And now that Dean Swift has helped me get rid of Tuffman, I'm going to go meet her tonight.

Chapter 9

WHERE RAUL LEARNS THAT SOMETHING HAPPENED IN THE WOODS

On Sunday my wolf mother and I return to the lighthouse. I'm always sad on Sundays. But this Sunday I'm worried, too. Something bad happened to her last week. When she met me Friday she had a deep scrape about eight inches long slicing down her left side. It was red and puffy. I could tell it had bled a lot.

There's nothing big enough in White Deer Woods to hurt her like that.

It has to be the new housing development. Because of it, she won't go as far north as she used to. White Wolf must be moving into another predator's territory. Maybe she's going south toward the fort to find food. But it can't be the coyote. A coyote would take one look at White Wolf and run off with flat ears and its tail squished up against its belly.

Something else is out there. I hope she stays out of its way this week.

A rabbit sits in the tall grass. We smell it before we see it. Twice its nose flutters open and shut.

White Wolf swings her head to look at me. *Go on. Get it.*

There's a reason people say "quick like a bunny." I charge into the underbrush. The smell of the rabbit is to my wolf nose what a paved road is to a boy's eyes. A path.

Rabbit scrambles under a fallen log and I leap over it. The air lifts me and for a minute I fly. I can't see anything but the chase. Boulder, ditch, log, thorn bush—my wolf body leaps and scampers and stretches and tumbles.

Rabbit turns. He's heading toward his burrow.

Bad idea, bunny.

The scent path opens up in front of us now. It's like he turned on headlights. He's been back and forth, in and out of that burrow so many times I can smell where he is going.

I corner him against a rock. *Snap.* I'm quick. Rabbit felt nothing. I promise.

I carry it back to her by the nape of its neck.

She makes a low growl. *Eat, Raul, eat.* She used to say that to me in a funny accent. It must be a line from an old movie she liked. I bet by now we would have watched it together.

I push the rabbit toward her. I'm returning to the world of refrigerators. She's recovering from an injury.

She growls, but I nose the meat toward her again. I

look at her, my neck straight, and my eyes speak to her. *You eat. You get strong.*

She puts her nose against mine.

Wolf kiss.

The bunny chase has brought us to the meadow where the wind has shoved back the trees. Every Sunday White Wolf leads me back to the lighthouse. There's a small growl that comes with a little nip that she only makes at the edge of the woods, and it means *Go now and be the boy you are.*

Her tail drops. She's sad to see me leave.

But there's more to it. White Wolf has regrets. I think she's sorry that we have to meet the way we do.

I lope toward the lighthouse.

White Wolf settles down under a big cedar and rests her head on her paws. The bunny is next to her. She better eat it.

My clothes are in the stove where I left them. As I put them on, I lose my wolf face and my wolf ways. When I walk out of the lighthouse, I'm no longer my second self, I'm no longer wolf me. I'm Raul, and the White Wolf who loves me is gone.

I head back toward the school. The sky is gray. A mist creeps up over the cliff, spreading a wet and glaring light into the woods.

The dean will be back by now, turning on the heat and the lights, making coffee and setting out cookies for the parents who take the time to come in. Some of the kids, like Mary Anne, just jump out of the car. Her parents don't even turn the engine off. They hit a button that makes the trunk pop open so that she can pull out her bags.

Dean Swift always runs down to help kids whose parents do this. He puts his arm around the boy or girl and takes the bag.

Sometimes I see Dean Swift look after the parents' car as it drives away, and his face looks like my insides feel—angry and sort of like he can't believe it. What kind of grown-up is too busy to carry his kid's suitcase up the stairs?

Thinking of the dean makes me feel better about going back. It'll be good to see Sparrow and hear about this weekend's disgusting casserole. His grandma throws everything she didn't eat that week into a pot for Sunday lunch—cottage cheese, refried beans, creamed spinach, spaghetti, fish sticks—if it's in her fridge Sunday morning, it's on Sparrow's plate at noon. She calls it Dutch soup, but me and Sparrow and some of the other kids like to make up different names for it. I draw pictures until someone guesses the name. So far we have barf bowl (Sparrow's), rat bath soup (mine), fungus 'n' feces (mine), poo punch (Sparrow's), dog drool dumplings (Dean Swift's), calamity casserole (Mary Anne's), and the newest one, stomach acid stew (Vincent's).

Maybe Mean Jack got to know Gollum. Do they pump your stomach for a mildly venomous snake bite? I'll ask the dean.

Maybe Vincent pranked his stepfather so good that he moved back out.

And maybe at dinner tonight Mary Anne will sit next to me at the counter.

I have a great idea. If I get there in time for drop-off, I can be the one to help her with her bag when her parents drive up. Dean Swift should be pretty easy to outrun.

Then I do what I do every Sunday when I'm halfway to the lake. I sniff until I find the stinkiest stick on the forest floor. It'll keep Bobo busy all week long.

I can tell by where the sun is in the sky that I'm earlier than usual, so I head toward the lake. I'm laughing over two new ones I thought up—scab surprise and maggot meatloaf.

But when the path opens out to the lake, I stop laughing pretty quick.

Tuffman is standing in front of the straw man.

"Was this your idea?"

I look at him. I remember the crazy idea I had about him on Friday afternoon—that he was one of my kind. I must be losing my marbles, as my dad would say. I think White Deer calls to people who need a second self because their first self has lost something so big it's not whole anymore.

Tuffman isn't the type who loses anything.

"You better talk to me, weirdo. I'm not playing games." He yanks the straw man off the tree. The heavy-duty ropes I used to tie it to the trunk snap like old rubber bands.

I can't believe it. The kids call me freaky strong, but the only word for Tuffman-strong is superhuman.

"You think it's funny to steal a man's clothes?" He strips the straw man.

The blood pumps in my neck. I want to run.

"This shirt means something," he says. "It means I'm a champion." He's ripping the straw man up as he talks. "Kids think they're the only ones with dreams. Grown-ups have dreams too. Dreams that die just like yours will unless you listen up and listen good."

He unzips his running jacket. He's not wearing a shirt underneath. The skin of his chest is smooth and tan and muscles bump and bulge. He turns around and points to a scar on his back. It's white and raised. It looks like he has two spines, almost.

"That's what happened to my dream. I was running in the woods one day, just like you." He steps toward me. "One wrong move, that's all it took." He tilts his head and I see his eyes glow. "They told me I'd never walk again. One wrong move in the woods, Raul, and everything changed. And now I'm a joke to you, huh?"

I shake my head. Nothing about Tuffman makes me

want to laugh. The scar is awful, like a thick seam of doubled-over skin.

"Bet you think that story has nothing to do with you. It has *everything* to do with you. You think you get to choose what happens next." He steps toward me again. "Well, you don't. Life happens to you."

He's about three feet away. I can sense he's about to grab me. The hairs on the back of my neck stand straight out.

"Listen, Raul," he says. His eyes fix on me. I can't move.

"Here's the moral to the story. Not just *my* story. *Your* story too. I was like you. I wasn't alone in the woods that day either. I was with a friend, Raul. More than a friend. She was family. I loved her like a little sister. She did that to me." He twists around again to show me the scar.

My mouth pops open. The scar has changed color. The muscles in his back twitch, and for a second I think it's a bloodred snake slithering along his spine.

"She broke my back. Maybe I had it coming. I'm the one that taught her to fight, that woke up the predator in her. I never thought she'd turn on me. I hate her sometimes, but I shouldn't. It's natural law. The strongest one wins. That day, she won."

He zips up his jacket.

"What are you doing out here, anyway? Is this your

territory?" He smiles a little, like he's teasing. But his eyes glow like he's not. He shifts.

I imagine the snake of a scar, twisting red with his every move. I remember the wounds in his neck that Mean Jack pointed out. My skin crawls. Everything about him is awful.

"Raul?" He says my name again.

I know better than to look in his eyes.

I run.

My second self is still awake. After the first step I go down on all fours and race wolf-style off the path and through the underbrush.

I hear Tuffman shout and curse, crashing down the path behind me. I barely have a head start, but I know these woods better than he does, and he only has two legs. I have four. I just have to make it to the road. It's drop-off day. Parents will be coming soon, right? Tuffman wouldn't want them to see him force-feeding me that bird's-nest toupee.

When I get to the road, I stand upright like a boy. The woods behind me are quiet, but I know he's in there, breathing hard and watching.

I brush my hands off on my jeans. I'm shaking. It's not just fear and adrenaline. It's shame. Tuffman saw me run on all fours like a wolf wearing the skin of a boy. It's like he saw me naked.

But that was a choice. I *chose* to run like a wolf.

I book it up the hill.

Please let Dean Swift be there. Please let the doors be unlocked.

I try the handle of the front door. I sigh with relief as it turns.

Bobo comes up and puts her nose in my pocket. *Give me the stinky stick.* Here's a conversation I understand. I give her the stick. She shoves her smooth head into my leg for a second. *Thank you.*

Welcome back to the world of doggy doors, kibble, and leashes. Where dogs are dogs and humans are humans.

I lie down on the blue sofa in the parlor. I feel like the straw man—like everything that holds me up snapped, and the stuffing got ripped out of me.

"What are you, sick?" a voice asks.

I scream a roller-coaster scream. "Eeeeek!"

Mary Anne is standing over me. She jumps when I scream and drops her notebook. I sit up and put my head in my hands. She sits down next to me.

"Sorry, Raul, I didn't mean to startle you," she says in a very kind voice. Then she starts to giggle. "That was funny, though."

It makes me laugh too. I can't remember the last time I laughed so hard. Maybe when Little John filled Mean Jack's shoes with crabs that had washed up dead on the beach. Or when Tuffman was showing us the proper form for sit-ups (*NO LIFTING YOUR BUTTS*

OFF THE FLOOR, YOU WEENIES), and he farted.

This is better, because there's no ghastly odor. Mary Anne smells like honey and daffodils. Trust me. If you had a wolf nose you'd know what a daffodil smells like, and it smells like it looks—yellow and frilly. Did you notice daffodils are always, always nodding yes at you? Remember that. Whenever you have a day where everyone is saying no to you, just find a daffodil. It will say yes.

Man. This is what Mary Anne does to me. Flowers and giggles. I make myself sick.

I stop laughing and look at her. Why is she here so early?

She reads my face. "My mom has to fly to Chicago tonight, so she dropped me off early. I got here before Dean Swift did." She frowns and then smiles quick to hide it.

I know how that feels. I wonder how long she sat on the front steps with her suitcase, waiting in the fog. No wolf coat to keep her warm. I pat her on the shoulder.

"No big deal. I'm working on a novel," she says. "I have the setting—Norway. And the villain—a sorcerer named Rodrigo who has a secret formula that will turn the world into a huge ocean. I have a heroine, a mermaid whose parents work for Rodrigo. But I need a hero."

She looks at me for a long time. Her eyes get very small like she's thinking hard.

"You could be a hero," she says slowly.

I look down at my hands. I got a few cuts during that tussle with the rabbit. Do not, I repeat, do *not* get the wrong end of a rabbit that doesn't want to be eaten.

Mary Anne's words make me feel so good it's embarrassing. I want to float away and bury my head under a pile of blankets at the same time.

Then I hear Mary Anne sigh. "No," she says in her serious voice, "no, the hero needs to be more . . . hmm." She pauses, scratching her chin. "More what, exactly? What is the word I am looking for?"

I feel a little irritated. I watch her from the corner of my eye. Just because I don't talk much doesn't mean I can't hear.

"More heroic," she says finally. "You'll make a fine helper for the mermaid. But the hero needs to be more . . . There's only the one word for it, isn't there?"

I get up from the couch and head up to the bathroom to take a shower.

What a day. Five minutes of conversation with Tuffman and I felt like I'd been doing sudoku for three hours straight. Five minutes of conversation with Mary Anne and I went from king of the world to feeling like a worm a bird pecked in half and then left because it didn't taste good enough.

There's been too much talking already today, and I haven't even said a word.

Chapter 10

A JOKE WITH NO PUNCH LINE: ONE DAY THIS PREDATOR WALKED INTO A FOREST . . .

Bad news at dinner Sunday night.

"Children." Dean Swift comes into the dining hall to make an announcement. "Listen! There is no call for panic, but it appears that a cougar has taken up residence near Fort Casey. Two guards and three tourists have described hearing the cry of a cougar while walking in the park at dusk." The dean clears his throat. He throws his head back and opens his mouth and makes a screech like a cat screaming and a dog snarling and a ghost sobbing.

The sound makes cold sharp fingernails walk up my spine.

But Mean Jack has to make a joke. "Was that a wildebeest burp, sir?"

Dean Swift doesn't even notice the Cubs laughing. "No, it's a cougar, Mean Jack, uh, I mean *Jack*," he answers, and then his face gets red and his eyes bulge because he said "mean Jack" twice now instead of once. "Scratch marks have been found about nine feet up on the trunks of several trees near the road to our school. This tells us it is a large cougar, and that it is actively roaming our grounds. Chances are good that it will move on shortly. But until it does, we must take precautions when we leave the building."

A cougar? The word gives me a strange feeling. It's like an itch in my brain I can't scratch. After a minute I realize it has to do with what happened in the woods this weekend. Sometimes what happens when I wear my wolf skin is hard to remember when I'm a boy.

My mind scratches around, and then Vincent sits down next to me.

"Don't look at me," he warns. "I'll die laughing if you look at me."

I stare straight out the window at the water.

"So I hid behind the bathroom door," Vincent says. "I put on the zombie mask I told you about. My stepfather was watching the game, and he drinks a lot of beer when he watches a game, right? So I knew he'd have to go to the bathroom, right?"

I look at him with a face that says, *Yeah, yeah, you told me all this on Friday*. There's a little piece of wolf worry left dangling in my head, and I'm not gonna feel like joking around until I rip it off.

"Okay, right. I told you that." He starts to giggle. "So look out the window, okay? I can't tell it without laughing if you look at me."

By now all the weirdos are leaning across to listen, and a couple of the kids from nearby tables have come over.

"So he comes into the bathroom, and he's unzipping his pants, and boom! I jump out at him and he *screams*." Vincent can hardly talk, he's laughing so much. "He screamed like a wee little girl, and then he peed his pants."

I can't help it. I laugh so hard I forget my wolf worries.

Nobody's eating anymore, everyone's laughing, and the story starts flying around the room. By the time it gets to the little kids' table, it's turned into *Vincent's dad went pee in his pants.* That's enough of a story for the Cubs, and half of them laugh so hard they fall out of their chairs and roll around on the floor. Little John ends up with nacho cheese mashed into his hair. Three peas get jammed up Peter's nose.

After dinner I realize it's no joke. Vincent has changed everything in less than a week.

Normally during TV time I sit in a ratty old armchair off to one side. All the other kids sit on the floor or the sofa. Nobody makes me sit where I sit. But nobody ever sits in my chair either.

Tonight, when Vincent walks into the TV room, everyone shifts around a little. Mary Anne scoots closer to Jenny to make a space for him next to her on the carpet. Mean Jack punches Little John in the shoulder to get him to slide down from the sofa to the floor.

Vincent doesn't notice them. He scans the room. When he sees me, he walks over and perches on the arm of my chair.

"Hey," he says. "I almost forgot. I told my mom about you this weekend. She wants you to spend spring break with us."

I can feel everyone's ears stretch toward us.

"Will your dad be cool with that?"

I nod. I can see the other kids look at me like they've never seen me before. Vincent has cool. It's contagious. Now I have it too.

All the chairs are turned toward the TV as usual, but the kids sitting in them are turned toward Vincent. He has a million and one jokes and stories. My armchair is the center of the room. Once or twice I start to open my mouth. I don't say anything. But I could have. I think they would have listened.

Later in bed I turn on my LED flashlight from the cereal box.

I hate the dark. It was hardest when I first got here. The sound of the madrona's branches scraping the window made me think of monsters. Even now I wake up sometimes in the middle of the night, and at first I'm half asleep and I forget that White Wolf found me. It's a feeling like night is inside of me.

Let's not talk about it.

Tonight I think I have a friend. It's a light inside me. But it scares me a little. I wonder how I can make him keep liking me. I wonder if he'll get tired of me.

There's no answer to that. I take out the code-cracking book Cook Patsy gave me. Last week I thought I'd need it to start up a conversation with Vincent. Like making friends was an uncrackable code.

I must fall asleep, because I wake up in the dark. The flashlight is on the floor. I hear footsteps in the hall outside my room. My heart bumps. A voice mumbles. My mind wants me to run, but my legs aren't listening.

A monster or a murderer jiggles the doorknob to the utility closet next to my room.

The next doorknob in the hall is mine.

Did I lock my door?

In my mind I see Tuffman's glowing eyes. I hear him saying my name. I can't move.

I wonder if they will find my last will and testament in my sock drawer. A cold sweat covers my body. I go over the distribution of my earthly possessions.

Sparrow will get my clothes and my books.

Cook Patsy gets my mom's box full of recipes. I've never opened it, so they will be good as new.

Dean Swift will get my shark-tooth necklace for his science cabinet.

My dad—if he's not too busy to come and pick it

up—will get the shoebox where I keep things that remind me of my mom: her velvet headband that used to smell like her, her gold bracelet with her name engraved on the inside and flowers and vines on the outside, a CD she used to play when she rocked me, one of her gloves that for a long time I put my hand inside whenever I slept.

Keys jangle. The utility closet door opens. I hear feet on steps. Whoever heard of a closet with stairs?

I scrabble my hand across the floor until I find the flashlight. When I flip its beam at the clock, I see it's midnight. This is a strange time for someone to be concerned about utilities.

I lie there for a long time. It feels like five hours, but the clock says it's only been two minutes. I tiptoe to the door and stand there with my ear to it for another five hours that turns out to be one minute. Slowly I open my door.

I look to the right. The door to the closet is ajar. I peek in and see a staircase. The stairs must lead up into the north turret, overlooking White Deer Woods. From the outside of the building it's obvious my room is just beside and below it. But from the inside I never thought of it as anything but a utility closet. Maybe because the sign on the door says UTILITY CLOSET.

I creep up the stairs. Somehow I know exactly where to put my feet on each step so that it won't creak.

Except on the third to the last one when I step dead center and the stair groans like a bull.

I stand very still. I get ready to bolt back down.

When my thoughts stop crashing around, I hear a scratching sound and the rustle of papers. Someone's writing up there.

Do assassins have diaries?

My nose twitches. I don't think that's Tuffman.

"Eureka," a man's voice says. "Perhaps the cougar saw the light."

The voice belongs to Dean Swift.

I hear a click like a button being pushed.

"Midnight. March seventeenth." He must be speaking into a recorder. "After years of searching, I have found Fresnel's secret treatise. It is titled most tantalizingly *On the Generative Power of Light*. My hunch was correct. Numerous prisms on the old lighthouse lens were never correctly installed. Using Fresnel's measurements, I have exponentially increased the power of the light beam. Is it mere coincidence that there are reports of cougar activity south of White Deer Woods? My investigation of its den on the fort grounds indicates it has been in the area for approximately one month. The timing corresponds with my first lighting of the lens since I applied Fresnel's secret calculations. Questions: Is this simply a predator displaced by the new housing development? Or, as per Fresnel's theories, did the light from the lens draw him to us?" A button clicks.

My mind is scratching around. *Its den on the fort grounds?* That was no coyote den in the Blackout Tunnel. It's the cougar's.

I stretch out and peer around the low wall that keeps people in the room from tumbling down the stairs. I'm looking at Dean Swift's back as he sits at a messy desk. Every once in a while he looks up at something in front of him. It takes a second for my eyes to adjust to the low light, but when they do, I almost somersault backward down the stairs.

It's an enormous lighthouse lens. And when I say enormous, I mean it's ten feet high and five feet wide. It fills most of the room beyond Dean Swift's desk.

Even though I've never seen it before, I recognize it.

I sneak back down the stairs to my room, my blood hot and my skin alive. I need to be sure.

I lie belly down on my bed and slide the books out one at a time. There are about twenty. It's my personal library on lighthouses.

I pull out my favorite, *Lighthouses of the Pacific Coast.* There it is, on page 127. A photo of the Point Reyes' first-order Fresnel lens, manufactured in 1867. First-order means it's the biggest kind. It has 1,032 pieces of glass. Twenty-four of those pieces are bull's-eye lenses so powerful they could start a fire if they're not exposed to direct sunlight.

That's a first-order Fresnel lens upstairs. Everything tingles. My skin, my hair, inside my belly, my brain and my heart.

Is it mine? The question burns in me. I've always wondered what happened to my light. The books all say that the first lighthouse on the island, named Red Bluff, was lit in 1861. Forty years later it was destroyed, and a new one was built a few miles away with a brand-new lens. I've figured out that the books are wrong about one thing. Red Bluff never got torn down. It's where it always was, at the edge of the cliff deep in White Deer Woods, where the meadow meets the cedars and the cedars meet the sea. I don't know why I'm the only one who knows about it. And I don't know why its lantern room is empty.

Because none of the books say what happened to Red Bluff's first-order Fresnel lens. You can't lose one of them. Those suckers cast a beam for thirty miles!

I'd bet my wolf skin that's my light in the turret.

But how did it get there? No way you could fit it up the staircase, or in through one of the little square windows.

There's only one way, and it makes me dizzy to think about it.

The school must have been built *around* the lens.

You know how an earthquake happens when two plates of the earth's crust slam into each other? My school-world and my woods-world just smashed together. It's all connected, but I don't know how. White Deer told me the lighthouse is my place between places. It's the door I walk through to find my other self.

But this school where I live was built to hold its light long before I was ever born.

Chapter 11

A RECIPE FOR A HERO

Monday morning.

I wake up to the sound of the madrona branch scraping back and forth across the window. Rain spatters. The wind howls.

My first thoughts are wolf worries. I hope White Wolf is dry and warm under our ledge. I hope she ate the rabbit. I hope the wound in her side is better and that the rain has washed the rest of the dried blood out of her pretty fur. Then I remember the lens and my lighthouse and Dean Swift's *eureka*.

The wind slaps the branch against the glass. The books are still spread across the floor. The dean said the light brought the cougar. I sit up. I finally scratched that brain itch I got last night at supper when Dean Swift first mentioned the cougar.

The cougar gave White Wolf that scrape. For a minute I can't move again, like last night when I thought Tuffman was lurking outside my door. This is worse, and it's true. A cougar attacked my mother.

I can't lose White Wolf.

I can't lose her and I can't help her. I sit on the edge of my bed in my underwear. My back hunches so my elbows touch my knees, and my hands cover my face. My skin is cold and my hands feel like ice.

The feeling is called Despair.

Nobody can help us.

In the dining hall I grab three boxes of cereal. Raisin bran, granola, and Lucky Charms cover the three major food groups—fruit, fiber, and marshmallows.

I need sustenance. I need a plan. I need to think this through.

I have to push past about ten kids to get to my usual seat. Vincent is on the stool next to it, and as I set my tray down, he lifts his jacket off of my stool without even looking at me.

Nobody has ever wanted to sit by me enough to save me a seat.

I'm so surprised that it takes me a minute or two to notice that the weirdo counter is really weird today. Kids from all the groups are hanging around, holding trays filled with their dirty dishes, listening to Vincent tell a story. Their fingers are white and blue from gripping the trays, and I can tell by how they shift from one foot to the other that they're tired of standing, but they don't want to miss a word.

After Vincent finishes talking and while everyone is repeating the punch line, he turns to me. Without saying a word, he pulls a plate from his tray and puts it on mine. Then he turns back around to answer some dumb question.

It's a plate full of bacon and sausage and ham. I haven't had hot food for breakfast in forever. It's cold by now, sure, but it *was* hot once, and that's good enough.

I don't say much. Vincent doesn't seem to mind. Everyone's listening, but after a while I get the feeling he's telling his jokes for me.

"Yeah," he says when I finally crack a grin. "I *knew* you'd be the only one to get it. We got the same sense of humor."

All this time I thought it was my fault that I couldn't figure out how to fit in. But now I see. You can't ever fit in like a number or a letter, because friendship's not a puzzle or a cipher. There's no answer that you get right or wrong. You don't "get" friends. You are one.

You have one.

I stare out the window.

Vincent keeps yakking away next to me, drawing a diagram on a napkin, making the weirdos laugh until they almost puke. You can't be a dummy and be that funny. He's got street smarts is what my dad would say—the kind of smarts that keep you alive.

"Are you done?" he asked as he scoots his stool back. When I nod he grabs my tray and stacks it on top of his.

"Save my place at lunch," he says, picking up our trays and heading off.

Maybe Vincent can help me protect my mom. I don't know how. But I think he would if he could.

How much would I have to tell him?

I've got kitchen duty, so when I'm done I put my plate on top of the other dirty dishes in the bus tub, pick it up, and head back to the kitchen.

"You like the meat plate special?" Cook Patsy asks when I swing open the doors.

"Thank you," I say.

She looks at me for a second and then taps her head, like she's just got an idea. She pulls a cookbook from the shelf. "You choose what we make for lunch. Anything you want. And then if we have time, why don't you let me teach you some wrestling? I was state champ in high school."

I stare at her, totally confused. Now *Cook Patsy* wants to wrestle me? Maybe it's a virus, a terrible pandemic, a contagion spreading through the teachers.

ChokeHoldococcus. PinaStudentitis.

"I cleaned the rubber mats and everything," she says.

I look down at the black mats that cover the kitchen floor. All the little wet bits of food and slime are gone. It reeks of bleach. So that's good to know. When my face gets pushed into it, it will be very sanitary.

"I thought about it all weekend," she says. She

looks worried. There are circles under her eyes.

Then I understand. She doesn't want to squish my face into the mat. She wants to teach me to squish *Tuffman's* face into the mat.

"I can't let you get pushed around," she says. "I can't let Tuffman bully you. But I respect that you want to solve your own problems."

She lifts up the cookbook. "It's the kitchen code. Follow the recipe. And my recipe always calls for a fair fight. So I'm going to teach you to defend yourself. But let me tell you, I don't think a fight between a teacher and a student can ever really be fair. So if I hear one more whisper of him picking on you, I'm going to the dean."

She hands me the cookbook. "You choose."

I look down at it for a long time without opening it. She turns around and punches the button to start the dishwasher. Cook Patsy is trying to look out for me. I bet my mom would've talked to me like that too. A little sharp, so it sounds like she's mad, but she's not mad, she's worried. About me.

I open the cookbook. Whatever we make for lunch, I'm not chopping onions. My eyes are already watery. It's allergy season, I guess.

I get a good idea. It must be all the protein. "Wait," I say.

I race out of the kitchen and up to my room. I come back down with the recipe box.

I mean, what if I don't die? She'd never know I wanted her to have them.

"Hmm." She thumbs through the cards. "Tuna Surprise?"

I shake my head.

"Beef Stew?"

I shake my head. She holds the box back out to me. "What, then?"

I've never really read the cards before. The sight of my mom's handwriting makes me smile and feel sad at the same time. I pick one card up just so I can touch it where she probably touched it. All that's between her hand and mine is seven years.

Cook Patsy watches me for a minute. Then she pats my shoulder and lifts the door on the huge dishwasher. Steam pours out. I feel her glance over at me.

I look at each card. There's no order to the recipes. It's not alphabetical like Apple Pie to Yam Surprise, and it's not in the order that you eat them, like appetizers to desserts. Meringues is the first recipe, and the one after is Ham with Pineapple. But I keep them like she left them. I want to read them the way she wrote them.

"They were my mom's," I say.

Cook Patsy reaches up and hangs a pot on the hook above the stove. "I figured as much. Let's make lunch a feast in her honor, how about that?"

I nod. My throat is tight.

I take the next two cards without looking at them and hand them to Cook Patsy.

"Bacon and Cheddar Omelet. Now that's a good lunch for a Monday," she says. "And Island Cobbler for dessert." She sets the cards down on the counter and opens the fridge. She goes back to read the cards. She looks up at me. A long line appears between her eyes.

I can tell she's really thinking about what she wants to say.

"Raul, was your mom a good cook?" she asks. "I mean, do you remember actually eating the food she made for you?"

I shrug.

"'Cause I want you to take a look at this and tell me if it sounds right. Maybe it's her handwriting."

I look at the recipe for Island Cobbler.

3 pineapple
2 sprigs mint
4 oranges
1 egg
3 cups milk
2 tsp cinnamon
3 oz liver
7 cps blackberry
1 cp sugar
7 pats Butter?"

When I get to the three ounces of liver I make a face.

"Yeah, right? You don't often see liver show up in a dessert recipe. Or a question mark, either." Cook Patsy looks like she doesn't know what to say. "I'm sure she was really good at lots of other stuff," she says after a minute.

I close the box.

She was good at being my mom.

In honor of my mom we decide to make grilled cheese sandwiches and canned tomato soup for lunch. Then Cook Patsy teaches me a couple of really good moves.

"The main thing," she says, "is to be aggressive. Don't let him choose what's gonna happen next. *You* choose."

After kitchen duty I go to my room. My mom was a rotten cook. Maybe it's weird, but this makes me happy. I know something about her now—something only her kid would know about her, something only I could tease her about. It's like Sparrow and his grandma's Dutch soup. I've got a joke with my mom now too.

I keep thinking about it, shaking my head. Liver in dessert? No wonder she messed up the recipe to change herself back.

Have you ever taken a joke too far? That's how that thought makes me feel. Bad and sad, like you would if you were teasing someone and took it too far.

How do I get her back? The question aches like a bruise. And how do I protect her from the cougar until I figure it out?

Last night it sounded like Dean Swift thought the cougar had something to do with the lens. My books are still spread out all over the floor. It sounds crazy, but I go ahead and look for words like "measurements" and "formula" in some of the BOBs. (That's what Ms. Tern calls the Back Of the Book.)

I find a few pages listed for the word "measurements" in a book about lighthouses during the Civil War. It turns out that in wartime lighthouse lenses got taken apart so enemy ships couldn't navigate the coastline. After the war some lenses got put back together wrong. That's not a big surprise, since all one thousand prisms have to be angled in just the right way. If the measurements are off, the beam won't be very strong.

It reminds me of what Dean Swift said about making the beam more powerful. I squint to remember how he said he figured out the correct measurements. Did he really say he found them in a "secret" book by Fresnel? I'm pretty sure the title was something like *The Generative Power of Light*. I pull out my dictionary. "Generative" is the adjective for "generation," and that means "to bring into being or existence." So to make something live.

I think about it for a while. Light makes things

live. But why would that be a secret? Even Little John knows about photosynthesis. We've all put dirt, water, and a bean in a plastic cup and set it in the light or out of the light or to the side of the light. The sprout is phototropic. That means it will grow toward the light.

I sigh. It's hard to believe that Dean Swift thinks the light made the cougar come here, like a sprout turns to the sun. A cougar is not a bean.

Maybe I didn't hear him right.

I feel like a dog biting his tail, going around in circles. My mom and her wolf skin and me and mine, the cougar and a light made by a flame and 1,032 prisms.

Then I stop. My mind sits down. It's all very simple. Who knows when Dean Swift will light the lens, or why he thinks the cougar has turned toward it. I can't control that—just like I can't tell my mom where to find her human skin.

But I do have a choice. There's one thing I can choose to do that will keep my mom safe and give us more time to figure out her recipe. I can get rid of the cougar.

A funny thought comes to me.

You want a hero, Mary Anne? You're looking right at him.

Chapter 12

WHERE RAUL LEARNS VINCENT'S PROBLEM

I wait until midnight. Then I put my flashlight in my pocket and stand at my door for a minute, listening. All is quiet.

"Come with me," I whisper to Vincent five minutes later.

He pokes his head out from under his covers. He screams. I hold the flashlight up so that he can see it's me.

"What are you doing in here?" he asks. "How did you get in?"

"I opened your door. It wasn't locked," I say. "I need your help for an undertaking of great importance."

He hops out of bed and pulls on his jeans. "Do I need a jacket?" is all he asks.

That's a friend for you. The kind of kid who grabs a jacket and goes with you—even when you are waking him up in the middle of the night to sneak out a window and climb down a tree taller than a three-story building and walk out into the pitch black to *hunt a wild cougar*.

I lead him out of his room to the end of the hall. The madrona that goes past my bedroom window reaches all the way up here. The window groans as I lift it. I go out first and then point the flashlight up so Vincent can see where to step.

He drops from the lowest branch and lands even more quietly than I do.

The flashlight makes a circle of light at our feet. Outside of that circle, we can't see a thing. We walk very slowly, since we are walking toward a cliff. Very. Slowly. We step off the mowed lawn of the school grounds and onto the zigzag path.

We walk one behind the other, Vincent in front and me in back.

"Maybe we should get Bobo," Vincent says. "Just to scare off the cougar if it's out there."

"No," I say. "That's our mission. We *want* to find the cougar."

Vincent stops so suddenly that I run into him and we end up taking a shortcut down the hill to the beach. In the beginning we do something very like somersaults, but by the end we have crashed into enough stuff on our way down that we have straightened out a little and are rolling on our sides like kids do down grassy hills for fun.

Only this hill is not grassy. And we are not having fun.

Of course I drop the flashlight when we meet the raccoon.

When we finally fall onto the wet sand at the bottom of the hill, we lay there for a while, breathing. The air smells good, like fish and salt and the tar they paint on wood that sits near water. Sand fleas are jumping all over us. I pull some leaves and small branches out of my hair. I'm bleeding—just a little bit—in about twenty places.

After a minute I start to wonder, why is the sand so wet this far up the beach? I get a bad feeling.

Then I hear it.

Keep in mind, it's pitch-black.

But I know a killer wave coming when I hear it.

"Get up!" I yell to Vincent. We barely have time to jump up onto the driftwood pile behind us before it hits.

We hang on to a big log as the wave washes over us, bashing us against the wood and leaving us sputtering and coughing.

"Move!" I shout as I hear another wave gathering itself up.

Vincent and I scuttle over the rest of the driftwood logs. We find the zigzag path and sit down. Our teeth are chattering. Sand crunches between my molars. My nose and throat have that scratchy feeling you get after you throw up.

"At least it washed all the twigs out of my hair," Vincent says.

"And the salt in the salt water is antiseptic," I say, trying to look on the bright side too. "That's why all of our cuts and welts and scrapes and abrasions hurt so especially bad."

"Yes," says Vincent. "It's good to think that we won't have to worry about any minor infections."

We find the flashlight at the top of the path, right near where we bumped into each other. I pick it up and we set out across the lawn to the school.

"Try again tomorrow night?" I ask.

Vincent takes a long time to answer.

"Listen," I say, "I'll get us headlamps. And I'll check the tide tables in Dean Swift's office to make sure no waves sneak up on us."

"Yeah, yeah," says Vincent. He sounds a little grumpy. "I'm in."

I sigh. I'm sticky, soaked, bruised, and battered. But I'm glad to have a friend like Vincent.

We start up the tree. When he gets to the window and I'm in the fork of the two biggest branches, we hear it.

The cougar's screech fills the night. I can see the sound like a funnel cloud, almost, narrow where it begins and then opening out into the sky. The sound is coming from the edge of the fort closest to the beach.

The cougar screams again, and a shudder jerks my head hard to the side. That animal is close.

It's on the beach.

Near the driftwood pile.

Where we were standing ten minutes ago.

We climb through the window. Vincent is shaking now, and I don't think it's just the wind and his wet clothes. I think he can see the cougar in his mind the way I can see it in mine, the huge cat pacing, sniffing the wet wood, leaping onto the pile and pausing, one paw up, its nose in the air, tracking a scent.

Our scent.

"Tomorrow night, same time," I say when we get to his room.

"But why are we doing this?" Vincent asks.

"We need to get that cougar," I whisper. "I think it's trying to hurt someone I love."

Vincent turns his back to me. He opens his door without saying a word.

I can't blame him for bailing out. The mission tonight was a ridiculous disaster, a miserable failure, a complete catastrophe. And that's only if you look at it in a really, really positive light.

He steps into his room and then turns around to face me.

"Then we'll take care of it. You and me together. We'll get it." His eyes are scared, but he bobs his head up and down like he really means it.

"You know why?" he says. He pulls me into his room. "It's a secret. Nobody at the school but Dean Swift knows. And he only knows part of it."

I sit down on the desk chair next to his bed. He sits facing me.

"This summer there was a fire in my house. Me and my baby brother were sleeping upstairs. I tried to run out the door, but there was too much smoke. I ran to the window. My mom was down there. She was crying. She said to get the baby and climb out the window. I couldn't move. I started shaking and shaking and I fell down. I was so scared. Then a fireman broke through the door. Another one came through the window. They picked us both up and got us out of there." He stops talking, and I let him. I'm soaked and frozen to the bone, but I know better than to rush a kid through his secret.

"The firemen gave me a sticker and said I was really brave. But that was a lie. I didn't think about my brother once. I didn't try to save him or anything." His mouth pulls out into a straight line, and I can tell he's trying really hard not to cry.

"I think it's why my mom sent me here," he says. "She wants me to get tough."

After a minute he looks up at me sideways, so I can only see half his face.

"You know how that fire started?"

I shake my head.

"It was me. I found some matches in my stepdad's jacket. I wanted to see what it felt like to light one. Right before bed, while they were giving my brother a bath, I hid in the coat closet and lit them all up. I thought I stomped them out. But I missed one." He covers his mouth with his hand. "You're the only person who knows. My mom would leave me here forever if she knew."

"I won't ever tell," I say.

Then all of a sudden he grins. "My mom blamed my stepdad for the fire. She almost kicked him out for it. Wouldn't that have been great? She made him give up smoking. He'd *kill* me if he knew it was me. Whenever they argue, she brings it up and says how his smoking almost fried us all."

I try to smile, but I don't think that's funny. I know Vincent hates his stepdad. But that's a whale of a lie.

"This time I'm not gonna let anyone down." Vincent keeps talking. "You're gonna put a rock in that sling of yours and you're gonna hit that cat between the eyes. You're gonna knock him out, and we're gonna hog-tie him. When we get back to school, I'll tell everyone the whole story and you'll be a big hero."

I imagine the look on Mary Anne's face when she hears about it.

"Yeah, then that Mary Anne will notice you for sure," he says with a grin.

My cheeks get hot.

"What, you think I didn't know you're crushing on her?" He rolls his eyes. "She likes you already, but this will show her what you're made of."

As I walk back to my room, I leave squishy footprints in the carpet and on the stairs. I'm cold. I'm wet. But I'm warm inside as I think about Vincent.

A hero and a storyteller. They go together. You can't have one without the other.

Chapter 13

WHERE RAUL LEARNS ABOUT COUGARS AND HUNTERS AND DRAWS A DANGEROUS DOCUMENT

I wake up thinking how last night I missed the cougar by ten minutes. Did it find White Wolf? The worry hooks into my heart like a claw.

And there's a new problem. I'm scared now. I can hear that shriek in my head. It put a bone-deep, teeth-chattering, knee-knocking kind of fear in me. What makes me think I can catch a cougar with a sling and a little help from a friend?

I need information. How much do they weigh? How fast are they? How well do they see in the dark?

I stop by Dean Swift's office on my way to breakfast. He's busy writing, but for once the words won't wait.

"Do cougars hunt wolves?" is the first question I ask. *Say no,* I think. *Please say no.* If the answer's no, then I'm barking up the wrong tree.

Dean Swift looks at me for a long time.

Maybe he knows I was spying on him in the turret, and he's so furious he doesn't even know what to say. What if he calls my dad about it? There's a can of worms I'd like to keep sealed.

Then I see that even though he's staring right at me, his hand is writing. The man isn't listening.

"Do cougars kill wolves?" I ask again.

The question finally sinks in. His eyes bulge.

"Well," he says. He stands up and puts his hands in his coat pockets so his elbows stick out a little. He looks like a penguin.

Bobo is at his feet. She sighs.

I sit down. I sigh too.

When Dean Swift looks like a penguin, we all know he is about to give a lecture.

Sometimes, when Dean Swift is very interested in and very informed about a subject—like cougars and wolves it turns out—he takes a very long time to get to the point.

I am very hungry. But I listen long and hard.

Here's the point: Cougars attack wolves, but only rarely. It has to do with territory. Sometimes a cougar gets "displaced," which means it doesn't have a territory of its own. Then it might try to move into a wolf's territory. Or a wolf might feel its territory shrinking due to human population growth. It may begin to hunt in a cougar's territory. Either way, there's bound to be a fight. If there's more than one wolf, then the cougar doesn't stand much of a chance. The wolves will follow the cougar around, and then when it makes a kill, the wolves will leap in and chase the cougar off and eat his dinner. Cool, huh? Well, not for the cougar. It spends so much energy making kills it can't eat, it eventually starves to death. Or it gets so hungry it does something risky—like pounce from too high—and ends up snapping its spine.

So much for the good news.

Here's the bad news: In a fair fight between predators—when there's only one wolf and one cougar—the cougar will most likely win.

First period is PE. It might as well be. It's not like the day is going to get better.

Tuffman calls my name for roll like usual. Maybe he's not holding a grudge about our voodoo doll in the woods. I don't see the bird's-nest toupee anywhere handy. He doesn't say much of anything to me. Instead he throws a ball out at us and barks, "Dodgeball!"

His feelings toward me become pretty clear though, when the first round ends.

"Raul, stand at the wall!" he yells. "And the rest of you little blue-haired ladies, don't tell me you can't hit him."

Oh yeah, he's still mad. Guess he decided that since I used the straw man of him for target practice, he'd turn me into a bull's-eye.

"I'll give a quarter to whoever leaves a mark," he hollers. He jingles the change in his pockets. They look very, very full.

I gulp. And dodge and duck and dart for my life.

Tuffman's pockets are empty in fifteen minutes. When the quarters run out, kids get dimes. Then nickels. The darnedest thing is that those kids throw just as hard for the pennies, in the end.

The good part is that every time Vincent gets the ball, he heaves it, granny-shot style, at the hoop at the other end of court. The bad part is that even though everyone laughs every time he does it, nobody copies him.

Of course Tuffman's gonna put a stop to that. The next time Vincent gets the ball, Tuffman booms, "What are you two, besties?"

He stalks over. "Vincent. You hit him fair and square, or you drop and give me fifty."

Vincent glances at me.

All the boys start to chant, "Hit him, hit him."

Fifty push-ups? Vincent doesn't have five in him.

Vincent lifts the ball. He stares at the ground. Then he looks up and takes aim.

My stomach jumps.

Right as he's about to throw it, Tuffman smacks the ball down.

"See?" Tuffman says. "Some things never change. It's always your best friend who betrays you in the end."

They don't even know what Tuffman's talking about, but all the boys hoot.

"Burn!" says Mean Jack.

Vincent looks off to the side.

All I can do is remember Tuffman's story about how his best friend broke Tuffman's back in the woods. Why is everything he says to me lately so personal? It's creepy.

Game over, people. I'm done.

"Where you going?" Tuffman asks when he sees me heading toward the locker room. "Don't be a quitter. We're only going after you because you're so good at running away. Heck, you can get down on all fours if you want."

My cheeks burn. I look around to see if any of the other boys heard. But Mean Jack is picking his nose, and Little John is scraping off the scab on his elbow and eating it, and Jason is walking around the room doing a chicken dance.

Tuffman sends the ball at Jason, so hard his last "squawk" comes out like a scream.

Vincent walks over to me. "I was going to take that ball and slam him with it," he says. "He wouldn't have known what hit him."

You promised your mom not to lie, I almost say to him, but instead I nod like I believe him. It's not easy to change. And it's hard not to do what Tuffman wants. It's the way he says your name.

I don't blame him. But I would've done all fifty push-ups with him.

Tuffman looks over at us, the ball raised high. I pick up the bathroom pass that's on a hook by the locker room door and hold it up to him.

"Wimp!" he hollers at me. Then he says, "Okeydoke, Mean Jack, you're up. You take Raul's place."

The last thing I hear before the ball starts slamming is Tuffman shouting, "I'm out of money, kids, so you're hitting Jackie-Girl here for the glory of it, all right?"

It almost makes me smile.

The nurse makes me ice my shins so long, I'm late to reading.

This is Ms. Tern's first teaching gig. I don't think she knows yet that the teacher is supposed to be mad at kids who come in late. She smiles when I open the door.

Ms. Tern always makes me feel better. I feel safe in her room. Is that weird?

Especially since she makes us read stories where dogs die and spiders die and moms die and sometimes a nuclear bomb falls on people and then they die later after being sick for a long time. If anyone complains, she says, "It's the curriculum." Her voice is so sad when she says it that even Mean Jack gets a wrinkle between his eyes and looks sympathetic.

She gets up from her desk and hands me a copy of the sheet she's reading from.

"Brilliant. I thought you might fancy learning something about the history of the island."

When she says "you" I realize she means me. Just me. I look down at my desk.

I wish I could tell her everything. I think she would believe me. I don't think she'd be afraid. Not with a right hook like she's got. She'd be a great cougar hunter, I bet.

Then she reads us the worst story I've ever heard.

Forty years ago some hunters got in little planes and boats and came to the Salish Sea and chased an orca family that scientists call the L pod. The male orcas and the grandma orcas tried to trick the hunters. They broke off from the mothers and babies and swam farther north to draw the hunters away from their families. But the hunters in the planes figured out what they were doing. They used loud noises and nets and got the whole pod trapped in Penn Cove. It's not far from Fort Casey. Then the hunters loaded the baby orcas onto trucks. They wanted to sell them to water parks where they would be trained to perform. The hunters let the rest go. But the orcas wouldn't leave. They waited in Penn Cove to see what would happen to their babies. They waited until the trucks drove off. Finally they swam away. Since that day the L pod has never returned to Penn Cove.

I'd rather spend the day bombed with dodgeballs than ever hear that story again.

Ms. Tern is a teacher, so she keeps reading. "Some of the mother orcas died that day trying to save their babies. They fought so hard they got tangled in the nets and suffocated. The hunters filled the bodies of the dead mother whales with rocks so they would sink to the bottom of the ocean floor. The hunters feared that animal rights groups would protest if they found out how many orcas had died. Eventually all these dark deeds came to light. Evil always does. And that particularly evil day has gone down in history as the Penn Cove Massacre."

Ms. Tern sets the book down. "Right." She wipes a tear away. Her voice is a little high up in her throat like she's got more tears bunched up in there. "I know a bit more."

Please don't tell me any more, I want to say. *Please.* I have the ache I get when I remember my mom tucking me into bed.

"As it turns out, two of the mother orcas were spirit whales," Ms. Tern says. She smiles softly. "That means they were pure white. They disappeared entirely. Nobody ever found their bodies."

My throat squeezes tight, but something in my belly jumps like it has little wings. Spirit animals. The story is sad, but now I have a name for something so important to me that I didn't think there could be a word for it. Animals that are white that shouldn't be white are spirit animals.

"Many cultures throughout the world prize spirit animals for their quote unquote 'magical' properties." Ms. Tern raises a skeptical eyebrow at me.

I stare back at her. Would she raise her eyebrow like that if I told her my secret?

She keeps talking. "Often times these animals are used in traditional medicines or sold illegally to wealthy individuals for private collections. International wild-life organizations believe a man named Luke Ferrier is the criminal mastermind responsible for the Penn Cove massacre as well as the disappearance of countless other spirit animals," she says. "He is a ruthless killer."

A chill of fear runs from my ears down my neck. I imagine a hunter in a red cap raising a rifle, white fur flashing through a screen of blackberry bushes.

"It is imperative that I find him before he further decimates endangered populations," she adds.

Have you ever looked in someone's eyes and seen the words they don't say? Like *I'm sorry.* Or *I love you.* Or *I just lied.* The words in Ms. Tern's eyes go like this: *I said too much.*

But I'm the only one listening. So I'm the only one who knows that when Ms. Tern should have said "they" she said "I." And that she meant it, or else why would her eyes look worried? Does Ms. Tern think she's part of an international organization looking for an infa-mous spirit-animal poacher?

I shake my head. Vincent's right. We do have the craziest teachers here.

"Right," Ms. Tern says. Her voice is very tidy and neat, like she's trying to sweep a little mess under the rug. "Now, let's have a look, shall we, at another document related to this issue." She begins to read aloud from a book. "The orcas of Puget Sound are called Southern Residents. The J, K, and L pods frequent these salmon-rich waters. Many facts about these animals would surprise you. Did you know that in local native lore the orca is related to the wolf?"

Orcas and wolves? Is that what she said?

But then my spine lights up. Gollum has returned. I turn, and she stops with the tip of her tail under the door. The gold ring around her body gleams under the fluorescent lights.

Mean Jack hollers, "I got a beef with you, snake!"

I remember Gollum's tail flicking out of Mean Jack's duffel bag last week. What did that snake do to that mobster over the weekend?

Mean Jack lunges at Gollum and lands flat on his belly. Half the kids are shouting, and the other half are standing on their chairs.

"Do *not* harm her!" Ms. Tern says in her popped-soap-bubble voice.

Cook Patsy and Mary Anne are right. Choices. You gotta make 'em. Ms. Tern needs a hand here. I pick up a big bin, dump out the crayons, and toss it to Mean Jack. He slams it onto the floor right on top of Gollum and shouts in a Cuban accent, "Say hello to my little friend!"

His aim is perfect. Almost. All I see is a flash of black and a glint of gold streak across the floor, over Ms. Tern's shoe, along the long wall, and back out under the door.

Mean Jack shakes his head at himself. "Man's gotta know his limitations."

Ms. Tern starts reading out loud again, but nobody's listening.

The classroom sounds like an F5 tornado. Paul, who gets to sit on an exercise ball instead of a chair, is bouncing across the classroom on it, smacking it and yelling "Yippee-kie-ay" and a bad word. Mark takes off the weighted vest they make him wear to keep him calm and starts swinging it above his head like a shot-put. Jason is making animal calls. He's good, and my pulse runs wild when he howls.

I put my hands over my ears, but then I can't draw.

Only the back corner of the room is quiet. A group of boys have pulled their desks around Mean Jack. They sit and watch carefully as he teaches them how to make a weapon out of a paper clip and a ruler.

"It's called a shiv," he says.

When the bell rings, Ms. Tern puts the book down.

The floor is covered with paper and broken pencil tips and Kleenex and paper clips, and each of Mean Jack's students has fashioned a perfect shiv.

"Beastly boys," I hear Ms. Tern whisper.

I'm halfway to lunch when I notice I forgot my drawing. Let's just say it's a dangerous document. I don't want it to end up in the wrong hands. It's a picture of a man getting chased by a hungry lion. The man's toupee is hanging from the lion's fangs. I kept the blood to the absolute minimum, considering the mortal injuries the victim has sustained.

Did I mention that the man looks a lot like Mr. Tuffman?

I run back to the classroom, but I'm too late.

Ms. Tern has taped my drawing to the blackboard.

My hands start to sweat. I'm going to be in big trouble. I don't get in trouble very often. I don't like it. Plus, Ms. Tern is my favorite teacher. I don't want her to be mad at me. I know she'd probably just give me sad eyes and whisper, "Raul. You know better than that." But is there anything worse than a teacher who never gets mad at anyone getting mad at *you*?

I step back into the hallway.

I peek in to watch as Ms. Tern picks up one of the shivs Mean Jack's crew was making. She walks to the back of the room. She glances at the door.

I don't move.

And then she sends that shiv flying. It slices the air. I hear a little pop and then another as the blade drives into the blackboard.

I push the door open a little wider and put my head in farther. I can't help it. It's what my dad would call professional curiosity. I'm a pretty good shot myself, but her form is phenomenal.

"Did you forget something?" she calls. She's standing at the blackboard, untaping my drawing.

I stare at the back of her head, frozen. My thoughts are frozen, my mouth is frozen. Should I ask her for the drawing? Does she hate Tuffman or just enjoy target practice? Will she rat me out, or does she believe in solidarity?

When she turns and looks at me, her eyes are sharp and intense like I've never seen them before. I'm used to Ms. Tern looking Defeated and In Despair. Right now she looks Tough as Nails.

"Would you like your drawing?" she asks.

My eyeballs feel dry. I've forgotten how to blink.

"It's a very good likeness," she says. "You're quite a gifted artist."

She walks over and hands it to me.

I don't look at the drawing until I'm out in the hall. It's not just her form that's phenomenal. It's her aim. There are two slits—one where the shiv hit Tuffman's heart and another where it tagged him in the head.

How did she make the blade *bounce* with such accuracy?

I turn back and stand in her open doorway for a second. It flashes through my mind that maybe Ms. Tern isn't delusional. Maybe she really is some kind of secret agent.

She's sitting at her desk. She looks up at me.

"Have we both got a little secret, then?" she asks. "Right. It looks to me like we'll just have to trust each other, eh?"

Can you be in love with two women at the same time? That's a question I'd like to ask my dad. Could I love Ms. Tern and Mary Anne both? Is it legal? Is it wrong?

I stop in the middle of the hall.

Could she do that to a cougar?

Chapter 14

WHERE RAUL FINDS OUT HE HAS FAMILY

After classes are over I head back toward my room. I have a lot on my mind. I want Vincent to like me enough to do fifty push-ups for me. I want Mary Anne to call me heroic. I want Ms. Tern to grab her shiv and help me get the cougar.

"Raul!"

The dean's voice makes me jump. I step into his office. Maybe he found out more about the cougar.

Dean Swift is at his desk. My nose twitches. Then I notice Tuffman sitting behind him, in the corner by the window. On the table next to Mr. Tuffman there's a lamp with a stained glass shade. It throws a blotchy pattern of light onto his face. Like he's wearing a coat of many colors.

"Mr. Tuffman and I were just having a little chat," Dean Swift says.

The drawing. Ms. Tern ratted on me. How could she?

"Someone gave the dean here the impression that

I've been picking on you," says Tuffman. "You got any idea who that might be?"

I almost smile, I'm so relieved. Cook Patsy must have got wind of the dodgeball disaster.

"You think that's funny?" Tuffman asks.

"No, no, Mr. Tuffman," says Dean Swift. "We're not here to accuse anyone, not Raul or you or *any* member of our staff. We are here to open the lines of communication."

The dean beckons to me. Ready to listen. Tuffman half stands. Ready to pounce.

I don't know what comes over me.

I bolt like a bunny in the woods.

Tuffman's on me before I hit the stairs. He grabs me by the back of my shirt. With his fist he gathers the material in tight like a straitjacket and steers me to the office.

"Keep your clothes on," he says in my ear. "Today you're gonna talk."

I shudder. Like that bunny in the woods when my wolf breath hit its neck.

Tuffman lets go of me before we get to the office. As we walk in, he rests his hand on my shoulder. He goes back to his chair in the corner.

I squeegee his spit out of my ear with the cuff of my sleeve.

"Have a seat, my boy," Dean Swift says. "I'm sure

we'll find that this is nothing more than a little misunderstanding."

"I've been coming on too strong," Tuffman says to me. "Let me tell you why." He leans forward. The shadows from the lampshade flicker across his face. I see that they are shapes—a red butterfly on his forehead, a playful kitten on his mouth. "We got history, kid, you and me."

Dean Swift looks back and forth between us, big-eyed.

"I didn't even know it until I got here and read your file. Then I thought it was best to keep quiet. I could see Raul was traumatized," he says to the dean. "And I was recovering from my last surgery. I didn't have the strength to tackle the problem. You get that, right?"

"Indeed, serious injuries like yours can take a grave emotional toll," Dean Swift says.

Tuffman clears his throat. "I knew your mother, Raul. I coached her at the university. When she went to Nationals she broke all the records. I bet she never told you, did she?"

His lies are getting personal again. I don't like it.

"I was the only one who could outrun her. Your dad couldn't come close to keeping up with her."

My *dad*? Now he knows my dad? Liar.

"Your mom had a real shot at the Olympics. It was your dad who put an end to all that. He got a job studying whales or something. She had to choose between him and the team. She chose him. Last I heard they were living in a one-man tent on Orcas Island."

I sit up. That part's true. I was born on that island.

The lampshade shadows shift. Now a running dog rests on Tuffman's cheek. His voice is soft. "Your mom was an amazing woman. *Kind*. No ego. Always putting everyone else first."

I stop hating Tuffman. I stop hating him because in his voice I can hear that he loved my mom too.

"Raul," he says softly. He comes across the room. He reaches out like he's going to touch me. I flinch. But I want to hear what else he has to say.

"When I got here and found out who you were and what all had happened to you, I thought that maybe fate had sent me for a reason. Your mom gave up her dream for your dad. She had disappeared a long time before she disappeared, if you know what I mean. You're a lot like her, the way you hide yourself. I started thinking that maybe if I toughened you up, you'd learn to put yourself first. My heart's in the right place, Raul. I didn't mean to scare you."

It makes sense, in a strange way. Maybe his heart *is* in the right place. "Thank you for telling me," I say. "I never knew my mom could've been in the Olympics."

It fills me up with pride. Since she left, my mom has become a shadow to me. A warm shape in a dark room in my mind. The more time passes, the darker the room gets, the harder it is to see her. Tuffman just walked into that dark room and turned on a night-light. I can see her better now.

I see my dad better now too. I don't think he means to be selfish. And I guess it's good to know that I'm not the only one he was selfish with. Forgetting about me has more to do with him than me. It's not because I'm so easy to forget. It's just who he is.

"Your mom and I were so close. I miss her." Tuffman's voice breaks. "See, I'm no good at all this." He puts a hand over his eyes. His Adam's apple bobs up and down. When he takes his hand away again his eyes are damp.

I put my head down in my hands. I knew he'd make me cry.

"So you gotta tell me how I can help you," Tuffman says. He kneels down in front of me. "You can't trust everybody you meet. Even best friends will betray you. But you can trust me, Raul."

I think of White Wolf and the scrape in her side and the broken-necked bunny I left for her in the grass. The relief runs over me like rain on your face when you look up into the sky. He will help me help my mom.

"Tell me about the woods, Raul." He opens his arms.

I slip from the chair.

"I know everything about your mom, Raul."

I can't say the wrong thing to him. He knows everything already. The words rush up. The whole story of how she found me and I found her.

"It started last year," I say. "I was so sad about my dad forgetting me." My voice is very small. It's because the words are so true. The truer the word, the closer to silence.

"Oh, we all were," Dean Swift says quickly and kindly. "We *all* were."

"Just tell us what happened, Raul," Tuffman says.

I lift my arms. I put them around him. He squeezes me to him. Warmth. Nobody has hugged me in a long time.

I don't mean to. But through his polo I feel a long raised river of skin. His scar. The second I touch it his fingernails plunge into my back. They bite into my skin through my thin shirt. My shoulders jump up, and, just as quick, he pulls away from me and pats me gently.

He looks down so I can't see his eyes.

I get a deep, bad, black feeling. The eight half-moons left by his fingernails on my back burn. This is the kind of guy who can hurt you when he hugs you. This is *Tuffman*.

I sit back in my chair. Far back. I almost told him everything! I watch him as he hangs his head. I forget to blink.

Finally he looks up. He's still sitting on his heels in front of me still. His eyes search the air above my head. He's looking for the words to make me forget those half-moons.

"Raul, I can't keep this secret anymore. Your grandma was my sister."

"Oh!" Dean Swift gasps. "Oh goodness. You're his family!"

I look at Tuffman. I don't see the resemblance.

"Your grandma was a lot older than me. Before she died I promised her I'd take care of your mom. I was barely twenty. She was around your age. I did the best I could by her, Raul."

Tuffman taps my knee to get me to look at him. He says my name again. *Raul.* He wants me to talk, but I can feel the sting of his nails in my back.

"I'm your great-uncle. What else can I say to convince you, Raul?" he asks. His voice has a hard edge to it.

I can feel how desperate he is. The more he wants my words, the less I want to give them to him.

He gets to his feet. His left hand reaches back. I think he's touching his scar.

"I loved her like a little sister," he whispers.

The words send a jolt through me. I've heard them before. Didn't he tell me that it was family who injured him? Someone he had loved *like a little sister*?

I shiver. My *mom* gave him that scar.

I smell it. Something wrong. Something bad. Story time's over, Tuffman.

But I can't look away from him. My neck won't let me. It's tight and stretched and forces my face in his direction.

He lowers himself into the chair by the lamp. His back must hurt from crouching in front of me for so long. Shadow leaves from the lamp flutter across his face. He looks tired out. He looks how I feel when I'm deep in the woods and I've spent an hour chasing a bunny and at the last second the bunny darts into a hole just big enough for my nose but too small for me to get my mouth open.

Dean Swift honks into his pocket handkerchief. "For the love of St. Jude, I never foresaw such a turn of events," he says damply. "Never in all my years. To witness such a reunion. Happy day. Happy day."

The bell rings.

I back out of the room.

Tuffman watches me through half-closed eyes. "We'll talk later," he says. He smiles softly at me. "There's more to the story, Raul."

I race upstairs. I'm out of breath, but I can finally breathe.

Tuffman was suffocating me. It's that feeling you get when someone stands too close or looks over your shoulder while you're reading or tries to get you to give them things you want to keep for yourself—like your dessert or your mom's soul. It's not just that he was in my space. It's like he was trying to climb inside of me.

I almost told him everything.

Vincent is standing at my bedroom door. He looks worried. "What happened, man? Did you get in trouble? I saw you running down the hall, and then Tuffman grabbed you and marched you into the dean's office."

"Later," I say. I'm done talking for the day. I push past him to open the door. I'm about to shut it, but Vincent has already stepped in behind me.

"Friends tell each other stuff," he says.

For a split-second I want to push him out of my room. But there's a look on his face that stops me. He wants to listen to me because I listened to him last night. He thinks he owes me. It's like sharing stuff, only it's not your baseball mitt or a book. It's words.

"Tuffman says he's my great-uncle," I say it quick, like ripping off a Band-Aid.

Vincent blinks. "No way. Tuffman?"

"Tuffman," I say. Then I say more. It just pops out. "It's so embarrassing. I'd rather have Mean Jack for a twin. Or Gollum for an aunt."

Vincent cracks up like the whole thing is just some crazy, random joke. It makes me smile too.

"My mom says you can't pick family, you just take what you get and lump it," Vincent says after he stops laughing. "But if I could, I'd pick you to be my brother."

He stretches out his hand. "Brother," he says.

"Brother," I say back.

We shake.

People always tell you talking will make you feel better. But it's not the talking that makes you feel better. It's the person listening.

Vincent picks up my code book and flips through it for a while. Then all of a sudden he sets it down. "So why's he being such a jerk to you, then?" he asks.

I shrug. "Maybe it's because he's a jerk."

"You know what? He's just like my stepfather. All he wants is to boss me around. It's like he's trying to get his claws into me, so I do what he says the second he says it."

I grin. I pull up my shirt. I can see the reflection of my back in the mirror when I turn to show him. Just above each shoulder blade are four red half-moons.

"He did that to you?" Vincent asks.

"Yeah, this is the side effect of a hug from Tuffman."

Vincent's eyes glint. "I'm gonna get him for you, just like I got my stepdad."

"Don't bother," I say. I'm happy he cares enough to want to. But I've got bigger fish to fry, if you know what I mean. I've got a cougar to hunt and a girl to win.

Vincent shrugs like it doesn't matter anyway. He holds up the code book and heads to the door. "Can I borrow this?"

"What's mine is yours," I say as he leaves. That's what my dad always said to anyone who wanted anything. And he meant it too. He's the kind of guy who would give you the shirt off his back. You ask for it, it's yours.

Tuffman's the kind of guy who will *take* the shirt off your back. Then he'll put it on and take a nap in your bed.

It makes me think.

Tuffman didn't lie about everything. But he twisted the truth like a wolf twists a bunny's neck.

My dad's not selfish. He'd give you everything even if it meant he'd end up with nothing. Maybe that's what happened when my dad lost my mom. He had nothing left.

Chapter 15

WHERE TUFFMAN GETS A GUN AND MARY ANNE MEETS A BULLET

I can't sleep. I wake up early. My plate is full of bacon and eggs and sausage and they're so hot the steam is coming off them. It cheers me up a little. Protein will do that for you.

Today I'm gonna ask Ms. Tern to help me hunt the cougar. She has skills, there's no denying it. And she's got a little more crazy in her than your average teacher. That's a plus in my book.

Mary Anne sits down next to me. "Vincent said to give this to you."

It's a plastic Easter egg. I crack it open. A paper clip and a strip of paper fall out.

I smooth the paper. Mary Anne leans over. Her eyebrows are pinched together.

"Paper clip code," she says after a second.

She takes the paper clip out of my hand. My hand buzzes when her fingers brush my palm.

I glance up and catch her staring at me. Right away she looks down. Her cheeks are a little pink. I get a fluttery feeling. Does Mary Anne like me, too?

"Now," she says in her teacher voice, "you lay the paper clip flat over the line of letters, with the double loop end to the right and the other end around the first letter. Whatever letter is in that double loop is the one you want. Then you slide the paper clip right, like this, so that the end loop goes around the letter the double loop was around. See?"

Together we spell it out. *LAKE. NOW. ALONE.*

We look at each other. I get off my stool and grab my tray.

"I'm coming," Mary Anne says. She sets her tray on top of mine, puts everything back in the Easter egg, and shoves it into her pocket.

Vincent said *alone*. But am I ever gonna tell Mary Anne she can't do something she wants?

As we run out the front door and down the steps, Bobo joins us.

The sun has just risen. It's very cold. The sky is filled with crows. I run hard.

We hear it before we get off the main road. *Crack*. The crows caw and croak. They swoop and tumble. Someone's shooting a gun in the woods.

I'm ahead of Mary Anne. I stop running and wave my hand at her to stop. We're not going into the woods if there's a hunter in there. But she races by me. Bobo is at her heels, and she looks back at me too, her tongue flopping out of her mouth.

"Come on," Mary Anne shouts as she turns off the road and onto the path to the lake. "That gunshot came from miles away."

For once Mary Anne is dead wrong. But they get to the oak tree with my bike stuck in it before I catch up. I sprint in front of her and block her way on the narrow path. Bobo sits and pants. Mary Anne puts her hands on her hips and looks at me, breathing hard.

"Stop," I say. Then the hairs on the back of my neck stand up. We're not alone in the woods. Is it the hunter?

My blood freezes.

The *cougar*? I reach toward my back pocket, but I already know there's no sling there. How could I be so stupid? Dean Swift said to stay close to the school.

When I turn to look behind me, toward the lake, Mary Anne darts ahead. "You worry too much. Last one there is a rotten egg."

Bobo streaks after her.

The early light is loose and filtered, falling through the fog and cedars. The lake is straight ahead. I look into the distance, just to the left of the path. I feel it. Something alive is in there. It's hard to see. The morning sunlight glares down from above, while the night still sits in the cold shade below.

I squint. Whatever it is, it's not moving. It's a man. The man's lifting something. It's a rifle. It's Tuffman. He's aiming at something on the other side of the path.

I'm trying to see what he's shooting at when I realize that Mary Anne is running straight toward the lake. My feet pound on the path before my brain screams *Run!* In a second Tuffman will be on her left. His target will be on her right. She's heading straight into the line of fire.

I hear the gun click.

"Don't shoot!" I yell. At the same time, I leap. The gun goes off. I grab Mary Anne and pull her down. She screams. We hit the path. The bullet whizzes over us. There's a sound like a bunch of little explosions, and we look to the right, where Tuffman was aiming.

Fireworks. Mary Anne and I sit up slowly and stare. Fireworks are popping and blazing out of something that looks like a busted-up piñata.

When I look the other way, I see Tuffman walking out of the trees toward us. He starts shouting. "I almost shot your head off!"

Mary Anne and I are sitting on the path side by side. She looks like she might cry. I put my arm around her shoulders. Bobo comes sniffing to see if we're alive.

"Who gave you permission to be out here at this time of day?"

We stare up at Tuffman. He's got two little spit balls, one in each corner of his mouth. He's frothing mad, but I can tell it's because he's scared pantsless about what he almost did.

A shadow falls across us. Tuffman wipes his mouth.

"What the dickens were you thinking, Mr. Tuffman?" comes Ms. Tern's clipped voice from behind us. We turn and see her standing over us in a jogging suit.

"I saw a cougar out on the road this morning," Tuffman says. I hear the nervous shake in his voice. "I got my gun and followed it. It was right there." He points to the thing with the fireworks popping out of it every so often. "I didn't see the kids until it was too late."

Ms. Tern looks over at the fireworks. "Your cougar appears to be a piñata in the shape of a lion. Either you have a very strange idea of a good time, or someone has played a rather complicated trick on you."

Mary Anne and I glance at each other. Vincent went a little too far this time.

Before we can blink, Ms. Tern snatches the rifle from Tuffman. He jerks his hand back and then holds it out and looks at it. There are four long scratches across Tuffman's skin where Ms. Tern's nails cut him as she took it.

Ms. Tern does something quick and clicky with the rifle to make sure it's not loaded. Then she puts her hand out and stares at Mr. Tuffman. "Don't make me go after them," she says.

Tuffman gulps. He rubs his hand, reaches into his front jeans pocket, and gives her some bullets.

Ms. Tern is now armed. Something tells me that if Ms. Tern aimed that rifle at the cougar, she wouldn't miss.

"Have you been injured?" she asks us. She helps Mary Anne to her feet. She makes a *tsk* sound at Mary Anne's ripped jeans and bleeding knees.

She glares at Tuffman. "I've got my eye on you."

"What about my gun?"

"That's the second time I've stopped you from trying to kill an animal. That cougar has as much right to be walking in these woods as you."

Here's a problem. Ms. Tern has the right skills and the firepower but the wrong attitude. She's never going to hunt the cougar with me.

She herds us down the path in front of her. "I'm taking you two directly to the nurse," she says.

I glance back at Tuffman. He looks angry and confused. He's made me feel that way often enough that it makes me a little happy. But he looks scared and sorry, too. He's a jerk, but even a jerk has his good side, I guess.

"You, young man," Ms. Tern keeps saying over and over.

I'm afraid she knows about Vincent's prank and thinks I was in on it.

Finally she says more. "I am speechless. I've known courageous men in my time. Men who would sacrifice their lives to make this world a better, safer place. But only rarely have I witnessed such bravery, such speed, such agility."

I'm proud and embarrassed. I didn't know she saw what happened. I'm glad she thinks I'm so great, but I just did what my gut told me to do.

Mary Anne nods. Her mouth moves, but for once she doesn't have anything to say.

At the oak, Bobo stops to sniff. My eyes follow her nose up into the branches of the tree. My mouth pops open. Vincent is sitting up there on my bike. He puts a finger over his lips.

I stare at him. I don't know what to think. That was one heck of a prank.

When we reach the driveway, Mary Anne takes my hand. "Thank you," she says. She gives me a hug. "I was wrong. There *is* a synonym for 'heroic.' It's *Raul.*"

Her hug pins my arms to my sides. I lean my head down toward hers. My cheek touches her hair. It's soft, like cherry blossoms.

Solidarity. Mary Anne and I don't say anything to anybody about what Vincent did. Ms. Tern would say that I am *conflicted.* Part of me gets all pumped up whenever I think about it. Cook Patsy taught me to wrestle Tuffman, Dean Swift made me talk to him, but Vincent scared the daylights out of him.

The other part of me knows it was the worst, dumbest, stupidest idea in the world. Obviously Vincent didn't expect Mary Anne to come running through that scene. But Tuffman, a gun, and a piñata full of fireworks? Nothing good's gonna come of that.

Vincent doesn't mention it either. He looks a little worried around Mary Anne at first, but she just tells us her usual stories about Samish princesses married to sea gods and children kidnapped by shape-shifting otters. In the dining hall Vincent sits to my left and Mary Anne to my right. Sometimes Mary Anne's shoulder brushes mine and neither of us pulls away.

Tuffman doesn't know what hit him or who got him. For a day or two he's a shadow of himself. He pulls out a parachute and lets us play popcorn in PE. Every once in a while he calls me "son." It makes me want to shove him away. *There's only one man who calls me that,* I want to say. *And it's not you.*

Ms. Tern has us read informational texts on gun safety. She's not going to help me get the cougar, I've figured that much out about her. But she gives me a little wink every now and then that makes me glow inside.

Nobody hears or sees the cougar. I bet it's gone away.

On Friday morning when it's my turn to help out in the kitchen, Cook Patsy gives me a hug.

“It’s nice to see you looking so happy,” she says. “You and your friends.”

I knew she liked me. But I didn’t know how much.

“Thank you,” I say. I always mean it when I say that. I hope she knows how much.

Chapter 16

WHERE EVERYTHING STARTS TO GO RIGHT BUT IS REALLY GOING WRONG

On Friday at lunch Dean Swift comes into the dining room to make an announcement.

"I'm sorry, children," he says. "Due to the high volume of phone calls from concerned parents regarding the cougar, there will be no fishing today. Instead, we will all enjoy an extra hour of free voluntary reading in our rooms."

All the Cubs moan and stomp their feet on the sticky floor.

I look out the window. The sky is the blue that makes the cedars so green. The air is cold and the sun is hot. There's enough wind to make your blood skip in your veins.

Nobody's heard that cougar all week. It's either long gone or sound asleep.

Vincent leans forward so he can see both me and Mary Anne. "I'm going fishing," he says. "Are you two in?"

Don't get me wrong. I love to read.

But I'm with Vincent. Mary Anne takes a second longer.

There's hot wet breath on my elbow. I look down. Sparrow. "Me too," he says.

I smile and mess up his hair.

"But keep your trap shut about it, okay?" Vincent says.

I shoot him a look. Nobody talks rude to Sparrow. Not even Vincent.

We sneak into the equipment room with the key Dean Swift gave me a few years ago. While I'm looking for a pole for Mary Anne, Sparrow shows Vincent the carving I made on his. Vincent traces his finger over the head of one of the wolves.

He looks up at me and whistles. "Wicked cool. This is some quality work."

"It's not done yet," I say. "I'm going to paint it, but I have to read a little bit more to make sure I do the colors right."

"It looks good to me," Vincent says.

"Dean Swift says there are rules about where you put which colors in Native American art," I explain. "It has to be authentic." I'm talking a lot. They all look at me with big eyes.

Sparrow pulls on the pole to take it back, but Vincent holds on to it a minute more.

"Will you make one exactly like it for me?" he asks when he finally lets Sparrow take it.

"No," I say.

Vincent opens his mouth like he can't believe it.

I try to explain. "I only make a pole once. It takes a long time to figure out the right carving for the right boy. The wood tells me what it wants to become."

Vincent raises an eyebrow. He's about to call me a weirdo. But instead he just nods.

I glance at Mary Anne. I can tell she likes something I said.

Now if I could just figure out which words, I'd say them again.

It's easy to sneak out the window in Sparrow's room, since it's on the ground floor. After the first bend in the road, nobody can see us from the school, so we slow down and relax.

Vincent has a big surprise for us when we get to the picnic table. "Look," he says, and opens up his backpack. "Candy feast."

Sour watermelons, candy necklaces, bouncy balls, tattoos—it's all my favorite stuff. There's enough loot for twenty kids. Mary Anne and I look at each other. We're thinking the same thing. We're thinking this is what you get when you gut a lion piñata to make room for fireworks and other incendiary devices.

"And I saved us some sparklers," he says.

Sparrow is jumping up and down. Mary Anne and I say thank you. Vincent shrugs.

Something tells me Vincent is trying to say he's sorry for almost getting us killed, but without actually saying it.

Mary Anne does a sparkler dance. Sparrow shows us some survival tricks you can do with bubble gum, pee, and some string. Vincent sticks a tattoo on his forehead.

Sparrow polishes off four packets of Pop Rocks and ten candy rings before we even notice him lying under the table singing a weird little song.

It's the best time I've ever had at the lake, even though the fish won't bite. In the end, Sparrow is the only one who catches something big enough to keep.

"It's my lucky pole," Sparrow says as I unhook the beautiful trout.

I get a glimpse of Vincent's face when Sparrow says that. He looks the way you look when the lunch lady gives the piece of pie you've been eyeing the whole time you're in line to the kid in front of you. Jealous.

It makes me feel bad and happy at the same time. I don't want Vincent upset. But I know all about jealousy. You only get it for the good stuff.

All of a sudden it starts to rain so hard, the ground turns to mud in seconds. With every gust of wind, the trees shake water down at us along with the sky, and so we all take off running back to the school.

This time I even outrun Vincent. Must be all the gummy peaches. Halfway up the main road I look back and see him standing where the path meets the road. He's hunched over like he's winded, but when he sees me staring he hollers for me to go on ahead.

"I dropped something," he yells. "I'm gonna go back and get it!"

His voice sounds funny—like it did when he lied and said White Deer hadn't spoken to him.

But why would Vincent lie to me?

After I change into dry clothes, I notice the recipe box sitting on my bedside table. I can't believe the whole week has gone by.

All my wolf worries hit me like a punch. Is White Wolf all right? What if the cougar *isn't* gone? What if it's out there and I did nothing all week but laugh at Vincent's jokes and think about holding Mary Anne's hand?

I can't watch the other kids leave today. I grab my duffel bag, run downstairs, and tell the dean that my dad got here early. Then I slip back into my room, lock the door, and keep the light off. Nobody will know I never left. After I see Dean Swift drive away, I'll sneak out my window and run to the lighthouse.

I lie on my bed and wait. The curtains are open and the light coming through is gray and wet. I'm mad at myself. Maybe this is what happened to my dad. Maybe he meant to do the things he was supposed to do but would forget right up until it was too late. I wonder if he has this same heavy dragging feeling when he thinks of me.

Ms. Tern said I was the bravest kid she'd ever seen. But I'm not. I'm a little chicken, afraid of a big cat. Why didn't I go after that cougar again?

I open my mom's recipe box. I flip through the cards. She feels more real to me now. I don't like Tuffman. He's a snoop and a jerk. But he did something nobody else did. He introduced me to my mom before she was my mom. I can't explain it very well. But I know her better now.

It's like what Dean Swift said about the mtDNA. Our family is a secret code, inside of us. I wonder if I'll ever crack the code of why my mom and dad did the things they did.

Most of the cards she wrote in blue ink. But right in the middle of the box there's one written in faded pencil. Tuna Surprise. I squint to make out the words. There's no tuna in it. But there are muffins. And coconut.

Nobody puts coconut and muffins in tuna casserole. *Everybody* puts tuna in it, though. My mom had to know when she wrote it that it wasn't right. You can't make that big of a mistake.

I get a tingly feeling.

My thought is typed out and italicized in my mind, just like the chapter title in the code book Cook Patsy gave me. *It's a List Code.*

What if my mom wasn't a terrible cook? What if her recipes are codes?

I grab my clipboard. I clip Tuna Surprise at the top. Then I take the inside of a candy bar wrapper and make a chart. For a list code you use the number in the front to tell you which letter of the ingredient to use. You ignore the measurements.

2 tsp ginger I
3 muffins F
4 tsp cumin I
2 oz meat E
3 oz liver V
5 pats butter E
2 tsp cream R

If I ever. I suck my breath in. It *is* a code.

I pull out the recipe after Tuna Surprise. It's Frog Eye Salad.

3 oz cod D
2 tsp ginger I
1 steak S
3 oranges A

1 tsp pepper
1 cup pearl pasta
5 frog eyes
1 apple
2 grapes

By the time I get halfway through Frog Eye Salad my hand is shaking.

I was wrong when I thought the cards weren't in order. They are. They're in the order of my mom's story. I keep going. It's five o' clock. I hear Dean Swift walking the halls, turning off lights. He jiggles the handle of the utility closet to make sure it's locked.

I stop taking the time to write out the ingredients and just copy over the letters. My mouth is dry like dust. After Crock Pot Spaghetti and Jim's Lasagna I put the pencil down.

If I ever disappear: I know his secret. T wants to kill me.

I look at my clock. It'll be sunset soon. I put the cards back in the box. My head feels full, like an overpacked suitcase. There's such a big mystery raining down all around me, and I can't see my way through it. I push the recipe card box far back under the bed. I throw the window open and scramble down the madrona tree.

I don't mind the rain or the cedars whipping in my face as I run.

I think about the questions Tuffman asked me. I

think about how he kept trying to find out where I go when I go into the woods. He's looking for her.

Maybe she didn't lose the recipe to turn back. Maybe she stopped using it. Maybe she turned into a wolf to escape him.

The rain stops. I slow down. Is he following me? Am I leading him straight to her?

What will he do if he finds her? Does he want to help her? Or does he want to kill her?

I stand real quiet and listen. I don't hear anything. I lift my face and sniff. The woods are wet and silent, and the little wind that rises tells me that they are all mine.

Of course. I exhale slowly. I tricked him today, without even trying. Usually I take the road down to the highway. He's waiting for me there. I get a sick feeling in my stomach when I remember how just last week he was hiding in the ash tree, waiting to pounce on me.

Chapter 17

IF YOU GIVE A BOY A ROCK . . .

As I get closer to the lighthouse I move more slowly. The rain stops, but the cedar fronds bob and drip. In the clearing at the edge of the cliff the sun has dropped right out of the clouds.

Worry tugs at me. I turn around and look at the path darkening behind me.

Through the trees I see something spark in the distance, back near the school. I freeze.

Is it Tuffman with a flashlight? Is it a cougar with glowing eyes? I take a breath and stare hard. The flashes are coming from the north-wing turret. Of course. Dean Swift has lit the Fresnel lens again. I squint, one hand shading my eyes, and the light swings at me, pouring through the tiny windows in the turret. Even the bricks of the building are glowing, like the light is coming through them, too, somehow.

The beam drenches me.

The light flickers in me like flames. It flows through me like waves. Fear and wonder quiver up my spine. That light makes me feel as if I'm wolf and boy at the same time. I'm wearing my two skins at once. The blood in my veins is thick and hot. Strength radiates from inside me.

The trunk of an alder tree is on the ground in front of me, fifteen feet long and maybe six feet around. The storm must have brought it down. I tap it with the tip of my toe. It flies thirty feet away into the horizon, off the edge of the cliff.

My strength is superhuman. It is superwolf. It's the light. Its power pulses in me.

It's magic, I whisper to the shuddering leaves.

The sun has wedged itself between the water and the clouds. Between the dark ocean and the dark sky is a thick slice of white and yellow. And I'm like that lemon-meringue pie of a sky. In my heart, hope jams itself between my fear of Tuffman and my worry about my mother. Because if I'm that strong, then how can Tuffman hurt anyone, or any wolf, that I love?

I run across the grass to the lighthouse.

I wait in my wolf skin on the doorstep of the lighthouse. The darkness of the woods deepens and spreads its shadows over the edge of the cliff and down into the blue-black water below. My hope disappears with the coming of the night.

White Wolf is late. And then she is later. And then she is very, very, very late.

What if the cougar found her?

I whimper. It's a sound that crumbles out of me.

At last I hear a whimper in return. Low and soft, the sound creeps toward me under the cover of dark and above the bed of quiet grass and bleeding hearts.

The moon comes up suddenly from below the line of treetops. I see a flash of white from the edge of the woods. In my wolf shape I lope from the lighthouse doorway to where she waits for me. *Thank you,* I say. *Thank you.*

She's weak and gets slowly to her feet. Her nose is dry.

Has she been waiting as long as I have? Waiting, but too sick to come to me?

I sniff her side. The wound has almost healed. But my nose tells me she is hungry and thirsty and tired. Was the rabbit I left for her on Sunday her last meal? It makes me ache inside to think of White Wolf alone and suffering without me.

Why isn't she eating? The woods are full of deer.

As I lead her to the lake, I catch the smell of the cougar here and there, coming at me on different currents of air. The cougar hasn't come into our territory, but he's roaming its edges. The scent of cougar gets stronger the closer we get to the lake.

I stand guard as she drinks. We're at the edge of the fishing area and White Deer Woods. We've never come this close to the school, but I need to find food for her and I know there are plenty of deer here. I sniff the ground. I smell Sparrow and Vincent. I smell human me. We've come so often to the lake that it would take more than a little rain to wash us away. I follow the whiffs and puffs of cougar scent that I pick up in the air. A pair of footprints in the mud near the picnic table makes my nose twitch. The prints are fresh and from not long ago. Expensive running shoes. Tuffman's the only one with feet that big wearing Pumas around here. The prints are his, but the smell is cougar.

My nose and mind work together.

Tuffman is the cougar. Tuffman, my uncle. Tuffman, the one my mom calls "T," the one who gave White Wolf that vicious scrape, the one my mom hurt in the woods long ago.

When wolves get scared, they get mad. My blood pops hot and slow, like boiling tar. That cougar's asking for trouble. He's gonna get it.

Once she's had enough to drink, I lead White Wolf back to the ledge. The cougar scent disappears inside White Deer Woods. He hasn't come into our territory. She's safe in here, for now.

All Saturday I hunt. I make sure White Wolf eats her fill. I kill everything I can and cache what she can't eat now so that she will have something during the week. The beam of light keeps pulsing in me. Nothing I chase outruns me. Nothing I lunge for slips past my teeth.

By Sunday morning White Wolf looks strong. Her eyes sparkle and her nose is damp and her fur glows white in the sunlight. I follow as she roams to the edge of our territory.

And then it happens.

One minute I'm looking off into the underbrush for a bunny snack and the next White Wolf is backing up. For a second I'm filled with her fear. Then I get a whiff of cougar.

When I'm in my boy skin, the cougar scares me. In my wolf skin it infuriates me. No litter-scratching cat is going to tell my mom where she can go, when she can eat, or what skin she can wear.

I push past her. She whimpers and stands still, her head tilted. She wants to go back and she wants me to come with her. But I'm not leaving her like this. Not for a whole week. If that cougar is up ahead, then I'm going to find him and finish him. I'll run him off the edge of the cliff.

I messed up during the week. Boy me spent his time eating candy and looking sideways at Mary Anne. But wolf me is going to take care of the problem.

I run harder as the cougar scent gets stronger. I head directly toward it, and a second later I feel her behind me. My wolf mouth smiles. Our feet beat in time against the hard dry dirt under the cedars.

Two against one. This is how wolves chase off a cougar.

We're so close to the lake I can smell the pollywogs Little John hasn't eaten yet. The cougar scent is so strong I almost choke on it.

Then I hear a whistle, and a split second later I'm lying on the path, a searing pain in my right shoulder. I can hardly breathe, it hurts so bad. White Wolf sniffs me. She whimpers. A second later she growls like a wild animal and dashes past me.

I struggle to my feet and follow her.

White Wolf's growl rumbles in the quiet woods ahead.

"I didn't know there were two of them!" a boy's voice screams out.

Humans.

I race through the pine trees. The lake is just ahead. I want White Wolf to turn around and come back. We hunt cougar, not humans.

What if they have a gun?

"Get up here on the table," a man's voice says.

I hear a boy sobbing.

"No!" the man shouts. "Get off the ground!"

As I come into the clearing, I skid to a stop, stunned.

White Wolf has brought Tuffman and Vincent to bay on the picnic table. They're wearing running shoes and shorts. There's a little stack of pink flags on the ground.

They are staking out the 5K practice run for PE. When did those two get to be such good buddies?

I look at her. My mother is a magnificent beast. Her teeth are sharp and gleaming. Her fur is standing on end so that she looks twice her usual size. And her usual size is about twice the size of any wolf you've ever seen.

"Stand up," Tuffman yells.

Vincent is on his hands and knees on top of the table, shaking with fear. Tuffman grabs him by the back of the neck and yanks him upright. He shakes Vincent hard.

"Pull it together," he says angrily. "I'm not about to lose her after all these years just because you're chicken."

Vincent has the slingshot I gave him. That must be how the rock hit me so hard. He's bawling his eyes out and shaking and trying to put another rock into the strap.

Rock or no rock, White Wolf is going to kill Vincent.

No, I want to shout. *Stop. He didn't know what he was doing.* My mother is going to kill my best friend. She's going to jump on him, pin him down, and do to him what we do to weasels and rabbits and deer.

I rush between them, barking and dancing around in front of White Wolf, trying to get her to calm down.

You can't reason with a wolf. Nose nudges and nips aren't going to stop her. Never—and I mean *never*—mess with a wolf mother's baby.

Whiz. Whack. Another rock hits me, this time in the back of the head.

White Wolf lunges to protect me, positioning her body between me and the table. She's barking so hard now she's like a machine gun.

I whimper but stay on my feet. I've got to get between her and them again. I'm the only one who knows everything. And one thing I know is that a wolf that attacks a human will be hunted down by the park rangers and killed within the week.

But when I look up at the table again, I see it's Tuffman who has the slingshot now. That last shot came from him. The smell and sight of him remind me of what he is. He's the cougar. He wants to hurt White Wolf. He asked me questions so that I would lead him to her.

Listen up, feline. Did you ever hear the saying: Curiosity killed the cat?

My fur goes electric. Every muscle in my body tightens. I turn to stand side by side with my wolf mother. Together we advance, growling fiercely. White Wolf shifts her weight, and I see she's about to jump. I gather up my strength.

Sorry, Vincent. This can't be helped. You're too close to my territory. I'm going to do whatever a wolf has to do to get you out.

Tuffman makes a little scream. Apparently, we are two really scary wolves. He drops the slingshot. He leaps off the table and is running before his feet hit the ground. Vincent follows.

White Wolf and I give chase. Vincent is still bawling, but he runs so hard he catches up with Tuffman. If I had a stopwatch and opposable thumbs, I bet I'd clock them at forty mph.

Before they even reach the road, White Wolf and I stop. We flop, panting, in the shade of the oak tree that is growing around my bike. As the thrill of the chase fades, I realize how bad my head hurts where Tuffman hit me with the rock.

I meant to take the cougar down with my sling last week. Looks like Tuffman found a rock with my name on it first. That is what Mary Anne would call ironic. I rest my nose in my paws. Why did Vincent hit me in the first place? I didn't give him that slingshot so that he could use it to hurt animals.

Before the sun reaches the middle of the sky, I get up and follow White Wolf back to the lighthouse. We're not the usual dynamic duo. I feel dizzy. There's blood in White Wolf's fur. I sniff it. It's the old wound. Running so hard must have reopened it a little. If the bunnies and deer have come up with any revenge fantasies, this would definitely be the time for them to act on them. They could pelt us with pinecones and green berries and we'd go belly up.

I'm worried when I walk into the lighthouse. But if

White Wolf stays near the ledge, she'll have plenty of food. And just because I'm not with her doesn't mean I won't be hunting cougar.

This week I won't get distracted. This week I'll remember what matters.

It takes me a long time to shift. I keep losing track of what I'm doing. I manage to walk out of the light-house fully dressed. I find out later my underwear's on inside out and my T-shirt is on backward, but at least I zipped my jeans. By the time I get to the school, I'm out of breath and dizzy. My head aches. My right shoulder burns.

Bobo meets me on the front steps. She jumps up and rests her paws on my chest.

Oh no. How could I forget her stinky stick? I gently help her down to all fours. She gets herself into a pickle like that sometimes where she has just enough strength to get up but not enough to get back down. Old hips, young heart.

I'm sorry, I whisper as I scratch just under her left ear. She licks my hand and then my cheek. *Forgiven*. It's simple between animals.

I see Mary Anne's suitcase in the foyer when I come in. She beat me again.

I walk into the TV room. I need to sit a second before I can make it up to my room.

Mary Anne takes one look at me and sets her book down.

"Dean Swift," she calls, running up the stairs before I can stop her.

I stand there and stare at her book for a long time. My brain can't turn the letters of the title into words. Finally I get it. *The History of Paris.*

The two of them come down half a minute later. I'm still staring at the book. It makes me feel less dizzy. Dean Swift's face is bright red from the dash down the stairs, and I can see that whatever Mary Anne told him has got him worried.

"See?" she says, pointing.

I look around. But she's pointing at me.

Dean Swift comes up and puts his face very close to mine.

"What have we got here?" he says softly. He touches my chin gently with his fingers and lightly turns my head one way and then the other. The pain in my head makes my knees buckle. Dean Swift catches me around the waist and settles me into a chair.

He kneels in front of me. "Mary Anne, bring me the flashlight from my top desk drawer."

She races back upstairs.

Before I can stop myself, I lean over the arm of the chair and throw up into a wastebasket.

Dean Swift pats my back. He hands me a tissue.

"Nice aim," he says, like it's nothing to be embarrassed about.

"Turn out the lights," he calls as Mary Anne comes back down the stairs.

"Now look into the flashlight when I hold it up to your eyes."

I do what he says, even though the bright light aches.

The dean whistles low. "Concussed, my boy. You have been concussed. How did this happen?"

"I was climbing a tree," I begin. "To get my kite. And I fell." I have to stop a lot because I'm making it up as I go. "Right on my back," I add. "And there was a big rock. I fell backward onto a big sharp rock." I pause. It throbs where Vincent tagged me with that rock. I better cover all my bases. "Two rocks. My shoulder landed on one."

I see Dean Swift glance at the phone by the front door.

"My dad knows," I say quickly. "He was there when it happened. We were having a picnic lunch at Fort Casey before he dropped me off. I told him I was fine. He said to tell you if I felt worse."

Dean Swift's jaw tightens. He can't believe my dad could be so heartless.

But I'm not done. "And you can't call him because he's flying to Paris tonight," I say quickly. Why did I say *Paris*, of all places?

"It must be that international conference for wildlife biologists," Dean Swift says, stroking his chin. "He's published some interesting work lately, your father."

I blink. Bingo. That was the lie to tell.

"I'll have to watch you carefully," he says. "If you're not better by this time tomorrow then I'll have to get ahold of him."

I sink back in the chair. I am now an official specimen in Dean Swift's curiosity cabinet. I will be observed. Conclusions will be drawn. I'm too sick to care.

Bring on the science. The magic's killing me.

"Stay with him while I call the doctor," he says to Mary Anne. "Don't let him fall asleep."

They only call the doctor when a kid is really sick. Is he going to give me a shot? Will they have to operate?

I touch the soft, sad, painful spot on the back of my head. When I pull my fingers away they are wet and red.

Mary Anne makes a little noise. Her eyebrows crinkle. She sees it too.

"Don't worry," she says. I can tell she is forcing herself to sound calm. "You'll be fine. Head injuries tend to bleed a lot. It's to be expected."

She takes some tissues from a box on the end table. "You should apply a little pressure. The doc will be here soon." As she stretches the tissues toward me, I can see her hand shaking.

I sit back in the chair. I close my eyes so that Mary Anne doesn't have to work so hard to pretend like she's not worried about me.

After a second she grabs my hand and squeezes it. "You have to stay awake. Okay?" She doesn't let go. "I'd read you my novel, but my dad says it puts him to sleep. *Best cure for insomnia ever.* Those were his exact words."

She frowns and then smiles real quick, like her dad's dumb, mean joke is actually funny.

Anger surges up in me. My skin burns. Wolf rage. *Hey, Mary Anne's dad, I've got an even better cure for insomnia. A nocturnal visit from a wolf. You'll never wake up again.*

I exhale slowly. I better calm down. I'm in boy world again.

I listen to her voice. I feel her press gently on my hand whenever I close my eyes. If all it takes to get Mary Anne to hold my hand is a rock smashing into my head, then bring on the meteor showers.

Because this is love.

The doctor is very jolly for a guy who spends his day jabbing people with needles. He explains what a concussion is.

"Your brain has been bruised," he says with a big smile. "Exactly like a melon that has been dropped on the ground. If your brain really were a melon, I'd suggest that you eat it up quick before it spoils, but since you're a boy, I suggest that you stay in bed for a few days and don't go doing those boy things that bruised your melon in the first place."

He's very pleased with his explanation, but I'm not. Eating my bruised melon brains? Where's that wastebasket again? And he prescribes bed rest. That's it. Not so twenty-first century. I wonder what he'd recommend for a sore throat. Leeches?

Chapter 18

WHERE THE HEARTACHE BEGINS

In the middle of the night I sit straight up in bed. I'm wide awake.

I remember the feel of the scar on Tuffman's back, the way he clawed me when I touched it. My mother did that to him, a long time ago. I remember the marks on the back of his neck that Mean Jack pointed out. White Wolf gave him those, I bet, when the cougar scraped her.

What else did she write on those cards?

I can't find my flashlight, so I flip on the bedroom light. I dig under my bed until I find the recipe box. As I'm pulling it out, my lighthouse books topple over and spill onto the floor.

Someone taps on the door. I stop scrabbling.

The tap turns into a rap. I am so quiet I stop breathing. My face feels like it's on fire. *I'm not about to lose her after all these years just because you're chicken.* That's what Tuffman said to Vincent.

Tuffman knows my mom is White Wolf. He's been hunting for her.

The door handle turns.

And he knows what I am too. He's come to finish what he started on the table by the lake.

"Raul?" Dean Swift peeks in.

I'm so relieved, I almost start to cry. I'm on my bed, the open box in one hand, the recipe for meringues in the other, my secret stash of books scattered out onto the floor.

"Oh, my child," Dean Swift says when he gets a look at me and my sad, scared eyes. "You must sleep. Give me that."

I shake my head.

"You can*not* read when you have a concussion." He takes the box from me gently. "I'll keep it safe," he says. But when he looks at it, his whole face sinks with sadness. He hands it back. "How can I take this from you? Please promise not to read them tonight."

I sniffle. I wipe my nose with the back of my hand. "Dean Swift," I whisper. "Tell me about the Fresnel lens."

Because I can't just ask him how to get rid of the cougar, can I?

The dean's spine straightens. I can feel him move away from me the tiniest bit. He looks at the wall that separates my room from the stairs to the turret. Then he looks at me. He looks at my books on the floor.

"Something tells me you know as much as I," he says.

"Please," I say.

I must look pretty pathetic with my face all wet and my head all banged up and my mom's recipe box on the pillow next to me like some kind of metallic, sharp-edged teddy bear.

He perches on the bed. "If you close your eyes," he says, "I'll tell you everything I know."

I tuck the box under my pillow and keep my hand on it. I close my eyes. I listen.

"My family has been the keeper of the Fresnel lens for three generations. This is how it began. Long ago there lived a French engineer named Augustin Fresnel, who believed that light traveled in waves. Most scientists mocked him. But Fresnel used mathematical equations to prove his theory. And then he applied everything he knew about light to design brighter lighthouse lenses. His innovations have saved countless lives from shipwrecks. After Fresnel died, his brother found that he had been working on a formula for a lens so powerful it could transform the energy of light and focus its life-giving properties. Fresnel's theories about what the lens could do were so unbelievable that his brother kept it secret. He didn't want to destroy the reputation Fresnel had fought so hard to earn. But my great-great-grandfather, Admiral Swift, got ahold of that formula." Dean Swift chuckles. "I'll tell you *that* story when you're older."

I hate it when they say that. *Tell me the whole story, you old baboon,* I want to shout. But I don't. Obviously.

"When Admiral Swift settled on the island, he had a lighthouse built in White Deer Woods, and he used Fresnel's secret formula to make the lens. For years he secretly studied the lens, and his first experiments apparently proved Fresnel's wildest theories. Admiral Swift began to tell people he had discovered something that would change human life forever. He invited famous scientists to come to a conference to study his claims. In those days it took years to organize such an event. In the meantime, a treaty was signed by the settlers that granted the return of White Deer Woods to the care of the local tribes, for whom the land was sacred. All the buildings that had been constructed in White Deer Woods, including Red Bluff Lighthouse, were torn down. Admiral Swift had helped to write the treaty. His wife, my great-great-grandmother, belonged to the Kwakiutl tribe. With the last of his seafaring fortune, he built this school to house the lens and provide a place for scientists to live and study it."

Dean Swift stops talking. The bed creaks as he stands.

"More," I say. The word is thick on my tongue.

The dean sighs and sits back down. "What happened next, nobody could have predicted. When the lens was moved to the school, it never worked properly again. Every experiment failed. It looked as though my great-great-grandfather had been losing his mind for quite some time. He became a joke—literally. Whenever a scientist formulated a particularly unlikely theory, others would tease, *Go measure your lens again, Admiral Swift*. He died a broken man. I never knew him. I wish I had. I don't think he was crazy. In fact, I know he was *not*. Because one day when I was a young man, I was in the woods and something happened. It made me wonder if Admiral Swift's first experiments had as much to do with White Deer Woods and its light phenomena as they did with Fresnel's special lens. I devoted my life to the study of bioluminescence, never quite knowing exactly what I was looking for. And then, not long ago, I was in the kitchen with Cook Patsy, selecting items to donate to charity. And do you know what I found folded up among the cookbooks?"

Sleep smothers me. I answer, but the words don't make sense. "A cougar?"

He stands up softly, his knees popping. He whispers, "Fresnel's secret formula."

The last thing I see before sleep crushes me is Dean Swift stretching his spine, his elbows pushed back. In profile he looks like a hawk launching himself from a branch.

I spend the night trying to wake up. I need to read the cards. My hand won't listen. It won't turn on the light, it won't open the box. My body is weighed down, stuck in the bed, but my mind wanders everywhere. Dean Swift has fixed the lens. Remember? He found Fresnel's measurements. The lens has a secret power. It has to do with the cougar. The cougar has to do with White Wolf.

The light behind my window shade is gray. Morning. My mouth is dry. My skin burns. The first thing I see when my eyes finally agree to open is the recipe box sticking out from under my pillow. I reach for it, but push it off the bed instead.

Dean Swift must hear the clang of the box as it hits the floor. He comes in and touches my forehead. His hand is ice cold.

"The cards," I whisper to him. "The whole story of my mom is written on them. She knows a secret, and I do too."

A drop of water falls on my cheek.

I look up. The dean's face is wet with tears.

"I'm going to put this in a safe place," he says, picking up the box. "I'm sorry. But we have to keep you calm."

"Please, please turn off the light," I beg. "For my mom."

He flips the switch as he leaves. But that's not the light I meant.

I fall asleep again. When I wake up the doctor is back. The doctor never comes twice. He says I have a fever. He says the wound in my head is infected and gives me pills. I have to take two of them three times a day. Each pill is the size of the rock that Vincent hit me with.

At the door I hear the doctor whisper to Dean Swift, "Don't be surprised by his fever talk. Children often say very strange things with a temperature running that high."

"He misses his mother," says Dean Swift, and the words sound full of tears.

"Don't we all?" the doctor says kindly. "Keep him hydrated."

The door closes.

Where are my cards?

All day people come in and check on me. Ms. Tern reads to me. Her voice is so sweet and she smells so nice that I can't tell her that her stories are like big boots stomping on my heart. She puts her hand on my forehead and smiles at me softly. "We'll have you sorted out in no time," she says. Dean Swift comes in and checks my pulse a lot. Really he's just holding my hand, but we both pretend he's checking my pulse.

The next morning I feel better, but they won't let me get up.

Cook Patsy brings me a diary. When she sees me look

worried because a diary is such a girl thing, she says, "You can live by those boy-girl rules everyone makes up for you, or you can make up your own. Your choice."

I put the diary under my pillow.

Mary Anne is in charge of bringing me soup and hot chocolate. I drink so much, I have to pee every half hour. But it keeps her coming back all day long.

Once I think I hear Sparrow breathing outside my door.

Later that night Mary Anne brings Vincent.

I'm afraid to look at him at first. Has he figured out that I'm the wolf he hit with a rock in the woods? Remembering what he did makes me want to lunge at him and take him to the floor. My chin juts forward. My muscles clench.

But Vincent just perches on the edge of my bed and shakes my hand.

"Are you better?" he asks. "Are you going crazy in here all by yourself?" He looks so worried for me.

I nod, *Yes* to both questions. I'm better and I'm crazier.

A shiver runs over me. It scares me, how angry I just got. A door in my mind opens. The thought behind it terrifies me. What would have happened if Vincent had tripped when wolf me was chasing him?

I shut that door quick.

I realize Mary Anne is talking to Vincent about me.

"No, he's not like *us*, Vincent. He's happiest alone. He's an artist. A scientist. An observer."

I can tell by the expression on her face that she thinks she's complimenting me. But the way she says "us" makes me feel like something scientists found in the deepest trench of the Atlantic ocean—pale, squishy, and one of a kind.

I'm a loner, but that doesn't mean I like being alone.

I'd tell her that, but I'm not sure she notices I'm alive right now. The way he's sitting on the bed and she's standing just inside the door makes it so that they're facing each other. I'm lying here behind Vincent like some unrolled sleeping bag.

I thought they were here to visit me?

Jealousy, like a wet little worm, squiggles in me.

"I didn't tell Raul what happened this weekend yet," Vincent says to her. "Should I?"

My jaw clenches. There's no way I can lie here like a lumpsucker and listen if he's found a way to turn those horrible fifteen minutes in the woods into a funny story.

The doctor said I should expect to have some trouble controlling my emotions for the next few weeks. It's part of bruising your brain. "You'll wear your heart on your sleeve. You'll be grumpy and sad," he said.

So I make my face as blank as I can. But neither of them notices me anyway.

Mary Anne looks like she's about to clap her hands.

"Yes! It's the best story." Then she does clap her hands. "You should write it down! It'd be a great first chapter."

Doc's right about one thing. I'm grumpy.

Vincent smiles. His teeth are white and straight. His skin is tan and his black hair gleams under the lamp.

Charming. That's the word for Vincent. I swallow it down like a piece of meat you can't quite chew and don't know how else to get rid of.

"Okay," he begins. "It's not really a story. It's more like a . . ." he pauses and looks at Mary Anne.

She mouths the word back to him.

"Right, it's more like a *development*."

She nods.

"I spent the whole weekend fishing on the pier with my stepdad," Vincent begins.

Mary Anne looks at him like it's a real cliffhanger of an opening line.

"All day long we sat there, shooting the breeze and hangin'. He let me bait the hooks. He showed me how to gut the fish *with his knife*. I mean it. He let me use his fishing knife. It's *that* big." He measures out about two feet with his hands in front of my face. I notice a big white bandage on his thumb. "Look!" He shoves it at me. "Ten stitches."

I try to smile, but my mouth feels stiff. I'm happy for him and his injury. I really am. So now he gets along with his stepdad. And Mary Anne loves him. And when his mom comes next weekend she'll tell him to pack his bag, because he's going home. And Mary Anne loves him.

Vincent looks worried. He can tell I'm upset. He should know why.

"Don't sweat it," he says. "I promise, next time we go to the lake I'll sneak into the kitchen and steal one of Patsy's knives. I'll show you how much quicker you can gut fish. You'll never want to use that Swiss Army knife again."

He's being so nice, how can I hold a grudge? He's willing to resort to thievery for me.

He takes the bandage off his thumb and shows me the stitches.

"It hurt like you-know-what," he says. "The doctor gave me a shot with a *huge* needle. I mean *huge*. Right in my thumb."

Mary Anne nods. "A local anesthetic."

"I'm telling you, it did *not* work. They started to stitch me up, and I could feel the needle going in and out. Do you know what it's like to have thread pulled *through* your skin?"

"Not good," Mary Anne says.

He's charming. She's pretty. He's witty. She's smart. Why wouldn't they get along?

He knew how much I liked her. Everyone else likes him better than me. I don't mind that. It makes me proud to be the best friend of the most popular kid in school. But couldn't he have let Mary Anne like me better?

My belly burns with the bad feeling. "Grumpy" is not the word for it.

"Won't Vincent make the best hero for my novel? He looks like a Nordic god, doesn't he?" she asks.

No, Mary Anne, I think. He doesn't. He looks like a kid so dumb he split his own thumb open with a knife.

After they leave I pull the diary out from under my pillow.

Cook Patsy was telling the truth. I'm gonna need this.

I pick up my favorite pencil, a number-two Staedtler, and practice my cursive on the first page. *Tuffman was right. Your best friend is always the one who betrays you.* I stare at it for a while.

I erase it.

My brain must really be bruised to think Tuffman could be right about anything.

Have you ever been sick with a fever and stayed in bed all day? At night you never really fall asleep. You toss around a lot and wait for morning. You might think about your crush liking your best friend better than you, and how that's nobody's fault, really, not hers and not yours and not his, either. You might think about the cougar invading your wolf territory. You might wonder if your mom is safe without you. You might wonder if her uncle is out hunting for her, and which skin he's in.

But then I hear the cougar screech.

My ears stretch upward, my mouth feels wet, my legs tighten, and I can actually smell the thing. It's the smell you smell when you go to the zoo and you watch the lions or other big cats pace. A little like old meat, a little like wet fur, a little stale.

White Wolf is out there alone.

I need the recipe cards.

I swing my legs out of the bed. I stand up. My head aches and feels empty at the same time. I fall down. The door opens. Ms. Tern helps me back into bed.

"My mom is a wolf," I say to her.

She pulls the covers up to my chin. Her hand is cool on my forehead.

"Mine was an orca," she whispers.

In the morning when I wake up, my pajamas and hair are soaking wet. Something happened in the middle of the night, but I don't know what.

As I look out the window, the memory of the cougar screech echoes in my head. Right after it comes the feeling of Ms. Tern's words brushing my ear. It makes my skin tingle to remember. I try to shake it away. The doctor said the fever would give me weird dreams. The weirdest thing about that dream is how it seems so real.

I don't have long to think about it.

When Mary Anne comes in with my breakfast, her eyes are red and puffy and I can tell she's been crying.

I bet Vincent has already broken her heart. I know it's wrong, but I'm crossing my fingers so hard my knuckle cracks. Please. Please. I would never break your heart.

"He doesn't want me to tell you," she says. "But I think you should know."

It's all right, Mary Anne, I know. He's charming. But I'm loyal.

"Dean Swift wants to tell you later. But I *hate* secrets." She starts to sob. "The cougar," she says.

My head pounds. Has the cougar hurt White Wolf?

"The cougar attacked Bobo," she says.

Bobo? I can't believe it.

"Bobo has been grievously wounded. The vet says her hind leg will have to be amputated." Mary Anne takes a breath. "I thought you should know that her chances of survival are slim. The truth, even when it is sad, is something we must all learn to live with."

I turn my face away from her. The ache fills my head and my chest so that I can't think or feel anything but it. A little later I hear the door shut.

What did Bobo ever do to him? Nothing. Bobo did nothing.

My skin is still hot from the fever, but inside I'm cold. What will he do to White Wolf? My mom knows his secret. And she's the one who cracked his back.

I need the recipe cards. I need to know how to get rid of my uncle.

Chapter 19

WHERE THE ENEMY MIGHT BE THE FRIEND

Thursday morning I get up and go downstairs before anyone can come and tell me that I can't. I need to see Bobo. I need the cards. My head hurts and I'm clammy. But the sooner Dean Swift thinks I'm healthy, the sooner he'll give me what I want.

I stop by his office to ask for the recipe box. The door is open, but he's not there.

I step in. Then I turn and look down the hallway, both directions. Nobody's coming. I close the door behind me. I open every one of his desk drawers. I know I shouldn't. But I need to learn the rest of my mom's story.

Why did she hurt Tuffman that day in the woods? What is Tuffman's secret?

I can't find the box. It must be in the turret. I'm going to have to get my hands on a key.

Next stop: kitchen. I left Bacon and Cheddar Omelet and Island Cobbler in there.

I sneak in the side entrance instead of going through

the cafeteria. There's nobody in the kitchen, either. The search takes a while. There are lots of drawers and cupboards to look through. Finally I think to look at the corkboard near the phone. An envelope with my name on it is tacked there. I pull it down and open it. Cook Patsy has slipped the recipe cards into plastic protectors so that they won't get stained by splatters when she's cooking. She's always looking out for me.

"Thank you," I say, even though she's nowhere around to hear it.

I look at the recipe for Bacon and Cheddar Omelet.

4 cubes Che"ddar	D
1 onion	O
5 tsp honey	Y
2 tsp yogurt	O
2 oz rum	U
1 walnut	W
1 apple	A
5 oz bacon	N
1 tsp thyme	T

I hold my breath until I figure out what's written on the next card.

Island Cobbler.

3 pineapple	N
2 sprigs mint	P
4 oranges	N
1 egg	E
3 cups milk	L
2 tsp cinnamon	I
3 oz liver	V
7 cps blackberry	E
1 cp sugar	S
7 pats Butter ?"	?

I must have done something wrong. Ignore the measurement. I change the *P* to *I*. *Do you want nine lives?* That's better. Or is it? What does that mean?

I shake my head and then stop because that hurts. I look again. Why are there quote marks in front of the *D* and after the question mark? I add them in. "Do you want nine lives?"

Is this part of a conversation?

I step out of the kitchen, tucking the cards into my pocket.

In the hallway I run into Ms. Tern. I scream like you do when you get caught doing something or being somewhere you shouldn't.

"Are you looking for Bobo?" she asks.

I stare at her. Maybe it wasn't a dream last night after

all. The memory of it feels so real. Finally I remember to nod.

"She's in here," Ms. Tern says. She walks to the storeroom next to the kitchen.

I don't follow. I don't want to see Bobo suffering.

"Don't be afraid." Ms. Tern comes back to lead me in. Her hand is cool like it was in my dream. "She's a bit groggy from the anesthesia," she says as she opens the door. "I put her in here since it's quiet during most of the day and warm because of the kitchen."

I step in. There's a pile of blankets on the floor. Bobo lifts her nose.

I don't think about it. I just do it. I lie down beside my friend.

"Oh!" Ms. Tern says. "Please get up. That floor is filthy."

I rest my hand under Bobo's muzzle and bring my face in close to hers.

I don't think I'll tell you any more of this part.

Ms. Tern leaves me alone with Bobo for a while. When she comes back, I let her convince me to get off the floor and go get breakfast. It's good to let grown-ups feel like they're helping you even when nothing can help. Everybody needs to feel useful.

What I see in the dining hall doesn't cheer me up. Vincent is on my stool. Mary Anne is next to him. When I come over with my tray, they're looking at something together.

"I like that scene," he says. "But what if you made the bad guy handsome?"

They look up when I sit down a few stools away.

"Sit with us," Vincent says like I'm crazy.

My new place is next to Vincent and not between the two of them. I try to look like I don't notice. But I feel like one of those reversible puppets. On the outside I'm a cheerful Little Red Riding Hood. But if you flip the puppet over you'll find a really angry wolf inside.

Dean Swift comes into the dining room.

Tuffman is behind him. A growl starts in my throat. Vincent looks at me sideways. I tap my chest and pretend it's a burp.

This weekend, Tuffman. You and me. In the woods. I get it now. It's the only way it can go down—when we're both what we are in the woods. Natural law, right?

"Children," the dean says, "the vet tells me that we must prepare for the worst. Bobo is an old dog. But a heroic one. The vet says that her injuries prove that she fought valiantly against her attacker. She lost three teeth in the fight." He gives a shaky smile. "And it is not unreasonable to assume that she left them deep in the beast's hide. The cougar will feel the bitter sting of Bobo's bite for many days to come."

I'm so proud of Bobo, I almost stand up and make a toast with my orange juice. *Here's to infected dog bites! Let there be pus and inflammation!*

But the dean keeps talking. "Nevertheless, we must be realistic. In preparation for a memorial service, please write down your memories of our dear old friend—" His voice cracks. He covers his eyes.

Tuffman finishes the dean's sentence. "And give them to a teacher. We're gonna make a memory book so we can always honor the good times we had with our four-legged buddy." His voice is high up in his throat, like he's got a lump of tears in there as big as mine. His mouth is turned down at the corners. His eyes are red and wet.

He's as sad as I am. I can feel it.

There's a word Ms. Tern uses: "gobsmacked." It means the look on someone's face after they get smacked in the gob. That's your mouth. My gob looks smacked.

Nobody can lie like that. Not even Tuffman. You would have to have two hearts and two brains and two tongues, not just two skins.

After a minute Dean Swift looks up again. "Well said, Coach. Because of this attack, nobody will leave the building without my permission."

The room erupts with chatter. Then above it all, Tuffman shouts, "We'll have that cougar in a cage by midnight tonight!" The anger in his voice sends an electric charge through the room. "Midnight tonight!" he shouts again, and we all stand up like soldiers, ready to fight.

Dean Swift nods and walks out of the room. Tuffman stomps out after him. Everyone is quiet for a long minute. Then there's a murmur, and the voices get shrill and loud and they're all talking about the cougar.

My throat clamps up. I'm about to start bawling. The doctor said the concussion would make me emotional. He said to try not to think about anything worrisome until I'm better. But *everything's* worrisome right now.

If Tuffman's the cougar and the cougar attacked Bobo, why would Tuffman look so broken up? And Bobo took a bite out of the cougar. Wouldn't Tuffman look a little worse for wear if he had three canine teeth stuck in him somewhere? Look at me. I'm living proof that a wound on one skin leaves a wound on the other.

My head hammers. I focus on my evidence. It's like I see it written out on a page in my scientific journal. First, set aside the science and the magic. The Fresnel lens, the spirit animals, and the mtDNA are all theories. Set aside the coincidences. Look at the evidence.

Item 1: Sneaker prints in the mud smelled like cougar.

Scents can get mixed-up. Especially after a rainstorm.

Item 2: Tuffman says a lot of weird things and stands too close to me and follows me around.

Little John practically stands on my feet half the time he's near me. And last week he walked up to me in the bathroom and said, "The thunder's moving east." What does that mean? But only a pollywog would accuse him of homicidal tendencies.

Item 3: My mom's recipe card said he wanted to kill her.

It said T wanted to kill her. T doesn't have to be Tuffman. It could be Ted or Tina or T. rex or Tinker Bell. Why would she call her uncle by his last name, anyway? Who does that?

But what really doesn't make any sense is this: Why would Tuffman have fallen for Vincent's prank if he was the cougar? When he was shooting the piñata, Tuffman *thought* he was shooting the cougar. My head whirls.

Conclusion: I can't make one until I have my mom's whole story.

I look around the cafeteria to calm myself down.

Little John is tapping the kid next to him on the head with a spoon. The kid is just shoveling cereal into his mouth like this is a normal part of breakfast. Mean Jack is twisting a wrapped-up string cheese around and around. Mark is wiping his face off with the dishrag that's for cleaning up spills.

At the little kids' table, Sparrow won't look at me. It hits me: He didn't come visit me. He didn't slide one of his drawings under my door, either, like he normally does when some nasty contagious stomach bug has half of us quarantined. And now, every time I try to make eye contact with him, he turns his back to me.

I try to pay attention to the funny story Vincent is telling Mary Anne. She laughs a lot and then asks, "Can I use this in my novel?"

I stop listening and start thinking about what's wrong with Sparrow. He's hiding something from me. It feels like an explosion in my chest when I realize what it must be. He must be hiding a bruise. His grandma must have let his mom come see him. She must have hit him again. He doesn't want her to get in trouble anymore because even though she's a terrible mom, she's *his* mom and he loves her. That's how love works. You can't always stop it, even when you probably should.

It makes me so angry. I can't take another bite. I put my tray in the dirty dishes bin and walk over to Sparrow's table.

I kneel down and put my hand under his chin and make him look up at me. There's no bruise on his face, but his eyes fill up with tears pretty quick.

I tilt my head so he can see I'm ready to listen.

"I lost it," he says, and makes a huge gulping sound. "I lost your fishing pole."

"What?" I ask. I spent so much time on that pole. It's the best carving I've ever made.

"I left it at the lake on Friday. When I went to look for it after Grammy dropped me off on Sunday, it was gone." He starts to cry really hard now.

All morning it's been cooking in me. Rage. And now it's like when frozen fries get thrown into a deep fat fryer and the oil spatters and jumps. Someone is gonna get burned.

"You promised. How could you?" First I whisper it. Then I say it louder because it makes me feel good to shout. "How could you?"

Sparrow's face crumples.

I don't stop. "Tuffman's right," I say. "You *are* a loser."

Everyone in the dining hall stops talking and eating. First they look at me, but my face must be even more scary than normal, because right away they turn and look at Sparrow. He can't stop crying, and now everyone is staring at him crying.

Good, I think. Now they'll think he's a baby, and he *is* a baby because a baby can't be trusted with important things.

Sparrow says something, but I can't understand it since he's sobbing so hard. I only hear the word "rain."

I stomp out of the dining hall and up to my room.

But before I even get to the second floor, I feel terrible. What is wrong with me?

He's only five. A five-year-old is going to lose things from time to time. When I was five, I lost plenty of things. Like the time I lost my mom's favorite bracelet. I remember how she almost started to cry, she was so sad, how she said she got it from her mother and her mother had gotten it from her mother and so on and so on. But did she yell at me? No. She hugged me and said she knew I felt even worse than she did and that even though the bracelet was a gift that reminded her of all the mothers who had made her, I was the gift who had made her a mother herself.

She found it a week later in the trunk of my Flintstones car, along with the remote for the garage door, an old slice of cheddar cheese, and twenty-five paper clips. How many times did I hear her tell that story to someone on the phone, saying it like it was the funniest, smartest thing a kid could do?

I turn around and head back to the dining hall. I'll tell him not to worry about it. We'll find the pole. And if we don't, then we'll go out to the woods and look for another straight branch so I can make him a new one. It won't be as great as the last one, that'll be the lesson for him, but it will still be pretty darn good.

Halfway down the hall I slap my hand to my forehead. *Rain.* That's what he was saying. It's why he forgot the pole on Friday. He wasn't being careless. It was raining so hard and so fast we all scrambled out of the woods like the cougar was after us.

I feel bad all right, but not as bad as I'm going to feel, because when I turn the corner, guess who is standing in front of me with a look in her eyes so mean it could shatter a window or make a building fall down or bend a telephone pole? You got it. Mary Anne.

"Was I wrong about you!" she says in a very quiet voice. "I thought you were different from all these other primates." She stares at me like I'm more disgusting than mushroom casserole. "Jack is a real Prince Charming next to you, you know that?"

I look down.

"You're out of the book," she hisses, knocking into me as she walks past. "You get that? You're *out* of my novel."

I hadn't known I was in it, but there's nothing she could say that would make me feel worse.

"I guess I shouldn't be surprised. There's a saying for it. The apple doesn't fall far from the tree. You didn't get Tuffman's looks, but you sure got all of his cruelty," she calls back.

I was dead wrong. She *could* say something that makes me feel worse. And that was it.

I can't believe Vincent told her I was related to Tuffman.

Chapter 20

WHERE RAUL LOSES SPARROW AND FINDS BOBO'S TEETH

I couldn't find Sparrow. After about ten minutes I had to stop looking and go to class.

Have you ever done something as bad as what I did? Lose your temper like that, make a little guy who looks up to you cry, make the girl you love hate you? But it gets worse. At lunch I don't see Sparrow at his table, so I go pound on his bedroom door. He doesn't answer, and when I hit it one last time the door opens a little. I peek around the corner. Maybe he's hiding behind the door. But he's not. He's not under the bed or in the closet, and when I've looked inside and under everywhere a five-year-old could hide, I notice how cold the room is. The window is open. It's a short jump to the ground even for Sparrow's little legs.

I run to Dean Swift's office and stand in the open doorway. Four teachers are hunched over his desk.

The math teacher is talking. "I think we're looking at a boy with anger management issues."

The social studies teacher clucks. "I'm not sure he

should be supervising the little ones on Fridays."

Ms. Tern shakes her head. "You're both mad. The doctor told us that the concussion could make him prone to irrational behavior. If anyone's at fault here, I am. I saw him acting strangely before breakfast. He was deeply affected by Bobo's injury. I should have taken him back to his room."

"Hey, Nicky, we all dropped the ball on this one," Tuffman says. "I should've checked on him first thing this morning. I can tell you from personal experience, a concussion brings out the worst in a man. Add that to the family temper and kaboom, whaddya expect?"

Have you ever walked into a room where everyone's talking about you? You know how part of you wants to run away and part of you wants to act normal so nobody can tell how much it hurts?

They all turn to stare at me, long wrinkles between their eyes. Ms. Tern looks worried. Tuffman looks sympathetic. Dean Swift looks disappointed.

In me. He's disappointed in me.

I hang back a little as we head into the dining hall. It's the middle of lunch and the noise makes me feel like someone stuffed a pillow in my brain. But the minute the kids notice the dean, four teachers, and me, all standing in the doorway, it gets as quiet as the library on a Saturday.

"Children," the dean says, "Sparrow has not come to

any of his classes. Please finish your lunches quickly. We will start a search. Students will work with a supervising adult."

Dean Swift doesn't look at me as he chooses his group, and Mary Anne flounces over to him before he even calls her name. Me, Mean Jack, Vincent, and Little John get assigned to Tuffman. The cafeteria bustles and booms as everyone starts talking and Cook Patsy distributes flashlights for the tunnels and walkie-talkies.

But when Dean Swift raises a hand, the room goes silent in a split-second. "Children," he says in a voice so serious it makes my skin tingle and my ears burn, "you must stay within sight of an adult at all times. *Do You Understand?*"

Why doesn't he just say the word we're all thinking?

Cougar.

I made a mistake. Everyone knows it. Me most of all.

And now I'm going to fix it.

"Come on," I say, pushing my way out the door. "I know where he is."

No one else knows it all. I know where Sparrow hides when someone he loves hurts him. I know his hideout is also the cougar's den. I guess we all know the cougar has three German shepherd teeth sunk in him and is getting meaner by the minute.

But I'm the only one who knows—who *really* knows—how dangerous a wounded predator is. Because I'm the only one who's ever worn that skin. I keep thinking how I charged Tuffman and Vincent down by the lake. What would I have done if one of them had tripped as he ran out of my territory? Would the boy in me have been able to reason with the wounded wolf?

I sprint down the zigzag path to the beach. I don't care how many spiderwebs break up on my face and arms. I don't care how many blackberry thorns rip my shirt and scrape my bare legs. I run. Tuffman and Vincent are right behind me as I jump from the path to the driftwood pile and then onto the sand. We are racing three across now, our feet pounding in the hard-packed sand. Behind us, Mean Jack stumbles over the driftwood. I glance back and see Little John at the top of the zigzag path. He's throwing rocks as hard as he can down at Mean Jack and whooping every time he hears the big kid curse and moan, "You're breakin' my heart Johnny, you're breakin' my heart."

We don't need them anyway.

I turn up the path that leads from the beach to the fort, and Vincent and Tuffman stay beside me. We're a team and we're running like one, our feet hitting the ground all at the same time.

Tuffman reaches out and punches me lightly on the shoulder. "We'll find him, Raul," he says. "You lead the way. It's your show, Raul."

I swallow hard. Tuffman drops back, like he knows

I'm about to cry and he doesn't want to embarrass me. Man, was I wrong about this guy. It's just been a misunderstanding, like the dean said. He's on my side. Look how he's treating me now, like he has respect for me. Like I made a mistake and he respects me enough to let me be the one to fix it.

Maybe he does know my mom is White Wolf. Maybe he's looking for her because he wants to help her.

Didn't he tell me *twice* that he loved her like a little sister?

The thought gives me a burst of energy. We pound across the field. A group of police officers is getting out of a squad car in the parking lot as we run by. They nod at us, and I feel another surge of energy as I see that our team is part of a bigger team. We're gonna find Sparrow. He'll be all right.

The Blackout Tunnel is on the far side of the fort, separate from the main building. It's a U shape, with two ways in or out. As we get nearer I put my finger to my lips. I signal to Tuffman to guard the first entrance to the tunnel in case Sparrow runs out that end. I try not to think about the cougar.

"Wait here," I whisper, and Tuffman gives me a sharp salute.

"You bet, Captain Raul," he says.

I've been thinking like a lunatic. This is what happens when you've got a bruised melon for a brain.

Thank goodness I kept my yap shut. One good thing about being the quiet type—even your fever talk is all in your head.

Vincent and I creep toward the other entrance. Then we hear it.

The cougar scream. It rings on and on with a cold, echoing sound, like it's coming to us from the bottom of a well.

When you were little, what scared you? Toilets flushing? Spiders? Or dogs? For me it was being alone in the dark. When I saw my mom's hand reach up to turn off the lights, my whole body felt like it was screaming NO!

That's how I feel when I hear the cougar screech.

I'm a big No. My legs are a jelly of No. My head has no thoughts but the word "No." My stomach jumps like a trampoline that squeaks the word "No."

I look at Vincent, and my eyes are so wide open, I wonder if I'll ever be able to shut them again. Vincent stares back.

"We gotta get Sparrow out of that tunnel," I manage to say.

Vincent starts to shake all over. He falls to the ground.

Looks like I'm on my own.

"Sparrow!" I shout. Halfway into the tunnel I trip over something. I scream. The thing on the ground screams. It jumps on me and starts scratching and clawing me.

It's not the cougar. It smells like maple syrup, for starters.

"Sparrow," I say after a second. My voice is very calm. The scratching stops.

"Raul?" his little voice asks.

"Yeah, it's me," I say. I try to pull him up, but I can't tell which end of him I've got.

We shuffle around for a second.

"Sorry," he says with a little sob once we're sitting shoulder to shoulder with our backs to the wall.

"No, Sparrow, I'm sorry. I acted like a total jerk. I know you only forgot it because of the rain," I say.

I stand up, because all of a sudden my legs want to run really fast. I sense the cougar. I try to keep my voice calm. "Okay, which way did I come in?" I ask, reaching down and patting around to find Sparrow again. I pull him up next to me.

"It doesn't matter," Sparrow says. "Either way leads out."

If either way leads out, then either way leads in. And I only know one thing for sure—the way I came in there was no cougar.

"Stay with me," I say. I walk with one hand on the wall to my left and the other hand holding tight to Sparrow's. It's so dark, I realize I've closed my eyes.

There's no point in keeping them open. I could not see my finger even if I stuck it into my eyeball.

The screech of the cougar echoes toward us. The back of my neck prickles. The tingly, chicken-flesh feeling spreads all the way from my neck up over the top of my head and then down into my ears.

I hear a sound like claws clicking on the cement. I look back. Two yellow eyes glow. Then I *feel* the cougar's low growl and the hot breath that carries it. I sense the cougar tensing its back, leaning into its hind legs, gathering all of its muscle into a force strong enough to knock the two of us down with one pounce. I can't explain what happens next. It's the wolf in me. It's the light in me. Without having any idea of what I'm doing, I scoop Sparrow up with one hand and then I leap blindly into the air, grabbing at a ladder that I somehow know is bolted to the wall in front of us. My hand grasps the middle rung and I pull us both up to safety in one insanely accurate jump into total blackness.

Below, the cougar pounces and lands on cement. I can hear him scrabble around, like he can't believe it, and then I can feel the air sweep beneath us as he stretches up against the wall and paws at the emptiness.

With Sparrow holding tight to my neck, his legs squeezing around my waist, I scramble up to the top of the ladder until my head hits the ceiling. We are out of rungs.

I push Sparrow up so that he is sitting on the top rung. I'm pretty sure the big field in the middle of the fort is above us. Some kid's up there flying a kite, I bet. In a minute, when I've caught my breath, I'll feel around on the ceiling for the hatch this ladder must lead to, but I doubt it'll open—it's probably been locked tight for half a century.

I hear claws scrape against something metallic. That cougar is trying to climb the ladder! I cling to the bar and curl my feet in. I'd sure like to keep them attached to my ankles.

Scrape, scrape. My ears flinch. I don't want to die in the dark.

Then I hear shouts.

It's Vincent's voice hollering at us, but I can't tell where he is.

"We're at the top of a ladder, but the cougar is trying to climb it," I shout back.

"Hang on, boys!" Dean Swift calls. "The police are going to fire a flare to scare him off. Stay where you are and plug your ears."

I put Sparrow's hands over my ears and mine over his and then I press down as hard as I can.

There's a flash of light and a loud bang.

A second later I hear the sound of a gunshot and then the screech of the cougar.

They've killed it.

We scramble down and head out of the tunnel as fast as we can in the dark.

As we come out into the daylight, Sparrow looks up at me. I can tell by the shape of his mouth that he's about to cry. I stop walking and kneel down so that I'm his height. It feels good to get low—my legs are wobbly. I hug Sparrow.

"I'm sorry," I tell him.

I look around as I pat him. We're all alone. This is where I left Tuffman. So much for calling me captain and promising to obey my orders.

Dean Swift runs over to us from the other entrance. A few of the teachers and some of the policemen follow. Vincent comes too, but he hangs back. He must feel embarrassed about how he acted when we heard the cougar.

"Thanks for going to get help," I say as I walk up to him. "You saved us." I say it loudly so that the grown-ups will remember to give him credit for doing the right thing.

His face gets red.

People start crowding around us.

Vincent leans in and whispers, "Promise you won't tell anyone."

Like I'd do that.

"Promise," he says again.

"I promise." I don't have much time to think about

it, but it bugs me a little that he doesn't trust me—that he needs me to swear to it.

Then the grown-ups are all over me and Sparrow, asking if we're okay and did we get hurt and are we frightened and do we need to talk and the counselor is waiting for us back at the school and here's some juice and brownies that the Fort Casey guards brought over for you.

When they quiet down for a second, Sparrow asks, "Did you get the cougar?"

Dean Swift and the policemen all sigh at the same time.

For the first time I notice Ms. Tern is standing there, holding a rifle.

One of the Fort Casey guards speaks up. "The durn thing got clean away!"

Dean Swift frowns. "Not clean away, you can't say that. The bullet nicked him. I saw it as he darted by. She managed to graze his cheek."

Ms. Tern bites her lower lip. "I hoped I could stop it without killing it."

Dean Swift shrugs. I can tell he wishes Ms. Tern had done a little more damage. But he just puts an arm around me and Sparrow and says, "I have been assured by the guards that it will be easier to track, thanks to the trail of blood. The suspense will soon end."

"Hey, there you are!" A voice cries out.

We turn around to see Tuffman walking out of the tunnel from the same side Sparrow and I had just run out of. The side where Tuffman saluted and promised to stand guard.

Tuffman is ready with an excuse before he can even see the look on my face. "I got worried. I went in to look for you. It's dark in there!"

My blood feels cold. My thoughts click together like puzzle pieces. How could he have gone in that side and not passed me and Sparrow as we were coming out?

Oh man. Maybe a wolf's nose is never wrong.

"I cut myself pretty good, huh?" Tuffman says. He's holding his bandana to his cheek. "There are some hooks stuck into the wall—right at face level. Wonder what the soldiers used them for."

How can it be a coincidence that Tuffman is bleeding in the same place where the cougar got hit?

The whole solidarity thing as we ran across the fort grounds—that was all just a big show, wasn't it? He was trying to distract me and make it easier to hide shifting into his second skin. His *cougar* skin.

"Missed it, Nicky? Well, it takes skill to use a gun that big," Tuffman says to Ms. Tern.

"Just because I didn't slaughter the animal doesn't mean I missed my shot," Ms. Tern says. She grips the stock of the rifle.

I watch them argue. I crack my jaw. It makes me

calm, to know the truth and to be certain of it. I'll take care of Tuffman in the woods.

But then I think of Bobo. Fury pulses in me. Because what would the cougar have done to me and Sparrow if I hadn't leaped onto that ladder?

It's not human—the anger in me is all wolf. I see and hear like I do when I'm deep in the woods. My nose is full of scents, each one resting above or below another, like layers on a tall cake.

Everyone is moving away from the Blackout Tunnel, crossing the field and heading to the beach and the school. Tuffman's at the back of the pack. He's wiping his cheek with his bandana.

I sense how he feels—frustrated but safe. He's tired and off his guard.

I move behind him slowly, tracking him. I stare at his back. The closer I get, the harder I sniff. I can smell his blood. I sniff deeper. I smell Bobo.

I found her teeth.

"Hey," I call to him. "Thanks for helping."

"And they say the kid never talks," he says in his jokey way as he turns to face me.

If he knew me better, he'd know that I always say *thank you*.

"Put it there, pardner," I say. I put my hand out.

He thinks I'm dumb as bricks. He reaches for my hand.

I don't think we've been properly introduced. Meet your nephew, the wolf.

I grip his hand tight in mine. With my left hand I pat him on the shoulder. I reach around a little to the back, where I can feel the shape of a bandage under his shirt. I sink my fingers into the wound. *Bobo wants her teeth back.*

He winces. His shoulder twists and drops down. I keep digging. He tries to yank his right hand out of mine. But I squeeze harder. I have my wolf strength in me.

"There's more than one way to skin a cat," I say to him.

I let go. I don't want him to start screeching. Not yet.

I turn to walk away, but he reaches out and swipes at me.

When I look back, his face is pale with pain but he's smiling. "Hey, pardner," he manages to say. "I had that coming. No hard feelings, yeah?"

My ears bend back. I want to snarl, but my mouth only works that way when I'm a wolf.

"What?" I bark.

"You two were in my territory, like the dog was last night. Remember the other day at the lake?" he asks. "Me and Vincent were in your territory, right?"

It's so strange to hear him say my secret out loud. He's talking about it like it's normal.

"Don't tell me you wouldn't have destroyed us if we'd given you half the chance," he says. "It's in our nature, that's all." His voice is calm and matter-of-fact, like this is just some weird family trait like a knack for math or bad teeth.

But it's true. I don't know what I would have done to them. I look away.

"You're strong, Raul," he says.

I shrug, but I can't help it—I feel proud. It's funny. Tuffman's the only one who could notice that about me. Nobody else sees what we can see.

"We need to work together, Raul," he says. "We can help each other—keep normal people out of our territory so they don't get hurt."

It all starts to sink in. What I've been hiding, why I've been hiding it, and now here it is out in the open. Someone knows my secret. And he's not afraid of me and he doesn't hate me for it.

He smiles. "I mean, it's not like we're monsters."

Mary Anne says I'm a loner because I want to be. But all this time, I've been a loner because I have to be.

He steps closer to me. "And, Raul, I can show you how to live forever."

His eyes wrap around me. I can't move.

Under the sharp March wind or above it is a puff of warmth. Spring. I sniff and smell the yellow stubs of sprouts and the white-green of rising bulbs and the cracking shells and cocoons of every insect and bird waking to life.

And I can't look away from his gold eyes and the promise that I know somehow is not a lie.

"Both of you," he says. "I can help her, too, Raul."

I blink. Of course he can.

He reaches back and rubs his shoulder where I dug my fingers into him. His hand comes away covered in blood. He stretches it out to me. "Shake on it?"

I begin to raise my hand. With a swipe so quick I don't even see it, his fingernail slices across my palm. I stare at the rising red line.

Blood brothers with Tuffman?

I drop my hand.

He steps closer. "Don't chicken out on me, kid. Here's the deal. A cat's got nine lives. A wolf can too," he says.

The words in my head are all in capital letters: DO YOU WANT NINE LIVES?

He made my mom the same promise.

I almost drop to all fours. I race to join Sparrow and the others.

The wind comes up off the water. The sky is whipped cream and blue. The grass along the cliffs is tall and golden. I smell salt and seaweed and driftwood.

Yeah, I want to live forever. But not with him.

I wipe my hand on my jeans. The cut isn't very deep.

On the walk back to the school everyone surrounds me.

I tell myself to look calm. Dean Swift will give me

the recipe box as soon as we get back. Until then, I'd best act like my brain isn't bruised and my uncle isn't a man-eating cougar who thinks he can live forever.

I say "Thank you" when Mean Jack says I make one heck of a capo. He wants to talk to me privately later about whether I'd consider taking the vow of *omertà*.

"Code of Silence, you wanna take that? Everyone knows you can keep your trap shut. But now you proved you got what it takes to be a made man," he whispers.

Mark, swinging his weighted vest over his head, hollers to me, "I woulda *Peed. My. Pants.* I mean it."

Little John grabs my hand. "Did you hear that joke? Is it wet on Uranus? Only it means the planet and it also means your butt. Right? You get it?"

When Sparrow takes my other hand, the pressure on the cut takes the sting away. He holds it like he'll never let go.

All the grown-ups tell me I must be the bravest kid in the world. But I know what I did. What I did was lose my temper, scare a little kid who looks up to me, and put him in danger. That's what I did. I acted as vicious as a wounded animal.

And I've still got to save my mom. Inside, the wolf rage dies down. The boy in me thinks. I might have messed up there, too. Maybe I shouldn't have let Tuffman know I know. Maybe I shouldn't have let him see how strong I am.

Who is he, really?

Cook Patsy comes over and calls me heroic. I look around to see if Mary Anne heard. It takes a while for me to spot her.

She's at the back of the crowd. With Vincent. A little drop of jealousy rains in my heart. Then it sprinkles when she whispers something in Vincent's ear. He smiles and nods like she said something reassuring.

Then it's a downpour. Because when she loses her balance and moves away from him a little, I see that they are holding hands. He pulls her back so that she doesn't fall.

It's a hurricane in my heart.

Chapter 21

WHERE RAUL FINDS THE KEY TO HIS QUESTIONS, BUT THE ANSWERS ARE WRONG

On the steps of the school, Dean Swift and Ms. Tern stop me. Their eyes drill into me.

"Straight to bed for you," the dean says.

I'm hot and sweaty. There's an 88 percent chance I'm going to barf. I sit down hard on the bottom step.

"He's knackered!" Ms. Tern says.

Dean Swift bends over me. Something small and metallic falls out of his pocket and lands on the step. A key. I point to it, but he has already stood up. His head is swiveling around, searching for help.

"We need a pair of strong arms to get you up to your bed," Dean Swift says.

I barely hear him. My eyes focus on the little key. The top of it is in the shape of a lighthouse. The key to the turret. I set my hand over it. I need the recipe cards more than ever.

"Mr. Tuffman," the dean shouts. "Mr. Tuffman, come here!"

While he's shouting, I slip the key into my pocket.

I hear Ms. Tern scolding the dean. "You're going to *humiliate* him. Really, Oliver, you haven't got a clue, have you?"

I look up and see Tuffman heading toward us. That's when I realize the dean wants Tuffman to carry me up to my bedroom.

Are you kidding me?

I jump up and take the steps two at a time. Dean Swift and Ms. Tern can hardly keep up with me. The sooner I get into bed, the sooner they'll leave me alone. I have the key to the turret, and the answers to all of my questions are in that recipe box.

Dean Swift flips on the light in my room. "You will stay in bed until tomorrow morning. We can't risk a relapse."

He turns to leave, then stops in the doorway. The air feels heavy all of a sudden. He's going to say something that maybe I don't want to hear.

"We all make mistakes, Raul," he says.

I nod. The scratch Tuffman gave me throbs. I'm glad it hurts, because I deserve it.

"It is through our failures—not in spite of them—that we triumph," the dean says softly. "You disappointed me this morning. You made me very, very proud this afternoon."

I swallow hard and look down.

"Pajamas!" he says as he turns out the light.

I put on my pajamas and listen to him and Ms. Tern bickering as they walk away. It's funny, they act like old friends even though she's new. I can't make out what they're saying, but I have a feeling it's about her shooting the cougar. I think she calls him a twit. Did he just tell her to put a lid on it?

I listen until the hallway is quiet. I open my door and peek out.

A second later and I've unlocked the utility closet. I glide up the steps. The recipe box is on top of Dean Swift's tape recorder. I grab it.

On the second step down the stairs I see the doorknob turn. For a split-second I'm so scared, I can't move.

"You forgot to lock it?" It's Ms. Tern.

"Never!" I hear the dean say as the door opens.

I turn around. I put the box back and dart under a small table pushed against the wall.

"You're an absentminded old duffer," Ms. Tern says as the steps creak and Dean Swift starts to puff-puff his way up them.

I pull a desk chair in under the table to hide myself better. I barely stop my scream. Coiled on the seat is Gollum. She lifts her head and looks at me. The back of my neck tingles. Then she drops to the floor and glides away.

"So you think this is why the cougar is here?" Ms. Tern asks.

They're so far from the truth they can't even see its tail end. The cougar is here for the wolf. I almost crawl out from under the table to tell them. But then I'd have a lot to explain. The key feels hot in my pajama pocket.

"It's a theory," says the dean.

"But it supports mine," she says.

"I don't see how." Dean Swift sounds tired.

"Luke Ferrier has spent a lifetime hunting rare predators. What if you're right? What if the Fresnel lens attracts them?"

There's a long silence. *Luke Ferrier*. My brain scratches around. Where have I heard that name before?

"It doesn't *call* them, exactly," Dean Swift finally says. "It's more complicated."

My ears stretch, I'm listening so hard.

"It's not a theory. It's a hunch. Perhaps the light of this lens has the power to open a kind of doorway in the natural world between different states of being. I think White Deer Woods is one of those doorways. And maybe certain types of predators are attracted to that power threshold."

I shiver. I'm hot and cold at the same time. The dean only has half the story. He's wrong about why the cougar's here, but he's right about the door. White Deer told me my lighthouse in the woods was a place between places. That's a good definition of a doorway, isn't it?

But here's what Dean Swift doesn't know. The door the light opens isn't White Deer Woods. When the light hit me last Friday on the edge of the cliff, it opened the door inside *me*—the door that separates wolf me from Raul me.

"What if you're right?" Ms. Tern asks. "Let's say that the light draws *certain types of predators.* What if Ferrier got wind of your experiments somehow, and decided to hunker down on this island and wait to see what your light would bring him?"

"If that were true, then the Fresnel lens would be like a baited trap!" Dean Swift sounds horrified.

"Precisely," says Ms. Tern. "Forty years ago, the Penn Cove Massacre brought Ferrier two spirit animals in one felonious swoop. Why wouldn't he return to the scene of his most successful crime? Especially if he thought that your light would lure his prey to him."

It clicks. Luke Ferrier is the criminal mastermind she told us about in class.

"I've been fiddling with the light for years," Dean Swift says. "Why would he show up now? It doesn't add up."

"It does, in fact, add up. This fall when you sent me the fundraiser flyer for your school and I saw the photo of your new coach, I knew it was him. The bio matches perfectly. I've been following Ferrier for years, always one step behind. Seven years ago the trail went cold. Interpol determined Ferrier must have died. I moved on to elephant poachers. But seven years ago—that's just about the time Tuffman broke his back, isn't it? It's been one surgery after another for him since then. No wonder he hasn't been in shape to hunt."

Ms. Tern should stick to tossing shivs and reading novels. Tuffman isn't Luke Ferrier and he isn't here to hunt the cougar. He *is* the cougar.

Dean Swift isn't buying it either. "How could *our* coach be *your* Luke Ferrier?"

"Look," she says. "It's a photo of Ferrier taken in August, 1970, just after the massacre."

"That photo is over forty years old!"

"Stay on topic, Oliver. The resemblance is uncanny."

"I am on topic. He looks thirty in that picture. Does Mr. Tuffman look like a seventy-five-year-old man? Or is he ageless? It's not rocket science. It's arithmetic."

I hear Ms. Tern's heels click angrily on the wood floor. "Didn't you see him try to kill that snake? Tell me how many coaches at primary schools carry hunting knives about in the pockets of their tracksuits. And do you care to know how I came by that rifle? Tuffman—*Ferrier*—was out hunting cougar with it. The man is a predator. And take our little prodigy, our little Raul, with his big eyes and sharp teeth."

What does she think I have to do with it?

And I don't know if I like that description.

"Raul *hates* him. That boy has instinct. Today, in fact, I saw him shake Tuffman's hand," her voice slows.

I hold my breath. I didn't know she was watching us. What did she see?

"I saw Tuffman's knees buckle. As if Raul—the skinny thing—gripped his hand too hard. And when I walked by just after, your coach's face was white with pain. Blood was seeping into his shirt where Raul had touched him."

Dean Swift doesn't say anything.

"Oliver?" she asks.

"Yes."

"You do realize that Raul is one of our kind?"

My eyes get watery. So it wasn't a dream the other night. She really did tell me her mother was an orca.

Her mother must have been one of the ones Ferrier filled with rocks or one of the white ones that disappeared. No wonder she hates him. My face is wet, and I turn my head to wipe it on my shirt. I think of White Wolf and how alone I would be if I lost her.

In the silence I can feel Gollum staring at me from some dark corner. I try not to sniffle. What kind *are* we?

You'd think it would make me happy to find out that it's not just me, my mom, and Tuffman. Instead, I feel a little angry. I don't know why. But shouldn't they be trying to help me?

The dean just stands there with his hand resting on

my mom's recipe box. I can't see his face. What is his second self?

"It's too early to know. It'll be years before he's called," Dean Swift says. "And you must be mistaken. Our kind or not, a child his size could hardly have injured Mr. Tuffman."

That was a low blow, dean. He's a mole, I bet. Don't they have eyes that can't see?

"I'm telling you what I witnessed. And, if Ferrier is Tuffman, and Tuffman is Raul's uncle, mightn't the boy be in danger? Shouldn't we warn him in some way?"

During the long silence that follows, I get nervous. My hands get damp and I can feel the blood beat in my throat. What are they going to do about me?

"We shouldn't be talking about this," the dean finally says. He smacks his desk with his hand. "Keep the woods in the woods, Nicolette. It's the way we survive. We know each other there, and that's enough. He's far too young to be shifting anyway. And even if he were, I can only help him if he asks. I'm not allowed to intervene. And you can't either. It's the way."

His words sink in. Finally something one of these two says makes sense. We know each other in the woods. We don't talk about it. We keep our selves separate. That's what my gut has been telling me to do all along. It's how our kind has managed to survive, the dean is saying, and hearing him explain it gives me a feeling of peace. I understand the rules—the way—of my own kind instinctively. It's why nobody can help me. I will figure it all out on my own.

"It's time we organize ourselves, Oliver," Ms. Tern says so softly I almost can't hear her. "It's time we make new ways. We must defend the wild."

"Silence is our only defense. The old way is the only way," Dean Swift says.

They're both quiet for so long my feet fall asleep.

"Turn off the light," Ms. Tern finally says. "Until we know what it does."

"How can I know, if I turn it off? Show me more than an old photo and a cold trail. Until then, I'll believe the most rational version of events. Ferrier is a very old man or a dead one. His days of destruction have ended. And Coach Tuffman is an Olympian who has boxed up his medals in order to forge a relationship with his long-lost nephew."

"There's no talking sense to you." Ms. Tern stomps down the stairs.

Dean Swift tinkers around at his desk for a while.

"Gollum," he whispers. The snake slithers across the floor, and he lifts her onto his desk. "Guard the light," he says with a little smile in his voice.

Then he takes the stairs slowly, his knees creaking as loudly as the steps. At the door I hear him mutter, "Now I must find that key."

Chapter 22

WHERE VINCENT WORRIES AND RAUL SAYS TOO MUCH

I take the stairs quick, two at a time. I want out of there before the dean decides to come back and look for the key. The second after I slip under my covers, I hear a tap at the door.

Vincent walks in with my dinner. I smile like I'm happy to see him, but I'm not.

I want to be alone, so I can think about every crazy thing I just overheard. I want the story and all its pieces out in front of me.

And I kind of want to cry, because I just realized that I left the recipe card box in the turret.

Vincent sets the tray on my desk under the window. It smells good. Fried chicken and mashed potatoes. Gravy—the good kind, homemade. And green beans with salt and basil. My stomach grumbles and moans and shouts and screams.

It's funny how good food can make you feel better.

Vincent sits down. He seems to have forgotten my dinner.

"Please promise you won't tell anyone what a loser I was."

"I won't tell," I say. Didn't we go over this already? I look at the food.

"Promise? I don't want them to call me chicken like they did at my last school."

Would it be rude to get my tray? Since Vincent is sitting between me and it, I'd have to climb all the way down the length of my bed. Or leap over Vincent.

I eyeball it. I could probably almost clear his head.

He blurts out, "*Everyone* likes me here. At my old school nobody would even sit next to me at lunch."

"I promise." I understand now. Vincent got typecast. That's when you get a reputation for being bad, or stupid, or a crybaby. You get stuck with that word and you can't get anyone to drop it. And when you come to a new school, you think you'll finally change that word.

There's nothing worse than finding out the word for you is always the same.

After a minute he walks over to my window. It's dark out, so all he can see is his own reflection.

I watch the steam coming off my plate next to his hand. I swallow my spit.

"So I know it and you know it. I don't want anyone else here to know it. Especially not Mary Anne." He whispers her name.

I get a mean little feeling. Because it's true—Mary Anne is looking for a hero.

But I say it nicely. "I won't tell."

"But you might."

"I won't."

"How can I be sure?"

"I won't tell." From here the gravy is looking less like gravy and more like jelly.

"It's hard to keep a secret," he says. "Are you sure you won't tell Sparrow?"

Starvation makes me desperate. He's not going to let me eat until I make him believe me. And I want to tell him anyway, don't I? I want him to help me make all the pieces of the puzzle into a picture.

"I have a secret too," I say. "What if I tell you my secret? Then you'll know something about me that nobody knows."

Vincent looks relieved. "Yeah, okay. But it better be bad."

What can I say, it seems like a good idea to a kid with a bruised brain and an empty stomach.

I tell him my secret. You know it already.

While I'm talking, I get up, go over to my plate, and devour my dinner standing up.

I tell him about the lighthouse and leaving the clothes in the old oven on Friday night and getting them on Sunday morning. I tell him that on the weekends in the woods I live in the skin of an animal. I don't tell him about White Wolf or Tuffman. Those aren't my secrets to tell.

I leave something else out. My melon isn't *that* cracked. I don't say "wolf."

Because he already met wolf me, and I don't think he liked me much.

When I'm done, he looks at me. "Do you think that's what the talking deer wanted?" he asks. "Do you think it was telling me I have a second skin too?"

I nod.

"A raven? Isn't that just a crow? I don't want to be a garbage-eating bird." He shakes his head. *No no no no,* like his body has to say the words even when his mouth doesn't.

He tucks his hands into his sweatshirt pocket to hide the trembling.

"I don't wanna change. And I don't want *you* to change either."

His eyes get big, like he just thought of something. "What animal are you?"

I look away. I don't want to lie to him.

Luckily, the more upset he is, the more he talks. "The woods are scary. Some cougar would snap me up in one bite. Look what it did to dumb old Bobo."

Bobo's not dumb.

"I'm not supposed to tell anyone, but something

happened to me in the woods this weekend. That scene with the cougar in the tunnel was *nothing* compared to it," he says.

This little talk is taking a turn for the worse.

"On Sunday I was helping Tuffman mark out the 5K race." He pauses. "You're *nothing* like him, I don't care what Mary Anne says. When I told her you were his nephew, she acted like it made sense because you're both antisocial or something. But you're nothing like Tuffman."

I think he thinks he's giving me a compliment, but it feels like a kick to the gut. Why'd he tell her in the first place? Didn't he know that was a secret?

I get a heavy, scared feeling. I think the word for it is doom. Because that secret really didn't matter much. But the one I just told him does.

I bet he knows the difference, right?

Vincent keeps talking.

"When we were down at the lake, a pack of wolves came out of nowhere. Twenty of them circled us, barking and snarling. I pulled out my slingshot. Pow. I hit one. Killed him cold." Vincent's moving around, acting the scene out. He doesn't look nervous anymore.

"Tuffman was useless. They chased us clean out of the woods and all the way up to the school. I've got bite marks on my calves." He lifts his pant leg up half an inch like he's gonna show me and then drops it again before I can see so much as a pimple.

"I barely managed to slam the door shut on them. They would've killed us if they caught us. *They're* the ones that got Bobo, bet you ten to one."

"Why didn't you tell Dean Swift?" I ask.

Vincent shrugs. "Tuffman. He said it was my fault for teasing them, but they just attacked me when I was totally minding my own business. He said the dean will always take nature's side in any argument—whatever that means—and that I'd get in big trouble with him. Plus he said they'd make him cancel the 5K run, and *that* would get me in trouble with Tuffman.

"So what kind of animal are you?" he asks again. "A chickadee? A squirrel?" he teases. Then he laughs. "Are you a werewolf?"

Man, I hate that question. "No, I'm not a *were*wolf."

I didn't mean to say the word the way I did.

Understanding ripples across his face like a wave at the tide line. He backs toward the door.

"Wait," I say. I try to make my eyes not so scary. "Listen. I think it's something genetic—you know, like coded in my DNA. My *mitochondrial* DNA. And it's White Deer Woods, too. It's a special place. It has something to do with bioluminescent fungi and the power of the light in the woods. I'm not sure how it all works, but it probably has to do with the wave theory of light and the measurements of the lens."

I'm mixing it all up and sticking it all together, everything I've heard and thought over the last few weeks.

He's staring at me like I'm a mad scientist who's been sniffing his test tubes.

"I don't hurt anyone," I say. "I don't care about humans at all when I'm in the woods."

He gets a look like he just figured something out. "What about dogs?" he asks.

I keep talking. I talk for a long time. I never admit to being a wolf. He doesn't ask again. But deep down, he knows I'm a wolf, and I know he's a liar.

After a while he starts to nod like he's convinced, but I can tell he just wants to get away from me. He's inching toward the door. He's careful not to turn his back on me as he steps into the hallway.

"The dean told us at dinner that Bobo won't make it through the night," he says as he shuts the door. There's a mean look on his face.

That's when I realize that he thinks maybe *I'm* the animal that attacked Bobo.

And Bobo won't make it through the night.

I get into bed. I should never have gotten out of it this morning.

My parents have come and gone. Teachers have come and gone. Kids have come and gone. But Bobo's been here with me the whole time. She's run through the woods with me and slept on the floor of my room. She's a tear licker, a heel nipper, a pillow, and a friend.

I never got to say good-bye to my mom. There are lots of things I would've said and done if I'd known the last time was the last time. I can't let Bobo leave without saying good-bye.

I get out of bed.

I can't let my best friend die alone in the middle of the night.

Maybe there's some leftover bacon in the kitchen. Dogs know love when you feed it to them.

I pick up my tray to take down with me. It bumps into my pajama pocket, and I feel the key. I take it out and stare at it for a second. I remember how the light made me feel when it pulsed through me. I remember how it made me so strong I could tap a tree trunk with the tip of my toe and send it flying across the meadow and over the cliff.

I grab the key and the tray and run out the door.

I run all the way down to the kitchen. I forgot to light the light. I smack my head, which hurts more than it would if I didn't have a smushed melon for a brain.

I run all the way back upstairs. Turn the light on first. Right? Doesn't that make sense? Turn the light on, get the dog, put the dog in the light.

Everyone's in the bathroom getting ready for bed.

Vincent opens the door and sees me run by. I see

myself in the big mirror. I look crazy. I've got a tray full of dirty dishes in one hand. I'm clenching the key in the other. My eyes are lit up and intense like Dean Swift's when he starts talking about fungi. There's a bandage wrapped around my head, and my hair is standing straight up around it. How many days since I washed it? Yikes. I'm one dirty dog.

Vincent just stands there and stares. Man, I could use his help. I don't know why, but I shove the tray at him. He takes it with a surprised look. The words are on the tip of my tongue, but he ducks back into the bathroom like he's afraid of getting stuck alone with me again. I hear the dishes clatter on the tray, and then the door slams shut.

I blink. I take a breath. My right eye twitches. This job I've got to do on my own. I wouldn't know where to begin explaining it to him, since I don't understand it all and I'm pretty sure the dean—the one who's in charge—doesn't either.

Ha! If the dean doesn't know, then nobody knows. If nobody knows, then anything's possible.

I race to my room. I stop and stand in front of it. I wait, quiet as a mouse. The hall is silent. I step one big step over and put my ear to the utility closet door. Silence.

It only takes me a minute. The matches are on the desk. The wick is ready.

Slash goes the match. Flicker goes the flame.

I don't even watch as the light fills the room.

"Guard the light, Gollum!" I whisper like a maniac as I fly down the stairs.

Everyone's awake, but I know where they are. The dean is in the basement, locking the gym doors. Cook Patsy is in the dining hall, wiping down tables and setting up for breakfast. Ms. Tern is monitoring the girls. Tuffman is monitoring the boys.

And I'm alone in the kitchen.

By the delivery door there's a low cart for moving big boxes. It's like a huge metal tray on wheels. I pile all the kitchen towels I can find onto it. Quick as I can, I wheel it over to the storage room.

The room is so quiet that it's only my wolf sense that tells me Bobo's alive, because she doesn't move.

I lift her. It's not easy. I know I hurt her. She whimpers, and I put my hand just above her eyes. *I'm sorry,* I say, but I don't have to say it out loud because she knows it already.

I push her back into the kitchen and out the delivery door.

I walk slowly along the edges of the driveway so that the noise of the cart wheels is muffled by the grass. The back left wheel creaks. I head toward the trees. I look up. Wings rustle in the oak. The crows are huddled there, each with one eye open.

Suddenly the driveway is flooded with light. I stop dead in my tracks. Someone must have seen me. Someone has turned on the lights. If I run with Bobo, she'll get tossed around. If I stay, I'll get caught. I shrink back as much as I can into the shadow of the great oak tree.

A second later and the crows have swooped down, silent.

At first it feels like I'm in the middle of a black feather storm, like there's no order or meaning to what they're doing. Then they settle. They surround Bobo and the cart, like a great dark shadow. They hover next to me, one above the other, sheltering me from the lights and the eyes that might be watching from the school.

Did Vincent call them garbage eaters? They're guardians, that's what they are.

Slowly I move on behind my shield of black feathers. I know that the woods love me.

As I push Bobo away from the school, I realize that must be why nobody ever sees White Wolf. It's why the cougar can't find her unless she leaves the woods. As long as she stays in White Deer Woods, the woods magic shelters her.

The crows wheel off, one by one, as we reach the lake. Bobo is so quiet. The path is rough. I wince every time the cart bounces. I can feel how it must hurt her.

As I get closer to the lighthouse, I catch flashes of

the light off to my left. I'm taking her to the meadow between the edge of the woods and the edge of the cliff, where the light struck me last week.

But it begins before we get there. Every time the beam catches my eye I feel it. It's so powerful that I flinch a little when I see it coming, the way you do before you touch something that you know will give you a little shock.

In the meadow I pull the kitchen towels off Bobo. I get down beside her and try to make her open her eyes. I don't know if the power happens when it hits your skin or your eyes.

The light swings at us. It drowns me. My skin hums. I look down at Bobo. Her fur is standing on end. Her eyes are half open. A tremor runs across her nose.

We stay there until the light goes out.

I imagine Dean Swift standing up there, scratching his head. "I do not recall lighting the lens," he must be saying to himself.

I cover Bobo back up. She looks awful. The light has made me even stronger. Pushing the cart is like pushing one of those toy lawnmowers with the popping balls.

When we reach the lake, I hear it. She whimpers. It's a sound of pain, but it brings tingles all over my skin. I stop pushing and run up to her. Bobo lifts her nose and sets it in my hand. Her eyes are open. I see the sketch of a tail wag.

Chapter 23

WHERE BEST FRIENDS FIGHT AND DON'T MAKE UP

Friday. I sleep late. At breakfast there are only weirdos at the counter. Mary Anne is with the Wolverines, whispering sadly about Bobo. Vincent perches on Mean Jack's table, telling them how he saw the cougar coming out of the tunnel and tagged it in the face with a rock. He says it so convincingly, I'd believe him too, except that I was there.

Vincent and Mary Anne don't look at me when I sit down at the counter, but I can tell they notice me. I have a heavy feeling inside. Are we still friends?

The dean walks into the dining hall. We can tell by the look on his face that he's here to tell us about Bobo. Even Vincent stops talking.

Dean Swift stands there for a minute. "Bobo," he says finally. His mouth is crooked and his voice is full of tears. He shakes his head and raises a finger.

The girl next to me starts to cry. I stare at the counter. I really thought the light would save her. Sometimes a bad situation is just a bad situation, no matter how hard you try to fix it.

Dean Swift clears his throat. "I'm sorry. I am overcome with emotion. The vet said Bobo will live. He said it is a miracle."

The room goes wild. Everyone starts to chant, *Bobo, Bobo*. The boys in the Pack and the Wolverines stand up, grab their chairs, and slam them up and down to the beat. The weirdos smack the counter with their open palms. The Cubs stamp their feet.

Cook Patsy walks over to me with a plate full of bacon. "I saw you," she says.

I freeze. Maybe she was the one who turned on the driveway lights.

"I saw you sleeping next to Bobo in the storage room," she says. "You're the reason why." She nods. "Love heals all, that's what they say." She pulls something out of her apron pocket and hands it to me. It's a friendship bracelet.

"Do you know why rings and bracelets always stand for friendship and love?" she asks.

I think about it. I want to give her a good answer. "Because they're like chains that lock us together?" I ask.

She laughs. "Well, that's one way of looking at it. But I always think it's because a circle never ends. It goes on and on, around and around, no matter what. *Nothing* can stop it, because it never ends once it begins."

I look down. She's a sneaky one. She's talking about my mom.

"Thank you," I say.

~

Right after breakfast a motorcycle roars up. A lot of us are in the upstairs bathroom, and we rush over to look out the window.

I lift Sparrow up to see. He weighs as little as a feather to me this morning. Bobo's not the only one the light fixed up last night. I'm wearing my bandages, but there aren't any bumps or bruises under them anymore.

We see Vincent tearing down the front steps, yelling, "Mom!"

I squeeze Sparrow a little tighter. Sometimes that's a hard word to hear.

Pretty Lady hops off and unstraps something tied to the side of the bike. She lifts it up and waves it at Vincent. "You forgot something, kiddo!" she says with a huge smile.

Even from up here, we can tell it's not just any fishing pole.

It's the one I made for Sparrow.

Vincent stops and glances up at us. Then he hurries toward her, his hands spread out in front of him like he's afraid of falling or like he's telling her to put that pole away.

On the last step Vincent trips and stumbles into his mom. She drops the pole to catch him and it falls in a long line going up the steps. We can all see it's about to happen before it does. He steps back to get his balance. The wood splinters as his foot comes down on it.

We all let out a big breath.

His mom bends down and starts picking up the pieces.

Vincent stands over her. "Why did you come so early today? Why would you bring that?" He chews her out. Like it's all her fault.

"I was vacuuming and found it under your bed," she says. Her voice is thin and confused. "I thought you go fishing on Fridays. I didn't want you to get left out. Vinnie, I took the whole day off work to bring it to you."

"You never get *anything* right," Vincent shouts. He kicks the Harley's tire and runs to the zigzag path, just like he did on the first day.

Only this time, no one is cheering about it.

No wonder his mom dumped him here.

I set Sparrow down. I rest my hand on the back of his thin little neck.

Vincent let me yell at *Sparrow*. My jaw crunches my teeth together. How low is that?

"That rat stole the pole and made the bambino take the fall for it?" Mean Jack can't believe it either. "What a *cafone*."

Mean Jack's got a way with words sometimes.

My chest hurts like I got punched. And I did—I got punched with the truth.

The truth is, Vincent's worse than Mean Jack. His dumb prank almost got Mary Anne blown to smithereens. He's the kind of kid who throws rocks at animals. And he's a liar. He lies even when it doesn't really matter. He lies until he thinks his lie is the truth. I never knew someone so low down.

And he broke my pole.

The other boys leave for class. I hear them calling Vincent a sneak and a cheater.

From the window I watch Vincent run.

Chicken. That's what they called him at his old school. That's what he is. Always doing the wrong thing and too chicken to admit it.

Since Dean Swift had to cancel fishing and outdoor time again, he decided to make it up to us by giving us an extra hour of PE. I like Dean Swift, but I don't think we have the same idea of a good time.

When I get into the gym, Mean Jack is on the bleachers with the Pack. "Me and Tuffman just had a little sit-down. I was telling him how Vinnie told us about clipping the cougar. Coach said forget about it. Coach says the second our boy heard that cougar, he hit the turf bawling. Coach says there's no way our friend so much as looked that cat in the eye, let alone whacked it."

Jason comes up, and Mean Jack tells him, too.

Jason makes little wings with his arms. "What a chicken, yeah?"

For some reason, I don't like it. I don't want them ganging up on Vincent. He's a jerk, but he was a jerk to Sparrow, not to any of them.

The gym gets quiet. I look up and see Vincent walking in through the side door that leads down to the beach. I don't think he was expecting us to all be in here. His eyes are red like he's been crying. His face is all scraped up like he got tackled again down on the beach. When is he gonna learn that when you run, they chase? It's called Consequences, Vincent.

He sits down on a pile of gym mats by the side door. He looks so sad that a weird thing happens. I start to feel sorry for him.

The Pack stares at him from the bleachers. Mean Jack cracks his knuckles. Little John puts his fists to his eyes and pretends to be a bawling baby. *Wah-wah.*

Anger flashes in me. I want to run over and shut them up. Vincent's *my* problem, not theirs. Fresnel fury, that's what I should call it. The light makes me strong for a while after I get hit with it, but it makes me angry, too.

I've got to control myself.

I start to walk over to Vincent. I'm still mad at him, but I understand about jealousy. He was jealous of that pole. Sparrow left it in the rain, Vincent went back to grab it. I bet Vincent meant to give it back. He just got in over his head. The lie went too far—like a bad joke. It's not his fault if I lost my temper and scared Sparrow. *I* did that. Not Vincent.

Friendship goes on and on like a circle, right? And Vincent's the only person I've ever known who would save me a seat or hunt cougar with me or try to make me laugh when I was worried. He invited me to his house for spring break. He may have stolen Mary Anne, but he made her notice me too—he made her my friend.

I'm halfway across the court when I hear it.

"Bok, bok, bok bok BAWK!" I turn around, and Jason's on the bleachers, doing his chicken dance. Everyone is pointing at Vincent, laughing.

Vincent glances at them and then stares at me.

"You said you wouldn't tell," he says.

He jumps up and runs at me. He wraps his arms around me and tries to take me to the ground, but I won't let him. He starts punching and kicking.

Strength pulses in me. One punch and he'd be on his back on the mats again. But I'm not gonna do it. No matter what Tuffman says, I'm not like him.

The Pack surrounds us, yelling, "Fight, fight, fight!"

I bob and duck quick enough that his fists go flying most of the time. When I grab his wrists he head butts me, and a second later hooks his foot around the back of my knee.

We fall to the floor. Twice he tags me on the head,

right on my bandage like it's a bull's-eye. Like he's trying to kill me.

I roll and get up on my feet. "Listen," I say. "It wasn't me. I didn't tell anyone."

Something feels loose in my mouth. I spit out blood and a tooth.

The sight makes the Pack hoot and howl.

He comes at me again, and this time I can't stop myself.

I pull my arm back. The shouting stops. Everyone stares as my fist connects with his chin. All anyone hears is the crack of my knuckles hitting his bone.

Vincent staggers back, back, back three steps and then lands on his butt.

Mean Jack starts counting.

"One, two, three!" Everyone counts along. Little John is jumping up and down, holding his crotch like he's trying not to pee. Jason's eyes look red, and Mark starts to unzip the weighted vest.

What if I broke his jaw? Will the police arrest me?

"That's enough," Tuffman says, shoving everyone aside. He winks at me. "I knew you had it in you."

How long has he been watching? I hate myself. I am what he says I am.

Tuffman drags Vincent up by the armpits. He inspects his chin. "You're fine. Don't start bawling. You had it coming."

Vincent stares at me like I'm less than dirt. "I know all about you," he says.

"I'm not the one who told," I say, but Tuffman is carrying him out of the room. "I didn't tell!" I shout after him.

I can taste blood. My tongue finds the hole where my tooth was.

"Where'd you learn to fight like that?" Mean Jack asks in a whisper. He pulls back like he's scared of me when I look at him.

Everyone is looking at me like I'm a monster.

I didn't want to hit Vincent. But I did. I'm turning into what I don't want to be—a creature that's half wolf and half boy.

There's a name for that.

I spend the rest of the day sitting on the floor of the storeroom with Bobo.

Ms. Tern tries to make me come out. "Do join us, Raul," she begs.

"Will you tell the dean I need my mom's recipes?" I finally say to her.

My eyes must look weird. Did I growl at her?

She backs out of the room, nodding. "Certainly," she says.

Chapter 24

WHERE RAUL FINDS THE TRUTH AND LOSES THE WORDS TO TELL IT

Finally there's nothing left to do but pack my bag to spend the weekend with my dad who never comes. I head up to the boys' wing. I sense Tuffman as soon as I step in the hallway. The door to my room's open. I smell burnt matches.

"Hey, kid," he says before I step inside.

He's stretched out on my bed, wearing my stocking cap. In one hand he's holding a silver lighter and in the other a recipe card. Tuna Surprise.

"Dean Swift said to bring these back to you. After all the hullabaloo, he thought you could use some time with family. And I'm all you got."

He grins and the lighter clicks. The card curls black, a little line of orange flame eats it all down to a corner. When the flame hits his thumb, he blows it out.

There's a pile of charred corners at the bottom of the garbage can. He drops in what's left of Tuna Surprise.

He takes five or six more from the box and makes them into a fan. "I appreciate her effort, you know, with the code. But it's a little obvious, isn't it? She put sawdust in her biscuits, just because she needed that *W*."

I reach over and bat the lighter out of his hand. It skids across the floor.

"Fine," he says. "Let's read them together." He squints at the cards. "'He killed a deer. Above the deer I saw the shadow of the head of a woman. I refused to eat. He was angry.'"

He tosses the cards onto the floor.

"I like her style. Good grammar. She gets right to the point, but there's attention to detail. And I *was* angry."

I pick up the box. It's empty.

"Go ahead. I'm done with it now. You want to know why I was so angry when she wouldn't eat?"

I stare at him.

"Have you ever tried to reason with someone who's going crazy? You try to be patient. But it's hard. Especially when you love that person the way I love your mom. I *raised* her, Raul. We were all we had."

He sighs and looks down. "So when she started to lose it, and I mean really lose it, it was hard for me. She always had a big imagination. When she was a little girl she thought she saw faces in trees."

I'm listening. He's telling me about her again. Things only someone who loves her could know. I saw faces in the trees too, when I was little. I still do sometimes.

He keeps talking. "You, me, and your mom—we change. Once the change happened to her, she went berserk. She didn't know where her second skin ended and her imagination began. She thought she could see human faces in the animals we hunted. She wouldn't eat. She'd get weak. Yeah, it made me angry. I couldn't stand watching her starve."

He stares at me. "Has she ever done that to you, Raul?"

It's been hard to get White Wolf to eat this spring. Is he telling some part of the truth?

"You don't trust me because of what happened with Bobo and Sparrow. I won't lie to you—when I'm an animal, I'm an animal. You go into my den, then that's what's gonna happen. I warned you, didn't I? I tried to put some fear in you so you'd stay away." His eyes hold me. "Raul, you and me are a lot alike. I had to run like the devil when you chased me and Vincent at the lake. And I saw you turn on Sparrow, I saw you knock Vincent across the room. Thing is, sometimes you act like a wolf when you're a boy. That's gonna get you in trouble."

I look down. He's not lying.

"Listen up. I've been tough. I've been nice. Now I'll be honest. You're younger than you should be. I've never known the change to happen so early. It wasn't until you went to my den that day Sparrow found the bone. I smelled the wolf in you. And you're stronger than you should be. Look what you did when you shook my hand." He stretches it out. On the back of it are four fingertip-shaped bruises.

He grins—like it's funny, like he's proud of me. "That's not normal. You can reach all your wolf strength in your boy skin."

That's true too.

"It's gonna take the two of us to talk some sense into her. You gotta lead me to her, Raul," he says.

My ears stretch at the sound of my name. I feel like I'm being called. "I need to think about it," I say.

"Raul," he says.

I look into his eyes. They're gold. I see a raised red scar in each of his pupils. But it doesn't scare me.

"Raul, I'm the only one that can help her. I know what she lost and I know where she lost it. I can take her back to the place where she can change."

He can help me. He has her recipe.

I feel light for a second. Like I've been carrying a backpack full of bricks and someone just reached down and lifted it off of me.

"She won't come with me. She attacked me a few weeks ago—chewed up the back of my neck and forced me to take a swipe at her. You saw her that day at the picnic table. But she'll trust you, Raul. See, I can't track her. For some reason, I lose her scent in the woods. I need you to tell me how to find her."

It's true, everything he says makes sense. The words gather in my throat.

"Raul," he says, "I got a question."

I nod.

His face is strange. Not nice. Not mean. I can't think of the word, exactly. "Your mom wasn't white when I knew her. She was a gray wolf, like you. Are there any other white animals in the woods around here, Raul?"

Hungry. That's the word. His face is *hungry*.

I take a step back. Stop saying my name.

I know his secret. That's what my mom wrote. I look at the ashes in the garbage can. He burned her words. What is he hiding?

"Bobo's going to live," I say. I want him to go away. I don't trust myself with him.

He looks me up and down. He sighs. "Well, I guess some dogs never do learn," he says. He stands up and brushes the ashes off his pants.

"We'll talk again later, Raul," he says as he opens the door to leave. "I'll give you a chance to pack for the weekend and change your clothes."

The last thing I see as he shuts the door are his eyes, laughing like it's a joke. It sends shivers up my spine.

I snarl at myself. What's wrong with me? Did he almost get me to take him to White Wolf?

I sit on the edge of the bed with my elbows on my

knees and my head in my hands. I keep talking to the wrong people.

At pick-up time I grab my duffel bag and join the rest of the kids on the front porch. The clouds are high and the sky is pale blue. Nobody comes near me. I don't blame them. I'm scaring myself lately too. Mary Anne looks at me sideways.

Did Vincent tell her? I swallow hard. Now that would be a rotten thing to do.

Sparrow's grandma is the first to show up. He jumps into her truck. At the bottom of the circle the truck lurches to a stop. Sparrow hops out and tears back to the porch.

"Wait, Grandma," he hollers.

"Look, Raul," he says when he gets to me. "I saved it." He stretches his hands out to me.

I smile at him even though I don't feel like it. I look at his little treasure.

It's part of the busted-up fishing pole I made him. The best part. It's the carving I did, of the wolves chasing each other around, tail to mouth. I trace the grooves with my finger. I was wrong. Vincent wasn't my only friend. He wasn't my best one either.

"I'll make you another one, but even better," I promise.

"No." He shakes his head and runs to his grandma's truck. "Not better. The same. The same is the best," he calls as he climbs in.

The bitter bad feeling goes away. Sparrow's forgiven me.

His grandma reaches over and hugs him like seeing him is the best thing that's happened to her all week. Then she hits the gas and the brake at the same time. The truck jerks and peels away. Blue smoke pours from the tailpipe.

I remember how Sparrow used to lie about the bruises his mom gave him. Back then I had a bad feeling about it all, but I never said anything to anyone. Sparrow's mean mom hit him a lot more times before the dean figured it all out.

I gotta use my brain here. Bobo almost died this week. Things could get even worse if I wait much longer to get help. I don't know what Tuffman wants or who he really is, but I do know one thing—I've got a bad feeling about it all.

I've got to tell Dean Swift.

I don't know why I've waited so long.

The words won't stay down anymore. I can tell they're important, because I feel them in my throat like the sounds I make when I wear my wolf skin.

Once all the other kids have gone, I'll walk up to him. I'll say, *Dean Swift, I have a secret I've been keeping. Can you help me?*

While I'm waiting for everyone to leave, I keep Bobo company. The tip of her tail moves gently while I stroke her side. Forty-five minutes to sunset. I press my forehead against Bobo's and tell her I'll see her soon.

I feel jumpy and nervous. I don't know where I'm going to begin the story. Does it start with White Deer? Or Tuffman?

But when I go into the living room, Mary Anne is sitting on the sofa, writing in her notebook. She doesn't look up at me. My hands are sweating and I can't sit still. Come on, Mary Anne's dad, come get your kid.

Out of the blue, Mary Anne starts talking.

"Some individuals are uncivilized. They do not understand the most basic elements of the *social contract*," she says to her notebook.

I'm pretty sure Mary Anne is just thinking out loud until she says, "I can't believe you told everyone his secret."

It's like she ripped the last of a hangnail off. It stings. *I didn't,* I almost say, but I can tell she's not in a listening mood.

"He's broken," she says. "He looks up to you."

I shake my head, because I don't know what she's talking about.

"Vincent doesn't know who he is or where he fits in. That's why he lies so much. He's hoping if he tells enough stories about himself, he'll finally tell one that's true."

She wants me to feel *sorry* for Vincent?

"You're not like everyone else. You *know* who you are. You're the strong one," she says.

My throat hurts. How can she be disappointed in me when she doesn't even know what happened? *I didn't tell.*

"And then you go and hit him? There's an expression. *Noblesse oblige.* It means that the stronger you are, the greater your obligation to take care of the weak."

She's wrong about most of it, but she's right about that. I *hate* her.

I hear a car honk. *Just leave, Mary Anne.* I need to talk with the dean.

The car horn honks again, louder and longer this time.

Mary Anne shoves her notebook into her bag and zips it up so quick that she catches the corner of her skirt in the zipper. She looks at the door and tries to undo the zipper. I hear the fabric rip.

A week ago I would have felt sorry for Mary Anne for having parents who can make their car horn sound like they're irritated with her when they haven't even seen her in a week. I would have felt sad to see her rush around and act nervous for making them wait for her for two minutes when she's been waiting for them for an hour.

You're just a kid like the rest of us, Mary Anne.

You've got to love them too, no matter what they do to you.

I don't feel sorry for her today.

I hear a car pull into the driveway. The front door slams. Mary Anne must have forgotten something. But it's Sparrow.

"I forgot!" he yells, even though he's standing in front of me. "I forgot and then I remembered. Here. Dean Swift couldn't find you. He says this is yours. He says it fell out of your box."

He hands me a card. Then he hugs me and runs out the door.

I look at it. I smile.

Skagit Oatmeal.

She must have been running out of cards. It's the longest recipe of them all and the craziest. Is *haggis* part of a healthy breakfast? And the seventh ingredient isn't food at all, it's just a number. 1750 what? Oat flakes?

But this is what it says: *Born in 1750. Preys on white ones. Their flesh makes him immortal. His power is your name.*

It's the last piece. And the picture the puzzle makes is a nightmare so bad, nobody's ever had it yet.

Ms. Tern was right. Tuffman is the spirit-animal hunter. Tuffman's the guy in her photo.

And the dean was right too, even if he meant to be sarcastic. Tuffman is ageless.

But neither of them could ever guess the secret my mom knew: that the hunter is one of our kind, and that he's ageless because he eats us.

Only one thing makes me feel better. It's awful, but it makes me feel better. He gets power over you by repeating your name. That's why I kept telling him stuff—whenever he'd say my name, I'd turn into his slave.

I jump up. My thoughts are zinging around in my head like a BB shot in a metal room.

What was it Tuffman said at the end?

Your mom wasn't white when I knew her. My ears bend back. He tracked her here to kill her so she wouldn't tell his secret. And now that he knows she's a spirit animal, he wants to eat her too. And I thought *Vincent* was a bad egg.

My skin creeps when I think of how he smiled at me when he shut my door. Like he had something up his sleeve.

I look at the clock. Sunset in ten minutes. It's time to go. I can't mess up the recipe this week of all weeks.

Dean Swift is standing at the door when I get to it. He's looking at me funny.

"How's the old noggin, Raul?" the dean asks. "Could I drive you down to meet your dad this week and tell him how sick you've been?"

I stand there with my hand on the doorknob, shaking my head. The clock is ticking, the sun is setting, the magic is happening. I don't have time to talk about it.

I'm not a dandelion. Tuffman can't puff me away.

Mary Anne got one thing right. I am the strong one.

Dean Swift puts a hand on my forehead. He's been doing it all week, checking if I have a fever. His skin smells like fire.

"Don't you need your bag?" he asks. We both look back to the parlor where my duffel bag is still on the floor.

"Did you light the lens?" I ask instead.

He looks startled. He nods slowly.

"Good," I say. "I'm gonna need it."

As I walk out the door, I turn around. The dean is standing in the foyer watching me. His face is gray and old and he looks so worried. I know if he could help me, he would.

"Thank you," I say. "I'll see you soon."

"I can only help you if you ask me," he says. "It's the way."

He says it sadly, like he'd give anything to save me. I'm tempted. But I don't have the time. I need to get to the lighthouse as quick as I can, and we've been over this, haven't we? When it comes to running, Dean Swift does *not* live up to his name.

"Just keep the light on," I say. "I've got it all taken care of."

Then I'm out the door and I'm running as hard as I can. My ears are stretching and my teeth are pulling and I can feel my body changing as I race. Every part of me is alive and alert and listening and sniffing for the cougar.

There's no time to talk.

Chapter 25

SOMETIMES THE GLASS IS HALF FULL BUT THE OVEN IS EMPTY

In the meadow the light blasts through me.

I stand in it so long my skin pulses. Then I walk into the lighthouse.

I step over the threshold with four legs. I'm a wolf with a purpose. I'm a wolf that means business.

I'm ready for whatever Tuffman has cooked up.

All weekend I watch and listen. I lead White Wolf to the lake, just outside the protection of White Deer Woods. But I never catch a whiff of the cougar or the man who wears its skin. We hunt and eat and sleep, but all I want is my chance to fight the cougar.

White Wolf makes me leave on Sunday morning. She nips and nudges me. I want to stay. How will I protect her if I'm not here? Two wolves together can defeat a cougar, right? But one alone cannot. My tail drags as I cross the meadow.

I wish we could speak to each other with words. *Stay in White Deer Woods,* I want to say. *The woods magic will protect you.*

There's a scent on the doorstep of the lighthouse. It makes me cold. I see them in my mind before their names come to me. A boy with hair the color of a raven's feathers and a man with a scrape on his cheek that could have been made by a hook stuck in a wall or by a bullet grazing his skin.

At first all I feel is fear. I race back to the edge of the woods to warn her. But White Wolf is gone. Will she be safe? Is this a trap? I stare into the woods. I listen. I sniff. Nothing moves. The cedar fronds sift the sharp gray light that falls across the green grass. The woods are still.

From a distance I watch the lighthouse. I am gray like the light, and I stay in the shadows of the trees as I walk the woods around the building. There's no sign of a boy or a man or the gun he might carry.

I nudge the lighthouse door open. I stop. I listen. But all I hear are wings above in the broken lantern room.

They've come and gone.

Vincent told Tuffman about my lighthouse. What will this do to the magic?

I put my nose to the ground and sniff. The scent trail leads from the door to the oven. The oven door is open. My clothes are gone.

In my wolf's mind's eye I see Tuffman's laughing eyes and the last words he said to me. *Change your clothes.*

Vincent didn't just tell him about the lighthouse. He told him everything he knew, and that was all Tuffman needed.

At first I'm stunned, like when someone hits you in the back of a head with a rock. It's that solid kind of ache like when a bone breaks—sharp and hurting the same amount of bad everywhere.

Then I wonder. Was Vincent laughing when he reached into the oven? Did he wear his zombie mask? If I open one of the kitchen cupboards, will golf balls come dropping out?

Does Vincent know this isn't a prank? This isn't stealing or lying. This is a kind of killing. He's stolen the boy in me, and forced me to stay a wolf forever.

It takes the air out of my lungs.

Has someone ever punched you or kicked you? It hurts, right? But what's worse is the way you feel ashamed, like you let it happen, like you had it coming, and now everyone can see how you are stupid and worthless and weak.

What will Dean Swift think? What will Sparrow think?

I know what it's like to lose someone. I don't want them to feel that way.

Bam goes my heart. Will they call my dad? He doesn't need to feel any sadder than he already does.

Tuffman will think he's won. He must be the one who

trapped my mom, too. This way we can't tell his secret. This way he can keep trying to kill us and nobody will know or care. Nobody goes to jail for shooting a wolf.

And Vincent? If there's one thing I know about Vincent, it's that when he does something wrong, he'll never admit it.

Remember the fire? He started it.

Remember the fishing pole? He broke it.

Remember my clothes? He stole them.

I stumble out of the lighthouse. I need White Wolf. I don't want to be alone.

But I am.

Maybe she only comes on Fridays at sunset. Maybe the magic only works at the moment I change.

I sit down in front of the lighthouse and put my nose on my paws. I feel the lump in my throat and I wait for the tears to come. But wolves don't cry. After a minute I swing my head up high and stretch my neck. I howl my sadness to the great gray sky.

When I stop howling, the woods fall silent. I think every bird feels my loneliness beneath its red or brown or blue feathers. The rabbits and the foxes, the voles and the moles, the frogs and the snakes, they all burrow down deep into the earth at the sound of my sorrow.

And then I hear a crack at the edge of the cedars.

When I look, I see White Wolf loping toward me. I

stand, my tail wagging with a joy so great only a tail can truly tell it.

Together we return to the woods.

We don't do much that day. We listen. I hear cars on the road below. The parents are bringing everyone back.

It may sound strange to be grateful for anything when you've just found out your best friend has stolen your life and that you'll never again eat with a fork or play pinball or baseball or wear shoes or read a book or watch a cartoon or fly a kite or use a straw to drink a soda.

But I'm grateful White Wolf returned when she heard my call. I'm grateful to find out that the magic doesn't happen just when I change. It's always there.

Chapter 26

HUNTED

Most of the time, I try not to think. I feel the sun in my fur. I chase a rabbit.

When I do think, I worry about what they told my dad.

The sun rises, and we stay under our ledge because we can hear the men and women and children searching. Most days I try to sleep through it.

The cougar is always a shiver of anger running along my spine. When the sun sets, sometimes we hear the cougar yowling. White Wolf keeps moving us deeper into White Deer Woods, sidling between shaggy cedars and widespread oaks and flowering chestnuts.

Trees have their own magic, I learn. The faces I once saw in their trunks—a wolf sees them too. But a wolf hears them sigh and sing, remember and regret, whisper and worry as well. It's all alive out here. Once you know what to look for, you see everything.

One morning I'm padding along so softly on a thick layer of pine needles that I startle a snake coiled on a rock, where the sun streaming down through the branches strikes it and heats it. I stop and raise one paw. Gollum. Her tongue flickers out toward me. When she looks at me, I think for a second that I can see the shadow of a girl's head floating just above her. Whoever said a wolf has no imagination? Quick as can be, she uncoils and slips into a crevice in the rock.

A warm feeling spreads through me. I'm happy to see this old friend.

The days grow long and the nights grow short. It must be almost summer.

After a while there are no more searches.

The 5K race comes. I hear the gun shot that starts it.

Did Tuffman get his rifle back? I hope when he comes, he comes as a cougar. There's no fair fight between wolves and guns.

The wind carries the scent of the runners to us as they follow the road that leads down to Highway 20 all the way around White Deer Woods to the ranger station. This is the first year I don't run it, and the only year that I could win it. If I raced in my wolf shape, that is. Ha-ha. A little dark wolf humor there.

Is Vincent sorry?

At first that's all I want. I want for him to be sorry. I want him to be terrified at what he's done. He's killed half of me. Doesn't he understand?

Many times, more than a wolf can count, I return to the lighthouse. Dean Swift keeps his word. The light of the lens is flooding a corner of the meadow every night I find myself there. I let it pulse through me until I feel too big to fit my skin.

White Wolf lets me come alone, to say good-bye to the part of me I have lost. I slink in slow, cautious. I stick my nose into the oven. It's always empty. Each time it surprises me. Each time it hurts.

After a while I just want Vincent to be terrified. He'd better not ride his bike too deep into the woods. A flick of my paw and he'd be over the cliff, swimming with the seals.

One evening the cougar attacks as I leave the lighthouse. He springs at me from a screen of fern and crushed bleeding hearts.

All I see from the corner of my eye is a flash of teeth and a red mouth coming at my throat. But I've stood in the light so many times. I'm quick. I dart away and he gets nothing but a mouthful of air.

I turn back and growl. The cougar jumps up onto a rotting stump of cedar.

Go ahead. Take the higher ground. It won't save you.

I've been waiting for this moment. All my anger—at Vincent, at Tuffman the man and Tuffman the cougar—surges through me.

As I gather my strength to charge, White Wolf streaks from the cedars, barking short and vicious barks. She's trying to protect me. Even she doesn't know what the light has done to me.

The cougar pounces. His claws dig into her back, his mouth gapes, and his teeth plunge toward her neck.

I leap at him, knocking him off balance. He twists and tumbles and just barely finds his feet. He hisses and turns to face us. White Wolf and I crouch. We advance, he retreats. We back him across the meadow and into the woods. White Wolf and I keep moving forward, our heads low. When the path narrows, White Wolf tries to push ahead of me, but I won't let her. Side by side, that's how it's gonna be this time.

You see, cougar, alone you can hurt us. Together we are strong.

Along the right cheek of the cougar is a hairless pink scar. The sight of it infuriates me, and I lunge at him.

I hear White Wolf warn me. My teeth pierce his skin, and I taste blood.

That's for the scrape in White Wolf's side, I rumble.

I shake my head as I bite down harder, ripping his hide. *That's for Bobo's leg.*

His huge paw comes up, claws stretched, and he bats me away.

The blow knocks me off balance. I stagger and fall against White Wolf. Before I can get back up, he's racing off ahead of us through the woods. We give chase, but everyone knows you can't catch a cougar. When we stop running, we are miles from the moon-dappled forest floor. Small lights illuminate the cement walls and rusty ladders of Fort Casey. The cougar has fled to his den.

A burning pain hits my haunch. Did I get shot? I didn't hear the rifle. But maybe the cougar led us here so Tuffman could shoot us.

I look at White Wolf. *Help,* I want to say.

She's dragging herself toward me, making sounds that mean *I'm coming. I'll help you.* Then her eyes cloud over and close.

Oh no, she got hit too. Oh no. Maybe we're dying. My head is dizzy and my haunch stings like something—a bullet? a thin sharp stick?—is stuck into me.

Then I see a ranger. I recognize the uniform. I stumble and fall to the ground beside White Wolf, trying to cover her with my body.

The man leans over me. His face is so kind and familiar. I feel safe.

"We got you, boy," the ranger says.

I can feel sleep pushing my eyes shut, but I struggle to stay awake. Who is he? What has he done to me?

"That's only a little tranquilizer shot," he says, stroking my side. "You two will be all right in the morning. We've been looking for you for a long time."

It's the most peaceful thought I've ever had. I was lost and now I've been found.

More voices join in. "Did you get the cougar?" one asks.

"No, but we got the wolves," says my man. "We can tag these two and release them up north." I'm glad he keeps talking. His voice is so familiar. I've been wanting to hear it for so long.

I can feel him looking me over; his fingers are deep in my coat. "I wonder what brought them all the way over here tonight. You think they got in a tangle with that cougar?"

Whoever he is, the clearest thought-in-words I've had in a long time comes to me as the strength in my wolf body fades. *I need to show him who I am.* It's the Raul me saying this. I fight the numbness that makes every muscle in my body feel like hot chocolate.

"My goodness!" the ranger says. He's surprised by what I do, but he doesn't move his hand away. "Can you believe it?" he calls to the others. "Look at this gray one here. He's licking my hand. Tame as a puppy."

I keep licking. He tastes like roast beef and cheddar cheese.

Feet surround me. Black shoes, polished. Hiking boots, expensive. Tennis shoes, very well used.

"Well, I'll be," someone says.

I lick the ranger's hand some more and then slowly

place my front paw on his hand. His face is familiar, his voice is familiar, and so is the feel of his hand in mine. What is happening? The hair on the back of my neck stands up, but not from fear. From wonder. The magic must be working again.

"Now, that's a new one. I never seen that before," says a woman. "That wolf is trying to tell you something, I think."

I do my best to nod my head and wag my tail.

I must have done a pretty good job, because they all stop talking.

"Did you see that?" the woman in the hiking boots finally asks. Good style *and* good brains. I reach over with my front paw and pat the toe of her boot very gently.

"I've got goose bumps," someone says. "That animal is trying to say something to us."

"I've never seen the likes of it." The woman sounds amazed. "Not in thirty years working these woods. He's thanking me for noticing. You realize that, don't you? That wolf's not just tame. He's downright civilized."

The ranger gets down low to study me; he must be crouching on all fours. He looks into my eyes. I bark a happy bark. I *do* know him. That's my dad.

In the distance a shot rings out.

"Got him!" a voice cries. "We got the cougar!"

Chapter 27

WHERE A WOLF IS NEVER WRONG

Budget. That's the word I keep hearing my dad say on his phone as he paces between a trailer and the kennel where White Wolf and I wake up.

To my dad, it's a bad word. He says a lot of real bad words when he's talking about the budget—worse even than the ones Mean Jack used to use. Sometimes he slams the trailer's screen door shut when he gets off the phone.

To me, "budget" is a good word. It's the reason why White Wolf and I are still here with him. The "budget" doesn't have the money to transport two wild wolves from an island in Puget Sound all the way to Montana and "integrate" them into a new environment. There's a red wolf exhibit at the Point Defiance Zoo, but they don't want us. Thank goodness.

The cougar went straight to Woodland Park Zoo in Seattle, where he has a cage all to himself. Since he tried to attack me and Sparrow, they consider him too dangerous to release back into the wild. *Ha.* Tuffman's too wild for the wilderness. They got that right, even if they don't know the half of it. Lock him up, boys, lock him up and throw away the key.

The trailer where we're staying is located at the ranger station on the far end of White Deer Woods. At first my dad keeps us out back in a big cage. It's a huge square of chain-link fence with a cement floor and a wooden roof.

Whenever my dad's not at work or yelling at someone on the phone about the importance of saving the wild wolf population of this country, I do what I can to show him that I'm not a wolf like any other.

When I see him, I sit on my hind legs with my front paws stretched out in front of me. Sort of like I'm bowing to him.

When he greets me with a "Hey, gray wolf," I yip in return.

One day, instead of stretching out in a bow, I sit up and offer him my paw. He blinks at me for a long time. Then he says, "Well, I'll be," and takes my hand and shakes it.

It doesn't take long to train him. He's a smart man. By the end of the week he opens the cage door and leads us into the trailer.

"Don't tell anyone," he says to us. "I'll lose my job if they catch me with wild animals for roommates."

I don't know who exactly he thinks I'm going to

tell. The blue jay who hangs out near the kennel? Yeah, he's a real chatterbox.

My dad lives in the trailer. It's his home.

In the last year he must have moved away from Seattle. He must have gotten a job as a ranger in the White Deer Woods.

But if he was living so close to the school, then why didn't he ever come see me?

Once we're inside, I realize he's been seeing me all the time.

There are pictures of us everywhere. Pictures of the three of us at the Woodland Park Zoo with the penguins. Me in a little kiddie car on the sidewalk in front of our apartment. Me and mom standing by the sound sculpture at Magnuson Park. Me trying to eat a pinecone at Green Lake. Man, I was a dumb baby!

I sit down in the middle of the room and look at the pictures.

The ranger kneels next to me. He puts a hand on my back. "My family," he says, and his voice sounds squeezed—like there's a lump in it that won't let the words past. "See," he says as White Wolf walks up and sits on the other side of him, "you two are lucky. You still have each other. I'm gonna make sure it stays that way too."

I learn things when he talks on the phone. I learn he took the ranger job so that he can live here next to my school. Sometimes he talks to the photos of us on the wall. He asks the picture of me why I didn't want to see him anymore, why I wrote him all those letters and told him to stay away. He says that if he hadn't listened to me, then none of this would have happened and he and I would still be together. He says he moved out here to be as near to me as he could be, until I was ready to see him again.

I never wrote him a letter. I don't know what he is talking about. Did someone play a trick on us? Was it Tuffman?

I sit close to him then. His sadness is the same as mine. We can't say what we want to say to each other. I guess I was wrong. I guess sometimes words matter.

One afternoon he has to go to town to get some supplies. He opens the trailer door and White Wolf and I walk straight into the cage.

"You two must really like it here," my dad says.

When he comes back, I hear voices.

"The wolves are out here," I hear my dad saying.

The back door opens. I smell him before I see him. Mean Jack.

Do you know what is strange? I'm happy to see him. I push my nose through the wire, and before my dad can tell him not to, Mean Jack has his hand right in front of my mouth. I lick him all over. Beef jerky and lemonade. This is my kind of kid.

"Never," my dad says sternly as he comes out the door, "*never* do that with a wild animal. Promise me you'll never do that again."

Mean Jack freezes and then yanks his hand back. "I'm sorry, Mr. Ranger. Please don't tell Dean Swift."

My dad puffs his cheeks up and blows the air out. "I won't tell him if you won't! I promised him I'd let you guys take a look, not get your hands bitten off."

Mean Jack nods. It's crazy how respectful he is with my dad. Maybe it's the ranger uniform. Or maybe Mean Jack is a nicer kid than I thought.

"Anyway, there's no real danger with this gray wolf, but he's somewhat of an anomaly," my dad says. "You know what that is? An anomaly is something unusual. And this gray wolf loves people."

"Anomaly comes from the Greek," I hear another voice say. "'An' is a prefix meaning 'not,' and the middle part, 'oma,' is a shortened form of *homos,* meaning 'the same' or 'equal.' So anomaly means 'not the same.'"

Mary Anne. The prettiest dictionary walking God's green earth.

I'm even happier to see her. I don't mind how mad she was at me the last time I saw her. Vincent had us both fooled.

"If this wolf is not the same as any other, then why *shouldn't* I do this?" she asks, and sticks her hand into the cage. Dean Swift always says she is too impertinent.

But I rush over and lick her hand like crazy. Wolf me is not shy, not one little bit. Sigh. Honey and blackberries.

My dad stares at her, but he doesn't chew her out. That's the power of Mary Anne. She can get away with anything. Words and beauty—a killing combination.

"I'm conducting research," she explains, even though nobody asked. "I'm penning a novel about a wolf family. I need to experience the precise texture of a wolf's tongue." She reaches through the fence and strokes my fur. "And its coat. Coarse." She pulls out a notebook and takes the cap off her pen with her teeth. "And a little . . . sebaceous." She lifts her hand and sniffs it, then makes a face. "*Sacre bleu!* For such a civilized specimen of *canis lupus*, he would do well to consider a bath."

After a minute my dad glances up to the trailer. "Where's the other one?" he asks.

Mary Anne shouts, "Come on, I thought you wanted to see them in the flesh."

"Is it safe?" I hear a worried voice ask.

The smell of him makes my nose twitch and my lip curl up. Vincent.

Then I see him in the doorway, chicken as usual, only this time he's got a really good reason to be.

"Of course," my dad says. "Dean Swift says you've been asking about these wolves since the day we caught them."

"If you nourish even the slightest hope of illustrating my story, then you had better come feast your eyes," Mary Anne says. "These animals are *magnificent*."

Yeah, Vincent, come on. Let me illustrate something for you with my teeth.

The growl starts low in my throat. Mean Jack hears it first. He steps away from the kennel. But Mary Anne stands her ground, watching me with her lips moving slightly.

Take a mental note, Mary Anne, because this is what a wolf looks like right before he attacks.

My hair stands on end. My muscles tense, but I stay perfectly still. Then the growl in my chest explodes into a round of barks so loud every other noise disappears. Even the trees stop talking to the wind.

I leap up against the fence. I'm taller than Vincent now, stretched long against the wire links, 155 pounds of rage. The cage rattles with the weight of me. I push my paws and chest against the metal and shake it so that it clangs and bangs.

Vincent screams and falls to the ground like a bird that has flown into a closed window. As he falls, his arm scrapes against the cage and my outstretched claws. A strip of his shirt rips away, and a thin line of red appears on his skin.

My dad looks at Mean Jack. Mean Jack looks at my dad. They both look down at Vincent. The whole time, Mary Anne stares at me.

So that's all it takes to get her undivided attention.

"No!" my dad shouts.

I jump down. I tuck my tail under and creep to the back of the cage. I curl up against White Wolf, who has watched it all so calmly. I sink my nose onto my paws. In one second I have ruined everything. My father will think I'm as wild as any other wolf. He'll forget all that I've done to show him who I really am.

"I've *never* seen that wolf do that," my dad says as he helps Vincent sit up. "Are you all right?" He pulls Vincent's arm out to look at the cut.

Vincent looks like he's seen a ghost. He should. I'm the ghost he made.

"It's a superficial flesh wound," Mary Anne announces after she glances at Vincent's arm. "It may or may not leave a scar."

"That wolf is dangerous," Vincent says, moving away on his knees. "You're gonna have to put it down," he says to my dad. "That's what happens, isn't it? When a wild animal attacks a human? It gets put down."

I feel a snarl start in my throat. I glance at White Wolf. Her body is tense. She moves forward slightly.

"Now, see here—" my dad starts to say.

But Mary Anne interrupts. "*Nobody* knows what you are saying, Vincent. *Nobody* saw that wolf attack you. I, for one, will testify that it was the fence and not the wolf that caused your injury. *Everyone* here will say the same thing."

My dad and Mean Jack nod. "I think the lady has made a fine point," says my dad.

There's a long silence, and then Mean Jack says in a voice like he can't believe it, "It was like the wolf had a score to settle."

I sit up. My humans are smarter than I thought.

"That wolf despises Vincent." Mary Anne nods.

Interesting. Whatever Vincent did to Mary Anne since I saw them last must have been pretty rotten, because she sure doesn't like him anymore.

"All I know," my dad repeats, "is that I have *never* seen that wolf act that way."

"Mr. Ranger here and me can vouch for this wolf. So, Vinnie, you gonna tell me why it thinks you're a problem?" Mean Jack asks.

Vincent starts walking really fast up the little steps to the back door.

"You wouldn't sink so low as to tease an animal, wouldja?"

I'll never call Jack "Mean" again, and that's a promise.

I slink over, really low to the ground. Then I push my nose out toward my dad. He scratches the top of it gently, the way I like.

All of them—even Vincent at the back door—stare at me. The blue jay comes to sit on the lowest branch of the cedar that shades the kennel. I could swear she winks at me.

Then Jack, Mary Anne, and my dad turn. Now all of us stare at Vincent.

My dad asks, "Dean Swift said you take your dirt bike out on the trails in the woods. Did you come across these wolves once and harm them somehow?" He glances back at White Wolf. He noticed the scar in her flank when we first got here.

Vincent looks at his feet. He digs his toe into the plank of the step and shakes his head.

"You can tell me the truth. It would be the right thing to do." My dad walks toward him.

Vincent runs back into the trailer. We hear the front door slam.

"There's a mystery here," Mary Anne says. She caps her pen and sits down on the bottom step.

Jack sits down on the step below. "Well, I, for one, ain't got nothin' better to do this summer than solve it," he says.

I sit down and look at them. I'm grateful. Even though I know Jack has the attention span of a fruit fly and Mary Anne will probably spend days looking up synonyms for the word "mystery." Even though I know the chances of the two of them working together well enough and long enough to figure this out are slim, to say the least. But it's funny to think that of all the kids I've ever known, these two are turning out to be my best friends.

The mobster and the novelist.

Chapter 28

WHERE TUFFMAN'S NEFARIOUS DEEDS ARE REVEALED

A few evenings later there's a knock at the door. Dad gets up to answer it. He must be tired because he forgets to send us outside.

"Hello, hello," a cheery voice says.

I sniff. My tongue rolls out of my mouth, I'm so happy. Dean Swift.

He comes in and sets a shoe box down on the table.

"It's been a few weeks since . . ." Dean Swift stops like he doesn't want to say the rest.

My dad finishes for him. "Since the search for Raul was called off."

"This has been a hard couple of months for all of us, and you especially," says Dean Swift. "But I have discovered something that might answer at least one question."

I stretch and crawl out from under the table. I come at Dean Swift very low, on my belly almost, with my tail droopy and my ears back. Dad is looking at me, waving his hand to tell me to get back under the table, but I know better than he does. If anyone can help, it's Dean Swift.

"Is that one of the wolves?" asks the dean. He doesn't sound as surprised as you'd expect.

"Yeah." Dad nods. He scratches his head. "The white one's over there, in front of the TV. She really likes prime-time dramas. This one stays close to the food. The darnedest thing—he loves cereal."

Dean Swift looks down at me. I scoot up closer and try to put words into my eyes so that he can see the Raul me inside them.

Instead, what I see stuns me. Above Dean Swift's head I see the shadow of an eagle's head. And behind him, I see wings. Well, not *really* wings. More like a hologram of wings—like I could push my hand through them. Like the ghost of a skin.

In his eyes there's a flash that tells me that above my wolf head he sees the shadow of my Raul skin. He smiles and touches me above my eyes.

We know each other in the woods. That's what he said to Ms. Tern. This is what he meant. This is the shadow my mother saw when she hunted with Tuffman. This is why she wouldn't eat his kills. This is how she figured out his evil secret.

Dean Swift takes a big breath. He smiles at me and then pushes the shoe box he brought toward my dad. "I found this among the belongings of our former PE teacher. He left us suddenly." The dean glances down at me. "In fact, he disappeared the night the cougar got shot."

There's a long silence. Then he says, "Jimmy, there is no question that I made a serious mistake. Not once have you blamed me, and yet you should. I should have kept track of where Raul went on the weekends. I thought he was with you. You thought he was with me. I've been trying to figure out how I could have been so negligent."

My dad looks sad, like he does whenever anyone talks about me.

"Well, here's part of the answer." The dean opens the box. "It was Mr. Tuffman." He pulls out a couple of yellow notepads.

"Do you see the traces here?" He points to the top sheet on one of the pads. "He pressed down so hard with his pen when he wrote that it left the imprint of the word on the next page. I took a pencil and gently shaded over the blank page."

He reads aloud, "'Dear Dad, We have been very busy. I go fishing with Sparrow and the Cubs. I have a lot of friends. I don't want to see you yet. You remind me too much of Mother. Please send more money because my shoes are too small. All my love, your son, Raul.'"

My dad swallows and his lower lip moves a little. *Don't cry, Dad. Please don't cry.*

"How much money did you send him?" Dean Swift asks.

My dad puts his head in his hands and shakes it. "I don't know. Couple hundred—a thousand. It doesn't matter. The money doesn't matter."

"If we could only figure out where Raul went during all those weekends, we might have a chance of finding him." Dean Swift pauses and then looks at me. "Of bringing him back," he corrects himself. "In the meantime, it's now clear that Tuffman took advantage of Raul's loneliness and your desire to do whatever Raul needed to cope with the loss of his mother. We'll notify the police. But I wanted to know how many letters he sent, and if you kept them?"

My dad nods. He gets up and walks with hunched-up old-man shoulders to the bedroom.

Dean Swift bends down and whispers, "I suspected you were one of my kind. But I thought it would be many years before your second self would call you. We can recognize each other now only because we are both wearing our second skins. It's the way of the woods. It prevents us from hunting one another."

I nod. He smiles. Then he stares at me, a long thinking line between his eyebrows.

"Are you hiding from someone in your wolf skin?" he asks.

I shake my head.

"Are you trapped?"

I nod.

"Have you lost your threshold?"

I tilt my head at him.

"The place where you shift."

No.

"Have you lost your light?"

No.

"Have you lost your clothes?"

Yes.

"Was it Tuffman?"

Yes.

Dean Swift runs his hands over his face. "I'm a fool. Ms. Tern warned me about him, but I refused to see the truth."

He jumps as a crash comes from the back of the trailer.

"I'm all right," my dad calls out. "It's a mess in here, that's all."

Dean Swift exhales and then leans back down to me. "So few of our kind harm one another that it seemed impossible. I went down to the fort the night they captured the cougar. When I saw the shadow of Tuffman's face above the skin of that cougar, I began to wonder if he had something to do with your disappearance. I searched his room but found nothing. This morning Mary Anne came to my office and told me about her visit here. She wanted to know about white wolves. It reminded me of Ms. Tern's strange theory that Tuffman is a notorious hunter of spirit animals. I decided to search his room again. What I found has led me to believe that he was trying to separate you from your father, and worm his way into your trust. But why? Was it simply to get to the white wolf through you?"

Yes.

My dad comes back with a stack of papers.

Dean Swift sits up straight and clears his throat.

"Here are all the letters," my dad says. He drops the stack on the table and slumps back in his chair. "And you're telling me Raul didn't write them."

I put my paws up on the chair and rest my head in his lap.

"No," Dean Swift says. "He didn't write even one of them."

"He must have wondered why I stopped coming," my dad says sadly. "He must have thought *I* abandoned him too. Now he'll never know how much I love him. That I think of him every second."

Dean Swift looks at me and talks to my dad. "I imagine he knows the truth. Children always do."

He stays until the sun starts to fall behind the cedars, cruising down toward the water, lighting it up so that the blue sea glows like my wolf mother's eyes. They don't talk much, my dad and the dean. But Dean

Swift's silence is a kind of hug, warm and filling the room with his understanding.

When he leaves, he bends down and scratches my ears. "I'll get you out," he whispers. "I will make inquiries. Have no fear."

Chapter 29

SOMEONE'S BEEN CLEANING MY LIGHTHOUSE

In the morning the phone rings.

"No," my dad says. "We can't separate her from the gray."

He listens. "They have to stay together."

He listens. "No. You can't put her in a zoo."

He slams the phone down.

I learn more when he calls a friend. "They're coming for the white one later today," he says. "It's all about money."

When he hangs up, he sits on the floor next to me. White Wolf settles down on the other side of him. I don't know how much she understands. Sometimes I think she's been a wolf so long she doesn't understand words.

I look at her for a long time. Ever since Dean Swift left, I've been looking at her. But no matter how hard I look, I never see the shadow of my mother's face above White Wolf's head. What does that mean?

Soon we will all be separated again. It will be like

when my dad stopped coming to get me and I hadn't found White Wolf. Only now I don't have Bobo or Sparrow. I don't have the other half of myself anymore either.

Cook Patsy is right. Love is a circle. It goes on forever. But I'm right too. It's also a chain that means you belong to someone. My family's chain keeps getting broken. When they take White Wolf from us, and me from the ranger, then I won't belong to anyone anymore. And nobody will belong to me.

I will have lost so much that there won't be much of me left.

I look again for the shadow of my mother's face. Maybe that's what happened to White Wolf.

I put my nose in my paws. It's despair. I can't change what's happening. Turn the light on me as much as you like, I'm just a dandelion seed floating in the wind—shining bright and alive but helpless.

That afternoon is so hot the trailer feels like the inside of a volcano.

"Come on," my dad says as he opens the back door. "You two will be more comfortable outside in the shade."

He trusts us. He knows we'll walk from the door of the trailer straight into the cage.

I nip White Wolf as she trots out the door. She

swings her head back at me. I make a low noise in my throat.

Right then we hear a truck coming up the dirt forest road that leads to the trailer. My dad turns at the sound. The blue jay darts up from her branch and flaps her wide indigo wings to the sky.

We bolt.

My dad hollers.

White Wolf is already at the edge of White Deer Woods. I'm close behind her. I slow down and stop, right in the shade of an enormous cedar. I swing my head back toward my dad. I give him one long last look. I make the sound that means *Good-bye.*

Then I hear him say it. "Go!" It's a whisper of a shout. "Go!" I can see him take his hat off and wave it at me. "Go!"

We run and run.

The woods are deep and dark and cool. The rabbits haven't missed us.

We return to our ledge deep in White Deer Woods. I know the ranger won't try to track us. We'll keep quiet and he'll keep quiet and soon the others will forget us.

We're free from our cage, but White Wolf and I are trapped. Nobody can help us. We'll be wolves until the day we die.

I'm melancholy. Do you know the word? If you were a melancholy wolf, your tail would droop. If you were a melancholy boy, you would shut the door to your room and listen to sad songs. If you were a melancholy kite, your streamers would straggle. A melancholy ball would go flat on one side.

At the lake I can smell the fish and frogs. I look to where the Tuffman straw man once hung. Now it's just a pine like any other. I look at the bicycle up in the oak. I look at it for a long time because something is different. I sniff. Fresh sawdust. I trot slowly toward the tree. I see the marks of a saw's teeth in the branches. Someone is trying to cut the bike from the tree. Soon every trace of me in these woods will be gone.

Late that first night, very, very late, I lope out to the lighthouse. By the orange light of an enormous moon I see that the shrubs and brush around it have been cleared. A small garden has been planted. I sniff. Broccoli, carrots, kale, basil. It makes me so mad I could growl. I'll never be able to eat those things again; to crunch and chew and taste something other than meat and bone and fur.

Who has uprooted the bleeding hearts and fern?

I nose the door open carefully. The room has been swept and cleaned.

I sniff. The smell is familiar—like the dining hall after Cook Patsy has sprayed the tables down with her special cleaner.

I look in the oven, even though I know it will be

empty. The ashes and bits of wood and charcoal have been swept out.

It has to be Vincent.

The wolf rage simmers in me. He took my skin and now he wants my lighthouse.

I'm going to play a little prank on him. I'm going to scare his pants off.

I come back often, staying in the shade of the cedars at the edge of the clearing, waiting. My gray fur makes me look more like a shadow than an animal. It's how I feel, too. I'm between skins, between shadows, between shapes.

One day I hear them.

They are coming out of the woods from the path I used to take.

"Are you *sure* Raul wasn't the one?" Vincent asks.

"*He* didn't tell me," Jack almost shouts, like he's been giving the same answer to the same question for an hour. "Give it up, already. Raul never told nobody nothin'. *Tuffman* told me you freaked when you heard the cougar. Then *I* told everyone else—'cause it was funny, that's why. Nobody ever told me not to tell."

As he gets closer, I can see Vincent's eyes darting all around. Is he looking for me? Good. 'Cause I'm looking for him.

I push the growl down. I'm not in a hurry. I've got him right where I want him, finally.

"How'd you know this was out here?" Jack asks as Vincent leads him toward the lighthouse.

Vincent stops on the threshold. "I'm fixing it up. In case Raul comes back."

"Why do you look so scared, Vinnie?" Jack asks. "You do something off the record?"

If he's scared now, just wait until I come charging out of these woods and run him right up to the edge of the cliff.

"You remember that gray wolf at the ranger's place?" Vincent asks.

I hold my breath. Is Vincent actually going to do the right thing?

The two of them step into the lighthouse.

A few minutes later they come out.

"We better get the ranger," Jack says. He's shaking his head.

"No grown-ups," says Vincent.

"Face it, it's too big for the two of us," Jack says.

"He's Raul's dad. He'll hate me," Vincent says.

"Well, you ain't gonna come out of this smellin' like roses." Jack shrugs. "But we don't have to tell the whole story, get it? Let Tuffman take the rap."

They're walking away from me now. My heart is beating so hard the blades of grass on the ground in front of me are trembling.

I can't stop myself.

I run out from under the cedar. I sprint across the meadow. They turn and see me. Vincent screams and falls down. Jack stays on his feet, but he looks scared. I trot the rest of the way to them slowly, tail wagging, tongue out of my mouth, lips drawn back in one wicked smile.

"Get up, Vincent," Jack says in a tired voice. "It's just Raul."

I jump and put my front paws on Jack's chest.

Jack scratches my ears. "Don't worry, we're gonna get your dad."

"Tuffman made me do it," Vincent says, his face pressed into the grass.

I walk over to him and sniff at his back. He's shaking like a leaf on a tree.

"I'm sorry, Raul," he says. "I'm really, really sorry."

What can I say? Nothing. Those are the words I've been howling to hear.

I wait at the edge of the forest. White Wolf waits with me.

The sun is high in the sky. It gets lower. Then lower still. The light of the setting sun streams down through a small opening between leafy branches, making a tunnel of speckled, spackled, dappled light from sky to earth. Through this tunnel of filmy light two boys walk. Behind them are two men. I take a big breath. Thank goodness. They brought Dean Swift.

White Wolf sits up. I nudge her with my nose. *Stay,* I'm saying to her. Because my only fear is that White Wolf will leave.

"I'm still not clear as to how you knew Raul's clothes were on the top rung of the ladder in the Blackout Tunnel?" Dean Swift asks.

"Tuffman told me," Vincent says. "But I didn't remember until just now."

Dean Swift makes a face like he can't believe what he's hearing. "You didn't *remember*?" he says.

Then he sees the lighthouse. He whistles softly between his teeth. "So they never destroyed it. Red Bluff has been here all along. I should have guessed." His face lights up like it does when he learns something new.

I get up and walk across the meadow. We meet in the middle. Tears stream down my dad's face, and he kneels to stroke my fur.

My dad looks up at Vincent. "This better not be some game."

Then he stands up. "Give him the clothes." He yanks Vincent by the arm so that he's standing in front of me. Vincent stares at the ground.

"Wait," says Dean Swift. "Let's put the clothes in the oven. Isn't that where Tuffman found them? And then the rest of us should step back into the forest."

Vincent doesn't look at my dad, but I hear him whisper, "I'm sorry, Mr. Ranger."

My dad nods, but there's an unforgiving look around his mouth.

Vincent takes a big breath and walks over the threshold.

Dean Swift tilts his head curiously. "So this is where Vincent has been coming all summer. He told me he had made a memorial garden for Raul." He scratches his head. "But how did he find the lighthouse?"

Jack pipes up, "Raul told him it was a place you could only find if you knew it was there."

Dean Swift looks at my dad. I can see them put it all together. My dad cracks his jaw. He looks after Vincent with pure hate on his face.

"Vincent knew about this all along, didn't he?" the dean asks Jack.

Jack lifts his left hand in a lopsided shrug.

Dean Swift's face turns purple. "Here I've spent endless hours reviewing every account of these kinds of occurrences, trying to find some way of bringing a boy back, and that little traitor had the answer the whole time!"

Now Jack and my dad look at the dean with surprise.

"You knew Raul was stuck in the gray wolf?" Jack asks the question before my dad can figure out how to say it.

"Thirty years of research has given me one irrefutable and entirely *natural* fact: These woods are magic.

Native cultures the world over and throughout time believe that there are places scattered over the earth where thresholds, or doorways, exist that allow us to move between the physical world and the world of the spirits. And in these special places, white spirit animals, like the wolf that accompanies Raul, are messengers between those worlds. The local tribes have always considered White Deer Woods to be one such sacred *locus*."

See how he does it? He only tells as much as he thinks you need to know. He's not going to mention that Fresnel lens. Even he doesn't know how the lens fits into the woods magic, just like he doesn't know that the white wolf is my mother. He knows more than anyone else, but he doesn't know it all, and he'll never tell all that he knows.

"So you're sayin' Raul's a wolf because of these woods?" asks Jack. "Can they turn me into a bear, then?"

"Well, yes, and I don't know. I believe the ability to shift between human and animal states and gain access to these thresholds is passed down genetically from mother to child." The dean speaks slowly. "The unusual forms of light in these woods are most certainly involved. Either these lights actually give special powers to certain people or they activate those powers in individuals who carry the code.

"I can only make observations," he says. "The light

phenomena in these woods spoke to me long ago—first as a scientist and then, well, then in the way that only Raul can understand."

He looks down at me. And I see the shadow of eagle wings on his back. The feathers ruffle in the breeze.

My dad looks skeptical, but he keeps his mouth shut. I mean, here he is in the middle of a clearing at the edge of a cliff on an island in the far west of the country, waiting for a lighthouse to turn a gray timber wolf back into his son.

So what's he really gonna say? That he doesn't believe in magic?

When Vincent returns, they all enter the woods.

I hug my old clothes when I pull them out of the oven. Joy, relief—I can't tell you how happy I am.

I found myself. I am right where I was.

Socks. My feet are warm. My jeans won't button and my shirt and shoes are snug, but I feel light, like I'm walking on two inches of air. My skin is smooth and my head is full of thoughts and words and things I have to say.

I run out of the lighthouse, and before I know it my dad picks me up and holds me tight.

"White Wolf," I say. The words come out like a creak and a growl.

We both look over to where we last saw her.

She's gone.

"It's Mom," I tell my dad. "I'm sure of it."

Dean Swift's eyes bulge. "That never occurred to me."

Dean Swift is flabbergasted, but my dad acts like I just told him mom got stuck in a traffic jam somewhere. Like it's no big deal. "Don't worry," he says. "We'll bring her back. We just have to figure out the right steps."

Do you see how quick a man of science can become a man of magic?

Seeing is believing.

"We'll fix it," he says.

He's my dad. So I believe him.

Chapter 30

ONCE UPON A TIME THERE WAS A HAPPY ENDING

Let me break it down for you. Even happy endings feel sad, so let's make it quick, right?

First we go back to the school.

Mary Anne skips down the steps, throws her arms around me, and squeezes me so tight I burp. How's that for a hero's homecoming? My belch cracks everyone up, but Mary Anne doesn't seem to mind. She keeps saying I'm the most heroic boy in school. I'm not sure what kind of lie Dean Swift has come up with to explain it all, so I just smile. Now, if I can figure out how to make the things I want to say to her sound like words instead of gastric distress, maybe she'll do a slow dance with me at the Christmas party this year. My armpits get sweaty just thinking about it. Ha! *There's* something I didn't miss when I was a wolf. Nervous perspiration.

Jack is my new best friend. He's rough on the outside but smooth on the inside. Like the birch branch we found last week in the woods. I'm showing him how to carve. For a mobster he has excellent fine-motor skills. Right now we're making Sparrow that rod.

Sparrow is still Sparrow. When he heard that I had come home, he ran and hid under his bed. He wouldn't come out until I had crawled under there with him. No easy feat, since I gained a lot of weight in the woods. Berries and raw meat apparently meet all of a wolf-boy's nutritional needs, and then some.

The police are looking for Tuffman. If they ever find him, he'll be charged with fraud for pretending to be me and writing letters to my dad and asking for money. I'd tell the police to go check out the new cougar at the Woodland Park Zoo, but then they'd send me off to the loony bin, and that has to be worse than being stuck in a cage or a wolf skin.

Vincent never says he's sorry again.

"Look," he says instead one day. "I sawed this from the tree and cleaned it up for you."

It's the red bike from the old oak. "A little grease, a lot of paint, and she's as good as new," he says. He spins the back wheel. He opens his hands, and I see the blisters and calluses he got from using the saw. On the inside of one arm he has a long thin scar, like what you'd get if you fell down against a sharp wolf claw.

"Thank you," I say. I know he really feels sorry for what he did. I just wish he had felt more sorry, sooner. A lot sooner. Like so soon that he had never done it.

I wish I could say I forgive him, but it's hard. I still

wake up some nights in a cold sweat, my head filled with the cougar's screech and the sight of him pouncing on White Wolf.

Vincent tries to explain it. One night he tells me how White Deer calls him Raven whenever he goes into the woods.

"I don't want to be a bird, Raul," he says. "I don't ever want to change. I want to stay the same."

I just look at him when he says that. Everyone changes. We can't help it. And maybe if he tries to be a raven, he won't be such a chicken anymore.

One day when I'm not so mad at him, I'll try to help him figure out that when you change, part of you stays the same. There's more than one of you inside you. Don't be afraid of that. We were made for this world and we belong everywhere in it, wearing all the skins that fit us.

And what about White Wolf? She came back, the very next Friday at sunset. She's not going anywhere. Love goes on and on. *That's* the magic.

The big problem is how to help her find whatever she lost. When the dean talked to me that night when I was a wolf with the shadow of a boy's head and he was a man with the shadow of an eagle's head, he asked me if I had lost my threshold, my light, or my clothes. My mom must have lost one of those things, or all three.

The day after I get back, I open the dean's office door.

"I have a question," I say. "And I'm afraid of the answer."

Dean Swift nods.

"I never see the shadow of my mom's face the way I saw the shadow of your eagle wings," I say. "Does that mean she's been trapped in her wolf skin so long that her first self is gone?" My mouth turns down. I've said most of it, but some of it I keep inside. I don't want to say it out loud because the words might make it true.

Is my mom dead? Is White Wolf all that's left of her?

Dean Swift's eyes are very soft when he finally speaks. "Think about your question," he says.

I think. He watches.

"Remember," he says, "shifters can only see each other's first-self shadow when they're *both* wearing their second skin."

My skin tingles when I realize what he means. "I understand," I say.

"Do you?" he asks.

I nod. I see him with different eyes. Dean Swift and my mom have something in common. It's their *second* skins that are human. My mom's first self is White Wolf. Dean Swift's is the eagle.

It's wonderful. And a little weird, too.

"When you're ready," he says, "I wonder if you'll

tell me what you know about the Fresnel lens?"

It's nice for once to know more about something than the dean.

"I love you," my dad says when he picks me up. Sometimes he just says it when we are opening a can of soup for dinner.

I was wrong before. Words matter. Those words my dad says matter to me.

The three of us—me, my dad, and the dean—we all agree on what to do. We all agree that not every family can be the same. Not every family can have a mom and dad and a house and two cars and two kids and money for vacations. But every family can find their own kind of happy.

So we all agree. I stay at the boarding school during the week.

In the mornings I carve in the woodshop before breakfast. At lunch Mary Anne sits next to me and tells me stories about soul-stealing shape-shifting otters. In the evenings Jack and I work on what the counselor calls our "social skills"—that means I try to talk more, and Jack tries to talk less. Cook Patsy is the new PE teacher. First thing, she burned the vomit troughs. Soon we will all be ripped. Ms. Tern doesn't come back. Something tells me she's parachuting into the jungle, a knife in her teeth and a rifle strapped to her back, looking for tiger poachers. On the first day of school, the new reading teacher rips up the curriculum and eats it in front of us.

Gollum's cage is still empty.

Jason made Bobo a little wheeled seat that attaches to her hind leg. She runs way faster than before.

There's a lot I don't understand. I think I'm becoming a wonderer, like Dean Swift. The less I know, the more there is to discover.

On Fridays I still take the Cubs fishing. On Friday afternoons my dad rides his bike over from the ranger station to pick me up. He hugs me. We bike out to the lighthouse together. My legs are finally long enough for that ten-speed. On Sunday mornings he meets me at the lighthouse again. We bike over to the ranger trailer. We draw maps. We make plans. We talk a lot, and we think even more.

We sit under the cedars by the lake, and we wait for White Deer. One day it will come back. Red flowers will pour from its mouth, and in each flower a word. And in each word, a clue to freeing my mom.

AUTHOR'S NOTE

In the late twelfth century there lived a noblewoman named Marie de France. She felt that as an author, her job was to take old stories that she had heard and write them down so that others could enjoy and learn from them. She often changed the stories to make them more meaningful to her audience.

One of her stories was called "Bisclavret." Bisclavret was a noble knight who became a wolf every weekend. When his wife discovered his secret, she was terrified. Nobody can really blame her, right? But instead of trying to understand and help her husband, she spoke with another knight who was in love with her. She got him to follow Bisclavret into the woods, steal his clothes, and trap him as a wolf forever.

There's more to the story. Believe me, Marie didn't let the wife and her partner in crime off as easily as I do Tuffman and Vincent. If you want to see how Marie went medieval on the bad guys, check out Project Gutenberg online for an English translation of her

"Bisclavret," or better yet, buy an English translation of *The Lais of Marie de France.* You'll find many more great short stories by her.

I've often wished I could thank Marie for all the joy her words have given me. A few years ago, I decided that the best way to make sure that everyone remembers her would be to do what she had done: take an old story and make it new.

ACKNOWLEDGMENTS

I wrote *This is Not a Werewolf Story* with my son, who was nine when we started it. Many of the ideas and words in the book are his. This story is dedicated to him. Without him, like most of the good things in my life, it wouldn't have happened.

The keys stop clicking when I try to express my gratitude to my husband, Mike. We've grown up together. Marie de France wrote it best: "Neither you without me nor me without you." I thank him for always thinking I can do anything I try.

My parents, Bill and Diane, filled my childhood with books. They read to me and my sister and talked with us. Above all, they gave us, and continue to give us, the precious gift of their time. Thank you more than I can say.

Nobody has believed in my dreams longer than my older sister, Kaye. She has always gone through everything in life first, and has made it all easier for me. I thank my nephew Evan and brother-in-law Jim for always cheering me on. I thank my mother- and father-in-law, Jane and James, who have shared countless books and conversations with me over the years. I thank my grandparents, Jim and Peggy, for always making a big deal about my reading and whistling skills.

I was ten when I started to write. Since then I have received hundreds of rejections for my poems and stories. I decided at some point that it didn't matter how many people said "No." All it would take was one person who said "Yes."

In my case that person was Minju Chang, my agent at BookStop Literary. To her I give my most sincere thanks for her faith, and for talking to me about my story as if it were a real book she had read. The next person to say yes to me was Reka Simonsen at Atheneum. I am so grateful for her willingness to work with a first-time author. Only with her guidance and insight was I able to find the shape of this tale. I thank Reka from the bottom of my heart. I am grateful to Debra Sfetsios-Conover for designing a cover that so perfectly captures the story, Maike Plenzke for an illustration that stuns me every time I look at it, and Adam Smith for catching so many of my errors.

I thank friends who bravely asked, "What's it about?" and then listened like they meant it: Sheri H., Kim K., Denise D., Tiffany, Derek and Ric M., Hans O., Jennifer C. I thank Michelle S., my son's compassionate and inspiring teacher during the year I wrote this. I thank the late Laura Hruska, who wrote me a rejection many years ago for an early attempt at a novel. Her letter, full of encouragement, has been taped to the refrigerator of every kitchen I've cooked in since.

I thank my teachers. Mr. Carroll, Professor Delcourt, Professor Vance, and Professor Stacey all thrilled me with their wit, intellect, and passion for old stories. I thank William Kibler, whose careful feedback allowed me to see my first scholarly article published in the journal *Speculum.* That success gave me the confidence to return to writing fiction. I thank Caroline Bynum and Peggy McCracken, whose scholarship influenced my interpretation of this story. I especially thank my students, whose kindness to one another, global awareness, and love of justice give me hope for the future.

SANDRA EVANS drew inspiration for this story from cultural sources, including the "sympathetic werewolf" stories of twelfth-century France, Celtic myths, and the folklore of the Pacific Northwest. In her research, she also studied everything from *ignes fatui* to mitochondrial DNA to wild animal behavior. She wrote this story for (and with input from) her nine-year-old son. Sandra is a native of Whidbey Island and earned her doctorate in French literature from the University of Washington. This is her first book for children.